SUPERIOR

SHOAL

A NUMBER OF VERY WONDERFUL PEOPLE HELPED ME PREPARE THIS
BOOK FOR PUBLICATION. EACH CONTRIBUTED SIGNIFICANTLY. THANK
YOU EVIE, ANDY, STEVE, JOHN, EMALEE, CHARITY, GEORGE, AND GAY.

A SPECIAL THANK YOU GOES TO LORA C. AND THE TALENTED MEMBERS
OF GRAND VALLEY ARTISTS FOR THEIR HELP ON COVER DESIGN.

SUPERIOR

SHOAL

MICHAEL CARRIER

GREENWICH VILLAGE INK

AN IMPRINT OF ALISTAIR RAPIDS PUBLISHING

GRAND RAPIDS, MICHIGAN

Copyright

SUPERIOR SHOAL

Author can be emailed at michael.jon.carrier@gmail.com. You can follow Michael's tweets at @MikeCarrier999.

ISBN: 978-1-936092-47-5 (trade pbk)
Printed in the United States of America

Library of Congress Cataloging-in-Publication Data

Carrier, Michael.
SUPERIOR SHOAL / by Michael Carrier. 1st ed.
ISBN: 978-1-936092-47-5 (trade pbk. : alk. paper)
1. Hard Boiled Thriller 2. Mystery 3. Thriller 4. Novel 5. Murder 6. Burglary 7. Lake Superior. 8. Michigan's Upper Peninsula.

A Foreword
by Author Robert Haig

Michael Carrier's approach to the topic of crime writing is substantially different from mine. He comes to the table with thirty years of experience in private security, while I bring my twenty-seven years of serving the public as a law enforcement officer with the Detroit Police Department.

I met him a year ago at a book-signing event in Mackinaw City, Michigan. I was discussing and signing my new book, "Ten Little Police Chiefs—A Detroit Police Story," and he was promoting his series of Jack Handler Thrillers. When he and I had the opportunity to discuss our respective backgrounds, and our love for writing about them, we found that we shared a number of common goals in the stories we tell.

For instance, even though the accounts I provide in the pages of my book are factual historic renderings of the events I experienced as a police officer in a major city, while the narratives Michael develops are totally fictional, yet we both paint word pictures of the strength and nobility of the human spirit.

Jack Handler, Michael's main character, definitely operates in an ethical world far removed from that required of those in law enforcement—especially when Handler is viewed in Michael's "Jack's Justice" series. Yet, Handler still exhibits many of the finer characteristics that could have made for a fulfilling career as a police officer.

For instance, Handler strives to be an honest and loyal friend. He is always brave, fair and consistent. And, like those who serve the law in the public sector, Jack Handler is bound by a code of conduct. Handler's code, however, is quite unlike the code I swore to uphold back in 1986.

But, the fact remains that each of us writes about what we know—that much, for certain, we have in common. It's just that our life pursuits took us in very different directions. Perhaps it is much the way Hemingway described it in "For Whom the Bell Tolls": "I have watched them all day and they are the same men that we are. I believe that I could walk up to the mill and knock on the door and I would be welcome except that they have orders to challenge all travelers and ask to see their papers. It is only orders that come between us."

Michael's latest book, "Superior Shoal," is, in my opinion, a fine example of crime fiction writing. It's nearly impossible to put it down. But, I think that can be said of all his Jack Handler books. – Robert Haig, Detroit Police Department (retired), and author of "Ten Little Police Chiefs—A Detroit Police Story."

What people are saying about the "Getting to Know Jack" series

If you enjoy this book you should consider reading the other books in this series. And, I would appreciate a short review on Amazon. You can do this by going to this book's page on Amazon. It is not necessary to have purchased the book from Amazon, only to have an Amazon account. Thanks, Michael

Top Shelf Murder Mystery—Riveting. Being a Murder-Mystery "JUNKIE" this book is definitely a keeper ... can't put it down ... read it again type of book...and it is very precise to the lifestyles in Upper Michigan. Very well researched. I am a resident of this area. His attention to detail is great. I have to rate this book in the same class or better than authors Michael Connelly, James Patterson, and Steve Hamilton. — Shelldrakeshores

Being a Michigan native, I was immediately drawn to this book. Michael Carrier is right in step with his contemporaries James Patterson and David Baldacci. I am anxious to read more of his work. I highly recommend this one! — J. Henningsen

A fast and interesting read. Michael ends each chapter with a hook that makes you want to keep reading. The relationship between father and daughter is compelling. Good book for those who like a quick moving detective story where the characters often break the "rules" for the greater good! I'm looking forward to reading the author's next book. — Flower Lady

Move over Patterson, I now have a new favorite author, Jack and his daughter make a great tag team, great intrigue, and diversions. I have a cabin on Sugar Island and enjoyed the references to the locations. I met the author at Joey's (the real live Joey) coffee shop up on the hill, great writer, good stuff. I don't usually finish a book in the course of a week, but read this one in two sittings so it definitely had my attention. I am looking forward to the next installment. Bravo. — Northland Press

My husband is not a reader— he probably hasn't read a book since his last elementary school book report was due. But ... he took my copy of *Murder on Sugar Island* to deer camp and read the whole thing in two days. After he recommended the book to me, I read it— being the book snob that I am, I thought I had the whole plot figured out within the first few pages, but a few chapters later, I was mystified once again. After that surprise ending, we ordered the other two Getting to Know Jack books. — Erin W.

I enjoyed this book very much. It was very entertaining, and the story unfolded in a believable manner. Jack Handler is a likable character. But you would not like to be on his wrong side. Handler made that very clear in *Jack and the New York Death Mask*. This book (*Murder on Sugar Island*) was the first book in the Getting to Know Jack series that I read. After I read Death Mask, I discovered just how tough Jack Handler really was.

I heard that Carrier is about to come out with another Jack Handler book—a sequel to *Superior Peril*. I will read it the day it becomes available. And I will undoubtedly finish it before I go to bed. If he could write them faster, I would be happy. — Deborah M.

I thoroughly enjoyed this book. I could not turn the pages fast enough. I am not sure it was plausible but I love the characters. I highly recommend this book and look forward to reading more by Michael Carrier. — Amazon Reader

An intense thrill ride!! — Mario

Michael Carrier has knocked it out of the park. — John

Left on the edge of my seat after the last book, I could not wait for the next chapter to unfold and Michael Carrier did not disappoint! I truly feel I know his characters better with each novel and I especially like the can-do/will-do attitude of Jack. Keep up the fine work, Michael, and may your pen never run dry! — SW

The Handlers are at it again, with the action starting on Sugar Island, I am really starting to enjoy the way the father/daughter and now Red are working through the mind of Michael Carrier. The entire family, plus a few more are becoming the reason for the new sheriff's increased body count and antacid intake. The twists and turns we have come to expect are all there and then some. I'm looking for the next installment already. — Northland Press

Finally, there is a new author who will challenge the likes of Michael Connelly and David Baldacci. — Island Books

If you like James Patterson and Michael Connelly, you'll love Michael Carrier. Carrier has proven that he can hang with the best of them. It has all of the great, edge-of-your-seat action and suspense that you'd expect in a good thriller, and it kept me guessing to the very end. Fantastic read with an awesome detective duo—I couldn't put it down! — Katie

Don't read Carrier at the beach or you are sure to get sunburned. I did. I loved the characters. It was so descriptive you feel like you know everyone. Lots of action—always something happening. I love the surprise twists. All my friends are reading it now because I wouldn't talk to them until I finished it so they knew it was good. Carrier is my new favorite author! — Sue

Thoroughly enjoyed this read — kept me turning page after page! Good character development and captivating plot. Had theories but couldn't quite solve the mystery without reading to the end. Highly recommended for readers of all ages. — Terry

* * *

Here are the Amazon links to my previous Jack Handler books:

Getting to Know Jack Series

Jack and the New York Death Mask: http://amzn.to/MVpAEd

Murder on Sugar Island: http://amzn.to/1u66DBG

Superior Peril: http://amzn.to/LAQnEU

Superior Intrigue: http://amzn.to/1jvjNSi

Sugar Island Girl Missing in Paris: http://amzn.to/1g5c66e

Wealthy Street Murders: http://amzn.to/1mb6NQy

Murders in Strangmoor Bog: http://amzn.to/1IEUPxX

Jack's Justice Series

Ghosts of Cherry Street: http://amzn.to/2n3lrRf

Assault on Sugar Island: http://amzn.to/2n3vcyL

Dogfight: http://amzn.to/2F7OkoM

Murder at Whitefish Point: http://amzn.to/2CxlAmC

Preview

The old man was still talking when Red caught a glimpse of movement on the screen of the CCTV system. He grunted and pointed at it.

Robby quickly spotted what Red was showing him.

"Looks like we've got company," Robby said.

The old man jumped out of his chair and hurried over to the monitor.

Red looked at Robby with an inquisitive scowl.

Robby shrugged his shoulders, but did not otherwise move.

The old man zoomed in on the image.

"Damn it! Why now!? … Boys. Get up and follow me. This guy cannot find you here. It will be bad for all of us. Get the hell down there," he barked he as pulled open the wood storage bin beside the fireplace. It was hinged to provide access to the basement.

"Get down there. The light will come on automatically. Hook the latch when I close the door. And don't open it for any reason. Not for anyone but me. This is a very dangerous man, and he can't find you here."

The boys responded only with their feet. While they did not fully understand what the old man was saying, they sensed his urgency. As soon as Red's foot hit the first step, the lights came on below. The old man slammed the bin closed behind them and commanded: "Lock it now, and don't open it back up for any reason. Not until I tell you to."

Robby was the one closest to the opening after they entered and so he secured the door behind them.

The old man looked around the cabin for any telltale evidence signaling that he might recently have had company. Spotting the screws the boys had removed from the shutter to gain entrance, he rushed over to the cupboard and scooped them up and stuck them in his pocket.

Knock! Knock! Knock!

The visitor pounded slowly but powerfully on the door.

"Unlock the damn door, Ren," the determined visitor ordered. "I can hear you fartin' around in there."

The old man took several deep breaths and then opened it.

But before he could utter a word, the visitor sent a crushing fist into the old man's face. The force of the nose-breaking blow knocked him off his feet and onto his back—his head bouncing as it crashed against the floor.

The force of his hard landing dislodged a Glock 9mm that was tucked under his belt and it slid a few feet across the floor. The visitor lunged on top of the old man and, at the same time, seized the pistol.

"What did you have in mind for this, Ren? Were you gonna shoot me? Is that what you were planning?"

The secret basement was well insulated and soundproofed. But, somehow, the boys were able to hear what was going on above. Red looked around and found the source of the sound. It was coming from a small speaker, and next to it was a fifteen-inch flat panel screen. He turned it on. The boys were then able to monitor in live imaging and audio all that was transpiring above them. Observing carefully, they remained silent.

With one knee firmly planted on the old man's chest, and the muzzle of the 9mm Glock pressed against the side of his profusely bleeding nose, the visitor slowly uttered his command.

"Ren. Now is the day you pay up. You knew this time would come. You've had twenty-six years—over twenty-six years—to plan for it. You knew I would find you. Now you will pay me what you owe me."

Chapter 1

The Stone House

(A brief backstory is provided in the *Cast of Characters* at the end of this book.)

Red and Robby, Jack and Kate Handler's two fourteen-year-old runaway foster boys, were hiding out at Pat Kozski's summer home on Sugar Island. The cottage was located south of the Handlers' resort. And, like the resort, it was situated on the bank of the St. Mary's River. That was significant in that it allowed the boys to fish for their food.

Pat had dug out a channel that practically extended right up to the front porch of the cottage. All the boys had to do was step out of the door and onto the dock, untie Pat's sixteen-foot aluminum boat, crank the twenty-three surface drive air cooled Mud Buddy, and off they would go.

Early on Pat became aware that they had been using the cottage. He knew this because he had observed the boys over the covert remotely controlled closed circuit camera system. Not only was he okay with having the boys as houseguests, he was pleased to have someone around to oversee his investment. And that's what he expressed to Jack Handler when he informed his friend that his two runaways were living in his summer residence.

When Jack offered to pay him rent if he would allow the boys to continue staying there, Pat told him that he absolutely would not accept payment.

"That's the least I can do for those boys," he said. "Besides, the cottage is much safer with them watching it than if it's left empty for six months. I'm only telling you that the boys are living there so you will know that they are safe and warm."

While at first the boys were not positive that Pat knew they were staying in his cottage, they soon sensed it because after Pat's second trip they discovered that he had left candy, evaporated milk, Cheerios, several pounds of butter, and three large cans of powdered eggs. Attached to the cupboard was a note: "To whoever reads this. Use as much from this cupboard as you need. I'm leaving it here for you. This is how you can repay me. There are lots of things here that need fixing. You will find tools in the pantry. Take care of the repairs, and we'll call it square. If for any reason you need to close up the cottage and leave, just be sure to lock the door behind you. Enjoy your stay and be safe—Pat the owner."

That note left no doubt in their minds that they had been found out. "Who else could he be thinking of?" they asked each other. "He has to know it's us, and he's good with it."

The boys developed a system for knowing when Pat was headed up to his cottage. Seven hours before he would arrive the gas furnace would kick in. The boys figured out that he had one of those remotely controlled thermostats, and that he would log on to it when he was preparing to head north from his house in Livonia, which is just west of Detroit in Michigan's Lower Peninsula.

The boys never turned the furnace on—they always heated using the wood stove. So, whenever they would hear the furnace running, they knew that Pat was on his way up north and that they should prepare to temporarily vacate.

They had discovered that there was a cottage only a few hundred yards upriver. And so that's where they would head first. It was unique in the area because it was constructed of stone.

When they needed to vacate Pat's cottage, they would always head to the stone cottage. As was the case every other time they arrived at the cottage, it did not appear to be occupied. They knocked on the door several times, but no one answered.

There were shutters over all the windows except for one. It was larger than the rest, and it was protected by a sturdy-looking virtually impenetrable storm window.

Once they had become firmly convinced that no one was home, they meticulously disassembled the shutters on one of the smaller windows and carefully opened it.

As soon as both of them set their feet down inside of the dark cabin, suddenly the lights switched on.

"Stay right where you are!" came a warning from the graveled throat of an old man.

The boys looked in the direction of the voice. Slumped over in a well-padded wicker chair only a few feet away was a haggard old man. And he was pointing a twelve-gauge double-barrel shotgun in their faces.

He had a moth-eaten dark gray wool sweater covering a well-worn pair of brown bib overalls. A fishing cap darkened and shaded his deep-set pale blue eyes. His hair was long and mostly gray. Wrinkles, some looking more like furrows, created a web-like pattern across his skin, making his face appear to be very old and worldly—perhaps like the king of the tramps.

Red's mind shifted into overdrive: *He was never here the other times we broke into this cottage. Why didn't he shoot us when he first spotted us? Why did he wait until we got all the way in? I don't think he wants to hurt us. But, here we are. He's gonna have to do something now ... too late to try to scare us. Maybe he's some kind of pervert. ... This can't be good.*

Red glanced over at his friend. It was obvious to Red that similar questions were racing through Robby's mind. ... And then he spotted it.

Next to the front door was a large CCTV monitor. It was probably only twenty or so inches diagonally, but because the cabin was so small, it appeared larger than it actually was.

Red stared at it long enough to observe a number of the images that were scrolling across the screen. *This guy's got at least half a dozen outside cameras. What could he be so worried about?*

"What, exactly, are you two young men doing in my house? … And, before you lie to me, understand that I know that this isn't the first time you pulled this shit. You've broken in two other times. What makes you think you can do that?"

"We didn't think anyone was home," Robbie said.

"Obviously. But that doesn't answer my question. How does your ignorance give you the right to break into my house?"

"We have no place to go. We wouldn't do any damage. … The court pulled us out of our foster home, and wanted to lock us up in detention. So we ran away. We've been living in a cottage just south of here, but the owner's coming up for the weekend, and we had to leave."

"So, the cops wanted to lock you boys up, and you ran away? Is that it? You're some kind of young *hoodlums*? Is that it? What the hell did you do that made them want to stick you in a kids' jail? Are you thieves? I hate thieves. Is that what you are?"

"I know it sounds bad," Robby tried to explain. "But we never stole anything. My parents are both dead, and so are his. We didn't do *anything* wrong."

"Then why the hell did they pull you out of your foster home and lock you up? You must have done *something* wrong."

"Actually, sir, we really didn't. Our caseworker decided that our foster home wasn't safe enough. So she pulled us out."

"You shittin' me? Not *safe* enough? Where was that foster home that was so dangerous? Did they beat you? I was in a foster care for a while … when I was twelve and thirteen. My foster parents were okay, but the other boys … they pulled some weird shit. I ran away *several* times. And then I went to live with an uncle. He beat the crap out of me every time he got drunk, which was just about every night. Is that what happened to you? Did your foster dad beat you?"

"Never," Robby quickly said in Jack's defense. "Uncle Jack *nev-*

er hits us. ... It's just that he's in a dangerous business. And sometimes bad people try to hurt him. And I guess that the court was afraid Red and I might get hurt if we continued to live with them."

"Them? There's more than one? Is this Jack guy married?"

"He's not married. He has a daughter, Kate. She's a cop in New York, but she spends a lot of time on Sugar Island. They own a resort here. The Sugar Island Resort."

"That wouldn't be Jack *Handler*? Would it? I think he's the one who runs that resort. Handler wouldn't be the fellow you're talking about. Would he?"

"Yes. Jack and Kate Handler. They're our foster parents."

"Oh, my God!" the old man said. "I've heard about him, all right. ... And, yeah, I can see how living with Jack Handler could be *very* dangerous."

The old man lifted the barrel and released both hammers, and then laid the shotgun across his lap.

"Okay," he said. "You two juvenile delinquents get your asses in here, and close up that window. You're letting the mosquitos in. Shut it up. Be quick about it. ... I'm not gonna shoot you if you do *exactly* what I tell you to do, and behave yourselves while you're doin' it."

The boys took a deep breath. Robby, who was still sitting on the cupboard, was closest to the window and so he pivoted around on his knees and shut it.

Red, who was standing just in front of the same cupboard, did not move.

"Hey, you. Carrot Top," the old man said looking at Red. "You sure as hell don't talk much. What's *wrong* with you? You afraid of me? That's probably smart of you. After all, I *am* the one with the scattergun. You *should* be scared of me."

"He ain't scared of you," Robby said, coming to Red's defense. "He has a problem with speaking. He damaged his voice box and he can't say words. But he ain't scared of anyone."

"So, he's a brave little sonofabitch. Is he? Not scared of anything."

"Not that so much," Robby countered. "Neither one of us is particularly brave. But we aren't scared of you, either. If you're gonna shoot us, then you just have to shoot us and clean up the mess. You're not gonna wreck your cottage like that. If you were going to shoot us, you'd have done it while we were still outside. Not on this expensive rug.

"But we're not here to steal from you, or damage your beautiful cottage, or cause you *any* harm. We just need a place to hide out for a few days. Until the owner of the other cottage goes back downstate. If we can hang out with you for a few days, we will chop wood, make repairs, or do anything you want us to do. And if you want us to take off, we'll do that too. You are the boss. If you've got some work around here, just tell us what you want done. … Or tell us to leave, and we'll do that. But we ain't scar—"

"All right. All right. I get it. You're not scared of me. Just shut up and get off my cupboard. I believe you. … Maybe I do have some chores you can do around here. You say you can handle an axe? You boys strong enough to chop some firewood?"

"Sure. No problem. We made up some sandwiches, so we won't be troubling you with feeding us. Your axes sharp? Can't do much with a dull axe. We can sharpen 'em if they're dull."

"I'll put an edge on them for you. But later. For right now, I want you to tell me a little bit about yourselves. I need to know what sort of hooligans I might be dealing with. I still might have to shoot you."

With that the old man smiled. He then broke the shotgun and removed the two shells.

The two boys took a deep breath. Although they tried not to show it, they were greatly concerned about having to stare down the barrels of a twelve-gauge shotgun, especially since it was being held by an old man with shaky hands. They were relieved when he reached up and rested the shotgun on top of two wooden pegs that were mounted in a substantial plank that was hanging on the wall to the right of the stone fireplace.

The old man followed their eyes as he pushed the cartridges into his pocket. *So much for their not being scared of my scattergun,* he concluded. *That was the blank stare of terror. … But that's good. At least they ain't stupid.*

"Go ahead and sit down," he commanded. "Right there on the rug will do. I want you to tell me all about this Jack Handler fellow. And, refresh my memory, what exactly is it that he does? What's *so* dangerous that it made the court pull you out of his home? And who is this Kate? Is that Handler's wife? No. You said Kate was Handler's *daughter*. Right?"

Robby looked over at Red to read what he was thinking.

"*Uncle* Jack, that's what we call him. He's not our real uncle, though. … But, he doesn't like for us to discuss his business. Not that we know very much about what he does, but he told us nothing good could come out of talking about him. So we shouldn't do it. … If that upsets you, we could just leave. If you want us to."

"No, I get it. I've heard that he is some kind of private investigator, or security contractor. Some shit like that. I can understand why he doesn't want you to talk about it. Especially if it is dangerous. You did say that the court pulled you out of the house because it was too dangerous. Right?"

"That's what *they* said. But we think they're wrong. Uncle Jack and Kate take very good care of us. They're the best. And they protect us very well. We couldn't feel safer."

Robby caught a glance fired at him by Red and he knew what it meant.

"Probably be best if we just moved along. Sorry to have troubled you. Don't think we did any damage to your window. Just took out a few screws. We'll fix it back the way it was and just take off. We promise we won't bother you again. Ever."

But as Robby started to stand the old man lifted his shirt slightly to reveal a nine mil. semi-automatic pistol tucked under his belt.

"Sit your asses back down," he growled. "I'm not done talking to you. You're going to sit right here in front of me until I'm finished with you. And then I'll tell you what you're going to do. This is my home. You don't get to tell me shit. Got it?"

The boys did not respond.

The old man was still talking when Red caught a glimpse of movement on the screen of the CCTV system. He grunted and pointed at it.

Robby quickly spotted what Red was showing him.

"Looks like we've got company," Robby said.

The old man jumped out of his chair and hurried over to the monitor.

Red looked at Robby with an inquisitive scowl.

Robby shrugged his shoulders, but did not otherwise move.

The old man zoomed in on the image.

"Damn it! Damn it! Damn it! Why *now*? … Boys. Get up and follow me. Be quick about it. This guy *cannot* find you here. It will be bad for all of us. Get the hell down there," he barked as he pulled open the wood storage bin beside the fireplace. It was hinged to operate like a door. Once fully opened, it revealed a set of steps leading downward into a dark cellar.

"Get down *there*. Hurry. The light will come on automatically. Hook the latch on the other side of this door when I close it. And don't open it for *any* reason. Not for anyone but me. Got it? This is a *very* dangerous man, and he can't find you here. Understand? Who knows what would happen if he discovers you. Move! Get your asses down there."

The boys responded only with their feet. While they did not fully understand what the old man was saying, they sensed the urgency. As soon as Red's foot hit the first step, the lights came on below. The old man slammed the bin closed behind them and commanded in a loud whisper, "Lock it now, and don't open it back up for *any* reason. Not until I tell you to."

Robby was the one closest to the opening after they entered and so he secured the door behind them.

The old man looked around the cabin for any telltale evidence signaling that he might recently have had company. Spotting the screws the boys had removed from the shutter to gain entrance, he rushed over to the cupboard and scooped them up and stuck them in his pocket.

Knock! Knock! Knock!

The visitor pounded slowly but powerfully on the door.

"Unlock the damn door, Ren," the determined visitor ordered. "I can hear you fartin' around in there."

The old man took several deep breaths and then opened it.

But before he could utter a word of greeting, the visitor sent a crushing fist into the old man's face. The force of the nose-smashing blow knocked him off his feet and onto his back—his head bouncing as it crashed against the floor.

The force of his hard landing dislodged the pistol that was tucked under his belt and it slid a few feet across the floor. The visitor pounced on top of the old man, scarfing up the pistol as he was landing.

"What did you have in mind for this, *Ren*? You old sonofabitch. Were you gonna *shoot* me? Is that what you were planning to do with it?"

The secret basement was well insulated and soundproofed. But, somehow, the boys were able to hear what was going on above. Red looked around and found the source of the sound. It was coming from a small speaker, and next to it was a fifteen-inch flat panel screen. He turned it on. The boys were then able to monitor in live imaging and audio all that was transpiring above them. They kept silent and observed carefully.

With one knee firmly planted on the old man's chest, and the muzzle of the 9mm Glock pressed against the side of his profusely bleeding nose, the visitor slowly uttered his command.

"Ren. *Now* is the day you pay up. You knew this time would come. You've had twenty-six years—*over* twenty-six years—to plan for it. You knew I would find you. Now you will pay me what you owe me."

"Yes. I have it right here. I didn't spend a cent of your money. Not one red cent. I swear. It's all here for you."

"Where? Tell me where it is right now. If you're tellin' the truth, I might let you live."

"It's all there. I wouldn't cheat you. … I would have come to visit you, but they would have found out where I lived. And they would have come and got your money. That's why I moved to Sugar Island. … No one gives a shit here. No one checks."

"*I* found you, didn't I?"

Renny didn't answer.

"Just let me up and I'll prove it to you. I have all your money. Let me get it for you."

"I'll give you one chance. That's it. If you try to pull anything on me, I'll kill you right here. … And that would be better than what I went through in prison. I took that rap for *you*. You sonofabitch. So you could have your freedom. Twenty-six years is a lifetime. It's more than a lifetime. In that hell hole."

The visitor stood to his feet and lifted the old man to his.

"Go get it. Get my money."

"Yes. Yes. I will."

But, before the old man could do anything, they both clearly heard a male voice shouting just outside the door.

"Hello. Anyone home?"

Even though the sound was muffled, Red and Robby saw the old man and his visitor turn toward the open door.

Red switched the monitor so they could view the outside cameras.

"Oh my God!" Robby exclaimed. "What are *they* doing here?"

Standing about twenty feet outside the front door were two deputy sheriffs, and Christina Baldwin, the boys' caseworker.

"Stay put!" the visitor told the old man. "We'll square up after I deal with these guys."

As he stood to his feet he caught sight of the old man's shotgun hanging on the wall. "What a damn mess this's turning into," he muttered. He slid the Glock under his belt at the small of his back, grabbed the old man by the back of the neck and pushed him behind the open door, to where he thought he could keep an eye on him. He then leaned out and greeted the visitors.

"Hello there," he said through his biggest smile. "What can I do for you?"

His hand rested on the pistol, and his finger on the trigger..

Chapter 2

Potosi

Four days earlier, another unforeseen adventure began to unfold that would soon have significant ramifications and provide a dramatic challenge with regard to the wellbeing of the Handlers and their friends. The unfolding events were set to be particularly impactful for Henry, Jack Handler's right-hand man, and Henry's eleven-year-old daughter—Lily.

The initiating incident involved a targeted attack on Henry by a recent inmate named Raymond Lee Munson.

Raymond looked like a genuine tough guy—even rougher than most of the other graduates of the Missouri State prison system. His stint there was largely responsible for his appearance. That's where he acquired the nasty scar on his upper lip and a severely bent nose.

He was not particularly tall. But he wasn't short, either. He stood just under five foot ten inches, and weighed one hundred and eighty-eight pounds. By today's standards, Raymond was about the same size as the average former prisoner. But that's where the similarity ended. By the time he had finished serving a combined twenty-three years behind bars, Raymond had risen through the ranks of the Aryan Alliance. He was, at the time of his *graduation*, the most feared and respected convict in the state's entire penal system—at least, the most feared and respected convict who had made it to the outside.

While he never bragged about his exploits—when he wasn't around, others did.

According to the stories, Raymond personally commuted the

sentences of six prisoners. Three of them with surgically placed shivs, and another three by inflicting fatal head injuries.

Originally, he had been charged with second-degree assault—a Class C Felony punishable by five to fifteen years. At the time that the original charge was brought against him he was a senior in high school. And the victim was the popular quarterback of his high school football team.

Raymond was the only one charged with a crime. His parents felt that the odds were stacked against their son from the beginning due to the fact that public sentiment sided with the football player. Unfortunately, the aspiring Joe Montana had broken his throwing hand against Raymond's very hard chin and was forced to sit out the remainder of the football season. While it was never clearly established which of the young men had thrown the first punch, since football was such a big deal in their little Missouri community, Raymond never stood a chance. It took the jury, all fans of high school football, less than an hour to find him guilty.

As is generally the case with first-time offenders, Raymond received the minimum—five years. That meant if he behaved himself he could gain early release, perhaps serving only three years or so. But, unfortunately for Raymond, that didn't happen for him. One month before his parole hearing he was attacked in the yard by three inmates. He managed to fight them all off, but in so doing, he struck one of the attackers in the nose with the heel of his right hand, driving bone splinters into his brain and killing him.

Of the six deaths he was alleged to have caused, he was convicted in only one case—the first one. But that was enough to earn him an additional twenty-year sentence. And because of his less than stellar record, and perhaps due to his affiliation with the prison gang, he ended up serving all twenty.

By the time he walked out of the prison gate at the age of forty-one, no one from his hometown even remembered his name, much less the circumstances surrounding his original conviction.

His parents had both long since died, and his only sibling, an older sister, had married and moved to St. Louis. Not only had she never visited him in prison, she made it clear that she wanted nothing to do with him once he got out. She had built a life for herself, and that was all she cared about.

The only object that he left with was a poster, which he had neatly folded and placed in a large manila envelope. It was a near-ly life-sized likeness of Rocky Marciano, the one hundred-and-eighty-eight-pound heavyweight champion boxer from 1952 to '56. His boxing record was forty-nine wins and no losses; which, until Floyd Mayweather came along, was the longest string of vic-tories ever compiled by a professional boxer.

Raymond had inherited the poster from a deceased cellmate years earlier.

It was his most valued possession.

While most prisoners leave the lockup with little more than the clothes they are wearing, and with virtually no prospects for significant employment, that was not the case for those with Ary-an Alliance affiliations. At least, it was not the situation for Ray-mond. His role as enforcer while on the inside afforded him some major perks on the outside as well. Not the least of which was a job and a bed for as long as he had need of them. And, most im-portant of all, a new name, along with all the necessary supporting credentials.

Raymond's name was to be *Lawrence William—LW—Chris-tian*. According to official records housed at the county seat in Galena, Lawrence William Christian was born in 1975 in Elsey, a small town in Stone County Missouri. He was subsequently issued a Social Security number, and was registered with the Selective Service in 1993.

It all appeared to be totally legitimate—except for the fact that the real Lawrence William Christian of Elsey, Missouri, was bur-ied five days after his birth in a small cemetery located just outside the little town. But that didn't matter to anyone who did not live in southern Missouri. And, as long as the new Lawrence William Christian didn't venture down into those parts of the state, odds are he would never be found out. So, Lawrence William Christian—AKA Raymond Lee Munson—caught a bus to Oklahoma City and never again ventured across the state line into Missouri.

The work the gang provided for him was very hard, but it paid enough for him to survive. His job was to load cattle onto rail cars. When he wasn't busy in the stockyard, he was bartending nearby. It was while tending the bar that he met and soon became friends with another former prisoner—Maynard "Slim" Truman. Even though no one had formally introduced the two men, they both immediately knew that they shared a common history.

That's just how it is for former long-term inmates of the penal system. Whether it's the way they always seem to be checking who might be approaching from the rear, or just the manner they carry themselves, cons can always spot a fellow traveler. But in this case it was pretty obvious to even a casual observer that both men had done time. Their prison tatts gave that away.

"Whaddya do for fun?" Slim asked. It was late—ten minutes before closing time. "And how long you been out, anyway?"

Lawrence stared at him coldly. He did not like to discuss his past.

"What the hell is it to you what I do for fun? Who the hell are you asking me that? ... What business is it of yours when I got out?"

"No offense, man," Slim said. "I got out two months ago. I just figured we might have something in com—"

"Three months ago," Lawrence said interrupting. "I walked out of Potosi ninety days ago."

"You're doin' okay for yourself, looks to me. ... You like slinging booze?"

"This ain't my real job. I just do it to make a few extra bucks."

"What's your real job?"

"Slinging beef. I work in the yard."

"You like it?"

"It's a job. I do okay. … Can't say that I like it *that* much. But it helps pay the bills. Whadda *you* do?"

"I work for my buddy in Little Rock. Driving, mostly. Making deliveries. Sometimes I pick stuff up. Shit like that."

"Getting' good money, are you? Making deliveries."

"Can't complain."

"That's cool."

"That's what I'm doin' here … picking up some shit, and then dropping it off over in Little Rock."

"What sort of shit?"

"Hell, I don't know. Whatever it happens to be. Sometimes it's sealed up in a box. I don't ask questions. Usually I just stick it in the trunk of my car. And that's it. … I don't much care what it is as long as I get paid."

"Need any help?"

"Maybe. I could check. You interested?"

"Might be. You say it pays okay?"

"More than you'd be making shuffling those steers around. I'm sure about that."

"Then I'd be interested."

Slim didn't respond immediately. Finally, he said, "They thought you would be."

Lawrence snapped his head up and stared coldly into Slim's brown eyes.

"What are you saying? *Who* exactly is it that thought I'd be interested?"

"My buddy and his associates."

"So, who's this buddy of yours?"

"You know him. At least, he says he knows you. From Potosi."

"What's his name?"

"Carl Milton."

"Carl? You work for Carl? … Damn. He was one very badass sonofabitch."

"Still is a badass SOB," Slim said with a cautious smile. "You can trust me about that. And that's exactly what he said about you."

"Then," Lawrence said, "the so-called package that you're here to pick up. There really isn't one, is there?"

"If there is, you'd be it. Just tell me if you want the job or not. I need to know right now."

Lawrence looked at his watch.

"Time to close up the bar. We driving to Little Rock now or in the morning?"

"How about your job in the stockyard?"

Lawrence flashed a glance at his new friend and smiled.

"Those stinky ass steers will just have to get along without me."

Lawrence lit up a Newport as the two men walked toward the door.

"What is it that Carl thinks I can do for him?" he said. "Does he need another driver?"

"I think he's got something different in mind for you. He'll explain it all when we get there. I'm not gonna try to speak for him."

Chapter 3

All Hell

Back at the old man's stone house on Sugar Island, all hell was about to break loose.

"My name is Deputy Jim Martin," said the deputy who appeared to be in charge. "And this is my partner, Deputy Donny Cochran. Are you the owner of this cottage?"

"Me? No. I'm just visiting my friend."

The visitor then turned to get a look at what the old man was up to. Seeing that he had turned around and was eyeing the shotgun, he called him to step to the door with him.

"Ren. Come over here. You've got visitors."

The old man hesitated for a moment, but then did as he was told.

As he reached the door the visitor took a step backward and gestured for the old man to address the new visitors. And again he complied, walking past his old associate and approaching the deputy.

"I'm the owner, officers," he said. "Reynold Chrysler's my name. I've lived here for over twenty years. Most people call me Renny."

"Everything okay here?" Deputy Martin asked.

The old man had wiped most of the blood from his face, and his nose had stopped bleeding, but there remained a lot of blood on his shirt and hands.

"Yeah. I'm fine. I took a spill while I was out chopping wood. That's why I called Wally, my buddy. But I'm gonna be just fine.

What brings the law here today? I hope you're not here to see me."

"No. You're not the object of our attention. We're here with Miss Baldwin. She's a juvenile caseworker with Chippewa County. We're trying to locate two of her clients. Two boys, both fourteen years old. Wonder if you've seen them, or know anything about where they might be hiding out."

"Two boys. No. I don't know nothin' about two boys. I live here by myself and mind my own business. I haven't actually talked to any of my neighbors in a year or more. Once a month I drive to the mainland and pick up supplies. But that's it. Ain't seen or heard about two boys. Sorry I can't help."

"Mind if we step in for a minute? Deputy Cochran here would like to get a drink of water, and maybe use your bathroom. Would that be okay?"

Wally, the old man's *buddy*, observed that Deputy Martin had already unsnapped his holster and was resting his hand on his Glock.

"Sure," Wally said as he stepped out of the house and took a position directly behind the old man. "There's bottled water in the fridge, and the bathroom is right beside the kitchen. Make yourself at home."

"Oh no!" Robby said as he and Red watched the situation develop on the monitor. "He's gonna shoot the cops!"

Chapter 4

A Job for Lawrence

The two men, Raymond Lee Munson, AKA LW, and Maynard Slim Truman, drove directly to Little Rock. There Truman delivered Munson to Carl Milton's office. It was located in a dingy bar on Geyer Springs Road.

"Raymond!" Carl said. "Old buddy! How's it hangin'?"

"Good as could be expected, I suppose," Lawrence said. "But people call me LW, or Lawrence, these days."

"Yes. Yes, of course," Carl said. "That's exactly right. Raymond Lee Munson no longer exists."

Carl was totally aware that his friend had changed his name. He had intentionally made reference to the old name merely to draw attention to the fact that a new identity had been given Raymond, and that it was he and his Aryan Alliance associates who were responsible for providing it.

"Glad you decided to pay me a visit," Carl said. "I'm sure we can find a way to work together. And I know it's gonna be mutually beneficial."

"I don't know much about what you think I might do for you," Lawrence said. "Slim didn't really have any information about the job, except that you would have to spell out the details personally."

"Yeah. That's exactly right."

Carl then addressed Slim, and said, "Slim, I think now is a good time for you to take care of your personal business. It looks like I won't have anything for you for the next day or two. But keep your cell charged in case something comes up."

"Right, boss. Thanks," Slim said. He was pleased to have a couple of days off.

"See ya around," he said to Lawrence.

"Yeah. See ya."

Once Slim had closed the door behind him, Carl took a seat behind his well-polished oak desk, and signaled for Lawrence to also have a seat.

After a long moment of silence as he fingered through some papers on his desk, Carl finally looked up at Lawrence and asked, "Do you have any idea about what it is I want you to do for me?"

"None whatsoever. But I'm hoping it doesn't involve a lot of driving. I don't much like being on the road all the time."

"No. That's not what I have in mind at all. Slim's my man for that shit. ... I need you to take care of other business for me. ... Sometimes things come up that require special talents. Abilities that you've demonstrated that you possess. It's not all the time. So, when you're not working for me, you'll be working for a buddy of mine. He owns a bar here in Little Rock. This one, actually. Slim said that you worked part-time as a bartender in Oklahoma City. Well, here you will work full-time at the bar, and then you will take off when I have an assignment for you. How's that arrangement sound?"

"Who pays me? You or him?"

"I pay you."

"Then it sounds good."

"Aren't you gonna ask how much?" Carl asked.

"Hell no. I'll let you know if I think you're shorting me."

"Fair enough. ... Don't you want to know what sort of jobs I've got for you?"

"Same answer," Lawrence said. "I know what my *special talents* are as well as you do. No need to spell anything out. ... When do I start?"

"Now. Tonight. I've been asked to deal with a man who has created a problem for some friends of mine. Some months ago he stuck his nose where it didn't belong, and seriously injured three of my friends … inside a federal facility. He needs to be eliminated."

Carl was alluding to the time Chuchip *Henry* Kalyesveh, Jack Handler's right-hand man, interrupted the contracted prison-camp hit on Jack. As a result of Henry's interference, three members of the Aryan Alliance were hospitalized, with one of them eventually succumbing to his injuries.

"I don't know nothin' about that," Lawrence said. "Never heard of either one of them. But that doesn't matter. If you want this guy gone, I'll make him gone. … Any preferences as to how I pull it off?"

"Oh, yes," Carl replied. "Lots of them. … First of all, the police report has to attribute it to robbery. Officially, nothing should point to the Alliance. And, I want him *really* messed up. Especially his face. I want Handler to get a good look at what we do to people who screw with us. … The guy you're eliminating is a Native American who goes by the name of Henry Kalyesveh. His real first name is Chuchip. But everyone calls him Henry."

Carl slid a picture of Henry across his desk for Lawrence to look at.

"Now, keep in mind that this Henry fellow is a very tough guy, so messing him up won't be easy. But, do *not* use a gun. I want him broken up badly, and killed. You might have to finish him off with a blade. But I'd prefer that he just be beaten to death. … Again, I have to warn you that he is a very tough character. He's fought professionally. He's going to be very cautious. It could be hard to get the drop on him.

"Does this sound like something you can do? And can you pull it off the way I want it done?"

"I'm sure I can. I just need to know how to find him."

"That part's easy. We've been monitoring this Henry guy for a few weeks now and I just learned that in about twenty-four hours he's leaving his house on Sugar Island. That's in Michigan's Upper Peninsula. He's driving down to Missouri. I guess on business. He works for his prison buddy—Jack Handler. Handler's a private investigator, and I guess he has him doing something for him in Missouri.

"You should get some rest right now. Plan to head up to Michigan at the crack of dawn, and we'll see to it that you run into him. We'll pinpoint his location along the way. We have a tracker on his car. And you can pick your spot—just make sure it's in Michigan. Don't wait until he leaves the state. Can you handle that?"

"Most definitely," Lawrence said. "But where do I sleep?"

"Here's the keys to your car and your apartment. Your new address is on the seat. Just plug it into the GPS. And, here's the cell I want you to use. After the job is complete, call me on it and let me know."

"Will I come back here after I take care of this fellow?"

"No. Not right away. After you kill the Indian, his boss, Jack Handler, will show up. He'll want to investigate. And, when he does, I want him eliminated as well. I don't care *how* you kill him. Shoot him if you want. He just has to die. I'll give you further instructions at that time."

Chapter 5

Blood in the Sand

The two boys huddled in closely around the CCTV monitor as they watched what was unfolding just outside the old man's house.

Robby's words of warning to Red had barely escaped his lips when the shooting began.

Using the old man as his shield Wally thrust ahead toward the three officers of the court. Assuming that the deputies were wearing protective gear, he fired off three rapid headshots, two of which struck Deputy Martin—one squarely.

His next three shots were aimed at Deputy Cochran, who had already dropped to his knees for a better firing position. One of the rounds caught him in the middle of his forehead. But before the second officer was struck he had managed to get off two shots, both of which hit the old man—one in the chest, and one in the abdomen. The old man tried to drop to his knees, but Wally, his *buddy*, forced him to remain on his feet until both lawmen were down, and then he shoved him back into the house.

Christiana Baldwin stood trembling but as yet unharmed. She was terrified. As soon as Wally turned his back on her, she bolted as fast as she could make her poorly conditioned legs run.

Wally heard her. He turned and fired four rounds in her direction. One struck her in the back of her right hand, and another in her right buttocks. She stumbled to the ground, sliding first on her hands, and then on the side of her face.

As she struggled to get up, Wally quickly ran over and knocked her back down with his foot. He then placed the Glock against the back of her neck, pulled it back an inch, and fired.

Robby and Red were transfixed. Before they realized just how bad this whole chain of events was about to become, they considered running to the aid of the deputies. But in a matter of seconds it was all over. The only ones to survive were the violent visitor, and the old man. And the boys were pretty sure that the old man was fatally wounded as well. They could do nothing to help. So, they decided to remain in the secret basement and try to wait it out.

"Maybe we can hide out here until the shooter leaves," Robby whispered. Red agreed.

The boys watched Wally walk back toward the cabin. As he entered, they switched the monitor to one of the cameras that covered the inside. At first they could not find the old man. Finally, Red spotted him. He was crouched up behind the couch. In his hands was the twelve-gauge shotgun.

Wally the visitor, upon not finding the old man where he had left him, stepped back outside.

"The old bastard's hiding," he said to himself. And then he checked on the rack where the shotgun had been hanging. "And he's armed himself. … Damn it! I need to get my money before I kill him. … Damn it!"

Wally walked around the house until he found the one window that was open—it was the one left that way by the boys when they broke in.

Carefully he peered over the sill. There he spotted the old man's boots sticking out from behind the couch. He took aim and fired off three rounds. It worked. Only one round did any damage, but it was enough to cause the old man to drop the shotgun and writhe in pain.

"Now, old man, break open that scattergun and remove the shells!"

The old man's hands were now shaking violently. He was crying in pain.

As soon as he had removed the cartridges from the gun he looked up at the visitor as if to get further instructions.

"Okay. Now throw them out of the door. Can you do that?"

"I need a doctor. You shot my toes off. I need help."

"Throw the damn shells out of the door!" the visitor shouted. "Do it!"

The old man whipped his hand in the direction of the door. Both of the shells flew toward the door, but neither one of them made it out.

The visitor flashed a look of disgust at the effort, and then said, "Alright, you sonofabitch. You stay right where you are. Don't try anything stupid, or I'll kill you right now."

"Nothing more painful than a good foot shot," he muttered as he quickly walked to the door and rushed the old man.

Grabbing the shotgun and flinging it across the room, he barked, "You stupid sonofabitch. You think you're gonna outsmart me? Never gonna happen. ... Now, let's get my money. Where you got it stashed? Talk while you still can, old man, or I'm gonna shoot *all* your toes off. Where is it?"

"I'll tell you. Just don't hurt me anymore. I told you I kept all of it for you. I wouldn't cheat you. It's right here under the floorboard. Right here."

"Right where?"

"Slide the couch over, and roll up this rug. There's a floorboard that comes up. It's there. All of it."

Wally grabbed the end of the couch and shoved it across the floor. The rug slid with it.

"What board? Where's the damn board you're talkin' about?"

"The short one. Just stick a knife under it. It will pry up. You'll see."

Wally pulled a three-inch mechanical knife from his pocket and flipped the blade open.

"If I break my knife screwing with this I'm gonna cut your throat right here," he barked.

The board lifted easily, and beneath it were stacked four bank moneybags. He opened the first to find many packs of one-hundred dollar bills. He pulled several bundles out and leafed through them.

"Cool."

He then checked the other three bags. He found that all four of them were full of cash. They all appeared to have not been disturbed since the robbery over twenty-six years earlier.

"See. Just like I told you. All your money is there. I didn't steal a penny of it. ... Now, can you get me a doctor?"

"Sure. I'll get you a doctor. Doctor Glock."

Wally then shoved the pistol into the old man's mouth and pulled the trigger.

"Click."

"The damn thing's empty. Can you beat that? There should have been two more rounds in that magazine. Damn glad I wasn't counting on fifteen. ... Guess you're gonna have to settle for Dr. Scattergun."

The two boys could not bear to watch.

"Boom."

The whole cottage shook with the blast of the shotgun.

Chapter 6

A Urinal — Most Dangerous Place on the Planet

Lily, Henry's eleven-year-old daughter, was happiest when she was with her father. She was now having an extended chance at that, and she loved it.

That was not the case during the first ten years of her life because, for most of that time, she was living with her aunt, while her father, Henry, was away doing his time in the federal prison system.

And Henry was loving his freedom. In fact, he had never been happier. For the first time in his life he had a job he truly enjoyed— he was employed as Jack Handler's right-hand man. Not only did he relish working for his friend, but one of the perks of the position was that it provided a nice cottage at the Handlers' Sugar Island Resort. This arrangement not only afforded a suitable living environment for Lily, but it was conveniently close to where best friends Millie and Angel Star lived. So, when Henry's job called him out of town, Lily could stay at the Stars' home.

On this particular day, Lily and her father were totally engrossed in each other's undivided attention. Not since Henry had regained his freedom had she spent an extended amount of time with her father. And that's exactly what was now happening. The two of them were driving all the way down to Missouri to visit Lily's aunt—Henry's sister-in-law—Grace Conklin.

Grace meant a lot to Lily. During Henry's entire stint in prison,

Grace lovingly served as Lily's caregiver. In fact, Lily viewed her "Aunt Gracie" more as a mother figure than she did her birth mother, Grace's younger sister.

"Are we in Missouri yet?" she asked. "It's already dark. You said it'd be dark when we got there."

"Yeah," Henry chuckled. "You're right. It's dark. But we're still in Michigan. You should try to get some sleep … so you'll have lots of energy to play with your cousins."

"I tried, Daddy. But I'm just not sleepy."

Daddy. How he loved to hear her say that.

"Since you're still awake, we'll stop for a bathroom break," he said as he slowed to pull into the rest stop.

"This is the last stop in Michigan. Before we enter Illinois."

"Illinois. Don't you mean Missouri?"

"We have to drive through a little bit of Illinois before we get to Missouri."

"We're never gonna get to Auntie Gracie's house. It's taking forever."

"Sure seems like it to me too. But, if you can just close your eyes. Probably, when you open them back up, we'll be there. Time passes faster when you're sleeping."

Lily closed her eyes as tightly as she could, just to test what her father had said.

"Not now, silly girl. Wait until you go. And then try closing your eyes. The next thing you know we'll be tucking you in bed at Auntie's house. And then, tomorrow morning, the sun will be shining, and you'll be out in Auntie's backyard playing with your cousins."

"Can I go in the boy's bathroom with you?"

Henry had spotted a man entering the Men's room ahead of him.

"I think you should use the girls' restroom this time. Just go in and see if it looks okay. If it doesn't look right, or you're scared, come back out and wait for me. We'll figure something out."

A great word to describe Lily is cute. In fact, in her case, the word cute begs an adverb such as exceptionally. Tiny for her age, Lily had already developed her own style. On this day she was wearing her favorite floral print leggings, white long sleeved shirt with "Yooper" in gold lettering across the front. She was a little disappointed that people might not be able to read her shirt because it was partially covered by her brand new denim jacket. She quickly learned that if she put her hands in her jacket pockets she could pull the jacket open so people could read her Yooper message. She was especially pleased with the way she looked in her new lace-up red hiking boots and red matching newsboy cap. The cap had a visor that helped keep her short-cropped hair out of her eyes.

Henry waited outside the women's restroom until his daughter emerged.

"All set?" he asked.

"Yes."

"Just wait for me here. There's a nice comfortable chair for you. I'll be right out."

Henry then entered the men's room and stepped up to the urinal. His mind raced as he began to relieve himself. Making pretty good time. He checked his watch. Will get there by noon. Or maybe early afternoon. Should stop at least two more times ... for Lily. And lunch. Don't want to arrive hungry.

Henry was so engrossed in thought that he neglected to exercise his usual level of caution.

When working on a case with Jack, he would never think of using the urinal in a public restroom. He always chose a stall—and usually a handicap stall, if one was available. Never know what might happen, he reasoned. And if I'm attacked, the additional space would provide more room to maneuver.

But, this time, because he was more concerned about the safety of his daughter than his own well being, he chose to use the urinal closest to the door. That way, if Lily had a problem, he would be able to detect and deal with it more quickly.

This choice did not turn out well for Henry.

As he began to release his bladder he no longer engaged his mind in contemplating his arrival in Missouri. Instead, he began silently counting off the seconds. Typically, it would take him around fifty seconds to complete the task. Longer, if he had waited too long between stops.

But, this time, he never reached his goal. At precisely the forty-second mark the lights went out … at least for him.

He never noticed the man who had just emerged from a stall a few feet away—not until it was too late.

He'd heard the door latch being disengaged. The click echoed off the white ceramic tile walls.

Even though Henry heard the sound, and was aware that some-one was walking behind him, he did not sense danger. Not initially.

By the time he noticed the reflection in the American Standard Urinal Flush Valve—that of a bald-headed man moving quickly toward him from the rear—it was too late.

Henry did not feel any pain as his attacker slammed an elbow into the back of his head, driving his face into the ceramic tile above the urinal.

The force of the powerful blow was delivered so quickly and forcefully that Henry did not have time to react. It broke Henry's nose, loosened several of his front teeth, and, of course, knocked him unconscious.

"Daddy," Lily said. "Everything okay?"

She had heard the loud thud caused by Henry's head smashing against the wall and she was concerned.

The baldheaded man in a second move thrust his knee into Henry's back and pulled a seven-inch Ka-bar from a sheath on his belt. Had the initial blow not rendered Henry totally incapacitated, Lawrence was prepared to slide his blade between the appropriate ribs and into the heart. But, because his attacker thought that the initial blow had killed Henry, and because he heard the voice of a little girl just outside the open men's room door, he did not immediately stab him.

Why make the mess out here? he reasoned. No need. The bastard's already dead. And what if that kid comes in here looking for her dad. Don't need for her to see a bunch of blood.

The baldheaded man guided Henry's body backward and then dragged him into an empty stall. He draped Henry's body over the toilet and searched him. He smiled when he pulled a money clip from Henry's pocket. He fingered through the bills quickly determining that there were at least five hundred plus dollars. He slipped the clip into his pocket.

There were three large chairs in the common area. Lily had picked the one closest to the Men's restroom.

After a minute of waiting, Lily spoke again—this time quite loudly, "Daddy. Can I buy some candy?"

There were a few vending machines where she was waiting, and one of them featured a selection of the more popular candy bars and assorted packets of candy—including Skittles.

"They've got sour Skittles. They're my favorite. Can I buy some?"

She waited for a response, but none came.

"Daddy—you almost done?"

Again, she waited.

While her words fell silent to her father, Lawrence heard them loud and clear.

"Must be he's got a kid," he mumbled to himself. "Damn it. Carl didn't say anything about a kid."

Lawrence hated loose ends. And a kid crying around for her father could easily become a huge loose end.

At first he contemplated scooping her up and taking her with him. Children were not his first choice, but he wasn't one to overlook low-hanging fruit.

But, then he heard other voices.

"Looks like I might have company," he said so only he could hear.

With that prospect in mind, he began to straighten up the restroom. He sat Henry up on the toilet and, using a pair of police-issued handcuffs, locked both of Henry's hands behind him around a water pipe that was running down the wall from the ceiling.

He again pulled out his knife. But he had second thoughts about it. What if I cut an artery, he'll bleed out all over the floor. If I just stick it in his gut, if he ain't already dead, it'll still kill him, just slowly, and he won't bleed out on the floor.

So, that's what he did. He pushed the knife into Henry's lower abdomen, and then retracted the blade. Henry never flinched.

I'll bet he's dead already, Lawrence reasoned.

Lawrence ran off thirty feet of toilet tissue, dipped it in the toilet, and used it to clean Henry's blood off the floor. He then shoved the wad of blood-soaked tissue into the unconscious man's mouth to gag him.

Scouring the restroom until he located a paper-towel dispenser, he removed over a dozen sheets, dampened them in a sink, and cleaned the remaining blood from the floor.

After shoving as many of the towels down his throat as he could, he removed Henry's belt and double-looped it around his head to secure the gag.

If you ain't dead already, then this gag will certainly finish the job, he reasoned. It's a cinch you can't breath through that busted up nose of yours.

"Daddy," Lily said again. This time she had taken half a step through the propped-open door of the men's room.

Lawrence spotted her out of the corner of his eye as he rubbed his hands together under the high-speed drier. But he pretended not to notice her until the blower had shut down.

"Is my daddy in there?" she asked.

"I'm sorry, darlin'. Whadja say?"

"Is my daddy in there?"

"No one's in here but me. What's your daddy's name?"

"Daddy."

"His real name. What do other people call him? His friends?"

"Henry. But I always call him Daddy."

"Hey. Henry," Lawrence said, turning toward the stalls. "You in here?"

He waited a moment as though expecting a response.

"Sorry, darlin'. Looks like your daddy might have headed out to your car already. Let's check and see where he is."

"Oh. ... Daddy told me to always wait for him. I don't think I should go outside."

"So, you like the sour Skittles. I heard you say that."

"Yeah."

"So does my little girl. Sour Skittles are her favorite. Let's see if I have some money. I'll buy some for both of you."

When he pulled out the money he had stolen from Henry, Lily noticed something that looked familiar.

"My daddy has a money clip just like that."

"Really? That's interesting. ... Looks like I've got a five here. Do these machines read bills?"

"My daddy was in a federal prison. When he got out, a friend of his, Mr. Jack, gave it to him. His is made of pure silver. Is yours?"

"I don't think so. I bought mine at a cheap store."

"My daddy's looks just like that. But his is worth a lot of money, I think. Mr. Wolf, the silverman on Sugar Island, made it specially for my dad."

"Mine's just a cheap imitation," Lawrence said, removing a five-dollar bill and quickly hiding the money clip in his pocket. "Yes, the machines look like they can take bills. ... Let's see. Can you push the button for the sour Skittles?

"Good job," he said as he retrieved his change and slid two of ones back into the machine.

"Hit it once more for my daughter.

"There. Now we're all set. Shall we go give this to Sarah, and see if we can find your dad?"

"Sarah. I really like that name. One of my best friends is named Sarah. She's from Missouri. … That's where I stayed while daddy was in jail."

"Missouri," Lawrence said. "I used to live in Missouri. Where in Missouri did you live?"

Before Lily could answer, Lawrence took her tiny hand and said, "Let's go see how Sarah's doing. And maybe we can find your dad."

Just seconds after the glass and aluminum doors to the restroom had closed behind them, Henry began to stir. Totally disoriented, and choking on the gag, the only thing that he knew for certain was that he needed to free himself, and then to check on his daughter.

Using his knee he managed to peal the belt and the gag from his mouth. And then, after taking a couple deep breaths, he mustered up the strength to call out.

"Lily!" he shouted a loudly as he could.

Unfortunately, neither Lawrence nor Lily heard his plea. They were already well on their way to his car, and in his weak condition, Henry was unable to project much in the way of decibels.

But the sound of Henry's distressed voice did stop a young woman as she was walking out of the women's room.

"Lily, are you okay?!" Henry shouted. This time his voice was noticeably louder.

The woman turned to see if there were any other people in the common area. Seeing none, she cautiously stepped over to the door of the men's room.

"What's happening in there?" she asked. "Are you okay?"

"No. I'm not okay. I've been robbed and cuffed to the toilet. Is there a little girl named Lily out there?"

"No. There's no one out here except me."

"Damn it. He must have Lily," Henry growled.

"If you have a phone, call 911. The bastard took my daughter."

Henry jerked and yanked on the cuffs, but could not pull his hands out of them. "Going to have to break something, and fast," he mumbled as he forced his left shoulder out of its socket so that he could squeeze his body to the floor beside the toilet.

With his back against the side of the toilet, bracing his knees against the concrete block wall he leveraged all of his strength until he felt the toilet begin to give way. He let up for a moment, and then gave one more mighty shove.

As the porcelain bowl yielded to his effort, the plumbing that still secured his arms broke off. Water shot out as he maneuvered himself to freedom.

"Lily!" he shouted. "Lily! Where are you?"

He staggered into the stall door. He could not force it open, but he did manage to cause it to bounce open enough for him to squeeze his body through.

He stumbled as he slipped on the wet floor, but somehow he managed to remain on his feet.

"Lily!" he shouted again, as he bumped past the young woman standing just outside the men's restroom door. She was on her cell trying to explain the situation, which she did not fully understand, to the State Police.

Smashing his good shoulder into the outside doors to force them open, he made it outside just in time to catch the glow of the interior lights of Lawrence's car. It was parked not far from his own. He could not be sure, but he thought he spotted his daughter about to get into the back seat.

"Lily!" he shouted as loudly as he could.

Lawrence had his right hand on Lily's back and was reaching under her arm with his left. But, he had not yet managed to talk Lily into his car.

Hearing the voice of her father, she stood straight up and turned in his direction.

"Daddy!" she screamed, as she spun around so that she could run to him.

Lawrence shifted his right hand from her back and grabbed her tightly around the upper arm.

"You're hurting me!" she screamed at him. "Let me go!"

But Lawrence was not yet ready to give up on her. Flinging Lily to the ground with his right hand, he shoved a Taser into her lower back with his left. He then triggered a horrible, incapacitating shock into her tender eleven-year-old body.

Lily lay motionless on the hard concrete as Henry rushed toward them.

Chapter 7

Henry's Driving Drop Kick

L awrence was faced with a snap decision. Should he take the time to toss the comatose Lily into the back of his car? Or, should he just leave her on the concrete and make his getaway?

Initially, he thought he'd load the powerless child into his car, and then take off. But the sight of Henry charging at him changed his mind.

Henry, even though his hands were still cuffed, and his shoulder dislocated, was rapidly bearing down on him. If he kidnapped the girl, he knew that Henry would somehow find a way to give chase.

If, however, he were to leave the girl where she lay, Henry would surely stay and tend to her injuries. He decided to try to avoid a confrontation with Henry. He slammed the rear door and jumped in behind the wheel.

But Henry, running toward him at full speed, was rapidly closing the gap. Lawrence shoved his car in reverse and hit the gas. Henry showed no sign of slowing down. In fact, the prospect of Lawrence escaping unscathed was not acceptable to him.

By the time Lawrence shifted into drive, Henry had reached the car and had gone airborne—both of his feet were off the ground and aimed directly at Lawrence's head inside his car.

Never in his entire MMA fighting career had Henry even contemplated such a maneuver. But, he could think of no other way to smash the glass in the door with enough violence to do damage to the man behind the wheel. The move looked like what is known in professional wrestling as a driving dropkick, or a "kangaroo kick."

As soon as Henry sensed his boot striking Lawrence in the head he immediately retracted his legs as best he could. The forward momentum of the vehicle aided his effort.

Of course, Henry was not able to observe the effectiveness of his attack. He had sensed the resistance Lawrence's head and shoulder had on the force of his kick. So, it seemed to him that he must have done some damage—perhaps even serious damage. But he didn't know whether or not it was significant. That was okay with Henry. He was good with it because he knew that at the very least his new arch-enemy would be fully aware that this was war, and that while he may have got the best of Henry in the first round, there would be a round two and more.

Fortunately for Henry his legs did not get tangled up or stuck inside the car. Lawrence had accelerated considerably right off the block, so Henry's body didn't follow him into the car. Instead his shoulder and head struck the left rear quarter panel with considerable force. And he tumbled and rolled onto the concrete.

For the second time that day, Henry was out cold.

The next thing he remembered was Lily's panicked voice pleading with him to wake up and talk to her.

"Daddy!" Lily screamed when she saw the blood on Henry's face and shoulder. "What happened?"

"Don't worry, darling. It's not as bad as it looks. Daddy's okay. … Actually, I don't remember what happened. … But somehow I seem to have got my hands cuffed to the toilet. … Darlin', do you have your cell phone on you?"

"No. I think I left it in the car."

Henry smiled and looked up at the same woman he had talked to earlier. She had followed him outside and was now comforting his daughter. "I know I look like a mess. ... And I don't usually wear my belt around my neck. But I could really use your help right now. If you would you dial 911 for me again. I'm going to need some keys to get these cuffs off."

"Daddy! Daddy! Are you sure you're okay? Please tell me you're okay?"

Slowly it began to sink in.

"Lily," he said. "Did he hurt you?"

"A little. But it doesn't hurt much now. It was kinda like when I poked that fork into the electric plug. Only a hundred times worse. I couldn't move for a while. But I'm okay now."

Lily was worried about her father and wanted to console him. But the emotions and fears of a little girl finally got the best of her when she got a look at the blood on the hand she used to brush her father's hair out of his eyes. Her fingers were dripping red.

"Oh, Daddy. What happened to you? Why did that man hurt me? He seemed so nice at first. And then he changed. Why?"

"He was just a bad person. That's all."

"Did I make him mad? I tried to be nice to him. He bought me candy. He said he had a daughter my age. She was in his car. ... But I didn't see her in there. Maybe she was using the bathroom."

"You did nothing, darling. He was just a bad person. And he was lying to you. He doesn't have a daughter. He was lying. ... But, it's all over now. You're safe, and I'm safe. It's all going to be fine."

"Why are your hands tied together?"

"Now *that's* a good question. I don't exactly remember why. Somehow I fell down and bumped my head. And the next thing I know, my hands are tied. We've got to get these things off."

Henry then addressed the woman.

"Any luck with the State Police?" he asked.

"I have them on the phone right now," she said as she held the phone over so he could talk in it. "They'd like to know your name."

"My name is Chuchip Kalyesveh. My daughter Lily is here

with me. … I was robbed and cuffed by a man out here at a rest stop on Interstate 94. Not sure about the mile marker, but it is located westbound just a few miles from the I-196 junction—before Benton Harbor/St. Joe. We were on our way from Michigan to Missouri. … The man also tried to abduct my daughter."

"We have already received a call from a female at that location. It is Rest Area 706 near Watervliet. We have a car en route. Along with an ambulance. The woman said that there was a man who was badly injured and was acting erratically."

"That would be me. But I'm not badly injured. I have some cuts and scrapes, but I'm okay. You need to catch the sonofabitch that tried to take my daughter. She's just ten years old—"

"Dad, I'm eleven years old."

"Eleven. My daughter's eleven, not ten. And the asshole Tasered her. … He just left the rest stop. He was headed west, but he's probably turned around or exited by now. I'm not sure exactly how long ago he left. I was out for a little while."

"Do you have a plate number?"

"No. I didn't see it. But it looked like a silver or gray late model Toyota. The driver's side—"

"Anything you noticed that might set the driver or the vehicle apart?"

"Yeah. The driver was bald, like skinhead bald, and the glass in the driver's side door is broken out. … And, I suspect that he might have some cuts on his face. But I don't know that for a fact."

"I'm not going to call the ambulance back. I want them to take a look at you and your daughter. The female who called it in said there was a lot of blood. So there must be some injuries."

"Yeah. Whatever. I got my nose broken. But it's not like *that* hasn't happened before. And I think that I might have been stabbed. … It would be good to have them check out my daughter. The sonofabitch Tasered her. I think she's okay, but it could have … it could have hurt her much worse than it did. I'm pretty sure she's going to be okay. If you hurry, you might be able to catch this guy. He's dangerous. I'm not a little guy. Yet, he had no problem taking me out and robbing me. He's pulled ... stuff like this before."

"You should be seeing our car very soon. We'll do what we can to find this guy as well."

Things did not go as smoothly for Henry as he had hoped. Sgt. Grover, the Michigan State Trooper who was first on the scene, balked at removing the handcuffs from his wrists even though it was obvious that Henry had suffered a severely dislocated shoulder.

Instead, he first called in the serial number from the cuffs. He quickly learned that they were registered to a Missouri State Highway patrolman who had been killed in the line of duty earlier that year—a gift from Carl.

"Here's what we've got, Lieutenant," he said to the detective in charge. "The injured party here, Mr. Chuchip Kalyesveh, is less than a year out of a federal Prison Camp. He has a record of violent behavior. And the cuffs he's wearing, they belong to a deceased Missouri Highway Patrolman. Something smells very fishy here. ... He *is* injured. According to the paramedics he has multiple contusions, a broken nose, numerous cuts and scrapes, what appears to be a stab wound to his abdomen, and a dislocated shoulder.

"I have to say that I'm not comfortable removing those cuffs. Everything he said could be a lie."

"Remove the damn cuffs right now and let the paramedics treat the man's injuries. How about the daughter? Is she injured?"

"No. It sounds like she got Tasered. But I think she's okay."

"Get those cuffs off now! Treat them as evidence. ... By the way, are you wearing gloves?"

"No."

"That's a crime scene, for God's sake! Put your gloves on and bag those cuffs!"

"Yes, sir. I'll do that."

"And treat the victim the way he deserves to be treated. *He's* the injured party here. We've no reason to think otherwise. ... And don't bring up his record again."

"Yes, sir."

Chapter 8

The Old Man's Dead

The shotgun blast ripped a massive hole in the old man's midsection. He now lay silent and motionless. Red and Robby were in shock. They did not know which way to turn. Red was an innocent looking freckle-face redhead with a thick mop of curls. On almost every occasion Red could be found wearing a plaid flannel shirt, denim pants and a gray hoodie—this day was not the exception. Robby preferred camo. Kate had made a note of this inclination, and so on his last birthday she had given him a new camo jacket and pants. She had bought them a bit on the large size so he could grow into them. Robby, with his straight brown hair and serious green eyes, was every bit as agreeable as Red, even though he didn't look the part. Both boys always wore waterproof hiking boots. Generally each of them carried a backpack with their survival gear inside. That equipment included a cell phone, water bottle, Swiss Army knife, matches, compass, first aid kit, whistle, fifty-foot nylon rope, cell chargers, Myron fish lure, and one change of clothes.

"Should we try to make a run for it?" they asked themselves and each other. "If we did that, what would stop the shooter from hunting us down?"

But if they stayed put, eventually he might get suspicious and search the house. *What if he were to discover the hidden steps? He'd then come down there and kill them.*

Robby looked at Red and whispered, "He's probably going to

get out of here as soon as he can. With all those dead bodies up there, he won't want to stick around. What do you think?"

Red agreed. He pulled out his cell and silenced it. Robby saw what he had done and followed suit, and then unscrewed the LED bulb that illuminated the basement.

Red then texted: "Ten fifteen minutes. If still up there, re-think?"

Robby nodded in agreement as he read the message Red was entering.

Both boys then turned to the monitor to see what was going on above them. They watched as the killer began searching for the old man's money.

"Okay, old man," the killer said loudly. "Where'd you hide what's left of your loot? You're sure as hell not gonna need it now. Must be around here somewhere. I'm sure you didn't spend it all."

After ripping open the couch and recliner, he began pulling the books off their shelves and searching for loose boards behind them.

"Surely you'd have hid it somewhere out in the open … easy to get at. Right? Ain't that whatcha would do? You'd wanna be able to get at it easily. Right, old man?"

After the killer had listened to those words coming out of his mouth he abruptly stopped his search and hurried over to where the old man was lying.

"You dead yet?" he asked as he pulled the man's left eye open with the thumb and index finger of his right hand. "You dead or are you just faking?"

He then examined the old man's right eye.

"I ain't no doctor, but I'd say you'd be completely dead."

But just as the killer stood to his feet, the old man's digestive system involuntarily released gas.

"Oh, shit," he moaned. "You're dead, all right. You wouldn't be fartin' right now if you were still alive. … Guess you ain't gonna be tellin' me nothin."

The boys were watching and listening to all that was transpiring above them.

When they saw the killer return to where the old man had hidden the four bags of cash, they panicked. The old man had apparently constructed the secret place to stash the money after he had completed the cellar, because there was no insulation sprayed over those boards.

Red immediately laid the monitor on its face because, as the only source of light in the basement, he was afraid that the killer would spot its light shining up through a crack in the boards. His concern was justified. The storage space was created by nailing a piece of plywood between two floor joists, and another one at each end of the pocket it created. While no light could travel through the bottom piece of plywood, there was no way for Red to know for certain that there were no cracks where the end pieces had been attached. After all, with the monitor entirely blocked off, the boys were able to see some light seeping through between the boards. And they knew if light from above could find the cracks, then so might the light from the monitor be visible from above.

They sat silently as they heard the killer poking around in the storage area.

When the light that had been shining through the largest crack went dark, they knew that he had lowered himself down and was trying to peek through the crack.

And then the boys heard a static sound. Red was first to remove his jacket and place it over the speaker.

"What the hell!" the killer complained. "What's goin' on now!?"

As soon as Robby heard steps leading toward the door he lifted the monitor enough so that he could determine what was happening.

Red watched with him as the killer ran out the door and over to where Deputy Cochran was lying.

Deputy Martin, though critically wounded, had revived sufficiently to retrieve a five-shot "J-Frame" .38 revolver from a holster that was strapped to his calf. With his bloodied hand shaking erratically he still managed to get two shots off before the killer reached him. Unfortunately, both of the rounds missed the target.

"You sonofabitch! What the hell does it take to kill you?" the killer shouted as he moved quickly to where Deputy Martin was firing and kicked the man in the head. The revolver dropped from the deputy's hand with the blow.

The killer stepped over the unconscious officer and picked up the deputy's pistol.

"Let's see how this works," he said as he pointed the pistol at the deputy's forehead and squeezed off the remaining three rounds. All of them exploded in the officer's brain.

"Bet you're dead now," he said as he tossed the pistol onto the officer's chest.

He stood there for a few seconds, and then picked the pistol back up and wiped it down.

Robby looked around the basement until he found a roll of duct tape. Without saying a word he tore off several pieces and began placing them over all the cracks that were allowing light to shine through from above. That involved only the spaces around the storage area where the cash had been hidden. All of the rest of the basement ceiling had been sprayed with foam insulation.

Once he had completed that task, he returned to the monitor. And from under Red's jacket the two boys continued to watch what was transpiring above.

They observed the killer walk back over to Deputy Cochran and check his neck for a pulse. It was obvious that he was talking, but he was too far from the mic for the boys to make out what he was saying.

"He must be dead," Robby whispered. "Everyone's dead except us. And now he's heading back into the house. We still gonna wait?

Right?"

By the light of the monitor Robby saw Red silently nodding his head. They watched as the killer walked out of the view of the camera.

"Where's he goin'?" Robby asked.

Red shook his head signaling that he really had no idea.

A few minutes later the killer re-entered the scene. He was dragging one of the bodies into the house.

"Oh no!" Robby moaned. "I think I know what this might mean."

Chapter 9

Bad to Worse
for Red and Robby

As it became clear to the boys what the killer was up to, they both began contemplating their next move.

"Looks to me like he's going to drag all the bodies into the cottage," Robby whispered. "And if he does, he's probably going to torch it. … We've got to find a way out of here."

Red nodded.

Using their phones for flashlights, the boys began searching for a path to the outside. They suspected that the old man would not have built this hiding place without providing himself with some sort of emergency escape hatch. But just where that might be was eluding them. And time was running short.

Red grabbed Robby by the shoulder as he slid his phone up so his friend could read his message. "Look for hinges," the unsent text read. "Or anything that looks like it could be moved."

Robby nodded.

Several minutes passed.

Red returned to the monitor to view what was going on above. He could no longer see the bodies of either one of the deputies, so he switched to the inside camera. There he spotted all four of the victims—the female caseworker, the two deputies, and the old man. But now the killer was not in view. At least not initially. Finally, Red spotted him entering the door. He had a one-gallon can of something. The video was in black and white, so Red did not know for certain what would have been in the can.

I don't think it's a red can, Red was thinking. *So it probably isn't gas. Maybe kerosene.*

Robby spotted his friend watching the monitor and joined him. Together they observed the killer pouring the contents of the can on his victims, the floor and on the furniture until it was empty.

Robby whispered, "It could take a few minutes for the flames to burn through the floor, especially with all this insulation. But it will suck all the air out, and kill us anyway. We've got to get out of here. Somehow. I just don't see any way to escape. … Doesn't make sense that there'd be no way to escape."

And then it happened. The boys watched as the killer struck a match and tossed it into the fuel. The inside of the cottage lit up like a giant torch, and almost immediately the camera went blank.

They could smell smoke. A lot of it. They both dropped to floor to avoid the searing stench. Soon a cloud of thick smoke was boiling a few feet below the ceiling.

The temperature rose rapidly. The uninterrupted power supply that ran the monitor began beeping, indicating that the power in the cottage was out.

The boys no longer worried about the killer finding them. They knew that if they did not escape within the next minute or two they would both succumb to the smoke and lack of oxygen. They would be dead. Their only chance of survival would be to find a way out. They pulled the monitor to the floor with them— not because there was anything to see, but because the monitor was now their only source of light.

And then that's when it happened. If it wasn't a miracle, then Red was convinced that it was probably the closest he would ever come to experiencing one.

Chapter 10

Red's Miracle

At first both Red and Robby headed toward the secret door that led up the stairs and back into the main level of the cottage. But as soon as Red touched the sizzling hot door latch he realized that path of escape had closed to them. He bellowed out a warning and headed back down the stairs. He grabbed Robby on the way and pulled him to the floor.

He looked into Robby's eyes and signaled a discouraged thumbs down. Using the light from the CCTV monitor he then frantically surveyed the surroundings, searching for the last pocket of clean air.

The whole area was rapidly filling with smoke. There remained only ten or twelve inches of clean air, and that was closest to the floor.

But something else did seem to be happening. Red detected a distinct movement within the thick cloud of smoke. It seemed to be flowing toward the north end of the basement. And the closer it got to the wall, the faster it moved.

Again he grabbed Robby, almost dragging him toward the point the smoke appeared to be heading.

Even though the monitor was still illuminated, the smoke had become so intense that not much light pierced it. Still, Red was certain that the smoke was finding its way out of their death trap. *And if the smoke is being sucked out,* he determined, *then perhaps we could follow it to safety.*

By the time they reached the wall there remained no clean air.

The smoke had grown even darker and hotter, and was swirling around what felt to Red like a rough-cut pallet, like the ones used in warehouses to store and transport merchandise.

It was leaning against the wall. When Red tried to move it, he discovered it was fastened securely—it would not budge.

Forcing his face to the floor, he gasped in two deep breaths of what remained relatively clean air. And then, holding his breath, he sat up, braced his right foot against the wall beside the pallet, and exerted every ounce of strength he could muster.

He felt it give a little with the first tug.

Still holding his breath he felt for the top of the pallet, and then gave all of his strength to one final pull.

When the pallet gave way he went tumbling backward.

The smoke was burning their eyes and stinging their skin.

With Red lying on his back after his fall, Robby slid the pallet out of the way and grabbed Red by his mop of red hair and began dragging him through what seemed in the darkness to be a steel-lined tunnel. The smoke was growing hotter and hotter.

"We gotta go fast!" Robby shouted. "Gonna be flaming down here very soon."

He was right. Every second the smoke grew thicker and hotter. While the flames above had not yet burned through the floor, both boys realized that it was only a matter of seconds.

The tunnel was barely large enough to crawl through on hands and knees. But, because they were young and agile, they were able to move quickly.

No longer could they keep their eyes open. Which, however, did not hinder their progress. It was simply too dark and too hot to see anything even had they been able to use their eyes.

Finally they reached the end of the tunnel. Realizing they could progress no farther, Red reached up. He felt something hard. *This must be the escape door,* he determined. But, again, he could not budge it.

Robby was thinking the same thing. So, using his back, he lifted alongside Red.

Finally it yielded to their effort. At first it moved only an inch or two. When that happened there was a huge surge of hot smoke from the basement. Knowing that they had only seconds left before the flames broke through into the basement, they both gave one more frantic shove. And with it, the escape door opened and both boys clambered through the opening.

Less than ten seconds after they had both rolled out and away from the opening, thick black smoke began shooting out of the shaft, followed by orange hot flames.

The boys stood to their feet and ran. They did not stop running until they had reached a small creek that ran through the woods barely a hundred yards from the old man's house. It was a very small feeder stream that dumped into one of their favorite rivers for fishing. The boys were very familiar with the area because they frequently fished the larger river, particularly the section of it just before it flowed into the St. Mary's River. Their clothes were still smoking when they jumped into the shallow cool water.

After what seemed longer than it was, the two boys took a long look at one another.

"You okay?" Robby asked in a smoke-induced gravelly voice. "Cuz you sure look like crap. No offense, Red. But your face is filthy. Your hair is brown, and it looks even curlier. You really do look like crap."

Red started laughing, and then scraping his open hand rapidly over the surface of the creek he sent a large spray of water into Robby's face.

That was Red's answer to Robby's question. Both boys had sore throats caused by breathing too much smoke. And both suffered singed hair and tender skin. But they were okay, and happy to be alive.

After the boys had finished washing themselves off as best

they could, Red grabbed Robby's shoulder and pointed toward the tunnel opening. It was still in sight and they could see smoke pouring out.

Red then pointed in the opposite direction as he clambered out of the water.

Robby knew what his friend was suggesting. The killer would have spotted the billowing smoke, and would certainly be investigating it.

They had to get out of there, and as quickly as possible.

Just as they crested a small hill in their escape, three rapid pistol shots reverberated through the Sugar Island forest. The boys knew they were the target, because rounds fired directly at a person have a special, sharper, soul-wrenching sound. Realizing the urgency of their escape, they moved even more quickly.

And then two more shots blasted behind them, but Robby heard only one of them.

Chapter 11

Robby's Hard Head

The killer had elevated his aim for the last two shots that he fired at the boys. Had he been thirty years younger he might have tried to chase them down. But he knew that he was too old and too out of condition to even have a ghost of a chance to catch them. His only hope would be to lob some pistol shots in their direction and maybe hit one or both of them. So, that's what he did.

And he did get lucky.

The last round that he fired ricocheted off a small green tree-limb and struck Robby in the back of his head. While the force of the blow was considerably diminished by the branch, it still did some serious damage. The impact ripped open Robby's scalp and concussed the right rear of his head. But, luckily, it did not penetrate his skull.

That was the good news. While it did not pose a life-threatening situation, the tumbling nature of the bullet's blow was sufficient to stun Robby. He fell head first into a large limb which was still attached to a fallen tree. He was out cold.

Red could not tell if his friend was unconscious due to the severity of the bullet wound, or because of the bump he took when he ran into the tree limb. Whatever the reason, Robby was immobilized, and Red was not about to leave without him.

The killer saw Robby go down with the shot. *Maybe now I*

could catch them, he reasoned. *At least one of them. Even if I can get close enough to make this pistol more effective. ... It's worth a try.*

"Robby! Robby!" Red pleaded. "Wake up!"

Of course, the raspy groaning Red articulated sounded nothing like the words he was attempting. However, had Robby been able to hear his friend, he would have got the message.

No more time, Red determined. *I've got to get Robby out of here right now.*

Robby was an inch or two taller than Red, and weighed about the same. So, for Red even to attempt to carry his friend would present an overwhelming challenge.

As soon as he realized that he was not going to awaken Robby quickly enough to avoid capture, he dropped to his knees beside him, ducked his head under Robby's left arm, and then tried to stand to his feet.

He was almost able to lift Robby, but not quite. Both boys toppled back to the ground.

He's too tall, Red determined. *This is not going to work.*

And then another shot rang out. This one struck a tree only a couple feet from Red's head.

Pivoting on his left knee, Red twisted his body around in the direction of the gunshot.

"He's comin'," he growled in a fashion only he could understand. "Got to get out of here. Somehow."

Employing all the strength he could muster, Red made another effort to lift his friend. This time, however, he was able to maneuver his shoulders to Robby's midsection for a better center of gravity. And, instead of trying to raise him to his feet, he draped him over his back and lifted his friend entirely off of the ground.

Red gripped the top of Robby's shirt with his left hand, and wrapped his right arm around Robby's left leg at the knee. He knew that he would not be able to sustain the effort, but, if he could only manage to carry Robby to the bottom of the hill, that might be enough.

Red knew that they were very close to the larger stream. If he could somehow manage to transport Robby's limp body to the water, perhaps he could ferry him downstream to safety. *Could be our best chance to escape,* he reasoned.

He did not even attempt to run. It was all he could do to keep his balance with a quick walk. Each step was a challenge. He knew that if he were to fall, chances are he would not have the strength or the time to lift his friend again.

His legs were rapidly growing weak. With every step he feared his knees would buckle. But, somehow he found the strength to struggle on.

Ten more steps, he gargled out. *Ten steps. I've got to do it. I've got to!*

Finally, his legs gave out. But, as the boys fell toward the ground, he gave one last mighty lunge, and at the same time, he ducked his head and hurled Robby forward. When his friend landed, the force of Red's final shove caused him to roll nearly to the bank of the river.

Red then propelled himself over the top of Robby's body toward the water. Grabbing his still unconscious friend by the shirt, he dragged him the final few yards.

The shock of the cold water on Robby's flesh shocked his system. He began to regain his senses. And when his head momentarily dropped beneath the surface of the stream, he struggled ferociously to cough the water from his mouth and nose. Red quickly slapped his hand over Robby's face to silence him.

At first Robby wanted to fight with his friend. But then he realized that Red was only trying to help him escape. Almost stoically, he then relaxed his muscles to allow Red to guide his body downstream.

At the point where they had entered the stream the water was not deep enough to swim in, nor was it sufficiently swift to carry them along unaided. So, like a raft floating down a river, Red eased Robby along until they reached a point where the water pooled and deepened.

At that point Red made a snap decision. If his plan worked, it would spare their lives. If not, it would seal their fate in a fatal fashion.

Chapter 12

The Hunter and his Prey

The boys could hear the killer rustling through the leaves and underbrush. It was clear to them that he was the hunter, and they were his prey.

We're not going to escape by sneaking along in the middle of this stream, Red calculated. *It's too narrow and too slow. We've got to find a way to hide out until this guy gives up. He's already killed four people, and he knows we witnessed it. He'll not rest until he's killed us. And for right now, our only hope is to wait him out.*

Red made sure he had Robby's attention, and then he placed his right index finger over his lips indicating that Robby must remain silent. He then pointed in the direction of the pursuing killer. Robby got the message.

Moving very deliberately, Red guided them over to a grassy bank at a bend in the river. There the rapidly flowing spring waters had washed out beneath the thick grass, creating a sizable overhang of sod that cantilevered over the now more slowly flowing river. Red's plan was to drag Robby beneath the grassy ledge, and there the two would remain until the killer had given up.

If there is enough room down there, Red reasoned, *and if we can somehow brace ourselves so that we don't succumb to the current, it could work. But those are very big "ifs."*

Red placed Robby's right hand on a root and signaled that he should hang onto it. Robby's head was still bleeding from where the bullet had struck him, but not so much that it would discolor the water and give their position away. And Robby felt like vomiting. Whether it was from the concussion caused by the gunshot, or from the river water he had ingested, or just simply from his nerves, whatever the cause, Robby found it a struggle to concentrate on the most important task of the moment—staying alive. So, Red was doing most of the thinking for both of them.

Without making a sound, and barely a ripple, Red ducked under the overhang. *This might work,* he determined. *There just might be enough room for us under here. We will have to be careful about where we put our feet, but it could work.*

Red ducked back out and signaled for Robby to hold his breath.

Robby took a deep breath, pinched his nose with his left hand, and closed his eyes. As soon as Red saw he was prepared to go under, he yanked Robby's collar, pulling him briefly beneath the surface of the water, and then lifted his head inside the small air pocket he had found beneath the overhang.

While it was dark beneath the grassy ledge, there was an adequate amount of light bouncing off the surface of the water for them to function—especially after their eyes had a chance to adjust.

Red nodded his head in an interrogating fashion. Robby responded with a similar nod.

The stream was very deep beneath them. And the current was slow. *All we have to do now is hold steady,* Red concluded. *And keep our feet out of sight.*

It was that last part of his plan, though, that posed the challenge. They were quite easily able to keep themselves positioned beneath the overhang. There was an adequate quantity of tree roots available for them to grip. But, as for hiding their legs and feet—that was a different story.

At first Red tried pushing up on the sloping bottom in order to gain some leverage. But he could not dig his heels into the silt buildup on the riverbed. So, instead of it providing stability, his effort merely kicked up mud and allowed his body to slide out far enough to be seen from the bank.

This is not going to work, he concluded.

He knew that Robby was weakened by his injury. And while he could not visually verify his suspicion, he surmised that Robby would not be physically strong enough to keep his lower body adequately drawn up under the bank.

So Red hooked his heels over Robby's legs at the knees and pulled them up until he could get a firm grip on the bottom of his friend's jeans. He then twisted his own body lengthwise under the bank until he was able to hook one of his feet onto a root.

This feels okay, Red thought. *For now.*

Robby was able to keep his face above water by hanging onto one of the very handy roots, while Red secured Robby's legs with one hand, and steadied his own position with his other hand.

Even though the frigid waters of the stream were sapping their strength, Robby was able to anchor his upper body by gripping roots with both hands. Also working in his favor was the fact that he could keep both of his hands out of the water.

That was not the case for Red.

His right hand, the one securing Robby's feet and legs, was totally submerged in the stream. And he was beginning to lose feeling in that hand.

There was nothing he could do to improve his lot. If he loosened his grip on Robby's jeans for even a moment, Robby's feet and legs would immediately begin to drift out into sight, and that would be fatal.

He could not even switch hands. If he were to relax his grip on the root, he would instantly begin drifting downstream.

I must not allow myself to think about the pain, Red determined. *I need to concentrate only on what I am doing. I must keep both of my hands right where they are—firmly gripping.* And then, without warning, it happened.

There was a loud splashing sound right beside Robby's stomach. The killer had stabbed the surface of the water above them with a large hardwood staff. He shoved the end of it down at the edge of the bank. It forcefully pierced through the water, sliding down Robby's stomach and sinking deeply into the soft riverbed below.

The impact on his body was glancing so it did not injure Robby. But it startled him, causing him to flinch just enough to wrench his right leg out of Red's grasp. Before Robby could react, his foot shot out from beneath the bank and into full view from above.

It took Robby less than a second to draw his foot back, but it had been out of control long enough for it to kick up a great deal of silt.

Fortunately, the staff itself had stirred the mud when the killer had initially rammed it down.

Red maintained his grip on Robby's left pant leg. There was nothing he could do about the other leg. Robby would have to take care of that problem now.

The killer had seen the movement below. But there was so much mud swirling in the area that he assumed that he had stirred up a fish, or a muskrat. He waited for the water to clear, and then shoved his stick down again. This time Robby was ready for it, and he held steady.

Robby hooked his right toe around his left ankle, and waited.

After the water cleared again, the killer shoved the stick down again. And again. But Red and Robby did not flinch.

And then there was nothing. For a long time dead silence prevailed.

How long do we have to stay down here? both boys wondered.

Just when it seemed like their strength was gone, they heard a welcome sound from off in the distance. It was a siren. *The fire department,* they both thought. *He's gonna have to get going now.*

After what seemed like another eternity, there was one final splash. But it was out toward the middle of the stream. The boys, concentrating their attention along the surface of the water in the direction of the sound, could clearly see what had caused it. The killer had tossed his staff away and it was floating downstream.

"If you little bastards can hear me," he growled. "You may *think* you have won this round. But I'll get you in the end. You can count on it."

Is he giving up on trying to hunt us down? At least for now?

A few moments later they heard him briskly striding away through the leaves.

But neither of the boys moved. *We've waited this long,* they both resolved. *We can hang on a little longer.*

Chapter 13

Henry, Where are You?

Henry. Where are you right now?" Jack asked his friend.

"I'm at the hospital. I'm sure I'm okay. Ended up with a minor shoulder dislocation, and a harmless nick in my gut. Not the first time for either. After the cops took the cuffs off I popped the shoulder back. I was actually in pretty good shape by the time the ambulance got me here."

"Which hospital?" Jack asked.

"Lakeland. Right in Watervliet."

"Not familiar with it."

"It looks like a great hospital. Quite modern. … But, I shouldn't be here very long. A good vet could've done the job. All I need are a few stitches and a bottle of alcohol. … And, I got my nose broken again. Nothing serious. A bottle of Jack Daniels, a couple aspirins, and a pair of cheap sunglasses. That oughta take care of my face."

"They'll want to keep you the night for observation. … When you got your nose broken—were you out?"

"Yeah. So I suppose I got a little concussed."

"Does your doctor know you were out?"

"Yeah. I was totally straight with the cops and the doc."

"They'll hang on to you for at least the night—guaranteed. … How about Lily? You said she was okay. But did she get traumatized?"

"She's seen me after my fights. She understands black eyes and broken noses. Fortunately, all she suffered was a shock from a Taser, and a little bump on her head. Probably got that when she fell on the concrete. The asshole didn't otherwise touch her. So, I'm pretty sure she'll be okay. ... I got hold of her aunt and she is on her way to pick Lily up."

"She's very lucky," Jack said. "Lily! He Tasered your daughter? ... Those Tasers are designed to take down a Chicago Bears lineman. Can't even imagine how it would feel to a little girl. Much less what it could have done to her. ... I called Lindsay. She talked to her father—who is her boss. She said she would drive down and help out with Lily. And I also talked to my daughter, Kate. She's not sure if she can get away. But if she can pull away for a few days, she'll give us a hand."

The *Lindsay* Jack was referring to was Det. Lindsay Hildebrandt, rookie detective in the Grand Rapids Police Department. She and Jack were involved in what observers called a *relationship*. But both of them were more comfortable referring to their arrangement as a *close friendship*.

Calvin Brandt, senior detective in Grand Rapids Police Department—and archenemy of Jack's—never missed an opportunity to badger his co-worker about her association with Jack, referring to it as a "friendship with benefits."

Even though Lindsay's father, Marcus Hildebrandt, was chief of police in Grand Rapids, Det. Brandt's hatred for Jack far outweighed his fear of his boss. And besides, Det. Brandt was so close to retirement, he knew that there was nothing that the chief or his daughter could do to him that would affect his pension. And so his constant mocking and bullying of the female detective went unabated.

Jack, however, was keeping score. While he was willing to allow Lindsay to handle the pressure for the short term, eventually he intended to straighten Brandt out. Justice would come to Brandt, and when it did, it would be totally on Jack's terms.

In fact, in the back of Jack's mind was the gnawing suspicion that Det. Brandt was behind the original attack on him in prison—the one where Henry rescued him.

"What do you know about this guy who attacked you?" Jack asked. "Do you suppose you might have encountered him before?"

"If he knew me, and if he's got a brain, he'd have known that he should have finished the job when he had the chance. ... I suppose it could have been a random robbery. He caught me while I was vulnerable. Taking a damn leak at a rest stop. I don't remember much about it, but he did hit me pretty good. And he was not a little guy. Busted my nose and loosened my two front teeth."

"Would you recognize him?"

"After he Tasered Lily. As he was jumping into his car. I got a good look at his left arm. Covered with tats. I'm sure he got them in prison. I know prison gang tats. He had an "88" on his shoulder. That's white supremacist shit. Eight twice, indicating the eighth letter of the alphabet twice, 'HH,' for 'Heil Hitler.'

"And he had a pretty elaborate black cobweb tat on his elbow. He *definitely* got that one in prison."

"Long termer," Jack said. "How old would you say he was?"

"Fifty. Maybe a little older. Well-muscled. Not particularly tall. Five nine or ten. One eighty something. Perhaps a little more. Trim. No fat. ... Built like a fighter. Might have done some boxing. ... I'd guess that he struck me with an elbow to the back of the head. He drove it right through. Damn near broke my neck. He knew how to deliver a big elbow."

"But would you be able to recognize him if you saw him on the street?"

"Don't know for sure. But I got a pretty good look at his face just as he was pulling out. I'm sure I gave him a headache."

"How'd you do that? I thought you had cuffs on?"

"I got a pretty good run down that sidewalk, and managed to plant my heel on the side of his head as he was driving off."

"That must have been a beautiful thing to see."

"Hardly. He was a moving target. I'm just glad the glass shattered, or I would have just bounced off the side of his car. There'd have been nothing pretty about that."

"So he would have had some cuts on his face?"

"I'd think so. But that tempered glass doesn't do too much damage like that—when it's flying at you. They had to pick a lot out of my leg. I got cut up a little because my leg slid across the broken plane. He was more or less showered by the glass. If it got in his eyes, and it probably did, it might have done some damage. But, about the only thing I can be pretty sure of is that I planted a fairly significant bruise on the left side of his head. I never saw him after impact. But I'd have to think that I left a mark."

"Cops tell you anything?"

"No. When they found out I had a record, it's like they shut down. Suddenly *I* became the bad guy. I'm sure they're working it. ... But he probably got off the Interstate as quickly as he could. It could have been at the Friday Road exit. That would be only a few miles west. Or, he could have taken one of those emergency vehicle cuts through the median, or exited at I-196 just a few miles further. I'm sure he had plenty of time to get off. After that, who knows?"

"Hell," Jack said. "He just might be in the bed next to you."

"Believe me, I thought of that. I told the detective that he might be needing some medical attention, and he put the word out. But, if he's the pro I think he is, he'll be lying low and privately licking his own wounds, if they're not *too* serious. ... That's what I'd do."

"Did they admit Lily?"

"Yes. Otherwise I think they would have had to call Child Protective Services. They admitted her, but then allowed her to come up here with me. She's sitting here coloring."

When Lily realized that she had become the subject of the conversation she looked up at her father and smiled.

"Want to say *Hi* to Uncle Jack?" Henry asked.

She immediately jumped out of her chair and ran over to her father.

"Hi, Uncle Jack. You should see Daddy. He's got stitches on his forehead. And, his nose looks pretty funny, too."

"You mean he's not as pretty as he used to be?"

"Daddy's not pretty. He's handsome. But, right now he looks kinda funny. He's got stitches—a bunch of stitches. His leg—it's all scratched up. His top lip is fat. And his nose is red and puffy."

"So, he looks like a clown. But is he smiling?" Jack chuckled. "Can he *still* smile?"

"Yes. Daddy can still smile. But he does look funny. He's all red around his eyes. He said that tomorrow he will look like a clown."

"Really," Jack said with a smile in his voice. "I'm not so sure he likes clowns very much."

"Me either," Lily said. "I'm kinda scared of clowns. … But I won't be scared of Daddy. Unless he puts on that stupid makeup."

"Here," Henry said. "Hand me the phone. I have to tell Uncle Jack something."

"Daddy wants to talk to you some more. Bye, Uncle Jack," she said as she passed the phone back to her father.

"Jack," Henry said in a tone waxing serious if not ominous. "I know you want to help. But I'm gonna have to take care of this myself. Once this sonof … once we get a fix on this guy. I want him. This must never go to court. You know what I'm saying. I know you do."

"Henry," Jack said. "I'm in the middle of a very untimely audit. No way am I going to be getting in the way. … And, yes, I most certainly understand your … frustrations. I'd feel the same way had some bastard gone off on my daughter. We're going to do everything we can to locate this guy. And as quickly as possible. Time is always critical in these situations. It's just unfortunate that I'm stuck here in Chicago dinking around with this audit.

"Maybe, once I'm done here, I can be of more help. In the meantime, Lindsay will be available, at least to a degree. … And maybe Kate. I do want you to keep me in the loop. You will do that? Right?"

"Of course, Jack. But you need to know that this is *my* problem to solve."

"Exactly right," Jack agreed. "I understand. That's how it has to be."

But, as soon as Jack disconnected the call he speed-dialed Roger Minsk, his friend in the Secret Service.

"Rog, we've got a problem here."

"Of course you do," Roger replied. "Why else would you be calling me?"

"I should say Henry's got a problem. And I need some help solving it."

Chapter 14

Roger to the Rescue

Does this have to do with that audit we talked about earlier?" Roger asked. "Because, if it does, you must keep in mind that Allison runs her own show these days. Since her stroke I don't have any pull when it comes to her and her agenda. And, hell, I can't exert *any* influence over there at Constitution Avenue—especially when it comes to *eleven eleven*."

By *eleven eleven* Roger was referring to the home office of the Internal Revenue Service, which is located at 1111 Constitution Ave.

Roger had intended his comment to serve Jack with a backhanded warning that the audit Former First Lady Allison Fulbright was orchestrating just might wind up in the hands of the IRS, in much the same manner as one did in the case of Al Capone.

Jack had contacted Roger earlier after he had become suspicious regarding a call he had received from his attorney about a New York law firm nosing around about some of Jack's business practices in Chicago. Because the inquiries had apparently originated in New York, Jack suspected that his long-time enemy, Former First Lady Allison Fulbright, might be behind it in an effort to force Jack into an IRS audit.

While Roger did work for the Federal Government, he actually had nothing at all to do with the court system. And, aside from his having to file his forms every spring just like everyone else, he possessed no inside information about the IRS.

Roger's full name was Roger Minsk—senior agent in the Secret Service. He was, in fact, the head of the detail responsible for protecting Allison Fulbright, the quasi-estranged wife of Bob Fulbright, the former president. This was a position Roger had held for over a decade and a half.

"Neither Allison nor the IRS are on my grocery list today," Jack told Roger. "The big issue right now is with Henry."

"Really. What's up with him?"

"He ran into an elbow. A big one. He was with his eleven-year-old daughter. Taking her down to visit her aunt in Missouri."

"So, where did this happen?"

"Southern Michigan. He's at a hospital in Watervliet right now. He's okay, he says. They're holding him there for observation. Could get discharged as early as tomorrow morning."

"Any idea who might have done this to him? Was it robbery? … Or something more?"

"He's convinced it was a random robbery. But I question that. Who in their right mind's going to try to rob that big sonofabitch? … Besides, I generally don't buy that coincidence shit. … Can't put my finger on it, but I think that there might be a lot more to it."

"Got a description of the guy?"

"Not a great one. Henry said he'd probably be able to identify him if given the opportunity. But I do have some info that might help limit the possibilities."

"Fire away," Roger said. "I'm just sitting here babysitting Allison. And watching the latest episodes of Harry Bosch … for the second time. Really wouldn't mind the challenge."

Allison had recently suffered a stroke and so was not getting out of her apartment very much.

"Can't believe you'd be getting into that series."

"Yeah. Love it. He reminds me a little of you."

"Don't give me that. I'm nothing like Bosch—that cynical old bastard. You've got to be kidding me."

"Well. What do they say about, 'If the shoe fits?' Anyway, I'll pause *Harry*, and you can tell me what you know about Henry's attacker."

"First things first. Within the past ninety minutes he would have been pointed west on Interstate 94. Heading out of the Rest Area 706. By Watervliet. Driving a later model gray or silver Toyota. With the driver's side window broken out."

"Ninety minutes is an eternity."

"I know," Jack said. "But I thought that maybe there were some cameras that could be accessed. Be nice to get a plate number."

"I'm putting it out there right now. We'll just have to see if it turns anything up. ... How about the perp himself? Anything specific about him?"

"Skinhead. Probably in his fifties. Well built. Henry said he sensed the guy might have some fighting experience. Maybe a boxer, or MMA. Henry thought he delivered the elbow like a pro. Right-handed. Henry got hit with a right elbow.

"Another thing about an elbow. Henry got a good look at the guy's *left* arm. He had a sizable black cobweb that pretty much covered the elbow. In fact, all the tats, and his whole arm had tats, were black. That strongly suggests prison tats, as black ink is all they have to work with.

"The guy's shaved head, along with a double eight on his shoulder, they both indicate that he sympathized with the white supremacists. Henry didn't point out any specific gang affiliation, but the supremacist shit strongly suggests that possibility."

"The fact that he still shaves his head on the outside," Roger added, "and that he's not covering up his tats, that could mean he *continues* to identify with that segment of society. ... And, about the boxing. Is Henry fairly certain about his buddy having boxing experience?"

"Henry's a pretty good judge on matters like that. If he thought his attacker had some significant experience, then most likely that would be the case."

"Back in the '70s, there were some prison fighters who were

granted furloughs to fight professionally outside the prisons. But now, about the only prison programs I know of are amateur boxing clubs, and they are mostly in Louisiana. The best known is the AABA—the Angola Amateur Boxing Association. That's not to say that professional boxers never go to jail—take Mike Tyson, for instance. But if your guy was a long-termer, and if he has maintained his boxing skills, then it follows that he had the opportunity to train aggressively in lockup. And, for that, the Louisiana system provides the most likely place to start looking.

"I'll pass your info along and see what it turns up down south. If this unsub didn't do his time down there, someone still might know something about him based on the description. ... I'll also do a search of related databases and see what it turns up. We should at least get some names. And that's more than we've got now."

"There's one more thing," Jack said. "If I'm not wrong, Henry has your number. Right?"

"He has my regular voicemail account. But not the number to my secure line."

"Right. He's thinking that he needs to deal with the attacker. *Personally* deal with him. Because his daughter was involved. I know you're already aware that he's on parole. One slip up and he's back in. And if he should ever show his face inside again he'll be dead that same day. Can't let that happen."

"What've you got in mind?"

"I'll figure something out when the time comes," Jack said. "But, for right now, if he should contact you I want you to let me know immediately. ... And any info you come into regarding our guy, filter it through me first. Henry will accept my help, but only in the hunt. He wants to finish the job himself. That smells too much like revenge. Can't let him go there. Those are the easiest crimes to solve."

"I get it," Roger replied. "But aren't you vulnerable yourself? There's a whole list of judges who would love to drop the gavel on you."

"Sure. But I'll be far less passionate in execution."

"I'm sure you'll be more careful. But that rap you beat. That judge can't be very pleased about it. You made him look bad. I've heard that he can't wait to get his hands on you. And the Brandt fellow. He has a lot of friends, and some of them are in low places. He might conjure up some evidence and try to punch your ticket. If he even suspects that you're in any way involved—it could be bad."

"Chance I have to take. I'll think of something when the time comes. … Hell, if I don't survive this audit, I might be up the creek anyway … or dead."

"Well, be safe and be careful," Roger encouraged him. "I'll see what I can turn up on your guy. Talk to you later."

Chapter 15

Fire Trucks Approaching

Even though the boys had clearly heard the fire sirens approach, and, subsequently, what sounded like the killer making a hasty exit through the forest, it was nearly half an hour later before they dared to venture out. Finally, Robby said, "Shall we take a look around and see if it's safe? Can't stay down here forever. I have *never* been this cold."

As soon as those words slipped through Robby's lips, Red released his grip on Robby's jeans. Actually, it wasn't truly a *grip*. His hand was so cold that all he could do was to hook his finger onto a twisted shoestring. He couldn't feel a thing with his right hand. So he wouldn't have been able to close it tight enough to grasp anything.

The bank was a little less steep above where Robby was hiding. So he made the first effort to crawl out and then up. Because both of his hands had been wrapped around a root, and therefore above the water, he was better able to use his fingers to climb up the bank.

Red was in worse shape. While his left hand was practically welded to the root he was using to anchor himself, he was at least able to use his fingers and thumb to some extent. But only those digits on his left hand. His right hand, the one he used to help Robby hide, was numb and totally unusable.

"Oh my gosh!" Robby said as he pulled his friend up the bank. "Your hands feel dead. Like cold raw hamburger. … You sure you're still alive?"

Even though engaged in a full-body shiver, Red could not

keep from laughing out loud.

"And your lips," Robby harmlessly chided. "You look like you just ate a piece of Blue Mouth Candy."

The boys wasted no time. They ran downstream to a point where the stream was shallower. They crossed, and kept running directly away from the black smoke of the burning cottage.

"Where're we headed?" Robby finally asked.

Red didn't break stride, nor did he attempt to answer. In any normal situation, he would stop and text his answer. But that was no longer an option—his cell, as well as Robby's, had been under water for well over an hour. And, besides that *minor* issue, he really did not know where they should go. Or could go. The killer had promised to hunt them down. The boys believed him.

Red's mind was working overtime. *When the fire department arrives, they are going to find four charred bodies inside that burned out cabin. There will be no evidence connecting the real killer to these crimes. In fact, there will probably be no evidence that this guy even exists.*

Most likely the sheriff will bring in dogs. And they will track Robby and me back to Pat K's cottage. And I think Pat knows exactly who it is that had been living in his cottage when he is gone—Robby and me. ... And, the sheriff will conclude that we have a motive for killing his deputies, and our caseworker. After all, she's the one responsible for pulling us out of Jack's house. The deputies were there only to support her. ... We're the ones with the motive. For sure, that's what the sheriff will think.

Those were the thoughts that were racing through Red's mind. He was sure about three things. He knew that the killer was serious about tracking him and Robby down and killing them. *That man is deadly. ... He didn't think twice about killing the two deputies. You've got to be some kind of crazy to kill a cop. He'll be comin' after us.*

Red also knew that no one would believe their story. *No one except for Jack, Kate and Henry. They'll believe anything we tell them. But who's going to believe them?*

And, the third thing he was sure of was that they could not go back to Pat K's cottage. Never. Those were the three things that he knew for certain, and all three were bad.

Finally, Robby caught up to Red and grabbed his shoulder.

"We need to get a plan," he said. "Where are we headed? We need some dry clothes, and someplace to hide out. … Any ideas?"

Red turned and crashed to the ground in a single motion. Robby collapsed beside him.

Red just feigned a big smile, raised his eyebrows, and shook his head.

"Me neither," Robby said. "You can be sure, there will be a major manhunt on the island. They'll bring in the State Police, helicopters, dogs, and everybody with a uniform. There will be no safe place to hide. Not once they decide that we killed those people. And that's what they are going to think. … I'd like to call Uncle Jack, or Kate. But we can't. … We don't have phones!"

Red pointed to the back of his head, and then at Robby.

Robby got the message.

"It's fine," he said, gingerly tapping his wound with his hand. "I can barely feel it anymore. It quit hurting about the time my whole body went numb from the cold."

He then examined his fingers to see if there was blood on them.

"Looks like it quit bleeding. That's good. … Uncle Jack always says it's good to thoroughly wash out a wound. I'd say I did a pretty good job doing that."

Red smiled.

Red then wrapped his arms around himself signaling that he was cold.

"Yeah," Robby said. "Me too. We've got to get some dry clothes. And right away. The cops are going to be all over this place real soon. With dogs. *Real* soon."

Suddenly Red's head shot up. It was as though he had just heard a noise. Or a familiar voice calling to him from the distance.

Robby recognized that look, and he sat silently waiting for Red to elaborate. However, this time around Red was significantly handicapped because they had no cell phones.

Typically Red would enter a text, and Robby would read it over his shoulder.

Red looked around, and then stood to his feet. He made sure he had Robby's full attention.

And then he pointed toward the St. Mary's River. The initial gesture was followed by a second. This one looped over the trees, indicating that they should go beyond the river.

"Are we gonna need a boat?" Robby asked.

Red nodded, widened his eyes, and gestured by spreading his hands as widely as he could.

"A big boat?" Robby said.

Red nodded.

"The ferry?"

Red shook his head.

"Not the ferry?"

Red shook his head again.

"What then? If *not* the ferry."

Red repeated his hand gesture.

"A freighter?"

Red nodded.

"Whoa! How would we do that? It'd be next to impossible to get on a freighter. … The ferry, yeah. But, *nobody* ever sneaks onto a freighter."

Red then began nodding his head, and signaling with his index finger. He pointed first at Robby's chest, and then at his own.

"We're gonna hop a freighter? Is that what you have in mind?"

Red nodded.

"Let me think about that. If we were able to do that, it would get us off the island. And outta the Soo, too. We've gotta get as far away as possible. As soon as possible. Right?"

Red nodded.

"Okay. Then, how do you propose we do this?"

It would have been handy were Red to have learned the standard American Sign Language. But, he had not. Kate did not permit him to learn it. Over a year earlier she had Red tested. The physicians determined that a relatively simple surgical procedure would have permitted Red to begin learning to speak. And that's what she wanted him to do. But Red was not willing to have the surgery. At least not yet. Kate believed that if he were to learn sign language, he might never submit to the operation. She never thought that it would become such an issue for him. But it was.

So, rather than employing the standard signs, he and Robby developed their own methods of communication. If they were able to use texting, that's what they did. But, in situations such as this, sharing ideas became difficult, if not totally tortuous.

Red first placed his hand on his chin as though stroking a beard.

"A man?" Robby said.

Red nodded.

He then placed his hand on top of his head, and then slid it down toward his chest.

"A short man?"

Red nodded as he held his hands to his eyes. He touched his index fingers to his thumbs.

"A short man with glasses?"

Red nodded.

"Does he work on a freighter?"

Red nodded.

There was only one man who fit that description. "Are you talking about Little Rich?"

Red nodded. And this time he smiled.

"You think he could somehow get us on his freighter?"

Red nodded.

"I think you're right. But how would we find him?"

Red looked around and got his bearings. And then he pointed in a northwesterly direction.

Robby followed his finger and figured out what his friend was suggesting.

"You think he might be at his house right now?"

Red raised his eyebrows, feigned a smile, and shrugged his shoulders.

"Worth a try, I'd say," Robby agreed. "He's about the only person outside Uncle Jack and Kate, who we can totally trust. ... Of course, we can trust Henry, too. But none of them could get us on a freighter."

Red nodded.

"Shall we give Little Rich a try?"

This time Red didn't nod. He simply turned in the direction he had just pointed and began running.

Both boys knew the way to Little Rich's house. It was not that far, either. Only a couple of miles through the woods. At the rate they were going, it would take them only a half an hour to reach his house—maybe a little less.

Once they drew within sight, Little Rich's dog started barking. He was a large black and brown mixed breed. Little Rich said he was mostly German Shepherd, but everyone else said he was at least half wolf. ... And that was what everyone except for Little Rich called him: "Wolf."

Little Rich had a different name for him, however. He called him *Dee-O-Gee*—which was *DOG* spelled out. Little Rich was so adamant that his pet was not mixed with a wolf, he called him Dee-O-Gee to help dispel the rumor.

Wolf was tied to a tree just outside Little Rich's house. He had broken his dog chain, and so Little Rich had tied him to the tree with a log chain—the same one he had used to lift the engine from his truck the previous year.

Even though the chain was extraordinarily heavy for a dog, Wolf dragged it straight out and was bounding around at the end of it like it was a piece of twine.

"Dee-O-Gee!" Little Rich shouted as he stepped out of the door. "What's goin' on out here? You see somethin'? What's up?"

When Little Rich called to his dog, he did it so that it sounded like a single word, with the emphasis on the *O*.

It was beginning to get dark. The boys observed that Little Rich was gripping a pump action twelve gauge at the end of his left arm, and a beer in his right hand. And he wasn't wearing his glasses. So, they did not want to expose themselves yet. *That probably isn't his first beer of the evening,* they concluded. *Better to just sit tight for now.*

"Hey!" Little Rich shouted in the direction that Wolf was looking. "Who goes there? Better show yourselves right now. Or you'll be dealing with Dee-O-Gee, and this here twelve gauge Remington. Who's out there?"

The boys didn't respond.

"I said, who goes there?" Little Rich shouted again. "Best to present yourselves now, before I start shootin'."

Still the boys remained silent.

"Okay. You've been warned."

Little Rich then carefully sat his beer down on the step, leaned the shotgun on the porch beside it, and released the animal's collar.

The dog then tore off toward the two boys like a wolf possessed.

Little Rich picked up his shotgun. He looked ready to shoot at anything that moved.

When Wolf reached the boys, Red rolled over on his back and

grabbed the huge dog by the ruff.

Robby joined in.

"Hey, Wolf, how ya doin'?" Robby said, eagerly petting his second favorite dog in the world.

"I know," Robby continued. "You wish we'd brought Buddy with us. But we couldn't. He's visiting with Uncle Jack right now. So, me and Red are just gunna *havta* do this time."

"Hey!" Little Rich shouted. "What the hell's goin' on out there? Who's out there?"

"It's just us," Robby yelled, but barely loud enough to be heard. "Robby and Red."

"Robby and Red? What the hell you doin' over here this time a night?"

"We need to talk to you. Okay?"

"Yeah, sure. Come on up."

The boys had waited until they were certain that Little Rich was not going to shoot them before they announced themselves.

"Well, I'll be damned," Little Rich said as they approached. "I thought I had me a bear, or somethin'. Wasn't expectin' a couple snot-nosed punks like you two. What the hell you doin' out here, anyway? Ain't you supposed to be hidin' out at Pat's cottage? That's what *I* heard."

Robby looked over at Red and said, "Little Rich, how'd you know about that?"

"Oh, hell. Everybody knows that you fellows have been holed up at Pat's cottage while he's Downstate. Isn't that the way it is?"

"Well. Yeah," Robby said. "I suppose we have. But, actually we *should* be back staying with Uncle Jack."

"I know about the judge," Little Rich said. "He took you away from the Handlers. ... Something about it being too dangerous for a kid. Somethin' like that. Yeah?"

"Yeah. *Exactly* like that."

"So, why you here spookin' Dee-O-Gee? You oughtn' be sneak-

ing around here like this. Not with that fire and shit goin' on. …
What's that all about, anyway? You know what's burning? Smells
like one of those cottages on fire. That what it is?"

"It is. That old man's place. The stone house. It burned down.
… Can we come in? Red and me? And dry off. We're wet and *very*
cold."

"Sure. Come on in. I'll kick up the fire. … How'd you get so
wet?"

"We fell in the stream, sort of fell, that is," Robby replied.
"We'll tell you all about it. And, we're gonna need your help. If
that's okay."

"Sure," Little Rich said. "I've got some dry clothes you can
wear. You boys just press in by the stove. I'll toss in another log."

"We're gonna need more than just a little help," Robby said.
"Red and I are in big trouble. So, if you decide to wash your hands
of us, we'll understand."

"What the hell did you boys do?" Little Rich said with a sly grin
and a chuckle in his voice. "You break Pat's favorite axe handle?"

"Way worse than that," Robby said. "But *we* didn't actually do
anything. It's what the cops are gonna think we did. … And what
we saw."

Chapter 16

The Boys Tell Their Story

Get over here, Dee-O-Gee," Little Rich barked at Wolf, coax-
ing him to accept the chain and collar. "Yur gonna like it
out here better than inside with the fire. Get *over* here."

"Attaboy," he said, patting Wolf on the head. "You let me know
if we get any more company. Ya hear?"

Little Rich then squeezed past the boys and opened the door.

"Come on. Let's get you boys cleaned up. … And *warmed* up.
Maybe some hot chocolate would help, too."

Little Rich put a large aluminum pan filled with water on top
of the wood stove. "It'll take a while for this to warm up," he said.
"So, maybe while it does, you can tell me about all this trouble you
think you got yourselves into."

Robby looked over at Red to get a read on what his friend was
thinking.

Red squeezed a tight smile, nodded, and held out his hands
palms up.

That signaled to Robby that he should tell Little Rich the whole
story. And so he did. He explained everything—from their breaking into the old man's house, to the killings, and the fire.

When he pulled his hair back to show the man the gunshot
wound on the back of his head, Little Rich lit up a Marlboro and
began to nod his head.

"I heard some shots from that direction," he said. "Thought
someone was target shooting. Could tell no one was hunting.
Sounded like a pistol. And they were spaced out wrong—for hunting. But we all mind our own business here on Sugar Island. As

long as the old man wasn't shooting at me or Dee-O-Gee, it's his affair. Not gonna stick my nose in his business.

"Now, just how sure are you that somebody got shot? Besides one of you. Did you actually see it? Or are you just supposin'?"

"We know for sure," Robby said. "The old man had cameras set up, and we watched it happen. We were hiding in his cellar."

"Maybe you saw a TV program. Could *that* be?"

"No. It happened. We're sure. Our caseworker, Miss Baldwin, and two deputy sheriffs. They all got shot. Dead. And the old man, too. He's dead. And the killer then set the cottage on fire. When we ran out the back, he tried to kill us. That's how I got shot. Red and I were running away. … When we reached the stream … you know, the one just over there, by the old man's cottage. When we reached the stream, we jumped in and hid under the bank. The killer followed us. And he threatened to come after us. … That's why we're here. We need your help."

"Holy shit. That's quite a story you're tellin'."

"Yeah. Except, it's not a story. It's all true."

"And how do you think I can help? You can get washed up here. And I'll give you some dry clothes. … But the best advice I can give you is to call the sheriff. And tell him the whole story. He can protect you, if this guy you're talking about, if he's seriously trying to hurt you."

"No one's gonna believe us," Robby said. "We're runaway foster rats. That's what they think of us. And, with two deputies dead. And our caseworker. For sure they're gonna think we did it. They're not gonna believe us. Not for one minute. As soon as we turned ourselves in, they'll quit looking."

"Who's this guy?" Little Rich asked. "The one who did all the killin'? … *Why'd* he do it?"

"He was an old friend of the old man's. They'd done some robberies, I guess. Stole a lot of money. And the killer ended up doing time in prison, while the old man lived here on Sugar Island.

Hiding out in that cottage of his. He had cameras and all kinds of electronics in there to watch his property. ... Well this guy showed up, right after us, and the old man hid us down in his cellar when his partner got there. Then the deputies and Miss Baldwin walked up. That's when it got bad. The visitor shot all three of them right in front of the cottage.

"And then he ordered the old man to give him his share of the money. A lot. Bags full of cash, it looked like. He then shot the old man, and set the cottage on fire. ... That's when we ran out. ... Somehow he spotted us running away. And that's when I got shot in the head."

"Holy shit. That's one unbelievable story you're tellin'."

"You don't believe us?"

"Oh, I believe you all right. ... But I doubt that the sheriff will. I think you're right about that. You boys are in a big pile of shit. Pardon my French."

"We know it. That's why we're here asking you to help us."

"This whole island is gonna be crawling with cops. As soon as they figure out that those deputies got killed. The fire trucks are over there right now. You can be sure the sheriff's there by now, or at least on the way. You don't have any time. ... Just what would you like me to do for you? As I see it, you don't have a shot in hell. ... What are you thinkin'?"

"The same thing," Robby said. "They're gonna be here very soon, looking for us. As soon as they figure out that we have been at the cottage. They're gonna have everyone in the county looking for us."

"So, what exactly do you have in mind?" Little Rich asked.

"You work on the freighters. Right?"

"Not any more. I got myself injured. Can't do the work anymore. I'm on Social Security. Disability. As of six months ago. Total disability."

Robby looked over at Red. Both boys were clearly disappointed.

"Tell me, how does it matter whether or not I'm still working on the boats?"

"We need to get off the island," Robby said. "And we even need to get farther away than that. We thought that if you could get us on a freighter, we could maybe go to a different city. And then call Uncle Jack and have him help us. Maybe even a different state. I think some of those freighters haul iron ore all the way to Cleveland. If we could get that far away, maybe we would be safe. … Not only are we trying to hide from the cops, we've got that killer on our trail as well."

"What could you do in Cleveland?"

"We don't know," Robby said. "Probably hide out for a while, and then contact Uncle Jack, or Kate. … Right now the cops are gonna be watching them real close. If we called Uncle Jack, we'd probably get him in trouble. He'll be looking for us as soon as he finds out we've got this problem. But, for the time being, we thought maybe you could get us on a freighter. And that could buy us a little time. … We don't know what we're doing. It's a sure bet that the cops are gonna be huntin' us down. And so's this killer. And they are not gonna believe us that there even is a killer. We're as good as dead if we don't do something soon. We're scared."

Little Rich began pacing back and forth across the living room.

"Let me think about this for a bit," he said, walking through the door leading to his bedroom.

He returned a few minutes later with a small stack of clean clothes.

"You boys wash up. That water should be warm enough by now. At least it'll take the chill off. You'll have to share it. Clean up and put these clothes on. They'll fit okay, I think. You get cleaned up, I'm gonna make a call. And then we'll have something to eat."

He then went back into the bedroom.

The boys could hear him talking on his cell while they washed up.

Five minutes later he walked back out. He brought two blankets with him.

"Wrap yourselves up with these until you get warm," he said. "And then we'll talk about what you should do."

Chapter 17

Little Rich's Plan

Finally, Robby and Red were getting warm. The hot fire, dry clothes, and blankets had done the job.

"This is pretty good," Robby said. "What is it?"

"Rabbit stew," Little Rich said. "Pretty simple. It's just rabbit and potatoes. But it does taste pretty good. If I say so myself. … Now, this is what I suggest you do. Are you ready to hear it?"

Red looked at Robby and nodded his head.

"Yeah," Robby said. "We want to hear what you think."

"Well, the safest thing to do would be to turn yourselves in. I could call the sheriff, and he'd pick you up. You'd be safer in lockup than you are out here. That's what I think."

Red looked over at Robby, and then down at his empty bowl. Slowly he shook his head.

"We don't want to turn ourselves in," Robby said. "The deputies already hate us. We ran away from them, and they've been trying to catch us for the past couple months. … That's what they were doing when they got shot. Looking for us. And Miss Baldwin. She hated us too. … They are going to think that we killed her and the two deputies. That's what they're gonna think. And, since there's no proof that this killer even exists, they're not gonna be looking for him. When they catch us, you can just bet that they'll throw the book at us. That's just how it's gonna be.

"We need to stay out of jail, and try to catch that killer ourselves. With Uncle Jack's help, of course. But we can't do anything if we're locked up."

"Then you're not interested in turning yourselves in?" Little

Rich asked. "Not at all?"

"No," Robby said. "And if you *can't* help us get on a freighter, then we'll just have to come up with a different plan. … We're very grateful for the food. It was really good. And the dry clothes. But, we'd better be getting out of here before the cops show up. It's only going to get you in trouble if they find us here."

"Not so fast," Little Rich said. "I told you that I thought you should turn yourselves in. That was my *best* advice. The safest route for you. But, if you are not willing to do that, and I do understand why you might not *want* to do that, then I have another plan."

The two boys looked at each other, and then at Little Rich.

"I have a brother who is passing through the Soo Locks in the morning," Little Rich said. "He thinks he might be able to help you."

Red signaled with his finger that he'd like to have a piece of paper and a pencil.

Robby picked it up and said, "Red would like to have something to write with. Anything will do."

Little Rich tore his supplies list from a small pad of paper and gave it and a pencil to Red.

"Why would your brother do that for us?" Red wrote, and spun the pad around so Little Rich could read it.

"Your Uncle Jack," he answered. "My brother Whitey knows him. *And* Henry. The two of them helped my brother resolve a property line dispute. This neighbor was coming over on Whitey's land while he was working, and he'd take down some of his trees. For firewood. Whitey owns a couple dozen acres just south and east of here. Not too far from the resort. He was talking to Henry over a beer on the mainland, and he told him about his dilemma.

"The next time Whitey sailed, Handler and Henry spent the night in Whitey's house. I guess they played poker and drank a lot of beer. According to my brother.

"And then, finally, early on Sunday morning they heard a chainsaw running. It was on the back of the property, but it was pretty clear that they had caught the guilty party.

"So the two of them took their Glocks back there. They set up a target fifty yards or so from the asshole who was stealing my brother's trees. And then they paced off thirty feet directly in line with the fellow running the chainsaw, and then stepped slightly to the side. So when they fired, the rounds that passed through the target would most likely come close to the stealin' bastard, but probably not actually hit him. But if they did hit him, most of the velocity would be drained, and they wouldn't do too much damage. Sort of like that bullet that bounced off your head.

"This poor guy never saw it comin'. All of a sudden Handler fired off six rounds. I'm sure the poor asshole shit his pants. He did a belly flop right on the spot, and started screaming and crying for them to stop shooting. Which they did.

"And then they casually walked over to the guy and apologized. 'We didn't see you over here. What's going on? Isn't this Whitey's property? Did he give you permission to cut his trees?'"

"I'm Olson. I live over there a bit. I must have accidentally come across the property line. My bad. I'm sorry. I'll apologize to Whitey when he gets back. So sorry. If you could hold your target practice off for a minute, I'll load up my tools and get going. Can you let me do that?"

"Well, I suppose," Jack said, holstering his Glock. "But Henry and I have a little more shooting to do. Haven't run any rounds through these Glocks in a while, wanted to make sure they still worked. We'll give you a few minutes. ... And I suggest you compensate Whitey for any trees you might have taken earlier. Will you do that?"

"Absolutely," Olson said as he packed up his equipment. "I do want to be a good neighbor."

"That was the last time Olson ever messed with Whitey," Little

Rich said. "They see each other in town, and sometimes at the bar—Olson and my brother—and that incident never comes up. He did send Whitey a check for the wood he'd cut earlier. Probably not enough, but better than nothin'. … Olson is scared shitless of your Uncle Jack. He doesn't want anything to do with him. In fact, now that all our neighbors know that we're friends with Handler, they all give us the respect we've never had before.

"So, that's why Whitey is willing to go out on the limb for you boys. Anything to help Jack Handler. … Of course, this has to be done right. If he ever gets found out, he loses his job. And maybe worse. But, he's willing to give it a shot."

Red then penciled, "How?"

"Still working out some of the details," Little Rich said. "We did run it by your Uncle Jack, but just in general terms. He said to proceed, and that he would get in touch shortly using a more secure connection. … This is what we've got so far.

"Whitey's the cook. He will onload some supplies while his freighter is passing through the locks. That's where I come in. He tells me what he needs, and I get it for him. Only this time, I'll have you two fellows tucked away in a couple of bags, and we'll load you on his boat.

"Once he gets you on board, he'll hide you away in the galley. Until he can move you. … But, you'd talked about going down to Cleveland. Well, his boat is headed west to Duluth. Hope that's not too big a problem. That's the best he can do. … But, you can't stay on the boat forever. He'll get you on, and hide you for a while. But then, you're gonna have to be ready to get off when and how he says. Is that clear? At least, that would get you off the island, and out of the Soo. I think that's what you wanted. Right?"

"Perfect," Red wrote. "Thanks."

"And, if you get caught, you can't spill the beans on him. That's a really good gig for Whitey, and he doesn't want to lose it. … Can you keep your mouths shut? If you get caught."

Red looked over at Robby and both boys nodded their heads in agreement.

"Absolutely," Robby said. "We'll not talk. … But, how do we get *off* the freighter in Duluth?"

"You don't go all the way to Duluth. … You boys do know how to swim, don't you?" Little Rich asked.

Chapter 18

Jack, Roger Here

Just before Jack fielded Little Rich's initial phone call concerning the problem the boys were having, Roger had called him.

"Jack," Roger said. "I hate to be the one to tell you this, old buddy, but about those calls from New York—just as you suspected, it does appear you've got a new problem brewing with Allison—possibly even involving the IRS, ultimately. … That part—the IRS—will most likely never materialize. While she might like to think she could take it there, I'd be skeptical about her ability to influence it in that direction. But the rest of it, the audit, you can count on. And, it's not a problem that is likely to go away quickly or easily."

Roger had a way of knowing about these things. So, when he called Jack to inform him about what was just over the horizon, Jack knew it was serious.

Jack sat back in his kitchen chair at their Sugar Island resort. He had just poured a fresh cup of coffee and he was ready to go. Now in his sixtieth year, Jack had barely lost a step in the last thirty years, and few would dispute that he was, in fact, in better condition than most men half his age.

It was not cold on the island, but an October chill was in the air. Typically, Jack would have been wearing his fall tan khaki jacket—the same fall jacket that he had worn every autumn day for the past ten years. But not on this day. Today Jack was wearing for the first time his birthday present from Kate—a vintage shearling bomber jacket that she had found in the Cockpit USA on West 39th Street.

Jack detested change, at least this type of change. *But,* he reasoned, *since Kate thinks I needed a new jacket, the least I can do is give it a shot. Maybe I'll like it.* He rolled up his Detroit Tigers cap and put it his left pocket, and tucked two Cuban cigars in the breast pocket.

"There you go, Handler," he said to himself. "You've got your Cubans and your cap. What more could you ask for?"

While Roger's role in the Secret Service did have many perks, by itself it did not provide him any special access into the inner workings of the other branches of government. His real sources of information were through his friendship with Allison's husband, the former president, and an even closer association with Albert Weissmann, the director of the National Security Agency. Roger and Weissmann, AKA "The Timekeeper," were classmates at Yale, and remained good friends throughout their professional careers.

As a favor to his friend Roger, and because Roger had specifically requested his help in this regard, Weissmann flagged a number of the names of people close to Roger so that whenever one of them bubbled to the surface, he would pass the information along to him. *Jack Handler* was one of the names recently added to the list.

"What else is new?" Jack quipped. "If the IRS does decide to come after me, it will be the third time in six years that I've been the object of their attention. I'm starting to get used to it. And now, with Connie's passing, my accountant tells me I should almost *expect* an audit."

Connie's full name was Conrad *Sticky Connie* O'Donnell. For the past several decades Jack had co-owned a bar on the south side of Chicago—it was called Sticky's. A little over a month earlier Connie was gunned down outside the bar after closing. He had been on his way to deposit the day's receipts when a gunman approached him from behind and fired four rounds into his back from close range.

While the robbery itself did not arouse much attention (being it occurred on the south side of Chicago) the fact that the robber was aware that Connie stashed the cash in an inside coat pocket, rather than in the bank bag he always openly carried to the bank—that made Jack wonder where the killer might have gotten his information.

"I realize that you've been under scrutiny before," Roger said. "But this time might be a little different. Now it is definitely Allison herself who has you in her crosshairs."

"Really?" Jack rhetoricized. "And you found out about this from her *directly*?"

"No. She told me nothing about it. And I haven't intercepted anything with regard to it from her communications. This is what happened. Early this morning I received a communiqué from my buddy over at NSA, and he informed me that you were being targeted by the Former first lady. ... I did call Bob, and he hadn't heard anything either. ... I do have to tell you that he had a good laugh when I told him about it. He chalked it up to her recent stroke. 'Allison's just not as sweet and charming as she used to be,' he said.

"But we know better, don't we, Jack? She's *always* been vindictive against those she perceives to be her enemies. And, of late, you've risen pretty close to the top of her *hate list*."

What Roger was alluding to was the animosity she felt toward Jack ever since he thwarted her attempt to assassinate the current president. She had, in fact, even attempted to have Jack killed. While that attempt also failed, Allison never forgave Jack for his interference. And, in spite of her being slowed down by a stroke, she never gave up on her desire to see Jack dead.

"So, you think I should be particularly concerned about this audit?" Jack asked.

Roger thought for a moment before he responded.

"Bob is skeptical that she'll actually want to get you audited by the IRS. Nevertheless, you and I both know that an IRS audit is like a gun. Even if it's not loaded or pointed at you, you should always respect its potential. ... But, when you can see the rounds in the cylinder, and it's pointed at you in the white-knuckled grip of an enemy, then you'd be wise to take your respect to the next level. One way or another, she's going to take you down if she's able. You can count on it."

"Yeah, I totally understand how that works. ... The crazy thing about it is I *always* pay more in taxes than is required."

"Allison might not be looking for tax *evasion*," Roger offered. "It's quite possible that this audit, if it ever fully materializes, will be a fishing expedition to entrap some of your clients. That wouldn't surprise me."

"Really? Anything specific make you and your spook buddy suspect that?"

"Actually," Roger replied, "there is. This, as I understand it, is the route of attack Allison has chosen. As you know, Conrad's son inherited his father's share of the bar. Allison is working through the son to come after you. That's what we think. ... Actually, that's what we know. The reality of that scheme has been borne out in the transcripts of telephone intercepts that I have seen."

"Really? How does that work?"

"You're intending to buy him out—the son. Is that right?"

"That's what he requested. And I've made him an offer," Jack said. "But he's not accepted it. Not yet. ... I thought my proposition was quite generous. I offered to let him stay on doing the *day-to-day*, just like his father had done. But he didn't express much interest in that. ... The kid ... he's in his late twenties, so I guess he isn't really a *kid*. Anyway, the son—Conrad Junior—doesn't much care for getting his hands dirty. At least not by working. Connie called him his *prodigal*. When he asked for a total buyout, I wasn't surprised. Hell, I was relieved. I don't have much use for the kid.

"So, Allison is working through the kid to get to me. Is that what you're saying? I'm not sure I get that. Maybe you can elaborate?"

"Here's how she intends to leverage the boy. As I understand it. Initially, he was going to ask you to buy him out. And, I think you just said that has happened. Right?"

"That's correct. He asked me to make him a cash offer. And I did just that."

"And you've not heard back from him?"

"Not yet."

"Well," Roger said, "I think you're just about to."

"And you know this how?"

"I'd really rather not say, but you know my friends. I'm sure you've already figured out that part of it."

"Your buddy, The Timekeeper?"

"Moving on," Roger said, obviously not wishing to discuss his sources of information. "Here is the verbatim text of a message I suspect you will soon receive: "Dear Mr. Handler. Thank you for the considerations given me since the passing of my father. I know that you and he were very close, and that his passing has been difficult for you as well. I trust that you will appreciate the fact that I do not wish to become actively involved in the operations of the bar, and I also appreciate the offer you made to buy out my inherited share. I think it looks very generous. However, my lawyer is not at all familiar with the bar itself, and so would like to see some numbers supporting the offer. I know you will appreciate his request. After all, he is a lawyer. This is what he would like to see:

1.   Federal and State Tax returns for the past three years.

2.   Accounts payable and accounts receivable for three years.

3.   Legal description of the physical property on which the bar is located, and a list of any debts or liens associated with it.

4. List of all property (and accumulated inventory) owned by the bar.
5. List of all persons or entities frequenting the bar or who have rented the associated banquet facilities. This should be for a period of three years."

"Yeah," Jack barked into his phone, cutting Roger off. "That's just about what that kid was asking from me earlier. All I thought of when I read it was that this kid's got to be shittin' me! Who the hell does he think he is? I made him a reasonable offer. *More* than reasonable. The bar should be valued at two million. I offered him a million two in cash for his *minority* share. … But I'm not about to provide him with a list of my customers. It's none of his business. What the hell is he thinking?"

Roger then continued: "This letter goes on to close pleasantly, and is signed, Conrad O'Donnell Jr. … But, it is clear to me that it was drafted by Allison's attorney, Abraham Stern. Even though it is written in a folksy manner, it appears under the attorney's letterhead. And on the bottom of it are instructions for the son. It tells him to copy the body of the letter in his own hand, and to send it to you.

"Jack, my friend, you need to see your attorney immediately. This is what is happening. Stern expected you to passionately react to the letter—just as you did. To be angry. And then to refuse to provide the requested information. Particularly that regarding your customers. Once you formally refused to comply, you would be faced with a demand, and then the whole matter would begin to go adversarial."

"And that's exactly what has happened," Jack said. "Then, what you are saying is, there is more to this matter than simply framing a basic buy/sell arrangement. Allison is behind it, and she—like always—has an agenda. A sinister agenda."

"That's about it. Let me read you a transcript of a telephone conversation between Allison and her lawyer. This one seems to be one of the first, if not *the* first, communiqué between Allison and this lawyer regarding your bar. After a brief greeting, she gets right to the point:

Allison: "This is what I have in mind. I know that Handler uses that bar to hide some of his income from his private security business, which, I must say, is very shady."

Stern: "I know all about Jack Handler."

Allison continues: "The bar and the banquet halls are all owned by the same corporation, *Handler O'Donnell Enterprises, Inc.* They are not separate entities. One tax return. The way Handler does it is like this. He performs services, of God knows what, for some of the most notorious figures in the country. And some abroad. Really bad actors. And these guys do not want it known that they've hired Handler. They want no paper trail. So, they pay him in cash. But, the payment does not go directly to him, he legitimizes it by passing it through the corporation. He rents out his banquet halls to them, and they pay him in cash. Supposedly the bar even caters events. But I'm sure that's a sham—probably like two Buds and a brat. Maybe not even that. I'm sure it's not much. All he's got is a microwave and a fryer. Sometimes the rentals are legit. In those cases they contract with a real caterer.

"And the size of those banquet rooms. They're postage stamps. Tiny. Yet he charges far more than comparable facilities. Not just top dollar—he's way over the top.

"Now, if you haven't heard, O'Donnell the senior recently met with an unfortunate end, and his son, O'Donnell Jr., inherited all of his father's holdings. These consisted of a rundown house on the south side of Chicago, and forty-five percent of the bar.

"The boy is going to ask Handler to make him an offer to buy his minority share. Once Handler makes him an offer, the kid is going to tell Handler that his lawyer is asking for documentation to determine the bar's worth. That part I want you to help him with. I want you to ask for every sort of information you can legitimately request. Even if his original offer is generous. My interest—*our* interest—is not so much in getting a good price for the kid. I want to rattle Handler's clients. If they think that Handler is fingering them, or even *might* finger them, they will turn on him. Especially if they think that it could end up in a full-blown IRS Audit. I want you to push it to the limit. Put as much pressure on Handler as you are able to exert. I know some of Handler's clients. They are very private people. There's a lot of them. It could turn out like Agatha Christie's *Murder on the Orient Express*. They will be lining up at the gate just to slide their knife into his heart."

"Okay," Jack said. "I get it. I didn't think that the son would be so savvy. Not that my offer wasn't generous. But when he came back looking for additional documentation, I really became suspicious. ... Now that I know who's behind this, it all makes perfect sense. I always thought that Sticky's kid was a lazy piece of shit. Do you think that he had something to do with his father's murder?"

"That'll never be proven ... not with Allison orchestrating the whole show. Good bet that he was a willing accomplice, but I doubt he pulled the trigger."

"How far along is this?" Jack asked. "Have they been in contact with my clients at this point? How concerned should I be?"

"I'm no lawyer, but the way it appears to me, the next move would be for you, or even better, your lawyer, to provide Mr. Stern the documentation he is looking for. Tell your lawyer what is going on, and then have him contact Stern. I'd think you're pretty safe for now. Any contact with your clients will most likely be conducted on the basis of the limited information they already have, and what they are demanding, and you have not yet complied. So, at this point, they should be in a holding pattern. Unless the kid has given them names from another list. Maybe his dad had a list. That could be. But you can't know what he has been up to. However, as soon as you comply, then watch out. ... Like I said, I'm not in a position to offer legal advice. So that's not what I'm doing. Huddle with your lawyer, tell him what I've told you, and come up with a game plan. … And, as always, leave my name out of it."

"That goes without saying," Jack replied as he disconnected.

Jack pondered all the ramifications of what Roger had just told him. And then he remembered a call that had gone to voicemail earlier in the day. It was from an old client—one to whom he was not eager to talk. Harry Weinstein was his name. He had known Harry ever since he was a junior homicide detective in Chicago nearly thirty years earlier. Jack had investigated a murder case— a mob hit—and Harry was the prime suspect. After helping the prosecution put together what Jack was convinced was an airtight case, Harry skated on a *technicality*—the murder weapon disappeared from the evidence vault. Of course, it did not help when the two eyewitnesses, a husband and wife, died in a mysterious automobile accident.

From that time on Jack viewed Harry Weinstein as a virtually untouchable stone-cold killer. *I hope I never run into that guy again,* Jack told himself. But, he did. Twenty-three years later Harry called him. By that time Jack had taken early retirement from the Chicago Police Department, and was in the process of building up his private practice. When he saw that it was Weinstein's attorney requesting his private security services, Jack had reservations. He knew what sort of a man Harry was, and so was concerned about the nature of the help his lawyer might be seeking. Jack's concerns turned out to be abundantly justified.

"Jack Handler. This is Brian Farnsworth. I'm a lawyer. I've been hired to represent Mr. Harry Weinstein. I believe you know my client. He says he knows you."

"Yes. I know your client. But only from opposite sides of a courtroom."

"Well, Mr. Weinstein would like to hire you, if you're interested."

"You're his lawyer. Right? That would suggest that Mr. Weinstein is in some sort of trouble. And given his reputation, my guess is that someone he knows ran into a slug. Is that about right?"

"A man was shot, but my client assures me he had nothing to do with it. He was arrested and charged solely on the basis of his reputation. And he can prove his innocence."

"If he can prove his innocence, why are you calling me?"

"He could use your help locating a man. He swears this fellow can totally exonerate him. He just needs to find him. … It will pay well. There's ten grand in it for just saying yes today, and fifty more if you locate the witness. You have only two weeks—that's the rub. We go to trial in two weeks."

Jack was relatively new at working in the private sector. He was used to earning a hundred dollars a day, plus expenses. Paying the rent and raising his daughter took every penny he earned, and more. Ten grand for two weeks' work sounded pretty good to him. And another fifty grand—that sounded great.

For a moment Jack recounted how, as a cop, he had let this killer slip through his fingers. *Maybe this time I should simply allow justice to run its course,* he reasoned. *After all, I know this man is a killer. What are the chances that he could actually be innocent this time around?*

But then Jack thought about his daughter, Kate. *Damn, I'd sure like to get us into a better neighborhood,* he thought. *And, I need to set up a college fund. This job could help.*

"You're pretty sure Weinstein didn't pull the trigger on this guy?"

"He assures me he is totally innocent. He gave me his word."

"Ten grand up front, and a hundred if I find this potential witness? Plus expenses?"

Jack believed that if Weinstein was willing to pay fifty thousand for a successful find, he'd be good for a hundred.

"We can make that work."

"And what if I have to travel? Say my investigation takes me to LA, or Florida?"

"That would be considered legitimate expenses. But you must locate the witness within that two-week time frame. Or else the bonus and expenses are off the table. Of course, you'd keep the ten grand. No questions."

"Then let's get started."

Twelve days later Jack received one thousand one hundred dollar bills from Farnsworth. And the next day, Mr. Perry Stiles, the witness Jack had located for Harry, committed *suicide* by jumping into the Chicago River. His ankles were tied together with a nylon cord, which was securely connected to a concrete block. Apparently the witness was able to exonerate Harry, but only through his death.

During the following two decades Jack never heard from Harry Weinstein. And then, three years ago, he had received a call.

"Jack. This is Harry. Harry Weinstein. Remember me?"

"I remember you. What do you want?"

"I need your help."

"I'm not your man," Jack said. "You need to call someone else."

"It's nothing like before. I've cleaned up my act. Totally legit these days."

"I'm not your man, I said."

"This is about my daughter. She's been kidnapped. I want to get her back, and you are the only one I can trust to do it."

"There's other private investigators who can do a good job for you. You should find one of them. I don't want to work for you."

"Jack, just hear me out. Give me one minute. And then, you do what you think is the right thing. Can you give me one minute?"

"One minute."

"Amy, my daughter, is twenty-five years old. She has been taken for ransom. I'm willing to pay it, but I need someone to deliver the cash, and make sure my daughter is freed. That's it."

"The FBI does shit like that. Call them."

"Hell, Jack, you know what that'll get me. I will lose my daughter. I know it. The guys who have taken Amy will spot a cop right away, and kill Amy. The FBI is out of the question."

"Why don't you do it yourself?"

"I would like to. They *refuse* to let me make the drop. They might know my reputation. Or maybe they think I would recognize them. ... You are the only one I trust to get her back. I'm paying the kidnappers five hundred thousand, and I'll pay you a hundred. ... One hour's work."

"What're you up to these days?" Jack asked. "You said you've gone legit. Just what is it you do?"

"I'm in the program—WITSEC. I can't tell you where I'm living, or what I'm doing. All I can say is that I'm totally legitimate. If I slip up, I get booted. No second chances. And I wouldn't last a day on the outside. ... About my daughter. All I can tell you is that she is being held in Chicago. Or at least *near* Chicago. I can send you the funds. And your payment. I'll let you know where the drop is as soon as they tell me. Once you're in position, I'll find out how they want it handled."

"You know how these things go," Jack said. "Most of the time abductions end badly."

"I know that full well," Harry said. "That's why I want you to do it. If anyone can get my daughter back, you can. ... But, if it fails. I'm coming to Chicago myself. To hell with witness protection. ... And I will square it with these assholes personally. Whatever happens, you keep the hundred grand. ... That's the whole story, as far as it involves you. ... You gonna help me ... and my daughter?"

"I might," Jack said. "But, first tell me why they targeted your daughter. They got something personal against you?"

"Come on, Jack. Half the city of Chicago has something against me. You know that. And some for good cause. I've never claimed to be an angel. ... Hell, I deserve whatever I get. I resolved years ago that eventually some of the old ghosts from my past would catch up with me, and put me down. I've come to grips with that. But, my daughter. That's a different story. She's a mom. And a schoolteacher. She's married to a schoolteacher. She's never done anything to hurt another human being in her entire life. Never.

"You ask me if the people who took her might have something against me personally. I'm sure they do. But I don't know who it would be. … I have narrowed the list down to maybe a dozen or so. But I can't whittle it down any further. And even then, I could be wrong. I'm not looking for revenge or anything. I just want to get Amy back."

"So," Jack said. "My job will simply be to drop off the ransom money, and pick up your daughter … if that's even on the table. Is that what you're saying? There's no contract implied? You're not expecting me to cap this guy?"

"No. Not at all. If it comes to that I will do it myself … but it'll be while I'm looking him in the eye—personally. … I think this guy is out of his element. Five hundred thousand—if he knew what he was doing he'd be going for a couple of mil. … All I want you to do is make the exchange, if such a thing is even possible. And bring my daughter home—if *that* is possible. That's it."

"Okay," Jack said. "But this is how it's going to go down. You have a courier deliver the five hundred K to me. Must be clean cash. Hang on to my fee. If I fail, you don't own me. Like I said, these things don't always turn out so good. … But, if I can get her out. Then, she can rent my banquet hall and catering service, and pay for it with my fee. That's how this has to go."

"The cash will be on its way in an hour. … But, there is one more thing. If you can figure out who this is that took Amy, I'd like to know. Maybe describe what the guy looks like. But you shouldn't even mess up his hair. If it goes south, I'll settle the score later. You just get my daughter back."

The ransom payment did arrive early the next day, just as Harry had promised. Along with it were thirteen images, one of his daughter, and twelve of the men he suspected might be responsible. Two days later Jack received instructions from the abductor as to how and when the money should be delivered.

The exchange plan was not complicated. Jack was told to come alone to a small restaurant on the South Side at exactly two P.M. on the following Thursday. He should wrap the cash up like a birthday gift, and set it on the chair across the table in front of him. When the waitress brought him the bill, he should hand her his credit card. Someone would pick up the package during this time. As soon as she returned with the slip, he should sign it and leave.

"Do not try to follow me," the instructions commanded. "You will find the girl in the back of a van in the parking lot. She will be alive and in good shape."

And that is almost exactly how it transpired. Jack entered the restaurant at precisely two P.M. He ordered the special, and set the gift-wrapped box containing five thousand one hundred-dollar bills on the chair across from him.

When he had finished eating, the waitress brought him the check, and Jack handed her his credit card. As soon as she had left, a young man walked by and scooped up the huge box of cash.

"Thanks, Handler," he said, looking Jack squarely in the face. He then hurried out of the door. Jack watched him as he turned left on the sidewalk and disappeared from view.

When the waitress returned, Jack thanked her and headed toward the door.

He looked to the right and to the left. When he reached the parking lot, he scoured it carefully with his eyes, searching for a van. But he found none. Finally, he spotted a large white well-rusted Chevy cargo van parked on the street nearly half a block away. *Maybe that's it,* he thought.

When he reached it he pounded heavily on the passenger door. Inside he could hear soft moaning.

The door was unlocked, so he opened it. There was a metal grid separating the van's cockpit from the rear compartment. He leaned in and looked in the back. Once his eyes had adjusted to the dark, he discovered the form of a woman lying on the floor. She was covered to her head with a wool blanket.

"Hang on, Amy, your father sent me to pick you up. You're going to be okay."

And, she was. As soon as Jack had removed the duct tape that was wrapped around her face she began to scream. He quickly placed his hand over her mouth.

"Stop! Your dad does not want the cops involved. He sent me here to help you. But you can't be screaming. Do you understand?"

Amy quickly got the picture and ceased her protest.

Two weeks later she did contract with Jack for a catered event at his banquet facilities. She paid in cash—one hundred thousand dollars.

Once Jack had been paid, he sent an image of the young man who had picked up the cash at the restaurant. Jack had been wearing a camera on his lapel.

Two weeks later Jack read a story in an online magazine about the shooting deaths of a whole family in the Highland Park neighborhood of North Chicago. He recognized the picture of one of the victims—it was the man who had picked up the cash in the restaurant.

Jack never asked any questions. The girl was safe. He had been paid. All was good.

But the recent voicemail from Weinstein begged the question: *what could this guy be looking for now—three years after the fact?*

Jack was not particularly eager to do any more jobs for Harry Weinstein, but he knew that it would be a mistake not to respond. *As soon as Roger and I are finished, I'll give Harry a call.*

Chapter 19

Roger Continues

A llison has specifically requested that Abraham Stern be assigned to your case," Roger told him. "And she also wants this guy, Jeffry Stokes—ever heard of him?"

"No. Should I have? … Does he have a reputation?"

"You could say that," Roger said with a chuckle. "He's worked for the IRS in the past. He's a CPA, and a member of the bar in the State of New York. In fact, if you were to pay a visit to Leavenworth, you'd be able to talk to several dozen inmates who could tell you volumes about Mr. Stokes. He's referred to as the *pit-bull* by his fellow auditors—his victims use a variety of terms for him, none of them complimentary. Once he gets a grip on your leg, he brings you down. … If Allison gets her wish and you end up with this fellow, you're going to want to be careful. If his treatment of you is true to form, he will seek to ensnare you in some sort of violation, and then get you to turn on one or more of your clients."

"Does she have anyone specific in mind? Are there any of my clients that you can think of that she might be going after?"

"Hard to tell at this point, Jack. From what I've heard, she's been tossing around some names. You and I both know your client list reads like a Who's Who of infamous bad actors. It could be any one, or any number of them. … But, I do have a theory."

"Yeah. And what would that be?"

"You and I both know she wants you dead. Right?"

"I suppose," Jack replied. "But I prefer to look at it as a love/hate relationship."

"I'd say you were half right—the part about the hate. But the love end of it—not so much. Really, Jack, you've known Allison for nearly as long as I have. You were Bob's right hand during his presidency. … God, that doesn't seem possible. That was over *two decades ago—twenty-two, twenty-three years.* Does it seem that long ago to you?"

"Roger, I know it's been a long time. But where were you going with your comment?"

"During that quarter of a century have you even known Allison to actually *love* anyone or anything? … Besides herself? But love? I don't think so. She sure as hell didn't love Bob. At least not while he was president. … Her daughter, maybe. But in her case, I think she regarded the girl as an extension of herself.

"Allison is probably the most narcissistic human being I have even known. Utilitarian might be a better word to describe her. If a person can serve her needs, she tolerates them. If that usefulness ceases to be the case, they're out. And, if she thinks they know too much, they disappear. … But I don't see love as part of her psychological makeup."

"Yeah, you're probably right. And I think I'm getting your drift here. You're suggesting that she might want to put the heat on a bunch of my clients. Until one of them decides that their life might be better if I were to go away. Is that it?"

"She's wanted you dead for a long time, Jack. And while she knows that you would never turn her in, she also knows that you're aware of where all the bodies are buried, so to speak. … She still has designs on being president, you know. And she's concerned about loose ends, or skeletons in the closet—whatever you want to call them."

"You've got to be shittin' me! She *still* thinks she can get elected?"

"I'm serious. It's true. She still thinks she can find a route to the Oval Office."

"And if she can scare my clients sufficiently one of them will put a bullet in me. That's her plan?"

"She doesn't confide in me so much anymore. But Bob usually has her number. And he gave me the heads up on what she might be thinking. And you know he's got great instincts. Especially where Allison is concerned."

"Actually, that's a great strategy," Jack admitted. "It could easily work. I can't run my business without seeing clients. And I have long-standing relationships with most of them. ... But, if they even suspect that I might be the conduit for opening up their re-cords to public scrutiny, I'm dead. That's a *great* plan. It reminds me of something I'd come up with."

"Well," Roger said, "at least you've been warned. I'm not so sure how you can go about fighting it. The courts have a lot of power, and far-reaching tentacles. Even Bob got a chuckle out of it. You know how he admires a devious mind. I asked him about your options, and he laughed again. His only suggestion was a big life insurance policy ... perhaps one naming him as beneficiary.

"But then he got a little more serious and said that he really didn't have a good answer. Only that the best thing I could do would be to warn you, and that you were about the most resource-ful person he knew—if anyone could figure out a way to deal with Allison and her pit-bull attorney, you'd be the guy. ... Sorry, Jack, but a warning is the best I can offer you."

Chapter 20

Another Word of Warning

A s was always the case, Jack took Roger's words to heart. And, given the seriousness of this ominous warning, he knew he had better begin preparing for the onslaught that was about to come down upon him. *But first, I need to see why Harry was calling me. Might just have something to do with this business.*

"Harry. Jack Handler here. What's on your mind?"

"Jack. I just received a disturbing call from Brian—my lawyer, Brian Farnsworth. It was about you."

"Really. I haven't talked to him for years. What's this all about?"

"He tells me that some squeaky little asswipe has been pressuring my daughter to provide proof that she paid you a hundred grand to rent your banquet hall. He even has been bragging that he's got some powerful friends that can bring a lot of pressure on me and my daughter if we don't *comply completely and quickly*. His exact words according to Brian—*completely and quickly*. Nobody talks like that to me or my people. Nobody. What do you know about this?"

Jack quickly surmised that Harry's lawyer had expressed to his client a high level of concern, and so felt it wise to be as forthright as he could in dispelling that concern.

"That *squeaky asswipe* would be Conrad O'Donnell Jr., Connie's son. Connie was my recently deceased partner. I made an offer to buy the kid out, but he's making it difficult. ... And as far as his powerful friends—I don't think the kid's got *any* friends. But he does have a powerful ally—Allison Fulbright. The former first lady. She's actually the one behind this whole fiasco. Wouldn't be surprised if she arranged my partner's death. Just to get that lever-age with the kid. It all seems a bit too convenient to me."

"C'mon, Jack. You've gotta be shittin' me. Why would she do something like that?"

"Long story. Suffice it to say that she wants me gone. … We go way back. She's tried stuff like this before. To get rid of me, that is."

"How's that supposed to work? If that's what it's all about? How does coming after me get rid of you?"

"You pretty much just answered your own question," Jack said. "Don't you think? Isn't your first reaction that *I'm* the immedi-ate source of your aggravation? And that if you eliminated me, it would solve your problem? If I were you, that's how I'd be think-ing. … And there's a hundred more out there who are going to be thinking the same thing. And, most of them are not going to be calling me to get my opinion."

"Damn. If you're right, if that's what she has in mind, she'd be one devious bitch."

"Oh, that's the plan alright. I just learned today, from an in-sider, that this is exactly what she is up to."

"I know you understand my position, Jack. I can't let this hap-pen to Amy. *I'm* pretty much untouchable, here in the program. And I've got a thick skin. But she doesn't. She's scared to death. What're we gonna do about this? You got a solution?"

"I suggest you stall them. Just because he tells your attorney that he needs the documentation yesterday does not mean you have to rush. … Give me a little time. Nothing is going to happen that quickly. His attorney has requested a whole boatload of docu-ments from me. It'll take a while to—"

"That's what I want to avoid. I don't know what all you have in your files. You have worked for me on a couple of occasions. If this *woman* is coming after you to get to me, anything you have on me or Amy could trigger an audit of *my* books, and create problems for my daughter. Especially if the only thing this bitch has in mind is to piss me off. You know what I mean?"

"I know exactly what you mean. … Give me two weeks. You can stall that long. Have your daughter take a two-week vacation. Do whatever you have to do to put this shit off. I'll come up with something. … Keep in mind, you and all my clients are best served if *I'm* allowed to handle this problem. I have a pretty good track record with shit like this."

"My advice to you, Jack, is to get this done. Now! Not in two weeks. Oh, don't get me wrong. I will send Amy and her family out of the country for a couple weeks. That'll take care of her and me for a little while. But somebody else. I called you to find out what was going on. Someone else in my position. Someone with a little less patience. They're just as likely to do you as they would be to smoke a good cigar. You'd better be careful. And quick. … I think the fancy word is *expeditious*. You should get this resolved expeditiously. Or somebody else is going to resolve it for you. … Just saying, Jack, not everyone will be as patient as me."

"You're not wrong. I've no doubt that this shit is going to make a lot of people very nervous. If I were in your place, I'd be pissed too. Especially if I knew that getting rid of me was the whole point. … I *will* get this resolved. And I'll do it in a way that protects you and all my other clients. Even this business with your daughter. I never provided anything that would have pointed to her. This kid must have given his lawyer a list that his father had made up. It didn't come from me. So there can't have been much to it."

"I believe you. But that doesn't make me feel much better. If *any* of these records can be accessed by the kid, then we still got a problem."

"You're right. But we can assume that he has already provided everything he is able to. And he could not have had much. They're fishing. … Just have your daughter hang on to her records, and give me a little time. I'll work it out."

"Two weeks," Weinstein said, "and then we'll talk again. Unless we don't."

Jack regarded his conversation with Harry Weinstein as a threat—a fairly friendly threat, but a serious one nonetheless.

For the next two days Jack huddled with his attorney, Randolph Calibret, contemplating strategy. On the third day he received a surprise call from an old friend on Sugar Island.

Chapter 21

Jack Learns About
Plight of his Boys

Jack. This is Little Rich. Do you remember me?"

"Yes, of course. You're my neighbor on the Island. Your brother, he works as a cook on a freighter."

"Yeah. That's us all right. I'm calling because of a problem involving your two boys—Red and Robby. I've got them here at my house. They've got a problem and they asked me to help them out."

"A problem? What sort of problem?"

"They witnessed a murder. Actually a few murders. And the guy who is doing the killing knows they saw him do it, and he's trying to hunt them down."

"Holy shit!" Jack said. "You got to be kidding me."

"Nope. I'm not. And the boys are sure that the sheriff is after them. I guess their caseworker—some lady named Baldwin, and two deputies. They were some of the people killed. And the boys witnessed it all."

"What are they going to do about it? What are *you* going to do about it? One thing for sure—the boys have to get off the island *right away*. No way is that sheriff going to believe their story. Especially not if this Baldwin woman is one of the victims. She's been a pain in our ass from the start."

"That's what we're thinking—the boys and me. They don't want to turn themselves in—at least not yet. But they're scared that the sheriff will be searching every inch of the island."

"So far I agree."

"I thought that if I could get them *off* the island, and *onto* my brother's boat, you could take it from there."

"Could you do that?"

"I think so. I think I can get them onboard. But they'll have to get off before the boat gets to Duluth. I figure I can fix them up with wetsuits, in case they have to spend some time in the lake. They can swim, right?"

"Yes, they can swim. But I'd like to think about this. It'd be *very* dangerous for them to try to swim to shore. Even on the calmest of days. … If we were going to attempt that, it'd have to be where the boat leaves Whitefish Bay. It comes in pretty close to shore right there. But I'd like to see if I can work something else out. … Let's keep in touch. Keep in mind that as soon as the sheriff can he'll get the FBI involved, and they'll be monitoring my calls. Proceed with your plan. I will be discarding this phone. I will get back with you ASAP on a more secure connection."

Chapter 22

The Law Swings into Action

Within hours both the Chippewa County Sheriff's Office, as well as the Michigan State Police, had mobilized to hunt down and catch Red and Robby. Their pictures were broadcast on television stations across the state, and even over the national news outlets.

Just as the boys anticipated, detectives, with the help of dogs, had tracked their scent from the stone house back to Pat K's cottage, and there fingerprints proved that they had been staying at the Kozski cottage. When Pat arrived the following day, he was greeted by an army of plain-clothed detectives, forensic technicians, and uniformed officers. Yellow crime-scene tape was strung around the entire cottage, including the adjacent parking area, and helicopters swirled in the air above them.

"My name is Det. Brent Fuller, Chippewa County Sheriff's Office. I'm sorry, but you cannot cross this tape."

"What's going on here?" Pat said. "This is *my* cottage. Why do you have tape around my cottage?"

"This is your cottage, is it?" Det. Fuller asked. "And what is your full name?"

Pat was not happy about the inconvenience, but Det. Fuller

quickly convinced him that he was quite serious about the investigation that was in progress, and that Pat would not have access to the cottage for an "undetermined" amount of time.

"I'll ask you one more time. What is your full name? Answer me truthfully right now, or I'll have a deputy take you away in handcuffs."

"Patrick Leonard Kozski. People usually call me Pat K."

"Were you aware that two runaways were staying at your cottage when you were not there? And I want to warn you just how serious we are about this. These two runaways, known as Red and Robby Handler, they are now being sought as material witnesses in a case involving multiple murders. … So, be careful how you answer my questions."

Pat thought about how he should respond, especially now that Red and Robby had been tied to the murders.

"Actually, yes I was aware," Pat replied.

"You knew that two fugitives were hiding in a property you owned, and you did not report it to the proper authorities?"

"I didn't know that they were fugitives," Pat said. "I knew them as two young teenagers who needed a roof over their heads. That's all. … I suppose that had I known that there was a warrant out for their arrest, I would have acted appropriately. … Was there such a warrant?"

Pat had seen the news and had tried to call Jack on his way up to the cottage but could not get through. And Jack, already having heard about the boys' situation from Little Rich, responded to Pat's attempt and called to warn him to be careful how he answered any questions. Jack told Pat that as far as he knew there was no warrant on file with any agency authorizing the arrest of the two boys, and so, technically, the mere fact that Pat was aware that the boys had broken into his cottage, and were using it for shelter, did not constitute a crime.

"The only crime the boys committed was breaking and entering," Jack told him, "but, if you did not report it, then it couldn't be construed as crime."

So, Pat stuck to that story.

As it turned out, the tracking dogs did not pick up the boys' scent at the end of the escape tunnel. Therefore, the investigators never found the spent cartridges the killer had fired at the boys, nor did they ever pick up the boys' scent leading to Little Rich's house. As far as they were concerned, the boys' trail extended only between Pat's cottage and the old man's burned out home.

Of course, because Red and Robby were obviously not to be found on Pat's property, the detectives expanded the search to include all of Sugar Island and northern Chippewa County. However, they were not aware that the boys knew Little Rich, so they expended no specific efforts concentrating on the Rich residence.

Instead, they swarmed upon Jack's resort. On the basis of Jack's relationship with the boys, they had obtained a search warrant for the entire Sugar Island Resort complex. Of course, Jack was in Chicago dealing with the Allison-inspired audit, so the sheriff's detectives gained entry into Jack's condo at the resort by breaking down the door.

Upon learning that Jack was not at that time in residence at the resort, the sheriff dispatched two detectives, Detectives Miller and Rosch, to his Chicago apartment. They had requested a search warrant for the Chicago residence but were unable to obtain one. So, they had to satisfy themselves with an interview—at least for the time being.

"Mr. Handler," Det. Miller said. "We have some questions for you regarding your knowledge as to the whereabouts of your two foster boys—Red and Robby. Would you mind answering a few of our questions?"

"Do I have a choice?"

"Look, Handler. You either answer our questions now, or we'll come back with a warrant, cuff you, and take you back to the UP that way. Your choice. How's it going to be?"

Jack had not heard anything directly from the boys for weeks. And, prior to his recent calls from Little Rich and Pat K., he had not received any information relating to the boys for an equally long time. While he had been concerned about their safety, he was at the same time pleased that they had not personally contacted him. *Never good to mislead an investigation,* he believed, *unless it's totally necessary.*

"I'll answer your questions," Jack agreed. "But, I have to tell you that I haven't heard from the boys in a very long time."

"How long has it been since you have communicated with either of them?"

"Weeks. Maybe months. Occasionally they will drop a note off at the house. But I never see them when they do. I haven't heard *anything* from them in over a month. Don't know specifically, but it's been over a month. Do you mind telling me what this is all about? Are the boys okay? You haven't come all the way down here to Chicago, threaten to put me in handcuffs, just to find out if I've talked to the boys. What's this all about?"

"This is a murder investigation, Mr. Handler. We've got four shot, including two of our friends—deputies out of our office. I'm not going to play games with you or anybody—"

"Murder! What could that possibly have to do with the boys? Are they okay?"

"We don't know," Det. Miller said. "All we know for sure is that there are four dead. All shot. Two of them are sheriff's deputies. A childcare worker for the county was killed. And a resident of Sugar Island. The two boys are wanted as material witnesses. Do you know where they are right now?"

"I just told you that I haven't had any contact with them in over a month. What is going on? Are the boys okay?"

"We have no reason to think otherwise. We are quite certain that they were present when the shootings took place. What role they played, if any, we just don't know. We want to talk to them. That's all. Like we're talking to you. If you hear from them, let us know immediately. Will you do that?"

"Yes. Of course. ... If I hear from them."

"Good. You do that. ... And, Mr. Handler. We are searching your house on Sugar Island, right now. As we speak. We have a warrant. ... There is a safe in that house. It's locked. It looks like a gun safe. Would you give us the combination? That way we will not have to cut it open. Or drill it. However it's done when you don't know the combination. It won't be pretty if we have to break into it."

"No problem, Detective," Jack said. "Anything to help."

Jack was relieved that the detective had asked him for help to open his "gun safe." Singular, not plural. Jack had a secret safe room in the basement of his resort home. And in that safe room were several safes, including two gun safes. Had the detective asked him to open his "safes," then that would pose a problem for Jack. Because, there were in those secret safes a large number of weapons that would by any definition be considered highly illegal. ... Not to mention, Jack's stash of Cuban cigars and superb Kentucky bourbon.

As he provided the combination to the safe, Jack made a point of verbalizing every number, along with the appropriate necessary directions, such as "twice right to forty-five, back once to twenty-two, etc." He noticed out of the corner of his eye that Det. Rosch was recording everything on his cell. And that was fine with Jack. The safe had cost him nearly five grand, and he wanted to make sure it sustained no unnecessary damage to it. Besides, there was nothing contained in that safe that he had to worry about. Or, so he thought.

"Hold on a moment," Det. Miller said as he hit his speed dial. "I'll see if that code works for Det. Fuller. He's at your house right now."

After the detective read off the numbers to Det. Fuller, he asked, "Handler says that should do it. Did the safe open?"

But Det. Fuller did not respond to the question. Instead, he barked out, "Back! Everyone back off. Stand back and shut up."

Jack heard what Det. Fuller had said and was taken aback by the tone of the detective's voice.

Det. Fuller singled out four boxes of ammunition, and slid them into an evidence bag, and labeled it.

"Deputy," Det. Fuller could be heard saying. "Those were Federal American Eagle 124s. ... Hell. Go ahead and remove everything from the safe and bag it as evidence."

And then Det. Fuller addressed his associate, Det. Miller: "The sheriff is with me right now. He says he would like you to bring Jack Handler back up to Chippewa County, he has some questions for him. That is, if he's willing to come. If not, we will get a warrant. Find out if he'll come willingly."

"What's *this* all about?" Jack asked. "There's absolutely nothing illegal about anything in that safe. And what's the big deal about a few boxes of Federal American Eagle 124s? There's nothing illegal or unusual about having that ammunition. I happen to own a Glock 9mm. It's legally registered. ... You *have* to know I have handguns. So what's the big deal?"

"I don't know," Det. Miller said. I don't think there's a problem. But the sheriff would like you to return with us. He's understandably upset about losing two of his deputies. ... He just has some additional questions he would like answered. Would you be willing to do that voluntarily?"

Jack knew Sheriff Green to be a no-nonsense sort of person. *If I don't return to Sugar Island of my own volition,* he said to himself, *he will see to it that a warrant is issued. Besides, returning with them will put me right up there where the boys are.*

Nine hours later Jack and the two detectives arrived in Sault Ste Marie. Sheriff Green was waiting in his office to debrief Jack.

"You're probably wondering why I wanted to get you back here in the UP," Sheriff Green said.

"Well, I assume that it's not because you just missed me," Jack replied.

The sheriff didn't respond to Jack's answer.

"The ammunition we found in your gun safe matches exactly with the spent cartridges we found at a crime scene. Exactly."

"Really," Jack responded. "And what would be so unusual about that? I think Federal American Eagle 124s are about one of the most common rounds run through a 9 mil. You'd probably find them in half the houses in the UP. The real question would be, did you find my prints on any of the spent rounds? I don't think so. ... Maybe you *were* just missing me."

"Go to hell, Handler," the sheriff, said tossing a handful of papers at Jack. "I just lost two of my good friends. They leave three children under ten. And you make jokes."

"Look, sheriff, I totally understand your frustration. But neither me or my boys are responsible for your loss. My boys did not commit those murders. I'm sure of it."

"So, you have talked to them?"

"No I have not. I just know my boys. They would not do that. That I know."

"Well, I'm not so sure about that. Right now, they have to be considered my best suspects."

"So, you're looking at them as suspects, not material witnesses."

"Call them what you will. We want them. And you had damn well better cooperate with my investigation. Or I promise I will fix it so you will have to leave the state. If you survive that long."

"I want to get this solved every bit as badly as you do, sheriff. But the boys did not do it. ... Do you intend to arrest me because you found some common ammo in my safe? Is that what you're planning to do?"

"Hell, no, Handler. You're free to go. Just do not leave town without my permission. I want to keep you around here until I get my hands on those two boys of yours."

"I'll stick around. You can count on that."

Immediately upon leaving the sheriff's company, Jack called Roger.

Chapter 23

Little Rich Goes to Work

At five A.M. the following day Little Rich was waiting at the Locks to load supplies onto the Arthur Fisher—his brother's freighter. Carefully packed among those articles were two fourteen-year-old male fugitives.

Little Rich had accurately anticipated a virtual lockdown of the island once the bodies had been found, and so he immediately loaded the two boys into the back of his pickup truck and fastened a tarp over them.

"You'll have to hide out on the mainland while I pick up supplies," he instructed. "I was thinking I could just drop you off at the rest stop south of the Soo on I-75. You could hide out in the woods, and if you needed to warm up, you could run into the restroom.

"And they have vending machines if you get hungry.

"Once I pick up what I need, I'll stop back for you guys. ... The important thing is to avoid being spotted. Any questions?"

Red and Robby did not question Little Rich's plan. They would have preferred to wait at Angel Star's house. She was their classmate, and good family friend. But they understood that so doing could put the girl and her mother in danger of being charged with harboring fugitives. *Best not to involve anyone else,* they reasoned, *at least not until the cops catch the real killer.*

And it was that matter that troubled the boys the most, because they knew that as far as the cops were concerned, the only ones they'd be looking for were the boys themselves.

* * *

"Ain't this a lot of shit to be pickin' up in the Soo?" deckhand Randall Misner asked. He been assigned to help Whitey with the supplies. "Didn't we just stock up in Detroit?"

"Mostly potatoes and onions," Whitey replied. "Had to toss much of what we loaded in Detroit last trip. They were sproutin' in the case. … Not fit for eating."

Little Rich had created a false bottom in both a case of onions and of potatoes. He packed Red under the potatoes, and Robby under the onions. The boys had flipped a coin to determine which crate they would ride in. Robby lost.

Whitey and his helper wheeled the supplies back to the galley and prepared to stow each item in its proper place.

"I've got it from here," Whitey said. "You get some sleep before breakfast."

Once alone in the galley, Whitey removed the potatoes and onions and freed the boys.

"This is how we do this," he told them. "I'll stand in for the deckhand on duty. And when I give you the signal, you sneak around and hide out in the aft lifeboat on the port side. Make sure you put on a life jacket.

"Be ready. I'll come around and tell you when to jump. And when I give you the signal, you'll have to go in immediately. We'll be empty, so we'll be riding high. Depending on Mother Superior's mood, you could be falling thirty feet or so. That means there will be a *terrific* impact. But you will be okay if you land on your feet and keep your arms hugging yourself.

"Those are pretty shitty wetsuits my brother gave you to wear. But they'll do the trick for this.

"When you come to the surface, swim toward shore. Remember, if the plan doesn't change, your jump will be just as the boat leaves Whitefish Bay. You'll be going in on the port side. So swim away from the boat. It'll be dark. Swim toward the lights. You'll see flashing lights onshore near the lighthouse. You'll be fine if you just push in toward them."

Whitey didn't mind helping the boys out as long as doing so did not jeopardize his job. And it wouldn't, unless the boys were to get caught and rat him and his brother out.

"Now, these plans are subject to change if Jack wants to change them. He might have a better way to get you off the boat. Don't do *anything* on your own. Just wait for my signal. If there's any kind of weather out there, you're not going in.

"Jack had Little Rich place a GPS transponder inside of each of your wetsuits. If anything goes south, it could help him locate you.

"And, if you guys get yourselves caught, keep your mouths shut about my brother and me. You got that?"

"We won't tell on you," Robby said. "No matter what happens, we won't tell anyone except for Uncle Jack. And we know he'll keep the secret."

"He ain't gonna talk," Whitey chuckled. "He's the one who's ultimately overseeing the rest of this operation, anyway."

Robby glanced over at Red. Both boys were surprised to learn that Jack was involved in the plot.

"Uncle Jack knows about the murders?" Robby asked.

"Of course. You think we'd come up with all this without his help? He'll be the one pickin' you up once you reach shore. ... Now, if any sort of weather comes up, we'll have to hold off on droppin' you fellows off. Or, if Jack has a different plan. So, don't go in unless you hear *specifically* from me. Got that?"

"Got it," Robby said.

"We might not be seein' each other again," Whitey told the boys. "That is, if all goes as planned. So, let's go over this stuff one more time."

"You're gonna stay put in the lifeboat until *I* give you the signal," he said, as he wrapped duct tape around their wrists and ankles to secure the wetsuits.

The wetsuits belonged to Little Rich. And they were not new. Little Rich was larger than the two boys, but not much. So the suits fit fairly well. But they were older, and had been stretched out through frequent use.

Little Rich's gloves and boots were also a little large for the boys, but with the application of a little duct tape, Whitey knew he could make them work. At least, the fit should be adequate to get the boys safely to where they needed to be.

The water temperature of Lake Superior is the coldest of all the Great Lakes. Averaging around fifty-one degrees in October, it would cause a man diving (or falling) into the lake without a wetsuit to quickly experience hypothermia, rendering his muscles useless within minutes and causing him to drown.

Little Rich's old wetsuits were the perfect solution. Once the whole matter had been resolved, Jack would replace the wetsuits, and Little Rich would be happy. However, were Jack, or anyone else in the area, at that time to purchase two new small wetsuits, the sheriff would undoubtedly hear about it, and figure out what Jack was planning.

Coordinating the caper was not straightforward. Jack had discarded his cell phone before the detectives had visited him in Chicago. He picked up some burners. While he believed them to be more secure than his known cell, the only totally secure line of communication Jack had available to him was the one that he could achieve with Roger, his friend in the Secret Service. So that's how he sought to interact whenever possible.

He called Roger and explained the problem. He told his friend about Little Rich, and that he had connections through his brother to secrete the boys out of the area onboard a Great Lakes Freighter.

"But," Jack said, "I have to be extremely careful about my involvement in the escape, and the pickup. The cops are going to be on my ass continually until they arrest these boys. I have no doubt that my calls outside this connection are subject to being monitored. And, I'm sure I'm being followed. … The best thing I can do is avoid anything that could lead to the boys."

"No problem," Roger said. "Get me the drop off coordinates. I'll get up there tonight and facilitate it."

"Thanks, buddy," Jack said. "That's the only way this is going to work."

"I think I've got a fix on who's responsible," Roger said.

"Really," Jack responded, obviously a little surprised. "And who would that be?"

"That old man, this Reynold Chrysler—the guy who owned the cottage. I got the forensics on him. Investigators pulled his prints off some tools in his shed, and they match those of one Reynold Wayne Fitzgerald. When he was younger—starting in his twenties—he established for himself a pretty extensive criminal record. Nothing that earned him hard time, however. And then, a couple of decades ago, he just seemed to drop off the grid. Haven't heard anything at all from him over the past twenty years. Hasn't even filed a tax form as Fitzgerald. He never signed up for social security. Nothing at all. It's as though he just fell off the end of the earth. Disappeared."

"Not until the boys found him hiding out on Sugar Island," Jack said. "What shitty luck. … Any fix on who it was that might have punched his ticket?"

"Nothing concrete. But I think I've come up with a workable *theory*."

"Let's have it."

"Understand that this is only *one* possible identification of your unsub. There's a lot more work to do before we can take this to the bank. But, you and I have both moved forward with less evidence. I think we have to pursue this angle until we can confirm or eliminate."

"For now, that's good enough for me," Jack said. "What are you thinking?"

"Nearly twenty-seven years ago, a buddy of Fitzgerald's, Walter Jon Kenny, was convicted of murder. He was sentenced to life. It was believed at the time that he had a partner, but he insisted he was acting alone.

"The two of them had been busted together before. So, there is definitely a connection.

"In this case, the murder victim was a well-known criminal. A convicted drug trafficker with Columbian connections. There was no proof, but there was suspected to have been a sizable amount of cash that went missing as well. The DEA believed that the money was taken by Kenny's partner, but there was never any solid evidence. Only the word of a confidential informant, and he refused to testify."

"How much money are we talking about?" Jack asked.

"That's unknown, but it could have been as much as five million. Estimates run between one and five."

"A lot of cash," Jack observed. "One man could easily live out his life on that amount. Especially if it were closer to the five mil."

"The way this whole thing looks to me is like this," Roger summarized. "Kenny took the fall, and Fitzgerald, or Chrysler, disappeared with the cash. He bought the cottage on Sugar Island, and then just hid out.

"Records do show that Reynold Wayne Chrysler did file federal and state income tax returns for the past two decades. He didn't earn a lot—he reported between eighteen and twenty-three thousand total income for each of those years."

"Then he had an employer?" Jack asked.

"Not really. He sold small wood trinkets that he made at his cottage. He worked at a dozen arts and crafts shows in the Upper Peninsula. And several gift shops carried his stuff.

"So, what we have is Reynold Wayne Fitzgerald disappearing, and after a couple years, Reynold Wayne Chrysler enters the picture. Looks to me like he paid someone to create a new identity.

Bought a bunch of first-rate woodworking tools, and set up a little business at his cottage.

"And then, when Mr. Kenny got out of prison, he tracked his buddy down. Maybe Mr. Chrysler didn't want to pay him his share, and so he killed the old man. And, unfortunately for everyone, the two deputies and the boys' caseworker just happened upon the scene.

"How is it that the boys managed to escape?" Roger asked. "Seems curious that a seasoned criminal like this Kenny guy would allow two teenagers to get away from him."

"Of course, the sheriff doesn't think that the boys escaped. He thinks they were the culprits responsible for the whole damn mess. I don't think that he is even looking for an alternative. … However, he did tell me that there was a basement to the cottage. That was unusual, all by itself. Not many of those cottages on Sugar Island have basements. I think it's possible that Red and Robby hid out in the basement for as long as they could, and when the killer started the fire, they ran. I have not talked directly to the boys, so I am not sure exactly how it went down. … But the scenario you present seems plausible."

"You worked out any sort of plan?" Roger asked, after a short pause in the conversation. "It's not going to be good enough to put this guy out of his misery. You've got to somehow exonerate the boys first. And do it convincingly."

"*Conclusively*," Jack followed. "The sheriff is not going to be easily convinced of anything. As far as he's concerned, Red and Robby are as good as convicted right now. In his mind. … This Kenny guy is going to have to sign a confession for the sheriff to even look beyond my boys. … To answer your question, I have *ideas*. But as far as a detailed plan—not yet. The only specifics at this time do not extend beyond the immediate protection of the kids.

"According to Little Rich, the boys told him that the killer swore he'd hunt them down. They are the only witnesses to his crime. He can't let them survive."

"Well," Roger said. "First things first."

"Where are you at the moment?" Jack asked.

"Well, let's see," Roger replied. "How about 46.335443, -85.259968."

"Coordinates," Jack chuckled as he plugged the numbers into his cell. "I suppose you can't get any more specific than that. ... That's going to be somewhere around Soo Junction, right here in in the UP. You're obviously flying. ... How'd you get here so fast?"

"I left New York as soon as I learned about your predicament. Figured you'd need some help."

"What are you flying?"

"My buddy's Piper—M350."

"There's no strips around there. And that plane is not built for STOL operation. ... Where you planning to set down?"

"Grand Marais."

"Really? There's a field there?"

"Sure. It's perfect. And this bird's a beautiful piece of equipment. It's all cool."

"Hell. You're setting down in the dark in a borrowed five million dollar Rolls Royce. I'll bet it's a turf strip. Right?"

"Absolutely. But, like I said, this is a great piece of equipment."

"It might be right now. But I think that you might end up buying that bird."

"You underestimate my talents, my friend. I'll call you after I get it tied down. We'll discuss logistics—where and how I need to proceed in picking up the boys."

Chapter 24

Jack's Lawyer Prepares for Audit

While Jack and Roger were formulating their plan to rescue the boys, both from Killer Kenny and from the clutches of the sheriff, Jack's lawyer, Randolph Calibret, was preparing a surprise for Allison's lawyer and their so-called audit.

One of Jack's biggest concerns through the years had to do with keeping the IRS happy. He had developed a system for dealing with the Feds. And, for the past thirty years, it had worked well.

Early on Jack came to the realization that he would not be able to report his income to the IRS in any typically legitimate manner.

Many of his clients were the sort of characters who liked to lurk in the shadows. They often paid Jack in cash. Frequently they offered payment in various types of non-negotiable properties such as real estate, gold, or diamonds. And on some rare occasions, they even bartered large quantities of firearms, which Jack would in turn dispose of to various foreign and domestic entities. He had even been known to accept as payment the promise of a favor. But, seldom did a client actually pay him with a check or with any other traceable forms of cash transfer. Such was the nature of his business, and the type of clientele he served.

That's why the Chicago bar he and a good friend owned came

in so handy.

Prior to Jack's buying into the bar, the establishment had always shown a loss. That's what three decades earlier had prompted his friend, Conrad *Sticky Connie* O'Donnell, to solicit Jack's help.

At that time Jack was in possession of just over five hundred thousand dollars in cash. And he did not know how he could deal with it as reportable income. The clients who had paid him in cash had informed him that they did not want there to be any way to trace the money back to them.

Jack had already invested a sizable amount in gold and silver, always keeping his purchases small and infrequent enough to avoid scrutiny.

But dealing with five hundred thousand dollars in cash—that, he felt, could present a problem. Especially in the event of an IRS audit.

So, following the advice of one of his other customers, a defrocked CPA, Jack invested in Connie O'Donnell's bar—*Sticky's*. Under the terms of the purchase, Jack owned the majority share of the bar. It was verbally understood that Connie would, in return for a generous salary, manage the day-to-day operations of the establishment for as long as he wished. And Jack stipulated in his will that should something happen to him, Connie or his heirs would inherit the bar. Or, if Connie were to die, his minority stake would pass to his heirs.

There were other stipulations insisted upon by the attorneys that were included in the final agreement and, after a little tweaking, both men signed off.

The first order of business was to convert the second floor of the bar into four banquet halls. By doing that, Jack was able to rent out the facilities to clients and their families, and thereby hide cash payments.

Jack did not mind paying the taxes on his income. That was never the issue. It was just that many of his customers did not want it known that they had contracted him in the first place. That's why they insisted on paying him in cash.

The addition of the banquet halls not only provided a creative means of disguising cash payments for the various services rendered by Jack, it also allowed him to file realistic looking tax data with the IRS. But, even more important to Conrad O'Donnell, the income from the banquet halls paid the bills.

For years the patrons of the bar had taken advantage of Connie's generosity. And he was good with that. He had a big heart. If his friends couldn't cover their tabs, he *comped* them out when he reconciled the books at the end of each month.

But now that the bar was under new ownership, Connie, as Jack's employee, was considerably more judicious with his dispensing of free drinks. Jack did, however, give him some latitude in that regard. As long as the bar came within putting distance of breaking even, Jack was good with it. It was simply more important to Jack that the bar maintain a large clientele, than seeing to it that every drink was paid for. Connie had a lot of loyal friends, and was gifted at providing a full house almost every night.

Two years earlier Jack and his accountants had their system put to the ultimate test—his books were audited by the IRS.

What Jack's attorneys and accountants termed every man's nightmare turned out to be a *walk in the park*. After ten days of laborious scrutinizing and double-checking, Craig Foster, the IRS agent in charge of the audit, shook Jack's hand and thanked him for his hospitality.

"Mr. Handler," he said, "if every business owner did as thorough and accurate a job as your people do, I would have to take a cut in pay. The only discrepancy we found was in your favor. And it was minor—one hundred dollars."

Jack had made every effort to accommodate the IRS audit. He directed his accountants to provide every document requested by Agent Foster, and to have them clearly tagged. To make the effort more pleasant, Jack freed up one of his banquet halls for the IRS to use. In it he provided unlimited snacks and coffee, and even offered to have lunches brought in by one of the caterers he frequently employed. Of course, Agent Foster and his team refused to take full advantage of Jack's hospitality on the grounds of appearance. But Jack made his point—he wanted it known that he would spare no effort to make the federal officers comfortable.

And, as far as his records were concerned, Agent Foster was correct. They were spotless. It was clear that Jack sought to pay every tax that he legitimately owed, and then some.

But then along came Allison Fulbright with her bulldog attorney—Abraham Stern.

Initially Jack was inclined to ignore their request altogether. But, after Roger's ominous warning, he decided he should come up with a strategy.

The first thing Jack did was to spell out Allison's plot to Randolph Calibret, his attorney.

After he was satisfied that Calibret fully understood the gravity of the situation, he asked, "Is there not *something* we can do about this? There must be a way we can legally refuse their request for all this documentation."

"Actually," Calibret said, "there really isn't. Stern is not *requesting* that we comply, he is demanding it. And he is within his rights to do so."

"I get it," Jack said. "And it would make sense that they would want to see certain records, in order to establish the value of the kid's share of the business. But that's not what they're really after. They couldn't care less about the kid's interests. Their sole purpose is to drive a wedge between me and my clients, and turn them against me. ... Like Roger said—*Allison is out to get me. And she's going after me with everything the legal system has at its disposal.*"

Calibret did not immediately respond, so Jack turned his statement into a question.

"Is *that* legitimate?" Jack asked. "Can a lawyer target my clients by auditing me?"

Calibret, who was sitting behind a well-worn wooden desk, looked over his glasses at Jack and smiled sarcastically. "Is it legitimate for the IRS to target specific groups on the basis of their political bias? That never happens, does it? ... If she has in mind going after your clients by targeting you, you can be pretty certain that she will do it, and may very well be successful in her attempt.

"Laws are not the perfect solution to every problem. Ideally, the law serves as a societal compass to determine minimally acceptable behavior. Among other things, the law regulates conduct, settles disputes, and establishes rights and obligations. But, in some cases, the law can be perverted. It can actually be weaponized and used to punish an enemy, or to gain an unfair advantage. I think that is what is happening here. Your old friend is using the law to trigger a desired reaction by—"

"Randy," Jack interrupted. "With all due respect, I understand what the law is *supposed* to be about. My question is this—what can we do to put an end to this travesty? ... Is there not *something* we can do about this? This is personal between Allison and me. The kid has nothing to do with it. He's being used by Allison. She is after me, and she is using him to get at my clients. I just want to put a quick end to this."

"Well," Calibret said, "I'll tell you what one of my buddies did when I was practicing down in Florida. It might not be very kosher, but it was effective. Got a forensic audit over with in record time. ... And the lawsuit dropped."

"I'm interested."

"Okay. You've got a third floor in the building where you have the bar? Right? Above the banquet facilities?"

"Yes," Jack replied. "But it's filthy. And not air conditioned."

"Perfect."

"Really?"

"Sounds *absolutely* perfect so far. Describe it to me."

"We use it for storage. It hasn't been cleaned out since before I bought the building. In fact, there's junk stored up there that might be from eighty/ninety years ago. ... And then when we remodeled for the banquet rooms on the second floor, we stuck all the shit we didn't want to trash out, put it all on the third floor."

"Like I said. That's *perfect*. Is there also an attic?"

"Sure," Jack said. "But it's got even more shit in it."

"Okay, this is what we do. We get a dumpster in here and stick all the stuff from the attic in the dumpster, and probably most of what is now on the third floor. Move what you want to hang on to up to the attic, and move your office temporarily to the third floor. Don't clean it up. Just clear it out a bit."

"The floors are just rough-cut tongue and groove boards," Jack said. "Some of them are even broken out. I'm telling you, it's a real mess up there. ... And, like I said, there's no air."

"As long as we can stick a desk in it, we can call it your office. It will work. We'll have to repair any holes in the floor. Wouldn't want some suit getting injured, and then suing you. ... Do you have electric on the third floor? And, is there a window or two? How about a working toilet?"

"Oh, sure. It used to be an apartment. Back in the day. It has all the necessary utilities. I imagine they all work. ... Just no air conditioning."

"Then we can use it. We'll make them as uncomfortable as we can. Legitimately, of course. We should move all your files off site. And bring in only what they specifically request. We'll give them a couple of desks, an old printer, and a light. That's it. That's all that we have to do. ... You should move your office up there as well. But I don't want you to taunt them. No matter what happens."

"Aren't they supposed to get started next week?" Jack asked.

"That's the time frame they stipulated. I'll see if I can postpone it for a week. That'll give us some time to get ready for them. ...

This is how we'll do this. I will have them specify *precisely* which documents they wish to inspect. I will make copies of the ones they list, and they can make copies of them, if they wish—provided they bring their own copy machine. But we will be keeping the originals in our possession. I think they'll be fine with that, because they will assume that since they are on-site, they will have access to more of the documents, and will then be able to broaden their investigation. If you're correct—that they are very limited as to the scope of their information—they will be eager for the opportunity to dig into the files. But, alas, they won't be able to because we will have moved offsite all the files not specifically requested.

"I'll take care of the arrangements," Calibret continued. "We will allow them five contiguous business days to do their work. And that's it. … This is actually going to be fun. At least I think it will. There is really no excuse for this. It borders on harassment. So, by the time they actually get here, we will have this set up like the audit from hell. We will make it so miserable that they will hate every day they have to show up here. Every *minute* of every day."

Jack just folded his arms and smiled. *God, I wish I could be around for this,* he thought. *But for right now, I've got too much on my plate. My first priority is to take care of those kids of mine.*

"I've got some other ideas, too," Calibret continued. "I've always wanted to do this, but never really had the chance. Yours is the first forensic audit I've ever prepared for where my client wasn't trying to conceal earnings from the IRS, or losses from stockholders. There's nothing anyone could find here that could land you in federal prison, or get you in trouble with investors. In those respects, your books are clean. All they are looking for is dirt on your clients. … And, ultimately, to incite one of them to kill you. Small matter—right? … Just kidding.

"Jack, we're going to give them something that they won't soon

forget… It'll be dirt all right. But not the type of dirt they're looking for."

Jack had no idea what all that *something* might entail, but he
was eager to let Calibret work magic on his behalf. Especially since
he had his own work cut out for him.

Chapter 25

A Tough Juggling Act

Jack believed what the boys had told Little Rich—that Killer Kenny was truly obsessed about hunting them down and eliminating them. And so Jack was equally fixated with making sure that did not happen. However, exactly how he was going to catch the killer, while at the same time protecting Red and Robby's safety—that was the challenge.

Little Rich had relayed the message to Jack early on that Robby had been nicked in the head, but that he was okay. He also explained that the boys had hid out in the creek for a while, and that this was after Robby had been shot.

That creek runs nearly a quarter of a mile from where the cottage stood, Jack was thinking. *So, I wonder if the investigators gathered up any forensics in that area. Or, if they even looked over there. I'll bet not. I think they assumed that the boys simply ran back to Pat's cottage.*

Jack's dilemma was this: for any forensic evidence to be admissible, it would have to be gathered by legitimate law enforcement. But, if Jack were to inform the sheriff regarding the escape tunnel, and the creek episode, it could then turn the investigation toward Little Rich and his possible role in helping the boys escape. And that would ultimately point to Whitey and the freighter. Jack needed to protect his friends' anonymity at all cost. He simply had to find an acceptable way to save the boys, and to get them off the hook for the murders.

In Jack's mind, it would be next to impossible to prove his boys did not kill the caseworker and the deputies. They had both motive and opportunity—that was indisputable. He felt that his best chance to clear the boys would be to present an alternative solution.

Fortunately, the law does not require that a suspect be proven innocent—only that he cannot be proven guilty beyond a reasonable doubt. So, all Jack had to do was to produce a viable option. Even if he were not able to keep the case from going to trial, if he could produce another suspect and demonstrate that there was adequate motive on his part for killing the victims, and that this suspect had the opportunity, then a good lawyer would be able to establish a reasonable level of doubt that Robby and Red were guilty of murder.

Of course, all of this investigation could be accomplished even if the boys were to be apprehended. But, in Jack's thinking, that would just not be acceptable.

He believed that once the boys were placed in custody, Killer Kenny would then be able to home in on the boys, and hire one of his buddies inside to kill them. *He certainly has enough money to get anyone hit,* Jack reckoned. *Especially if he knows where they are. I've got to keep the boys out of lockup and out of Kenny's reach. And, at the same time demonstrate that it was actually this Kenny character who pulled the trigger.*

Of course, if Kenny were to somehow defeat the legal system, and gain his freedom, Jack would see to it that he didn't survive one day on the outside.

Nevertheless, that scenario was fraught with danger for the boys and therefore totally untenable for Jack to consider.

Chapter 26

Bumpy Landing

*W*ham!

"Holy shit!" Roger barked as his Piper bounced along the 2600 foot 5/23 Runway at Grand Marais Airport. "Jack could be right. I just might end up buying this machine by the time I get it back to New York."

Roger was aware that AirNav listed Y98, the organization's designation for Grand Marais Airport, as having "poor" turf runways, but he was still taken aback at the severity of the head jolts.

Next time I won't come in quite so hot, he resolved, as the plane bounced to a stop with a couple hundred feet to spare. *Hope I didn't break anything.*

He then turned the plane around and taxied back to the tie-down area.

Chapter 27

Jack Engages Kate

D ad," Kate said in a surprised tone. She'd just pulled a small
burner phone out of a concealed compartment in her
purse. "Using the burners, I see. … *That's* never a good
sign."

As was usually the case, Kate was right.

She had spent early morning at her new second home office—the twenty-four-seven Starbucks on Broadway in Midtown Manhattan. She had just purchased her favorite morning treat, a Blonde Roast Venti, and was quietly allowing heat from the gas fireplace to quell her October chill. She was still just sipping her drink, not yet having removed her laptop or files from the new Porteen book bag that she balanced on her lap. It was a recent birthday gift from Don Maze, a New York literary agent and Kate's frequent evening companion. Both of her hands rested on it.

As was her habit, Kate had left her house on Long Island by four-thirty A.M. She liked to spend an hour or so planning her day and reviewing the cases that would require her testimony. Therefore—the files in her bag. Today she had showered, dressed in her browns, blacks and grays, and blow-dried her now shoulder-length auburn hair. And to complete her outfit—a touch of mascara and lip gloss. Right at that moment, all was well in Kate's hectic world.

Jack's call did not catch her by surprise. Whenever he needed to talk to her he knew that if he rang her between five and six in the morning he would catch her at a coffee shop or in transit. Little by little, Jack was formulating a plan. While he was keenly aware that at that time Kate was tying the bow on a couple major homicide investigations in New York—and so it would be next to impossible for her to pull away and join him on Sugar Island—he believed that Kate could help him dramatically by simply making a couple of phone calls from her office.

"We need to use the burners," Jack said, "because I have every reason to believe we need to exercise extreme caution. Phone might not be bugged, but can't take a chance."

"Then, you are being surveilled?"

"Without a doubt. They're not even trying to conceal it. Not that I wouldn't pick it up out here on the island, even if they tried to be sneaky. The only reason for tailing me around out here is that they must suspect that the boys are still hiding out on Sugar Island. That's a good thing."

"Can I assume our connection is secure?"

"It's as safe as it could be," Jack replied. "As long as we don't attract the attention of one of our federal agencies. And as long as no one's bugged your house. I might call you there tonight."

"I sweep it weekly, at least," Kate replied.

"Then we're good—at least for what I want you to do today."

"What's the latest on the boys?"

"Right now they are hiding out on a freighter. They are on Whitefish Bay heading toward Duluth."

"Really? How does that work?"

"Not sure it's going to," Jack said. "But at least it's got them off the island and out of the Soo. ... This place is crawling with cops. They must think that the boys are still here."

"Are the Feds involved?"

"No. At least I've not yet run into them. I expect that they will get here, eventually."

There was a long moment of silence, and then Kate spoke.

"I know you called me for a reason, Dad. But, I really can't get away right now. At least not today. So, is there something I can do from here?"

"There sure is. I need you to kick the bushes. Make as much noise as possible. See what runs out."

"Who's the target?"

"Walter Jon Kenny. He just left the system after doing a long stint for murder. Roger dug him up. He seems likely to have committed the murders on the island. All four of them. And up to this point, he's been flying under the radar. The sheriff's not even aware of him, as far as I know."

"And you think that if I start poking around, the sheriff might want to know why?"

"In part," Jack said. "It'd be nice if somehow the sheriff could be made aware that this Kenny guy exists. He's got a fix on the old man's real identity—the old guy that got killed. It wouldn't be too much of a leap of faith for him to tie the two of them together. Maybe you could give him a nudge in that direction."

"What did you mean with that "in part" comment?" Kate asked. "There's more?"

"There's always more," Jack said. "Roger texted me a list of contacts for this Mr. Kenny. People in his past—family members, friends, men he's done time with, but who are now on the outside. Some of them will be staying in contact. It's not like he's being hunted, or anything. He's not wanted. So, if you stir up enough attention, someone will pass it on to Mr. Kenny."

"What do you want me to say?"

"Let it be known that you have a couple witnesses on Sugar Island who saw Walter Jon Kenny shoot and kill Mr. Reynold Wayne Fitzgerald, two deputies, and a female county childcare worker. Ask them if they know Mr. Kenny's whereabouts."

"What do you want to accomplish?"

"I do not want Mr. Kenny to take off. He's got a whole shit load of cash. If he flees the area, we might never be able to tie him to the killings. I want him to be worried about the boys. So worried that he tries to do something about them. And hopefully makes a mistake."

"I'm pretty sure I get it," Kate said after thinking about it. "Roger can't help with this because the sheriff is unable to monitor what he does. But, with me, that's not the case. My office records my calls. I couldn't hide what I've been up to even if I tried."

"Exactly," Jack said. "We want the word to get out. Go ahead and talk it up with your co-workers."

"I'll get right on it," Kate said. "Right now."

And she did.

The minute she disconnected Jack's call she began jotting down the list of contacts Roger had given to Jack. And then she tucked the burner cell back into its place in her bag. And then she walked the four blocks to her precinct.

"Hello," the voice said after a dozen rings.

"Arthur Kenny?"

"Yeah," the man said after he'd cleared his throat. "Who the hell's calling at this time of morning?"

"This is Lieutenant Kate Beckett. I'm a New York City homicide detective. I have some questions I need to ask you."

"Go to hell," the man barked as he hung up on her. But before he had closed his eyes his cell rang again.

"I'm in Colorado. Just north of Denver. Do you know what time it is here? This is *Mountain Time*. It's four-thirty here. ... What the hell do you want?"

"You're related to Walter Jon Kenny?"

"Yeah. He's my worthless piece of shit brother. Why?"

"We're trying to locate him. We have some questions we'd like to ask him. Do you know where he is, or how we might contact him?"

"No. I haven't seen him in over twenty years. He's still in prison, as far as I know?"

"Mr. Kenny was released a week ago. The last we heard he was in northern Michigan—Sugar Island, to be specific. Could you corroborate that?"

"Like I said. I haven't seen him for over twenty years. … What the hell's he doin' in Michigan?"

Kate found Arthur's last comment to be most interesting. Roger's notes on the brother stated that he had visited Walter in prison several times through the years, the latest being less than a month before he gained release. Therefore, she had suspected from the start that he was lying—that he was actually totally aware that his brother had been released from prison. So, when he expressed surprise that Walter Kenny was in Michigan, she became even more convinced that he knew significantly more than he was letting on.

Someone has done some major legwork in locating old man Fitzgerald, she reckoned. *Kenny could not have done that from inside. Could very well be this Arthur fellow was Killer Kenny's eyes and legs on the outside. The mere fact that once he woke up he was eager to talk to me. That sounds suspicious. If he was as irritated at my call as he let on, he would have simply turned his cell off. This guy wanted to find out what I knew.*

Following that line of thinking, she decided to plant some seeds.

"We have reason to think that your brother has located his old partner, one Reynold Wayne Fitzgerald. He was living in Northern Michigan. On Sugar Island. Mr. Fitzgerald has been living there for the past couple of decades under the name Reynold Chrysler. We believe Mr. Fitzgerald, AKA Reynold Chrysler, had helped your brother rob and kill a well-known drug dealer, and that Mr. Fitzgerald had hidden the cash they had stolen at his cottage on Sugar Island."

"No shit!" Arthur said. "How much money was it?"

With that comment, Kate became totally convinced that Arthur was deeply involved—if not in the initial robbery and murder, then at least in the attempt to recover the loot. Kate decided to inflate the numbers to trigger suspicion in Arthur's mind.

"Upwards of fourteen million dollars."

"You're shittin' me!" he blurted out. "That much? I'd thought it was a few million at most."

"No. It's closer to fifteen. Possibly even more. ... It was drug money, so we don't have an accurate fix on the exact amount. But reliable witnesses place it at around fifteen million dollars. That's a lot of money. Certainly worth even a heavy prison term. ... Your brother appears to have recovered the cash. So he is a very rich man right now."

"I guess so," Arthur said. "If I hear from him I'll let you know. Got a phone number where I can call?"

"Should be on your phone. You can call that number. Ask for Lieutenant Kate Handler. Homicide."

"Are you pretty sure that he's been up to see this Fitzgerald dude?"

"Oh, yeah," Kate replied. "He's paid his old friend a visit, for sure. We have two eyewitnesses that not only put him at the old man's cottage on Sugar Island, but that will swear that your brother did, indeed, shoot and kill Mr. Reynold Fitzgerald, along with two Chippewa County sheriff's deputies, and a county child welfare worker."

"Eyewitnesses?"

"That's right. Two teenage boys saw him shoot and kill four people—two of them law enforcement officers. ... So, be careful. Your brother is a *very* dangerous man. Anyone who comes into contact with him is in danger. But, since you haven't been in contact with him during all that time, odds are that he won't seek you out.

"However. Should he contact you. Or, should someone reach out to you on his behalf, give me a call immediately."

"Yes. I will do that."

The instant Kate disconnected the call, she called her father.

"Dad. We got a live one."

"Arthur?"

"Exactly. I'm quite sure he's been in contact with his brother. Maybe he's even the one who located old man Fitzgerald. You should have Roger track down his calls. I'm sure he's calling his brother as we speak."

"Done," Jack said. "Roger's people are already on it. If Arthur Kenny is calling his brother, then we're going to get a fix on our killer right away, and I'll be paying him a visit. ... I assume you told him about those two boys being witnesses of his crime."

"Oh, yeah," Kate said. "Better keep a close watch on them from here on out. He's comin' after them."

"I figure he'll be asking around at the bars. I've put the word out. Expect to hear something before long."

"Where are the boys right now?" Kate asked.

"They're still on the boat. Headed toward Duluth. As soon as Roger gets positioned, I'll have them jump out. ... He's just landed at Grand Marais. Initially I was going to have them go in as they passed the lighthouse at Whitefish Point. But, that's when I was planning on doing the pickup. But the sheriff's tightened his surveillance on me. I don't dare give their location away. So we'll wait on Roger."

Just then Jack spotted an incoming call.

"That's Roger now," he said. "I need to take his call."

"Hey, buddy. What's your 10-20?"

"Just got my little bird tied down. But, Jack, I'm afraid I've got some disturbing news about your boys."

Chapter 28

The Kenny Brothers Team Up

After Roger had securely tied down his M350, he climbed back in the cockpit to check his messages. One text message in particular grabbed his attention. It was from *Jasper*, one of his associates. It was time-stamped one minute ago, and it read: "Roger. Have some news about your Michigan boys. Call me."

Roger did just that.

"Hey, buddy. Roger here. What's up?"

"Just monitored a call from a man named Arthur Kenny to Walter Kenny. They're brothers, I assume. Arthur informed Walter that the cops were looking for him. The news that the cops were looking for him caught Walter off guard. Apparently he didn't suspect that his name had been connected with the killings of the two deputies, the old man Fitzgerald, and a female. That there were witnesses, the two boys, who could ID him, that did not seem to surprise him.

"But, here's the kicker. Somehow this Walter Kenny fellow had learned that the two boys were on a freighter headed west toward Duluth. Apparently someone who knew the guys that were helping arrange the pickup was talking at a bar. Must have had one beer too many, and spilled the beans. I thought you'd want to get that info to your friend ASAP."

"Did he say what his plans were?" Roger asked.

"Not specifically. He did seem intent on 'terminating' his problem. We both know what that means. But he didn't spell anything out. He almost sounded a little hesitant to talk about it on the phone. Maybe there was someone sitting close to him who he feared might be able to overhear. "

"Where was he at the time?"

"At a bar in Sault Ste. Marie."

"Not still there, I'd bet," Roger said.

"Don't know that. Walter did seem a little rattled when Arthur told him the cops were looking for him. Now, to my knowledge, that's not true ... that the cops were looking for him. I heard Kate Handler tell Arthur that, but I don't know where she got her information. Do you?"

"Yeah," Roger said. "You're right about that. There's no warrant out for Walter Jon Kenny. Not yet. And, I am pretty sure I know where her story came from. But, I'd rather not say. The whole point was to force Arthur to make that call to his brother. That part of it worked. But what we were not counting on is for Mr. Kenny to find out that the boys were on the freighter. That changes everything. It puts the boys in real imminent danger. I need to pass this on to Jack Handler."

Immediately upon closing out his conversation with Jasper, Roger called Jack and informed him.

Jack's first reaction was, "Oh shit!"

"That's what I thought," Roger said. "Your buddy on the island—that Little Rich—must be he couldn't keep his mouth shut."

"I doubt it was him," Jack said. "He's a pretty cool guy. Must be one of his nosey neighbors, or someone on the boat. But I doubt that it was Rich or his brother. Those freighters are huge, but not much happens onboard that someone doesn't find out about. ... At least we got the boys off the island and out of the Soo. That's where the search is centered. ... But, if word has gotten out that the boys are on the boat, won't be long before the sheriff gets wind of it as well.

"And this Walter Kenny. Do we know where he is? I suspect he could be on the boat as well. If so, those boys will not be able to hide out forever."

"They did take on a new crewman at the Locks," Roger said. "Don't have any info on him right now, except for a name. William Franks. Just a name. That's all we have."

"Stay with your plane for now," Jack said. "I might need a pilot. And give the Coast Guard a call, Homeland Security, and have them look this guy up and send a picture of him to you, and you forward it to me. And then see if you can bring up some video for when the freighter passed through the Locks. See if we can find anything on it. I'll head down to where you are right now."

Jack then called Little Rich and asked him what he knew about a crewman named William Franks.

Little Rich told him that he'd never run into anyone by that name. "But that doesn't mean anything," Little Rich said. "There're new guys that come through all the time. I wouldn't necessarily know that many of them. And he's one that I've never met. Besides, I've been out of circulation for a while now. ... I'll get hold of my brother and see if he knows anything.

"And, Jack, I didn't breathe a word to anyone, except for Whitey. But, on those boats, it's almost impossible to keep anything totally quiet. It could have come from someone onboard. Someone could have made a call to his girlfriend."

"I know you didn't talk. This stuff happens. We'll just have to play the hand we're dealt. Do let me know if you can find out anything about this William Franks. If anyone knows him and can provide a description."

Jack did not wish to waste any more time. He knew what he had to do, and he was eager to set about the task.

"Roger, I need you to drop me onto that boat," Jack said as he jumped out of his Tahoe. He slid beneath the rear undercarriage and removed a magnetic tracking device. He looked around until he found a newer model pickup truck, and attached the device beneath it.

"Right," Roger chuckled. "Who do you think you are? Evel Knievel? … Or, better yet, who do you think *I* am? Even if I was flying a chopper, I couldn't set it down on a freighter without breaking every maritime law in the book. … And probably busting up the chopper as well. And then, I'd lose my license, my job, and my reputation … and possibly even my life."

"You've got pretty good instrumentation on that bird, don't you?"

"Yeah. It's set up fine. … What have you got in mind?"

"All you have to do is calculate the forward motion of the boat, and wind speed and direction, and I'll do the rest. That is, provided you have a decent parachute on your plane."

"Pretty sure I've got a couple Hi-5 Ram Airs. Would one of them work for you?"

"Perfect. I need you to get me up, and drop me from ten thousand feet. I'll fly it down. If we can get to this while it's still dark, you can cut your lights, and no one will ever see me coming … or you going. Hopefully."

"I suppose you've got a wetsuit."

"No time. Besides, I don't intend to miss that boat. It's a thousand feet long and a hundred feet wide. How could I miss a target that size? … You ready the plane and calculate the logistics. I'll get to the strip as quickly as I can."

Both men knew that this would be an incredibly dangerous jump. Hitting a stationary target under good conditions is difficult enough. But the freighter was anything but stationary.

First of all, they had to deal with its forward motion. Using radar, they would be able to determine just how fast the boat was moving. Being that it was empty, it would be operating at its optimum speed, which was sixteen knots.

The winds were also a factor. On this night they were out of the west-northwest at four knots, with gusts up to eight.

Cloud cover was another factor to be considered. Right at that moment the sky was amazingly clear. There was a thin cloud layer at three thousand feet. But it was very scattered. As long as Jack jumped at the right location, and remained on course during free fall, the clouds should not present a serious problem.

He could have opted to wear a wetsuit. And that would probably have been advisable, because without one, he would not survive were he to miss the freighter and land in Superior.

But he did have his reasons to forego that safety factor. For one thing, if he was to miss the boat, there would not be a way in which he could get picked up and put on the boat in time to save the boys. His success required speed and surprise.

Another reason he decided against a wetsuit was wind resistance, or the lack of it. He had jumped many times before, and in every case he wore the typical jumpsuit. Not only was he comfortable in one, he was familiar with what to expect with regard to wind resistance during free fall. It would be during that forty-four-second period of time that he would need to *fly* into the optimal position to deploy the main canopy.

Of course, were the main canopy to fail, he could jettison it and use the reserve parachute. But he knew that he would not be able to land on the freighter using the round reserve. So, he did not give that possibility a second's thought.

But a million other thoughts and concerns whirled around in his mind on his drive to the airfield.

What if Kenny never actually got on the boat? That was a real possibility. So far he did not have any confirmation that the killer had made it that far. Jack did know that Kenny was aware that the two boys—the only witnesses who could testify against him—were on the boat. But that's all Jack knew for certain.

What if Kenny decided to drive to Duluth and wait for the boys there? Maybe. But not likely. If he knew that the boys were on the freighter, he also knew that there would have been a plan to get them off somewhere en route. ... No. He's on that boat.

But, what if he's already found the boys?

That possibility was not acceptable to Jack. *I just can't allow myself to go there.*

And then, in a moment of weakness, Jack violated one of his principle tenets. He allowed himself to second guess his decision. *Should I have simply called the sheriff? Or, maybe the Coast Guard? After all, that's their job.*

"Damn you, Handler!" he shouted out loud. "What the hell do you think you're doing!? *No* one is better able, or more motivated, than *you.* So cut the shit and get your sorry ass on that boat!"

After that short exchange with himself, Jack ceased debating the matter and concentrated on how he would pull the rescue off.

Chapter 29

Planning and Preparation

During the final nineteen minutes of the drive to Grand Marais airfield, Jack played his jump over and over again in his mind. As to exactly what he would do once on the boat, that he would have to improvise depending on what he found. And he had no control over what that might be.

"You sure you want to go through with this?"

Those were the first words out of Roger's mouth.

Jack did not respond to his friend's question.

So, Roger dropped it.

"We don't have much time, Roger," Jack said. "But, I'm sure you know that already. … Any problems landing? I've heard that the field is a little dicey."

"It was a bit rough. But this Piper is a nice piece of equipment. Should be okay."

"Got enough strip to get it back up?"

"I came in on fourteen because it was a little longer—2800. But I think I'll use five to go up. It's a little shorter, but it's within this bird's limits. I think I ran into a patch of sand coming down. Don't want to do that on the way up."

"We don't have time to check it out," Jack said. "Let's just do whatever's quickest. We're running light, anyway."

"You're right in more ways than one," Roger said, as Jack was strapping on his harness. "About not having time. Looks like we're getting some company."

"Who is it?" Jack asked. "Does it look like the sheriff?"

"I'd say so. It's not the State Police."

"I removed the tracking device before I headed out here," Jack said. "Must be they had physical eyes on me as well."

"I'm taking fourteen up," Roger announced. "It's closer. Get ready for a bumpy ride."

"Whatever," Jack said.

He was duct-taping the bottoms of his trousers and his sleeves as Roger turned the plane around at the end of the strip.

Roger reviewed his instruments, applied the brakes and throttled up.

He then released the brakes and throttled fully.

The patrol car, with reds and blues flashing, had pulled across runway fourteen in order to block them. Roger did not back off.

"Looks like they want to play chicken with us," he said. "How well do they know you, Jack?"

"They'll move," Jack said without ever looking up.

And they did.

By the time the plane was within two hundred feet of the patrol car it had become clear to the deputies that either they moved their car, or there was going to be a serious accident. The driver wisely shoved the car in reverse to avoid crashing the plane and the county's car.

Just as Roger and Jack sped past the patrol car, on their way up to takeoff speed, the left wheel caught the edge of a sand patch, but by then they had reached speed and Roger was able to correct.

"That wasn't so bad," Jack said. "Do you know exactly where we need to look for the boys' boat?"

"Yeah, I've got it," Roger said. "You should check your cell. I'm sending you a picture of that William Franks fellow."

Jack checked it out, but didn't comment.

Roger climbed as quickly as the Piper could and headed out

over Lake Superior.

"You all set back there?" Roger asked.

"As much as possible. What's the cloud cover look like?"

"Right here it looks pretty good. Some patchy clouds at three thousand. But who knows what we're going to find blowing in from Canada out over the lake. ... I think that the best we can do is get you in position as quickly as possible. And you jump. I will guide you down as best I can. It's moving at fourteen and fifteen knots. ... With a little luck, you *might* miss the water. ... Make that with a *lot* of luck."

"I'll engage the main canopy at forty-four seconds. And aim behind the center of bow. Hopefully land in the middle of the boat. Anyway, that's the plan."

Both men knew that this particular plane was neither designed nor set up for skydiving. So, it was going to be a fairly tricky exercise.

Not only did Roger have to maneuver perfectly to the jump point, he needed to be in a position to render aid to Jack should something get hung up.

The plane was equipped with USP, Underspeed Protection—a feature designed to dip the nose should the speed approach the point of stalling. Roger decided to disable the USP because he wanted to force the plane into a stall at precisely the moment Jack was to jump.

He had two reasons for this approach: First, to serve as a clear signal for Jack to jump. Were Jack to jump too soon, he would risk flying into the starboard side of the boat, and ending up in the lake. Too late, and he would sail entirely over the freighter, and end up in the lake on the port side.

The plan was for Roger to bring the plane into position, pull back on the yoke, and cut the engine. Jumping at exactly the right moment would give Jack the best chance at a safe landing on the boat.

In addition to the stall serving as a timing signal, it would ensure that Jack would clear the right horizontal stabilizer, as it would allow him to fall vertically, and not strike the tail section.

"I'm going to count down from twenty," Roger said. "You ready, or do I take another pass?"

"Do it," Jack said.

Roger double checked his instruments, and began counting down.

"Twenty, nineteen, eighteen. ..."

As the countdown progressed, Roger cut the engine and pulled the yoke toward him.

"Five, four, three, two, one."

At that point, the engine stalled, and Jack jumped.

The plane lurched as he did, and Roger adjusted.

Three seconds after Jack jumped, Roger dipped the nose and regained power. At the same time he was counting off the seconds of Jack's free fall. When he reached fifty he said, "Jack, do you copy?"

"I'm flying the canopy. All is well. I see the boat. How does it look from up there?"

"Looks to me like you should be on target. ... The boat hasn't changed course."

Jack had passed through the cloud layer and was approaching two thousand feet. The freighter was nicely illuminated. Jack observed that the smoke from the diesel engine was flowing toward the port side at almost a forty-degree angle with the stern. This told him that the wind remained from the west-northwest. He adjusted accordingly.

"Jack. Make sure you clear the bow radar tower. ... How does it look to you?"

"Shit! Like I could use a stiff drink."

There was not a good way to make this landing. And Jack knew it. No matter how nicely he came in, he was going to have to set down on hard steel in motion, with a head wind of over eight miles per hour, compounded by the force of the boat's forward motion into that wind.

Jack was not concerned with the forward radar tower. His approach from starboard was well behind it. His biggest concern was in having an inflated canopy drag him across the top of the freighter. The covers for the cargo hatches would not provide a friendly landing strip for a body in motion. He would need to release his canopy immediately on touchdown—before the twenty-knot air differential could launch him over the port side and into the frigid waters of Lake Superior.

Roger knew better than to distract Jack at this sensitive point in the task. So he simply circled around and tried to get a visual. In a worst-case scenario, one in which Jack was swept off the boat and into the water, Roger would radio the Coast Guard. Of course, by that time the Coast Guard could arrive on scene, the operation would be one of recovery, not search and rescue.

Jack steered himself in for a landing. He flared his canopy a little lower than he would have liked, but he did not want to risk a gust pulling him back up and over the other side of the boat.

And, as is the case with flaring so close to hard objects, he struck the deck with tremendous force. He did, however, successfully release the canopy almost immediately. He rolled forward, crashing hard into a steel hatch cover. He lay still for a long moment nursing a lump on his head. Finally he spoke to Roger.

"I'm down. Bruised up and bleeding a bit, but nothing broken."

"I spotted your canopy floating off the port side. Glad you're not still attached."

"Me too."

"What do you see?"

"Don't see anything. I came down pretty close to midship. ... But, I do hear sirens sounding. Not sure what they mean."

"See anyone?"

"No. Nothing's moving."

"That's good. Then no one saw you coming in. They might have spotted your canopy floating past the bridge. But, if no one's looking for you, then you should be good. ... Wonder what that siren's about."

"I'm ditching this helmet. I'll be switching to the radio."

"The one thing I can think of that would explain your siren. That freighter might be equipped with a warning system. Like a dead man switch. If it is, and if the pilot doesn't reset the timer periodically, it will go into alarm. ... Is the siren ship-wide, or just localized?"

"I can hear a horn in the bow, and the stern."

"Do you see anyone moving about?"

"I have been down for five minutes, and I have spotted no movement. I'm going to head to the bridge."

Just as Jack started to get up he spotted a man hurriedly moving away from the bridge.

"Wait a minute," Jack said. "I see a man heading in my direction. He's running."

Jack had still not stood to his feet. He pushed himself up enough to get a better look.

"You never run on the deck of a ship," Roger said. "Something must be wrong."

Just then there was a rapid burst of fire from an automatic weapon. It sounded to Jack as though six rounds had been fired.

"Holy shit!" Jack muttered to Roger. "The guy who was running toward me. He just got shot."

"Who's firing?" Roger asked. "Can you make out the shooter?"

"Three hundred feet away. Maybe more. I saw the muzzle flash. Pretty sure it's a MAC-10 9mm. Lit him up pretty good. But I can't make out the shooter. He's too far away. Looks like a big guy. Could be Kenny. ... Can't be good. Shot the victim in the back while he was running away."

"Everyone else must be in hiding," Roger said.

"Or dead," Jack said. "Wouldn't be too difficult to take over a boat like this. These guys are sailors, not soldiers. I've got to get myself in position. Can't stay hiding out here forever. It's only a matter of time before he finds the boys."

"Do you know where they're hiding?" Roger asked.

"Supposed to be in the port side lifeboat," Jack said. "But, who knows. Could be they've changed location. I should be able to pick up one of their GPS transponders, but I'm not getting any signal. That's troubling. ... I'm going to try to find Whitey, and see what he can tell me."

"Jack," Roger said. "I'm thinking there's a problem with your boat. You're now moving at sixteen knots, and I'd say you were a little off course. Like, enough off course to be a problem. You're on track to clip Lighthouse Island. There's a significant shoal surrounding it. ... In fact, you couldn't be headed more directly at it if you tried."

"No shit," Jack said. "How long do I have?"

"Right now you are approximately twenty-two minutes away from impact. That would be the maximum. You are several degrees off course. The lighthouse lies a couple miles south of Caribou Island. I don't have a suitable maritime chart showing what's beneath the surface along where you're heading. But I am showing a serious sandstone shoal running out from the lighthouse. It's only a few meters beneath the surface. I can state this much unequivocally—that lighthouse is built on a rock, and you're headed right for it."

"Roger," Jack said, still horizontal on the deck. "You need to get out of here. Fuel up and wait to hear from me. Nothing you can do here right now. ... There's a small airstrip just south of Munising. Might be a good one for you."

"Roger that," Roger said, as he got his bearings and angled south toward Munising.

"Hey, buddy," he texted. "I'm going to need your help. Call me."

Roger was sending a message to Former President Robert Fulbright. Because Roger had served in the White House for six years as the head of the former president's Secret Service detail, whenever he needed a favor, he frequently turned to Fulbright first for help.

Roger knew that there would be a complaint issued after his narrow escape from the sheriff's grasp at the Grand Marais airstrip, and that there would be some probing questions resulting from suspicions of his involvement with the freighter, especially if it was to run aground around Caribou Island. … And then there would be the matter of the body, or perhaps bodies, on that boat.

Roger was fairly confident that the former president could and would issue him a *Get out of Jail Free* card, but he wasn't so sure how his immunity could be construed so as to also cover Jack. *Maybe Bob will have a good solution,* he thought.

Chapter 30

Jack Finds Kenny

Jack did not have time to be concerned about the future, except as it might involve the fate of his two boys.

"There he is," Jack mumbled to himself.

The killer stepped forward as though straining to get a better look across the expanse of steel hold covers that stretched the full length of the ship. For a moment it appeared that he was staring directly at Jack. But then he shifted his gaze toward the bow and stepped forward.

Jack was busy affixing a suppressor to his Stealth Recon Scout A1 Covert. He had chosen this piece of equipment as his weapon of choice because it was extremely compact for a sniper rifle—measuring only twenty-seven inches. *The smaller the better,* he believed, *when a man's jumping out of an airplane.*

While he wanted to keep Kenny alive until he was certain he would be able to locate, extricate, and exonerate the boys, he was not sure he would be able to accomplish all three tasks without at some point being forced to take him out.

Ideally, Jack would like to hand a living Walter Jon Kenny over to the sheriff, along with evidence sufficient to absolve the boys of all wrongdoing. But, given the fact that the sheriff had been unable to turn up any evidence at all suggesting that Walter Kenny had ever set foot on the crime scene, it seemed unlikely to Jack that he would be able to accomplish this task without some sort of a confession. And Jack was well aware that *dead men don't talk.*

But there were some things Jack had going for him. By dropping out of the sky, he had managed to gain proximity to the killer without having been detected. *At least he's not hunting me,* Jack determined. *He is hunting, but not in the same fashion that he would be if he knew I was onboard with a sniper rifle.*

Jack cautiously lifted his head above the cargo hatch cover.

"Five hundred feet," he said to himself. "I've got to get closer. Or coax him over to me."

It was not a matter of Jack's being unable to take the killer out from that distance. He knew he could do that with a single well-placed shot from his A1 Covert. But his goal was to capture, not kill. At least, that was his intent at this point in time.

I wonder how many are dead or wounded? And are there some that are armed? If any onboard are armed, they're going to shoot me if they get a chance. … If I could find Whitey. He'd know where the boys are. They're supposed to be in the port side lifeboat. I can see that from here. If they're in there, I hope to hell they don't move. Eventually Kenny's going to check it out. I need to stay close enough to it just in case they're in it.

The sirens were still sounding. At first he found it to be distracting, but as time passed he started to get used to it.

And then he had an idea.

He slipped on a tight-fitting pair of latex gloves. He then took aim at the siren closest to him. It was mounted on the aft end of the boat. He then cranked his head around to check on Kenny. After nearly a minute, the killer turned his back on Jack in order to check out a noise he had heard behind him.

Jack rapidly re-aimed his rifle and fired a single shot. The 180 grain 308 soft point blew the entire siren from the wall.

Kenny spun around and fell to his stomach—gun drawn. He had heard Jack's suppressed round. But, because of the nature of a suppressor, he could not get an accurate fix on its source. Especially when his back had been turned.

Jack pulled the bolt back slowly, and retrieved the spent brass with his fingers to prevent it from making noise when it struck the steel of the deck. He slid the bolt forward. This pushed a new round into the breech. He then locked the bolt.

Jack thought that Kenny would investigate. And he was right. The killer slowly rose to his feet and proceeded to cautiously move toward the stern—his MAC-10 leading the way.

This might go well, Jack was thinking. *The guy obviously doesn't know what he's doing. That MAC-10 is no competition. Not from any distance at all. If he knows his target, and is close enough, that thousand rounds a minute can be a challenge. But, if I can get off one clean shot, that's all I'll need.*

Jack was positioned between cargo hatch twenty-one and twenty-two. Kenny was slowly making his way back. As he approached the space between hatches, he scoured each with his eyes.

Jack did not intend to wait until the killer reached hatch twenty-one. *After he checks out twenty, he will turn toward the stern. At that point I should have a clean shot at his gun. This 308 will knock it to hell. Soon as I disable it, I'll charge him. ... Unless he pulls out a reserve. He used a Glock to kill the deputies. He probably has that with him. I'll give him a few seconds to produce another weapon. If he goes down, I'll charge him anyway. His gun hand will not be functioning very well.*

Bang!

Kenny's MAC-10 flew from his hand. The killer screamed like a frightened child.

Jack wasted no time. He drew his own Glock and charged the still-standing Walter Jon Kenny.

Jack started barking commands at him: "Get down on your stomach! Now! Get down! Stretch your hands out in front of you! Now! Down! Down! All the way! On your face! Now!"

Jack's round, another 180 grain soft point, struck the MAC-10 just above and in front of the trigger guard. It smacked with such force it caved the metal in from the trigger guard to the magazine. It ripped the submachine gun out of Walter Jon Kenny's hand like a discarded toy and sent it flying across the starboard walkway. It bounced off the railing and slid harmlessly back toward the bow of the freighter.

The killer was stretched out on the deck writhing in pain.

"You damn near broke my hand. You ruined it. You shot me for no reason."

When Jack approached the fallen killer he intentionally stepped on the man's hurting right hand as he reached down to remove the Glock that was sticking out of his belt in the small of his back.

"You won't be needing this," Jack said, sliding it under his own belt.

"You bastard," Kenny shouted. "I need a doctor! You damn near shot my hand off! Get me a doctor right now!"

"Yeah," Jack said. "I'll get on that right away."

Jack stood to his feet to survey his surroundings. As he did he surveyed his surroundings. With his right foot firmly planted on Kenny's tailbone, Jack scrutinized the path the big boat was on.

"There it is, all right," he muttered. "That damn lighthouse! … Roger was right!"

Dead ahead and slightly to the port side was the Caribou Island lighthouse. There would be no missing the rocks surrounding it, and running just below the surface of the water all the way to Caribou Island. The big boat was crashing through the waves at nearly fifteen knots. The five-eighths inch steel plate that kept the freighter afloat would be no match for the glacier-carved rocks lying just beneath the surface of Lake Superior—especially those lurking around Caribou Island. It was, after all, one of these shoals that was believed to have doomed the SS Edmund Fitzgerald on that fateful November night in 1975.

"So, what's this all about, jackass? Why you trying to run the boat aground? What could you possibly gain by doing that?"

Kenny did not respond.

Jack reached down and pulled the killer's quivering right hand behind his back and slipped the restraint over his wrist.

But before Jack had time to secure his other hand, a voice boomed from behind him: "Stop right there. I saw you shoot Mr. Franks. Let him up. Now. Or I'll shoot *you*."

Jack did not move.

"This is *not* William Franks," Jack finally said. "I'm sure that William Franks is dead. And this man killed him. ... This is Walter Jon Kenny. He's wanted for killing two deputy sheriffs, and two other innocent people."

"Get off of him right now!" the man commanded Jack. "I'm the First Mate. I'm in charge here. And this *is* Mr. William Franks. I saw his ID. It is *you* who don't belong on this boat. I don't even know who you are or what you're doing here. But, I do know Mr. Franks. He works on my boat."

Instead of yielding his position, Jack firmly squeezed Kenny's wrist, and pivoted his body around enough to look the First Mate in the eye.

"Handler," Jack said. "My name's Jack Handler. I'm a licensed private investigator.

"I need to secure this man, and you need to get this boat stopped. Surely you realize that we're about to run aground. Let me secure my prisoner, and then I'll address your concerns."

"He's lying!" Kenny blurted out as loudly as he could. "*He's* the killer the sheriff's looking for. ... My name is William Franks. I can prove it. And I can also prove that I have been working undercover on this freighter for Homeland Security. We've been tracking this guy who *says* he's Jack Handler. Not only is he a suspect in those killings, he's a person of interest for terror threats against the shipping industry. Get him off of me and I will prove it to you."

"Back off. Let Mr. Franks get up!" the First Mate barked.

Reluctantly, Jack released Kenny's wrist, and then slowly removed his foot from Kenny's spine.

"Tell him to back off," Kenny said, still lying face down on the deck. "I don't trust him. Look what he did to my hand."

"Step back. Give Mr. Franks room to get up."

Jack complied. He took one step back, but remained close enough to engage.

Slowly, using his left hand, Kenny pushed himself up to his knees. And then, while greatly favoring his throbbing right hand, he managed to get to his feet. However, he kept his back turned toward the First Mate.

Jack kept a wary eye on him, but he stood just out of Jack's reach.

"I've got my badge in my pocket," Kenny said. "I'll get it for you."

I have his Glock ... and I broke his Mac-10, Jack was thinking. *Could he have a third weapon?... Working undercover—and carrying his badge in his pocket. I don't think so.*

"No!" Jack shouted. "He's got a gun."

Unfortunately, the killer managed to quickly extricate a small hammerless Smith & Wesson five-shot Military Police J-frame from his right pocket, and using both hands he squeezed off three shots, striking the First Mate with two of them.

At the very moment Kenny swung the pistol toward Jack, the big boat lurched forward, throwing off him off balance before he could shoot Jack.

The screeching of metal on rock was nearly deafening. The torquing and ripping seemed to go on forever. The shock of the boat hitting the rocks knocked Kenny off his feet. While he was still able to hold onto the .38, he was unable to right himself enough to get off a shot.

Jack pounced on the killer, striking him in the face with a crushing right elbow, while at the same time grasping Kenny's pistol hand with his left. He bent Kenny's wrist backward and wrested the pistol from it.

And then, gripping the small pistol tightly, Jack delivered three hammer blows to Kenny's head and face rendering him unconscious.

As Jack again stood to his feet, it was clear to him that all forward motion was dramatically slowing. Under normal conditions it would take several miles for a ship that size to stop—even in full reverse. He looked out and was shocked to see the lighthouse barely one hundred feet off the port side of the boat. And it did not appear to be moving—which actually meant the boat was no longer moving.

"We've run aground," he said out loud.

It seemed to him that someone other than he had just uttered those words. "Hell. It's worse than that. I'm sure something must have ripped open. We've got to be taking water."

The boat had hit the rocks under full power. Now it was dead in the water, yet the motor was still spinning the screws.

I should have figured the captain would have been carrying a weapon, Jack deduced. *And you, you murdering sonofabitch, you killed the captain. And now the First Mate. ... And just about everyone else, I bet.*

Jack stretched his back and then took a closer look at the lighthouse. *This was all by design. Running aground—everything,* Jack determined. *No accident. He must have something bigger in mind for this boat. More than just running it into the rocks. ... And where's the rest of the crew? So far I've seen two. The deckhand that Kenny shot when I first got here. And now the First Mate. ... And where's Whitey?*

The ASP Restraint was still partially secured to Kenny's right wrist, so Jack flipped the unconscious man over on his face again and finished securing his hands behind his back. And then, using a second ASP Restraint, Jack secured one of Kenny's ankles to a hatch fastener.

"Don't think you'll run very far dragging that around with you."

"Got to find those boys," Jack said to himself as he bolted toward the lifeboats. They were located off the poop deck aft.

"Red!" he shouted. "Robby! Can you hear me? It's safe now. You can come out. Boys, it's your Uncle Jack. Where are you?"

When he reached the first lifeboat, he began pounding on the side of it and shouting for the boys to show themselves—that it was now safe. But there was not a sound.

He then ran over to starboard. But, still no sign of his boys.

If I could locate Whitey, Jack reasoned, *dead or alive, I would find the boys. Whitey would surely have kept the boys close to him if there were to be trouble. I'll try the galley.*

The galley and the eating areas were accessible off the poop deck aft. Jack ran up the steps that led to where the meals were prepared. When he reached the top he stumbled slightly as he cleared the last step.

As was typical of Great Lakes freighters, the galley was located between and forward of the eating areas. To the port side was the crew's mess. It was set up with two tables, each of which sat eight men. Behind the mess was the officers' dining room. It consisted of four square tables each accommodating four officers. To the starboard side aft was the owner's dining room. It had a single table and could seat eight. Jack got no further than the galley.

Lying on the floor in front of the refrigerator was Whitey Rich. He was dead. A single bullet in the center of his forehead had put an end to his life. But it was clear to Jack that death had not come quickly. His face and hair was matted in blood. Most of his front teeth were either broken off or missing altogether. Both of his hands, which were tied together, evidenced severe abrasions and gnarled broken fingers—as though they had been stomped upon. His empty wallet had been tossed beside him, and its contents strewn about on the floor.

"My God, Whitey," Jack said. "What the hell did you just go through?"

Jack dropped to one knee beside the body and searched his blood-soaked shirt pockets. In one of them he found a single small piece of paper. On it was written the name, "William Franks?"

It was the question mark after the name that piqued Jack's attention.

Did Whitey question the identity of this fellow calling himself William Franks? Jack wondered. *Is that why he's dead? Or, was he tortured by Kenny, trying to compel him to give up the boys? And did he tell Kenny where the boys were hiding? Every man has his breaking point—every man. Even tough seamen like Whitey.*

Chapter 31

Jack Refuses to Go Negative

N o good, Handler," Jack said out loud. "You can't even go there. The boys are alive, and they're on this boat. Now it's up to you to find them. So get your ass in gear!"

"Red! Robby!" Jack shouted from the galley. "Boys, can you hear me?"

And then he stood silent, listening for a reply. But there was none.

He repeated their names, and waited again. Still nothing.

Then Jack got to thinking: *I've spotted only three men—a crewman, and two officers. This boat must have a crew of twenty-five or more. So, where are they?*

Jack then bolted for the engine room, which was located directly two levels down from the poop deck aft. When he reached the door of the main engine compartment he found it chained from the outside. He pounded on the door and shouted through the thin sliver of the opening.

"Anybody hear me?" he yelled. And then he pounded again.

After his third effort, he heard a muffled sound, but he couldn't make it out. *What the hell was that? Did someone respond to me?*

"Hey! Anyone down here?"

"Help us. Please, help us."

Jack forced the door open as much as he could. "Can you come to the door?"

"Yeah," the man moaned, "But I've been shot. I'm bleeding pretty bad. It'll take me a while."

Over a minute later Jack spotted the man making his way toward the chained door. His midsection was covered with blood.

"Good," Jack said. "Very good. Just keep trying."

Just inside the door Jack spotted a fire extinguisher. And so he shouted to the wounded man: "Is there a fire axe on the wall? I see an extinguisher—is there a fire axe?"

The man stopped and stared at Jack. "Who are you?" he asked. "I don't recognize your voice. Are you with that Franks bastard? The one who shot us. You with him?"

"No! My name is Jack Handler. I think my two boys are on this freighter. I'm here looking for them."

"So was that Franks guy. That's all he talked about. Everybody who did help him look for the boys, he shot. Most of them are dead. He thought I was dead, too. Or he would have shot me some more. I think I'm dying. It's hurting like hell. I'm weak and cold. Barely walk."

"Do you know where my boys are?"

"Whitey, the cook, he knew. But he wouldn't talk. Franks killed him. Because he wouldn't tell him where the boys were hiding. I don't know where they are. … But, I can tell you something. This engine room is a disaster. He flooded it out with diesel fuel. I managed to stop most of the flow after he left. He thought I was dead. That we all were dead. … They *are* all dead, except for me. I checked. … I think he was planning to burn the boat up once he found the boys. That's why he ran the fuel down here. He's got something like that in mind."

"Is there an axe down there?" Jack asked again. "A fire axe. Do you see one? Would probably be near or with the fire extinguisher. An axe. Is there a fire axe?"

"Yes. Yes."

"Then, would you slide it through this crack? I might be able to break the lock with an axe."

"Yes. I'll get it."

"You say he ran fuel out down there?" Jack asked. "I can smell diesel. That's what he ran?"

"He busted a pipe and let it dump out on the floor. … Lucky for us that diesel fuel won't burn. At least, not like gasoline. It has a much higher flashpoint. You can toss a lit cigarette in it and it won't burn."

"What's the temperature down there?" Jack asked

"Eighty degrees."

"If you can keep the temperature at eighty, you won't have a problem with fire. But, if something else catches on fire, or if he were able to detonate an incendiary device of some sort, then it would burn like hell."

"I don't know nothin' about that stuff," the man said. "I suppose it might be right, if you say so. I just know I can barely breathe, and I like the smell of diesel."

He then slid the handle of the axe through the cracked door.

"Here's that axe," he said.

Jack did not respond, except by pulling the axe out of the room as quickly as the man inside produced it.

Taking careful aim, Jack swung the axe downward, striking squarely the top of the padlock that secured the ends of the chain.

The padlock was not constructed of very good material, and so it quickly gave out. Using his fingers, Jack was able to force it the rest of the way open, and remove it. He slid the chain out from its moorings and removed it altogether. He then opened the door and reached out to help the man inside. But as he did, the wounded man collapsed to the floor.

Jack knelt beside the man and felt his neck for a pulse.

"Damn it," Jack muttered. "He's died."

His eyes slowly surveyed the room.

"Holy shit, what a mess," he said.

What he saw was a scene of carnage—the place was in shambles. There were perhaps seven or more men who were lying face down in what appeared to be at least seven inches of diesel fuel.

"He's absolutely right, they are all dead," he muttered.

This stuff might not burn like gasoline, he reasoned, *but if there were some heat added, like a fire bomb of some sort, the diesel fuel would burn hot as a blowtorch. It would be an inferno. I've got to find my boys and get the hell off of this thing. And do it right away.*

Just then Jack spotted a large pile of rags and what looked like bed linen. It was piled on top of a large piece of equipment, and it appeared to be soaked in a liquid of some sort. Jack thought it was probably diesel fuel, or some other type of petroleum product.

That looks weird right there, he thought. *Why would anyone pile something like that in a place like that—on top of the machinery? Doesn't make sense.*

Back at hatch cover twenty-two, the last surviving member of the freighter's crew had finally emerged from hiding. He had felt the impact of running aground and was on his way to the bow of the boat to inspect the damage when he spotted two men lying between hatches twenty-one and twenty-two. He had concealed himself under luggage and clothing in a storage area located just forward of the recreation room on the spar deck aft.

First he knelt over the First Mate and checked for a pulse.

"Oh my God!" he said almost in tears. "Billy's dead! Oh my God!"

He then crawled on his hands and knees over to the still form of Walter Jon Kenny, known to him as Crewman William Franks. He checked his pulse.

Just as he checked Kenny's neck, the man groaned lowly and moved.

"Franks!" he said. "Thank God, you're alive."

"Oh. My God," Kenny said. "I'm hurt. Cut my hands free. Please. Before the killer comes back. Hurry."

"Who's the killer?"

"Handler. Jack Handler. He's killed several people on the boat.

And he's still on it. Cut my hands free before he comes back and kills us both."

"I don't know anyone named Jack Handler. He's not *on* this boat."

"Yes he is. I saw him. He's the one who shot me. Somehow he got onto the boat. And now he's going from bow to stern killing everyone. He'll be back here at any time, and he'll kill us both. Cut me free right now."

"I don't have anything to cut it with."

"Check to see if the First Mate has a knife," Kenny said. "Hurry. Before Handler hears us screwing around and comes back to shoot us. Check the First Mate's pockets."

"I don't feel right going through a dead man's pockets. It's just wrong."

"Sure it is," Kenny said. "It *is* wrong. But if Handler comes back, he's gonna kill both of us. That's not right, either. ... Now just do what I tell you. Get his knife and cut me free. Do it now!"

The crewman pulled up the First Mate's jacket and saw that he had a small knife strapped to his belt. He removed it from its sheath, and cut Kenny's hands free.

"Give me that knife," Kenny said. "Just give it to me."

The crewman complied with Kenny's command and reluctantly handed him the knife.

"Attaboy," Kenny said, taking the knife and cutting the ankle restraint.

After rubbing his tender ankle, Kenny leaned forward and stood to his feet. As soon as he had his balance, he reached into the crewman's hair and grabbed a handful. He then pulled the man's head toward him and rammed the knife deep into his neck, severing the left carotid artery. The man screamed and stepped backward, stumbling over the body of the First Mate and falling onto number twenty-two hatch cover. Within a minute he was dead.

Standing over the two bodies, both still warm, Kenny said,

"You are two stupid bastards. *Stupid* bastards. You *both* deserve what you got. You deserve to be dead."

He then turned to face the aft portion of the boat.

"I can't shit around anymore."

He reached into his jacket pocket and pulled out a small electronic device. He extended a shiny retractable antenna, and pushed a button.

When he did, a signal was sent to an explosive device located in the engine room. It ignited a container of magnesium strips, which in turn kindled a very hot flame inside the pile of oil-soaked rags that Jack had found. Immediately Jack recognized what was happening, and he slammed and latched the engine room door.

"Damn!" he muttered. "Just what I was afraid of. It's only a matter of time now, and all that diesel fuel will turn this boat into an inferno. I've got to find those boys."

Jack shifted his mind into overdrive. *If Whitey died in the galley, then chances are the boys will be nearby. He wouldn't have had them hid far from where he was stationed. They've got to be somewhere in the galley as well, or at least nearby.*

Jack ran back up to where he had found Whitey and began searching. He then ransacked the three eating areas. But he didn't find the boys.

Next he dropped down to the sleeping areas on the spar deck. First he searched the cabins on port side, and then starboard. Still no success.

"Where the hell could they be?" he muttered quite loudly.

And then he heard something.

He stopped dead in his tracks.

He heard it again.

"Uncle Jack? Is that you?"

"Robby!" Jack shouted as loudly as he could. "Where are you?"

With that announcement, Jack heard boxes and suitcases shuffling and overturning. And, finally, the two boys emerged from the storage room. The same one where Kenny's last victim had been hiding.

Jack bolted around the corner just in time to see the two boys run out—Robby first, and then Red.

"We knew you'd find us," Robby cried out, running over to Jack and nearly knocking him off his feet. Jack grabbed Robby first and swung him under his right arm like a sack of potatoes.

Red then ran full speed and leapt into Jack's left arm. Jack lifted Red up and planted a huge kiss on the top of his mop of red hair. And then he dropped to his back on the floor, still gripping both boys tightly.

"I was afraid that you boys might not have made it," Jack said. "I thought you were wearing a GPS transponder. Didn't Whitey put one on each of you?"

"Yeah," Robby said. "He did. But just before he hid us that last time he took the transponders and tossed them in the lake. He said something about a guy looking for us, and that he had a GPS receiver."

Robby finally broke free and rolled onto his knees. Looking square into Jack's face, he asked, "Uncle Jack, are you crying?"

"Hell no. I'm not crying. My eyes are sweating. It's getting too damn hot in here. We've got to get off this shit-ass boat. Right now!"

"How about Mr. Rich?" Robby asked. "Whitey. Aren't we going to find him first? He needs to go with us. Right?"

"Boys," Jack said. "There's no nice way to say this. But that man you witnessed at the cottage. The one who killed your caseworker, and the deputies, he somehow managed to get on this freighter, and he has killed a lot of people. And Whitey was one of them. As far as I know you two boys and I are the only ones left alive on this boat."

"Handler," Kenny said. "Are you forgetting about me? … I'm still alive and kicking. And in a minute, I'll be the lone survivor.

Thanks for finding the boys for me."

Jack knew there'd be no time to think. If he didn't act immediately, the boys would be dead, and so would he.

Jack saw that Kenny was wielding the 9mm Glock. He knew that there was less than a second separating him from death. But, if he could get to Kenny, while suffering anything less than a dead-on headshot, he could kill the man before he could harm the boys.

Jack knew that even a shot to the heart would not incapacitate him instantly. All he needed was one second to knock Kenny off of his feet and pin him to the floor. There he could drive his knife into the man's chest.

Kenny was standing less than ten feet away. Jack bolted. Kenny's first shot grazed Jack's face just above his cheekbone, but did not penetrate his skull. He was by then almost within striking distance.

Kenny this time aimed for the center of Jack's chest, and squeezed off another round. But with that shot, the strangest thing happened. Just as Ren's 9mm misfired when Kenny was trying to shoot the deputy, it again failed.

By the time Kenny realized that the pistol had misfired, Jack was on him. He caught Kenny in the throat with a driving forearm, knocking him on his back, and killing him almost instantly.

Even though Jack thought that he had already crushed the man's larynx with his initial blow, he was not about to take a chance. And so, with Kenny lying on his back, and with Jack on top of him, using the mechanical knife he had pulled from his pocket on the way down, Jack drove it into Kenny's chest and through his heart.

Jack had watched the pistol fly from Kenny's hand, so he was no longer concerned about his harming the boys. Jack continued to lie silent, as though anticipating some reaction from the man beneath him.

Finally, he rose to a position over Kenny, with one knee on either side of the man's chest. With his body blocking the boys' view, he pulled the knife from the Kenny's chest.

"There you go, you bastard," Jack said to himself. "I just killed you twice. Once for each of my boys."

For a moment Jack contemplated shoving the blade into Kenny's dead heart a second time. *That would be in memory of Whitey*, he reckoned. But he thought better of it, and, after wiping it clean on Kenny's shirt, he retracted the blade and slid it back into his pocket. *No need for revenge.*

He stood up and faced the boys.

"I am truly sorry that you boys had to witness this. I would give anything I own to have avoided doing what I just did. In front of you like that. ... But, unfortunately, some men just need to die. Sometimes it's the only option."

The boys observed that blood was running profusely from the wound on the side of Jack's face, but they said nothing. They had seen Jack bleed before and knew that it would eventually stop. And, as long as he was walking and talking, there was nothing to worry about.

"Now," Jack said, "let's get off of this boat. It's on fire."

Jack began playing in his mind the whole scenario—just how it would be perceived by the sheriff.

The man is not wearing gloves, Jack observed. *That means his prints are all over that MAC-10. And his hands and clothes will be saturated with GSR. ... How about this Glock. Wonder if there are prints other than his on it? Can't have that.*

Jack retrieved the pistol and wiped it down. He then placed it in Kenny's hand and squeezed his hand down on it. Once satisfied that Kenny's prints had been applied, he removed the Glock and slid it back to where it had been.

He looked around on the deck and found a large bucket and a mop. *Someone must have been cleaning up. Got to have some sort of cleaning chemicals in it. Should do the trick.*

Jack wiped down the knife he had just used to kill Kenny and tossed it into the soapy water. *That ought to corrupt any DNA.*

By that time the whole aft end of the freighter was ablaze.

"We'd better commandeer one of those lifeboats before they burn up," he said. "Let's go for the starboard boat. ... Closer to Canada."

The freighter was equipped with a relatively new single arm davit that dropped a fully enclosed diesel powered lifeboat.

Jack first had the boys put on latex gloves, and then he ushered them into the boat, and swung it out over the side. He remained on the freighter until the boys had safely reached the surface of the water, and then he slid down the cable to join them. Once he was onboard the lifeboat, he opened the release hook and started the engine.

"Where we headed, Uncle Jack?" Robby asked.

"North and east," Jack said.

"Canada?" Robby asked. "Red thinks we're going to Canada. Are we?"

Jack smiled and nodded his head affirmatively. "That's my plan," he said. "We'll have to see what Roger can arrange. ... But first, we're going to want to disable the GPS locater. Otherwise we'll have Canadian Coast Guard dispatching on us. It's going to be hard enough to sneak in without announcing our presence."

It took Jack less than a minute to disable the transponder, and another two minutes to cut off all running lights.

"Red," Jack said as he referred to a set of waterproof charts he had brought with him. "Drive this boat. Hold it steady on an east-northeast course. We should be good—I don't see any hazards for the next ten minutes. Hold the speed steady. I'll see where Roger wants us to head."

Just as Jack reached Roger, there was an enormous explosion onboard the freighter.

"Holy shit!" Jack roared, "The damn boat just blew up."

"The freighter?" Roger asked. "Or your lifeboat?"

"The freighter," Jack replied. "Must be a parting gift from Mr. Kenny. It was a good-sized blast. If it was placed right, it could sink that boat."

"Single hull," Roger agreed. "That boat has a single hull. If it was a strong enough explosion, in the right place, it surely could take it to the bottom."

"It was at the aft end," Jack said. "Looked like it was on the outside. Probably attached with a magnet to the hull, just below water level. Lake is deep there. I'd say she'd be taking water. ... It'd be a damn shame if it does go down. I wanted the sheriff to find Kenny lying there on the deck, with the murder weapon right beside him. If the boat sinks, so does the evidence."

"Nothing we can do about that," Roger said. "But how do you suppose that blast was activated? Someone onboard trigger it?"

"I'm pretty certain there are no living souls on that boat," Jack said. "It must have been set to go off on a timer. Maybe half an hour after the first blast. He knew the first explosion would ignite the diesel fuel. And that the second would take it to the bottom."

"Where should we pick you fellows up?" Roger asked. "That is, of course, provided you make it past the Canadian Mounted Police."

"This is what I'm concerned about—the CMP," Jack replied. "We'll take it in toward Lizard Islands. It's about thirty miles from where we went aground. The Trans-Canada Highway passes close to Lake Superior around there. We'll come around from the south of the islands, and then northeast to Robertson Cove. Have someone meet us there with a camo tarp. Drop your guy off at Katherine Cove. That would be just south of Robertson Cove."

"The tarp would be for what purpose?" Roger asked. "I'm guessing to hide the lifeboat."

"That would be the plan."

"That would be one hell of a big piece of material," Roger

chuckled. "You really don't think they're going to have planes up there looking for survivors?"

"I'm sure they will," Jack said. "And they will find the boat, too. But if it would give us another twenty minutes, might be all we'd need. Just looking for a little edge."

"How're the boys?"

"Great. Just great. Robby has a little knob on his head, but other than that, they look pretty good to me."

"I'm probably looking at the same charts you are," Roger said. "I'm sure you can see that once you come around the south end of that string of little islands, Lizard Islands, all you've got are a bunch of rocks right beneath the surface of the water. It's going to be tricky navigating through them ... even with charts. At that point you're going to be dealing with the Canadian Coast Guard on the water, and in the air, the Mounted Police on land, and Davy Jones chomping at your toes from beneath the big lake. ... Does that sound about right?"

"All in a day's work, my friend," Jack said. "These boys can handle whatever comes along. ... Latitude 47.443157, and a negative 84.748320 longitude."

"And exactly where does that place us?"

"That would be Katherine Cove ... the pickup point. Robertson Cove, where we're planning to ditch the boat, is just up the lake a bit. The coordinates I gave you provide a site right next to the lake—should be easy to spot."

"I'm on it," Roger said. "Give me a shout when you're ready."

Chapter 32

Tremble

R oger disconnected from his call with Jack, and began scrolling through his call list until he found the number he was looking for: "Tremble." It stood for Eric Tremblay, an officer in the Canadian Security Intelligence Service, otherwise known as CSIS. The organization was the Canadian version of the American Secret Service. In other words, Mr. Tremblay was Roger's Canadian counterpart.

"Need some help over in your neck of the woods," Roger said.

"And greetings to you as well, Roger. ... Now, what exactly is it that my exuberant American friend is asking of me and my government?"

"Not your government, buddy. Just you. ... I've got a situation occurring right now in Superior. I need you to extricate three of my good friends. Within ... say, forty-five minutes, give or take."

"In Superior, as we speak? I heard that there is a boat on fire up by Michipicoten. One of your boats, I believe. Would that have anything to do with your friends?"

Michipicoten was a Canadian island located just north of where Jack's boat went aground.

"You might say that. I've got one of my oldest and best friends, and his two teenage boys. They are going to be at a place called Katherine Cove shortly. Would you like the coordinates?"

"I'm a well-trained, professional intelligence officer, thank you very much. I know exactly where Katherine Cove is located. ... Thirty minutes, you say?"

"Can you help me out?" Roger asked.

"Are these fugitives?" Tremblay asked with hesitation. "And, if so, fugitives from what? Or from whom?"

"Not from the Canadian Government," Roger said. "I can assure you of that. As far as them being federal fugitives, that would not be the case either. I do understand that the county sheriff—Chippewa County, in the Upper Peninsula—he might be looking for the two boys … as witnesses in a case in Michigan. But, as far as my friend is concerned, Jack Handler, there's no warrant out for him. At least none that I know about."

"Jack Handler," Tremblay said. "Now, there's a name I've heard before. And not all of it good. He's always showing up on my radar. … Wasn't he recently rung up on federal charges? I thought he was still in prison."

"His conviction was overturned. He's got his PI license back. He's as innocent as you and I. … Well, at least as innocent as I am. I don't know anyone as pure as you."

"Enough of the bullshit, Roger. … So, spell it out. What exactly is it you want me to do for you?"

Roger laid out what Jack was expecting, including the huge camouflage tarp, and the time constraints he was working under. And just as he had completed his instructions, he spotted a parade of law enforcement vehicles storming the little airport.

"Hey, buddy," Roger said to his friend, Eric, "looks like I've got some business to attend to here. I'll get back to you a little later. Okay? And thanks. I'm going to owe you one."

Chapter 33

Hands up — Don't Shoot

L et's see," Roger said to himself as he fingered through a large white envelope he had tucked away among his important papers in the cockpit. "Ah, yes. This ought to do the job."

By the time he looked up, the entire plane was surrounded by State Troopers and sheriff's deputies—all with guns drawn.

Roger smiled and raised his hands so that they could be seen from the ground. He then opened a small vent window and addressed them.

"Officers. How might I assist you?"

"Stay right where you are," the sheriff commanded. "And keep your hands where I can see them."

"Yes, sir," Roger said.

As they were approaching, Roger offered to open the door a crack.

"The door is open," he told the sheriff. "If you'd care to pop up here. I've got some info I think you'd be interested in. How about it?"

"Sit tight, and keep your hands up where we can see them."

One of the State Troopers opened the door to the plane. He pointed his Glock at Roger and told him to get out.

"Can I bring this with me?" Roger said, pointing at a neatly folded letter that was lying on his lap. "There's some information here that I'm sure the sheriff would be interested in seeing."

The trooper grabbed it and said, "I'll give it to the sheriff. Now, you slowly get out of this plane."

Once Roger was on the ground, one of the deputies began cuffing him.

"Deputy," the sheriff said. "I need to talk to this man ... in private."

"Agent Minsk, would you please step over here for a moment."

The sheriff then turned to his deputies and the troopers, and said, "Excuse us for a minute. This gentleman and I have to discuss something."

"Is this for real?" the sheriff asked. "Are you really a member of the Secret Service?"

"Yes, I am. I think if you will check in my wallet, you will find my credentials are quite legitimate."

"And you are here at the behest of the former president? Is that correct?"

"If you care to call the phone number on that letter you have in your hand, you will find that the former president will vouch for me."

"May I ask what you are doing here right now? This is a private airstrip, and you have no authorization to—"

"If you call the number I gave you, I think you will find that I have all the authorization I require."

"You are here on official business?"

"Sheriff, I am not authorized to provide you with any additional information. If you care to call the number I provided for you, your questions will be adequately answered. That's all I am going to say. I do suggest you remove these cuffs this minute, or you will be dealing with some very unpleasant circumstances. Your choice."

"Let me give that number a call," the sheriff said as he slipped on his glasses. He turned away and began walking toward his car.

"Deputy," the sheriff said. "Keep an eye on our friend here. I'll be back in a minute."

When he reached his car, he opened the door and sat down behind the wheel. He feigned that he was studying the paper Roger had given him as he dialed a number on his phone. Instead, he was dialing the number of FBI Special Agent William Dollar. Special Agent Dollar had worked a case in the Upper Peninsula a year earlier, and he had told the sheriff that if he ever had a question involving federal law enforcement, he should feel free to give him a call.

"Special Agent Dollar, this is Sheriff Bill Green of Chippewa County. In Michigan's Upper Peninsula. We worked a case up here together a couple years ago. Do you recall?"

"Oh, yes. I remember."

"You'd told me that if I ever had a question on a federal matter, that I could call you."

"Right. What's up?"

"I have a gentleman here in my county. He just illegally landed a small plane. He says his name is Special Agent Roger Minsk with the—"

"With the Secret Service. Right?"

"Yes. Do you know him?"

"He's one very bad ass. Try to keep out of his way as much as possible. Just trying to give you some good advice. He is very good friends with Former President Bob Fulbright. In fact, I think he might still be in charge of the Former first lady's detail. ... But, none of that is what brought him up to your neighborhood. He's there on personal business. You can bet on it."

"*Personal* business," the sheriff said. "What sort of personal business?"

"You can bet your socks that he is working with Jack Handler. Those two go back decades. They both used to work for Fulbright—when he was in office. The two of them are nothing but trouble."

"Got it. Thanks."

"Deputy," the sheriff said after disconnecting the call. "Please remove the cuffs. This is a fellow officer of the law, and he is on official Government business. We will be extending all professional courtesies to this gentleman. ... And will all of you please holster your weapons. This is Special Agent Roger Minsk. He's a member of the Secret Service."

After the deputy removed the handcuffs, the sheriff again asked that he and "Special Agent Minsk" be given privacy.

"Special Agent Minsk," the sheriff said as he folded the paper Roger had given him, and handed it back. "Is there anything that my office can do to be of help?"

Roger fully understood what the sheriff wanted. He was seeking information from Roger regarding the specifics of his mission. And, of course, Roger had no interest or desire to share anything with the sheriff.

"Did you talk to President Fulbright?" Roger asked.

"I talked to one of my people—a friend. He actually knows you. He backed up your story."

Roger correctly assumed that whoever it was the sheriff had talked to, he had confirmed his identity and most likely also filled the sheriff in on the fact that Jack Handler might also be involved in the matter. If that were the case, then Roger ought to create a little subterfuge to draw the sheriff off the real purpose of his being in the Upper Peninsula.

"Actually," Roger said, "there is something that you could do that would be useful to me."

"Just let me know what I can do, and if possible, I'll help you in any way I can."

"I need to fly into Grand Rapids as soon as possible. But, I do not want it to be as a federal agent. It would create too much chatter. If you could arrange for me to land there under the auspices of your office, that would be most appreciated. I would owe you one."

The sheriff thought for a moment, and then said, "I see no

problem with that. When would you want to do this?"

"Immediately. I would need to fuel up first. I should be able to get off the ground within an hour. Flight time to GRR is just under two hours. So, between two and a half and three and a half."

"Consider it done."

"Are you sure you wouldn't mind?"

"Hell no. As far as I'm concerned, you're on official Chippewa County Sheriff business. ... Deputy Minsk. How does that sound?"

"Maybe I should ask about the benefits package first."

"Okay," the sheriff said. "I think we're done here. I wish you well ... down there in Grand Rapids. Ever been there before?"

"Oh, yes," Roger said. "I was there with the former president for the dedication of the Gerald R. Ford Presidential Museum. Nice city. Good restaurants, if I remember correctly."

"That's right. And they've got some new ones. My favorite is Ruth's Chris. It's right downtown, in the Amway Grand. Great steaks."

"I might give it a try. Only going to be there a short time. But, if I get a chance."

"Nice to meet you," Sheriff Green said. "Ever get back in the area again, be sure to look me up."

"Sure will," Roger said.

As they were parting company Roger smiled and thought to himself, *that bastard didn't believe a word I said.*

And Sheriff Green was also having some thoughts of his own: *He's lying. He has no intention of flying south. He's working with Handler. ... And if I keep tabs on this guy, he just might lead me to Jack and the two boys.*

Chapter 34

Roger Cools His Jets in GR

A fter Roger had fueled his plane, he signaled to the sheriff that he was leaving. And off he went—heading south.

This has got to be messing with the sheriff's head a little, Roger was thinking. *I'm sure he's expecting me to circle around and set down somewhere on or around Sugar Island. But, I can do what I have to do from Grand Rapids just as well.*

Roger could not erase his smile.

"Eric," Roger said. "Have you been in contact with my friend Jack?"

"We've talked. He's looking for my guy to pick them up within the hour."

"Have you decided where you're going to put them yet?"

"Oh, yes. Nothing fancy. We've really got nothing over there of a permanent nature. We'll be picking them up in a Winnebago, and then take them on a little fishing trip."

"All set with the camo tarp Jack wanted? Something to conceal the lifeboat?"

"He and I talked and came up with a better idea. I'm dropping off an inflatable, and one of my men. He will tow the lifeboat out, run it on some rocks, and torch it. Somewhere not close to where I'm meeting them. … Where are you going to be?"

"I'm going to hang out in Grand Rapids for a while. Until I'm needed somewhere else."

"How does Grand Rapids figure in? And is that Grand Rapids, Michigan or Grand Rapids, Minnesota?"

"Michigan—the Lower Peninsula. And it really doesn't figure in at all," Roger said. "I thought it might deflect some attention if I got them looking down there. Besides, there are some great restaurants in the city. You'd like them."

"I know about Grand Rapids," Eric said. "That's the home of Founders Brewing Company. Right? They brew some of the best craft beers in your country. ... Their Kentucky Breakfast Ale—it's to die for."

"You've actually tasted it?" Roger said. "It's hard to come by. ... I can't believe you've actually been able to buy it in Canada."

"No. No. No. Not up here. I've got friends in Grand Rapids. They help me out."

"I guess I'll look you up when Jack runs out."

"Well," Eric continued, "it's like I said, we're going to do some fishing. You should join us."

"Another time. ... I'll be in touch regarding Jack and the boys. Not exactly sure how that's going to work out. I guess I'll leave the details up to Jack and you. ... Using a satphone to communicate with him. Right?"

"Right."

"Keep me in the loop," Roger said. "I'm here to help."

Chapter 35

Minefield of Rocks

Jack cut back on the throttle and slowed the lifeboat to five knots. The dramatic change in speed aroused Robby's and Red's attention. The two boys exchanged looks of concern.

"We almost there?" Robby said. "That why we're stopping?"

Jack then trimmed the throttle to under three knots.

"Not really," he said. "But we are entering a hazardous area. … This is a virtual minefield of rocks around here. This boat can handle a lot, but a sharp rock will tear it up in a hurry."

"Can we help?" Robby offered. "We could go out on the bow and watch for rocks."

"I think that's the only way we'll get through this," Jack said. "According to my chart, we've got about a mile of it. And then it's mostly sand. … Red, you get on the port side, Robby on starboard. As soon as you see something, raise a hand. … If it's dead ahead, raise both hands. Yell out if I have to stop and go around anything. I'll let you know when we're through the worst of it."

As the boys were taking their positions on the bow, Jack's satphone rang.

"George here. How's it going?"

Jack and Eric Tremblay had earlier determined not to use their real names or locations, nor even to speak using standard law enforcement jargon. Jack understood that this George fellow was actually Roger's associate, Eric Tremblay.

"Moving slowly right now," Jack said. "We should be at the location within the half hour. How about you?"

"We're already at the cabin. But are planning to greet you when you arrive."

"I'll give you a shout just before we reach land," Jack confirmed, as he slammed the boat into reverse.

Both boys were waving their hands in the air and signaling for Jack to stop.

Robby turned around and said, "Big rock straight ahead. Several of them. Better back out of it and move to the right … to starboard."

"Moving though some heavy traffic right now," Jack said to Eric. "Will touch base with you just before I get there."

Even though the chart clearly indicated that there could be rocks beneath the surface, he suspected that the higher water of Lake Superior that year would raise the boat above them far enough to allow safe passage. But such was apparently not the case.

Jack did as the boys had suggested. He backed the lifeboat up and turned starboard. As he eased forward again, he, too, spotted the rocks that had attracted the boys' attention. "Yeah," he said to himself. "They are a little too close to the surface. The boys are doing a good job."

"I got to pee," he told them as he cut power, and directed a copious stream off port side.

The boys looked at each other and chuckled.

"Uncle Jack," Robby yelled. "Red and I ain't gonna eat any more fish out of *this* lake. … Besides, you're probably gonna kill 'em all, anyway."

Jack smiled but did not acknowledge the comment.

When he had finished, he again eased the throttle forward, and corrected the boat's drift.

"Here we go," he yelled. "Now, you boys need to keep us off

those rocks. You understand me?"

Jack double-checked his position on the chart. It looked as though they had made it through, but he wasn't positive. They were past the Lizard Islands, but were still over two miles off shore. *Another five minutes,* Jack resolved, *and we'll gun it through to the cove.*

Once he was confident that they had passed all the rocks that were noted on his chart, he called the boys back off the bow.

"Okay, boys, get back here. Fasten your seatbelts. We're going to rock and roll."

Red looked over at Robby as if to say, "What's got into the old man?"

"He's got to be kidding," Robby said. "We don't have seatbelts on a lifeboat."

As soon as the boys crawled back under the cover, Jack hit the throttle and barreled full speed ahead toward the beach at Robinson Cove.

"We're coming in," he said to Eric, and then disconnected.

When the boat began to touch sand he cut the engine.

A man in a wetsuit was waiting there with a motorized inflatable boat. Virtually no words were exchanged. Jack and the boys got out of the lifeboat, and the man in the wetsuit tied onto it, and off he went. Jack and the boys pushed the boat back off the sand, and off it went undertow.

"Where's he taking our boat?" Robby asked.

"We're done using it. Right?" Jack said. "He's returning it to the freighter."

"But, the freighter's on fire."

"Exactly," Jack said. "Maybe someone else will want to use it."

Again the two boys looked at each other in amazement.

"I forgot that Uncle Jack had such a great sense of humor," Robby said to Red.

Red laughed and shoved Robby face first into the water.

"Let's go, fellows," Jack said. "I think our ride's here."

As the three of them bolted up the beach toward the pickup point on the Trans-Canada Highway, Jack's burner phone vibrated. It was an incoming call from his Chicago attorney, Randolph Calibret.

"Randy," Jack said. "What's up, buddy?"

Chapter 36

Calibret Calibrates

The call had come in to Jack while he and the two boys were waiting for Eric to pick them up at Katherine Cove.

"Jack," Calibret said, "is this a good time? I know you're busy, but I thought you might like to hear a progress report on your audit."

Jack, though thoroughly amazed that the call reached him on that remote Canadian shore, was eager to find out how the preparations for the audit were going. He was anticipating a call from Weinstein, and he wanted to be able to put Harry's mind at ease. He positioned himself close enough to the highway to be able to monitor traffic and said, "Sure, I might have to cut you off—I'm waiting to meet a friend. But, in the meantime, fire away."

"Okay," Calibret said. "If you have to pull away, just do what you have to do. I'm going to show you a little Facetime video of the stage I've set for your auditor friends. It should take me about five minutes. I'll explain what I've done as we do this little walking tour. Sure you've got time?"

"Let's do it," Jack said.

"These are your new offices," Calibret said, as the video started. "Right now I am getting off the elevator on the third floor. As you can see, I have had the workers move all the equipment you had stored here. It is now either in the dumpster, or in the attic."

"This is the first time I've seen the third floor in years," Jack said as Calibret stepped off the elevator. "Since before we renovated the second floor and put in the banquet halls. … I'd forgotten just how unfinished this area is. Can't believe you got rid of all that junk. I'm sure it didn't all fit in that little attic."

"Yeah," Calibret said, "we moved a lot up there. You wouldn't believe how much shit we squeezed into it. But we did throw a lot away too. We nearly filled up that roll-off forty-yard dumpster we had dropped off."

"How about the plumbing?" Jack asked. "Everything still work?"

"We brought in a plumber to check it all out before we turned the water on up here. He had to make a few repairs. But, all told, there was nothing major. … Toilet works. Kitchen sink works. We even moved in a refrigerator and a coffee brewer for them to use.

"And, Jack." Calibret paused a moment for effect. And then he continued. "Only thing is, the refrigerator doesn't get cold, and the coffee maker doesn't get very hot."

"Damn, Randy," Jack chuckled. "You are one mean sonofabitch. Depriving these poor bastards of their coffee and Coke."

Jack could hear the bare floorboards squeak as Calibret walked over toward the bathroom. It was located off the main office working area, which was formerly the living room when the area was used as an apartment. It shared a common wall with the small kitchen. Neither the kitchen nor the bathroom had a window. Light for the bathroom was provided by a small, round florescent ceiling fixture.

Calibret opened the bathroom door and triggered the wall switch. Nothing happened at first. After a couple seconds the fixture made a slight popping sound and then illuminated—but not fully. Instead, it flickered erratically between off and dim, each time emitting that same irritating popping noise.

Calibret rotated his phone in a panoramic fashion for a few moments and then switched the light off. "That's grating," he said.

"But not as offensive as the odor. Wish you could smell that."

"Odor? Really? What is it?"

"Here," Calibret said holding his camera to show the back of the flush tank. "Let me show you. It's pretty disgusting. What we've got here is a small nylon net hanging on the bottom of the toilet. It contains the decomposing carcass of a large mouse. Could be a small rat—it's pretty big for a mouse. There's another one attached behind one of the file cabinets. And a third one in the kitchen. It's attached to the hot water pipe beneath the sink. So, every time someone turns on the hot water, he will get an extra strong whiff of a dead something."

"That is *disgusting!*" Jack said. "Anyone trying to do some serious work there … it'd just be impossible. Don't you think that they're going to insist on moving to a more conducive area?"

"They can *insist* all they want," Calibret said through a large smile. He had pointed the camera so that Jack could see his face. "But it ain't gonna do them any good. They have already agreed to access and view the records here, in your office. We correctly stipulated the minimum number of square feet they'd have to work in, and the number of desks and tables. They signed off on it. Now they have no choice. Not under the terms of our agreement."

"Okay," Jack said. "I guess we'll have to see how it goes. I just can't see them dealing with this unpleasant situation. … These are not your typical Chicago lawyers and accountants. How many of them are coming?"

"According to Abraham Stern, they will have one attorney from his firm. I doubt that he will be it. Probably a junior partner. And two forensic accountants. I believe one of them will likely be the notorious Jeffry Stokes. All from New York."

"Stern's firm is your quintessential *white shoe* outfit," Jack said. "The accountants will be of a similar caliber—such as Jeffry Stokes and his two thousand dollar suits. … That shitty smell will saturate their clothes. … They're going to object. You can count on it."

"That's what we want. If we can distract and discourage them, we will have accomplished our goal. They are not going to be as motivated as your friend Allison. From the way you describe her, she'd be willing to work by candlelight in an outhouse. But, she's not the one we've got to scare off—it's these suits.

"But, Jack, that's not the only dirty trick we're going to subject them to. Let's head back down. I've got a special treat for you in my car—I call it my *secret weapon*. You're gonna love this."

"Are you telling me there's more?"

"Oh, yes," Calibret said as he led Jack to the elevator, and then out to his car. He opened the rear of his black Escalade. "There," he said, "What do you think of these?"

At first Jack did not recognize what he was being shown.

"What the hell have we got here?" Jack asked. "Looks like a few large baby food jars, with little holes poked in the lids. What's this all about?"

"These, my friend, are two hundred live cockroaches," Calibret said in a tone clearly exuding pleasure."

"What the hell are you planning to do with those?"

"One hour before they are scheduled to arrive I will release three jars at various locations on the third floor. One in the kitchen."

"Randy," Jack said. He was startled. "We *can't* do that. I've got my bar in that building. And the banquet halls. I'll have the city inspectors closing me down if we get this building infested with cockroaches."

"Relax, my friend. It'll be just fine. No worries. These are *special* cockroaches. They have all been sterilized. They can't reproduce. … And they are mature. They will all die within a few days."

"What? How does that work?"

"These cockroaches are German cockroaches. That's a common variety of cockroach, I just learned. They have been treated with a product called Gencor. It's an insect growth regulator. What it does is saturate young cockroaches with a high dosage of hormones. This prevents the insects from maturing, and it renders them sterile. These particular cockroaches have neared the end of their life cycle, and will soon die. But, because of the Gencor, they cannot reproduce.

"The bugs we distribute just before our guests arrive will live long enough to make the visitors miserable, but they will die before they can present themselves downstairs. And, besides, I've scheduled to have the whole building treated immediately after this sinister audit."

"You're sure they can't reproduce?"

"The product works. These cockroaches *cannot* be impregnated. Their bodies have been physically altered by the chemical. You can even tell by looking at them that their growth has been arrested. If these *visitors* report you to the health department, by the time you get inspected, you will be free of cockroaches. They'll all be dead. ... All we'll have to do is run a Dyson around the third floor, and the entire bug problem will go away—picked up with the trash. ... Along with your *Allison* problem. We hope."

"We can hope," Jack chuckled. "I just wish they made Dysons large enough gather her up."

Calibret laughed at Jack's humor, and then said, "There might be a good market for a product like that."

Before Calibret had completed his comment, Jack's phone vibrated.

As Jack and Calibret wound up their pre-audit tour of the third floor, Jack excused himself to take the new call.

Jack recognized the number. It was Harry Weinstein.

Chapter 37

Harry's Treat

Jack answered the call: "Yes, Harry. Jack here."

"Jack, I'm just checking in to see how you're coming along with that kid's audit ... or whatever the hell it is. Seems more like a fishing expedition to me. Whatever. What can you tell me?"

"Three things. Day after tomorrow. Ten A.M. He's scheduled to have two accountants and a lawyer here to dig through my books. But—"

"That's exactly what I *don't* want to hear, Jack. I smell something bad coming out of that. And the foul smell is drifting in my direction. ... So, what's the other two things?"

"Yeah. I get it. You're right about the stink. We will not let anything damaging leak out of here. ... The operative word in what I was saying is *scheduled*. They are scheduled to be here. But we have a few surprises for them when they show up."

"I hope one of your surprises is a MAC 10. ... You said there were three things. What would that third one be?"

"They think they are using my office to do their work. The kid has his father's keys. I'm sure he's taken them around the bar and showed them my office when I wasn't there. With its three five-foot locked file cabinets. That's where they think they're camping out. But we've stashed all the file cabinets off-site. And moved my office to the third floor. We're providing for them just the files they specifically requested. And, we've sanitized those files. They will see nothing that could possibly implicate you or your family. In fact, none of my clients are specifically named in any of the info they are reviewing."

"That all sounds good, Jack. I just wish that this shit storm wasn't headed my way."

"It's not. I'm telling you there will be nothing available to them that could possibly lead to you."

"Jack. If there is one person in this world that I trust, it'd be you. You're like the captain of a ship. I believe you'd go down with it before you'd abandon your crew. Hell, I know you would. But these audits, when bastards like these guys sink their teeth into something, they chew away at the red meat until they hit the bone. They won't be satisfied with the taste of blood. … If you don't have what they want the first time, they will keep coming back with new demands, and court orders, until they get what they want. I know how this works. … Are any of your records on a computer?"

"No. And even my attorney doesn't know where I've stored the rest of the physical files. But, to answer your question, absolutely nothing's online."

"Who does know?"

"No one else."

"So, if I put you down, all your files would go down with you?"

"They sure would. … No doubt, that'd be one way to solve the problem. And, if I were in your shoes, that would certainly be on my shortlist of options. But, I do have a plan. It's a good one. Very good chance that it will work. Should know more once they get here.

"There is a fourth aspect to what we came up with. If they are as persistent as you suspect they might be, then we'll simply stonewall them. My attorney says we could delay the whole audit for a year if need be. That would give us time to implement other measures."

"That part sounds good to me. The thing about implementing *other measures*, if you know what I mean. I suppose you could say that was my specialty—implementing other measures. … What you tell me all sounds good, Jack. And I do trust you. Maybe more than I should. Hell. I don't really trust anyone except myself. Not totally. … So, this is what I propose. You do what you have to. Whatever you think is going to put an end to this horseshit. We'll see how it works. If you can then convince me that none of the stuff about me or my family will ever see the light of day, then we all go on like nothing happened. But, if the wind keeps blowing the shit my way, then I'll do what I have to do. I know you understand me completely. Like you said, you can put yourself in my shoes."

"Nice talking to you, Harry. Hope next time it's on a more pleasant topic."

"Take care, my friend. Make good stuff happen. For both of us. … And, I hope we never talk a—"

"Harry," Jack interrupted. "Sorry to be so abrupt, but I've got to catch my train."

Jack hung up. He did so for two reasons. Had he responded to Harry's frustrated threat, it would not have helped the situation. *Better to hang up on this bastard now*, he determined, *before I put him in his place. No point in burning bridges.*

But the main reason he cut Harry short was that Christopher May had indeed arrived with the Winnebago.

Jack slid his hot cell phone into his pocket and the three of them hurried up the bank of lake sand and Superior rocks.

Chapter 38

Ship in Distress

Sheriff," Deputy Anderson said to Sheriff Green. "Looks like the Coast Guard has a situation on the lake. There's a freighter, licensed here, operating between Duluth and Cleveland … and it's on fire. They think it might go down."

"Where is it?" Sheriff Green asked.

"By Caribou Island."

"What the hell! There ain't any weather out there. What happened? … Caribou. That's in Canadian waters. Right?"

"Yup. Just barely, but it's in Canada, alright. … There's no storms. According to our Coast Guard, it's the *Arthur Fisher*. Owner is *Amalgamated Shipping*, outta Cleveland. Apparently it just drifted over into Canadian waters, and ran aground at the lighthouse by Caribou Island."

"Boats don't usually sink when they run aground," the sheriff said. "There must be something else going on."

"There's a fire onboard. A *big* fire. And for some reason the boat's taking a lot of water at the stern. … It's still afloat, but the thinking is that it might go under within hours."

"Any casualties?" the sheriff asked. "Or did everyone get off safely?"

"So far we don't have any report of survivors. And no floaters, either. Not yet."

"That don't make any sense at all," the sheriff said. "What's up with the lifeboats?"

"One's still with the Arthur Fisher. One's missing. And it's not been spotted."

"No distress calls?"

"None reported."

"How about GPS? Anything with that?"

"Nothing."

"That's impossible," the sheriff said, noticeably irritated. "A boat that big can't just run into a lighthouse without anyone knowing about it. Somebody had to have radioed it in. Something—"

"Hold on, sheriff," the deputy said. "Dispatch is telling me that a Coast Guard helicopter has spotted several people—at least three—on the boat's deck. All apparently injured or dead. And the engine room appears to be burning out of control.

"They can't tell how the fire started, or why it seems to be taking water, but they are pretty certain that it's going to sink."

"They're not going to board it—or are they?" the sheriff asked.

"Too dangerous. It's still hung up on the rocks by the lighthouse. But if the ass end of it starts to go down, it'll lift the bow and pull it down backward. And it *is* going to go down, they say."

The sheriff turned and walked away from his deputy. He was deep in thought. Finally, he turned back to the deputy and said, "It's that asshole Handler. I just know it is. Every time his name is mentioned, people start dying. *Every damn time. Never* fails. You can make book on it. ... First we get that Secret Service guy, Roger Minsk. He's like Handler's partner, practically. Whenever Handler gets in trouble, he calls this Roger guy, and then more people begin dying.

"I'd bet a year's salary that Handler's somehow involved. If he didn't kill those people on the Arthur Fisher, then he knows who did. ... Could have been those two teenage hoodlums he's been raising. First they kill two of my best deputies, and their caseworker, and then three people are killed on the boat. Probably more than three—if we still have a lifeboat attached. ... Who knows how many have been killed. And, so far we don't have any survivors. How in hell could two fourteen-year-old boys do so much damage? Those boats can't just catch on fire. Yet, somehow, they manage to burn one up. And now it looks like they're going to sink it. ... Two asshole kids!

"Handler's turning them into killers just like he is. ... But, there's one major difference. We've never been able to make anything stick when it came to Handler. With those two boys, though, we've got hard evidence that they're killers. We've got their prints all over that stone house—especially in the basement. They are the only ones who walked away from that place. *They're* the killers. You can be sure of it."

The deputy remained on his cell phone with dispatch during the sheriff's rant. He stood listening to the sheriff and his dispatch officer at the same time. He made constant eye contact with his boss even while listening to his cell.

As soon as there was a break in the sheriff's tirade, the deputy interjected, "The boat just slid under. Still no survivors spotted. ... They're searching for the missing lifeboat."

Chapter 39

Escape in a Winnebago

The four-wheel-drive Winnebago Revel motor home had proceeded several miles south along ON-75S, otherwise known as the Trans-Canada Highway and was about to turn onto the dirt road leading east toward Batchewana, Ontario, when they confronted a makeshift roadblock set up by the Royal Canadian Mounted Police.

"May I see your driver's license, please?" the uniformed officer requested.

"Certainly, sir," Christopher May responded. He then removed his driver's license from his wallet and handed it to the officer.

"Thank you," Officer Jared Swearengen said.

He examined May's driver's license and then requested proof of ownership and insurance.

Mr. May promptly provided the papers the officer sought.

"Any passengers with you today?" the officer asked.

"No, sir. I'm by myself. Except for my dog. Bill is keeping me company."

"Is that his name? Bill."

"Yup. B-I-L-L."

"Where are you headed?"

"I'm on my way fishing."

"Really? Where are you fishing at?"

"Batchewana."

"You're kidding me. Right? That's a terrible road. You can't possibly be driving this beautiful piece of equipment on that road."

"It's four-wheel drive. I've taken it in worse places. As long as it's not flooded out, I'll be just fine."

"Isn't this a Winnebago?"

"It's a Winnebago Revel. It's built on a Mercedes frame. ... And, like I said, it's four-wheel drive."

"Do you mind if I take a look in the back?"

"Help yourself."

"Would you come around and open it up for me?"

"Sure, officer. Happy to accommodate."

Mr. May stepped out of the vehicle and walked around to the rear door. He opened it, and stepped back.

Officer Swearengen pointed his flashlight inside, even though it was thoroughly illuminated.

"That's very attractive," he said. "All self-contained and everything. You could probably live out of this, if you wanted. I'd bet you could. Very nice. ... You expecting to have company in Batchewana? Or will you be by yourself?"

"I'm not expecting anyone. I just like to get away. Me and Bill."

"Okay," Officer Swearengen said. "You may leave. Hope you catch a lot of fish."

Mr. May just smiled and got back in the Winnebago.

He slowly pulled out and continued down the highway until he arrived at the gravel/dirt road that led east toward Batchewana. And he turned down it.

After nearly a mile, he stopped the vehicle and opened the divider that led to the rear of the camper.

He knocked on the roof and said, "Mr. Handler. Would you like to come down now?"

Mr. May popped the cover off of the twelve-volt light and

pulled a ring. When he did, it released a latch and allowed him to slide a section of the roof back. Jack promptly gripped the edge of the opening and lowered himself.

"It can get a little breezy up there," he said. "But that is one of the charms of these Mercedes tall vans—not only can a man stand up in one, you could probably hide a small army on top of one, if you were so inclined."

"Don't you think you could have driven a little slower?" Jack said in a joking tone. "Especially over those bumps—I'm not as young as I used to be. There's not much for padding up there. ... I'll bet those boys are not too happy all cramped up. Can we let them out too?"

"Absolutely. I think Bill would like to have someone to play with."

When Mr. May lifted the top of the bench over the tire well, Robby and Red crawled out.

"Wow," Robby said, "that was getting a little stuffy. ... It wouldn't have been too bad, but Red kept farting. ... And not just once. He *kept* farting, and farting."

"I can't believe how calm your dog is," Jack said. "He's a very good sport—putting up with all these strangers."

"He *is* a good dog. He's actually a puppy. Five months."

"He looks a lot like a Weimaraner," Jack said. "Is he a mix?"

"That's right. He's a Labmaraner—half Chocolate Lab. Still has the blue eyes."

"Beautiful animal. I was concerned that he might give us away. But he was great."

"He's *always* great. He's about the only person I can get along with all the time. We're always together."

"I'm sure the boys are going to enjoy hanging around with Bill. We've got a Golden Retriever, Buddy, I think he's our best friend. ... About that fishing. Are the boys going to be able to drop a line someplace? Or is this fishing story just that—a story?"

"Mitchell Lake," Mr. May said. "It's real, and the fishing is real. We're going to park the Winnebago on the lake, and we're going to do some serious fishing. Until I get orders to pull out."

He then turned to the boys and asked, "How does that sound to you fellows? Ready to do some fishing?"

"You bet," Robby said.

"Red doesn't talk," Jack said. "But don't let that fool you. He's smarter than I am. He just has a physical condition that won't allow him to speak."

"I wish more people had that condition," Mr. May said. "Well, if you fellows will strap up, we'll start the drive. It's a rough one."

"How much farther?" Jack asked.

"Thirty kilometers give or take. And it's very bumpy. Some of it's over a dried up river bottom. It's all very rough going. ... But that's a *positive* thing. It means that it's unlikely that anyone will accidently venture back here. So that's all good."

"It's all good until we have to get out of here in a hurry," Jack added. "And then it's not so good."

"What's your connection to Roger?" Jack asked.

"Roger? I don't know any Roger. Well, I can't say that, exactly. I did go to high school with a Roger. But that's not who you meant. Other than that Roger, I'm not familiar with any other person with that name."

"Who do you take orders from?" Jack asked.

"I work for CSIS. I take my orders from Officer Eric Tremblay. *He* may be familiar with the man you call Roger. But I wouldn't know about that."

"CSIS, that's the Canadian Security Intelligence Service—it's like our Secret Service. Isn't that right?"

"I think you could say that," Mr. May said. "But I'm more of a private contractor. I've not had formal training. There are a lot of guys like me in the CSIS. I think they like us because we work cheap. But, it's a good job. Most of the time, like right now, I'm really not doing much. Maybe fishing. But I still get a small stipend. I can't complain."

"I can tell you that the boys and I are genuinely appreciative of your assistance. Not sure how this would have turned out had you not been available to bail us out."

"Hey, it was really nothing," Mr. May said. "It's been nearly a month since they've called on me for anything. After a while I start to feel a little useless. Like maybe they've forgotten I exist. Thankfully they don't forget to put money in my account. So, I guess they haven't forgotten about me. … But, then I get the call. Like today. And off I go. Makes Bill and me feel like we've got an important job to do. Like we count for something. So, I should be thanking you and your boys for that good feeling. You know what I mean, eh?"

"Yeah," Jack said. "I get it. But you did really come through for us. And we do appreciate your professionalism. I heard you dealing with that cop."

Jack took a seat in the front, but he had not yet fastened his seatbelt. The boys in the back were all set to go. They were already growing very attached to Bill.

"Let's get going," Mr. May said, "before we end up with some unwanted company."

Just as Jack latched his seatbelt he spotted a flashing red light in his rearview mirror.

"Damn," Mr. May barked. "No time to hide. I'll go back and talk to them. If it doesn't work, you should get out of here as best you can. This is all wheel drive. And you've got GPS. If this goes south, you're on your own. … I'll see what I can do."

Jack unhooked his seatbelt, and then watched what transpired in the mirror.

"Something's wrong," he muttered. "Boys, keep your belts on, and your heads low."

He watched a man get out of the car and approach Mr. May.

"No uniform, and a red flashing light on the roof, but not centered," he said to himself. "Might not be a real cop. This does not make sense."

Jack began breathing deeply as adrenalin surged through his system.

Bang! Bang!

The sharp sound of two rounds of a 9mm reverberated through the cool Canadian air. Mr. May turned and took a few short steps back toward the Winnebago. And then a third and final shot dropped him in his tracks.

"Down! And stay down!" Jack shouted at the boys as he clambered over the center console and slid in behind the wheel. He slammed the shifter into drive and hit the gas.

The shooter fired three more rounds, two of which struck the back of the vehicle, but did not hit any vital components.

The boys, who were strapped to the bench, lay down as far as they could. Red grabbed Bill around his neck to protect him from getting bounced around in what he suspected would be a very rough ride.

"Never thought I could be this grateful for a bad road," Jack said to himself. "It looks to me like that fellow bought, rented or stole the only two-wheel-drive vehicle in Canada. … But he's not doing too badly. So far."

Jack looked down at the GPS screen as he bounced along.

"Looks like this two-track almost goes away. We'll see how he does then."

"Keep your heads down!" Jack shouted back at the boys. "We're not out of the woods yet."

Jack observed that the vehicle following him stopped abruptly. "I wonder what that's all about?" he muttered.

He soon found out. The trail curved sharply to the right, and when it did it exposed the entire right side of the Winnebago to his pursuer.

When Jack turned, he was unable to monitor the car behind him in his mirror. Even though the distance between the car and his camper had increased substantially, Jack was clearly able to distinguish the sounds that were now cracking from behind.

"Oh, shit!" Jack barked. "That's a high-power rifle. That could do some real damage."

The first round appeared to have missed the vehicle altogether—at least Jack sensed no impact. The second shot was a different story. That round tore through the vehicle and scored a direct hit on the engine. It struck it so soundly that Jack not only heard the impact, but he was convinced that he even felt it.

"I don't see steam or smoke," he said to himself. "That's good."

Jack knew that a round from a high-power weapon, such as a 30-06 or a .308, could actually crack an engine block. And if it were to strike a hose or any electronic component, it could quickly disable the vehicle.

He pointed the Winnebago into a clump of trees and slammed on the brakes.

"I'll be right back," Jack advised the boys as he grabbed the Stealth Recon Scout. "I've got to do something about our friend back there. Stay low, and keep Bill with you."

When the shooter saw that Jack had ceased moving, he suspected that he had hit Jack, or somehow disabled the Winnebago. He jumped in his car and closed the distance between them. As soon as he believed he would have a clear shot, he stopped again.

Jack could see him looking in his direction with a pair of binoculars.

Jack had a dilemma. He did not have any notion as to who it was firing at him. Or why. *I've already killed the only man I know who could clear my boys of murdering the deputies and the caseworker. Maybe this fellow has somehow partnered up with that Kenny guy. So, if I take this fellow out, I win in the short term, but I still won't be able to exonerate my boys.*

Jack scoped his target. But, instead of going for the kill, he zeroed in on the rifle, and fired.

After the recoil, he slid another round in the chamber, and eyed the target again through his scope.

"Damn!" Jack said. "I love this gun."

He stood and walked back to the Winnebago.

"Okay, boys, you can relax for a while."

He was still smiling as he fastened his belt and started the engine. What he had seen through the scope was a significantly deformed barrel on a long 30-06 rifle. His round had actually clipped the shooter's weapon and ruined it.

"That must have felt like hell when my round hit," he said to himself, out loud and laughing.

Just before he pulled out, Jack tried to call Roger on his satphone. It didn't work, so he looked around for a place to plug into an external antenna.

Finding the appropriately marked jack on the dash, he declared, "That oughta do it," as he plugged in.

"Roger. I just had some joker taking pot shots at me and the boys. Any idea what that could all be about?"

Chapter 40

Arthur's on the Prowl

Yeah," Roger said. "That doesn't surprise me. The agent charged to get rid of the lifeboat. The Canadian Coast Guard just pulled his body out of Superior. He'd been shot."

"Who the hell is pulling this shit? … Can't be law enforcement. I know Sheriff Green hates my guts, but he's not going to come over and start shooting up Canada. Who the hell could this be?"

"I'll offer my theory," Roger said.

"Yeah."

"That brother of Kenny—killer Kenny. We tracked him to the UP. He's up there right now."

"Okay," Jack said. "This starts to make some sense. … I hate to have to tell you this, but, whoever it is, he killed this May fellow. The man Eric sent to pick us up."

"Did you take him out?" Roger asked.

"No. I couldn't. I did not have any idea who I was dealing with. If it turned out to be the law … the last thing I need is to kill a Canadian cop. Or *any* cop. Even if he does happen to be shooting at me. Just can't go there.

"Besides, now that Kenny is out of the picture, I'm going to need another witness. Someone who can clear my boys. That's what this was all about from the start."

"So, if I'm right about this guy, what do you suppose he's up to?

Avenging his brother? Somehow he doesn't strike me that much as a caring sort of fellow."

"He's after the loot," Jack said.

"My thoughts, exactly," Roger agreed. "He flew up to the UP to get some of his brother's cash. ... He was probably boating out in the lake, following that freighter and just waiting to extricate his brother from it, once the boys were dead. ... And, now, he must think that you're his only chance to get his hands on the money."

"Makes sense," Jack said. "That's why he was trying to take the engine out, and not to kill me outright."

"Where's he at right now?"

"I don't think he's moved yet."

"Well, he will be coming after you. ... And I have to warn you. You're pretty much on your own. I cannot set foot in Canada. And, I sincerely doubt that Eric is going to be much help anymore, now that the lead is flying. I'd have to say that you're going to be on your own from here on. I might be able to pull you out when the time comes. But that's about it. And that's even questionable. Can you deal with it?"

"Sure I can," Jack replied. "It certainly helps just knowing who it is I'm dealing with, and his motivation. ... I'll figure something out. ... One thing for sure. I'm going to see about getting me one of these Winnebagos. This would be great for driving through the Porcupine Mountains."

"Handler. You're a real messed up guy. Here you've got half the people in Michigan shooting at you, and all you can do is plan your next outing."

"Roger. Have you driven one of these?"

"Goodbye, Jack. Call me when you get in position for a pick-up."

"Thanks, Rog."

Jack turned the key and started the engine. When all the gauges met his satisfaction, he backed it up a bit, and then shifted to drive.

"Okay, boys, you may sit up now. Everything should be fine for a while."

Bill felt the Winnebago moving and made his way to Red. He placed his head on Red's lap and whined his concern.

"C'mon, boy," Red gurgled. "Get up here."

Bill happily accepted the invite and sprang onto Red's lap, giving him a kiss on his way up.

Jack saw what was going on and laughed.

"Is that fellow still back there?" Robby asked.

"He is, but I think he's going to want to wait until dark before he tries anything again. We've got a little time, I think."

Red tapped on Robby's shoulder, pointed back at the shooter's car, turned his palms up and shrugged his shoulders.

Robby knew exactly what his friend was *saying*.

"Uncle Jack, we were wondering who that man was, and why he was shooting at us."

"Fair question," Jack said. "We think he is *Arthur* Kenny, the brother of Walter Jon Kenny—the man who killed the deputies and your caseworker."

"Why is he trying to kill *us*?"

"Not so sure he is. I think he might want to find out from us if we have his brother's loot."

Red looked wide-eyed at Robby.

Robby nodded his head.

"You don't have his money, do you?"

"No," Jack said. "But *he* might not know that. And I'm quite sure he won't be taking my word about it, either. ... We're going to have to find a good way to make our point."

"And that part you haven't worked out yet," Robby said. "Right?"

"That's about it. So, if you fellows come up with some good ideas, let me know. I'm open to suggestions."

234   *Michael Carrier*

While Jack seemed to be kidding with the boys, he was not dismissive. They and he knew that if either one of them came up with a good strategy; Jack would be more than willing to entertain it. And if he deemed it superior to his own plan, he would execute it.

"Did that man damage the van?" Robby asked at Red's bidding.

"No," Jack said. "But I don't think he knows that either."

Jack pulled ahead about fifty yards, and then parked in a small growth of pine trees.

"He did put a couple rounds into us, but I don't think that he damaged any of our vital mechanics. That's what I was just trying to determine. Everything seems to be okay as far as this vehicle is concerned."

"He hasn't given up, though, has he?"

"No. He'll be back. … And most likely sooner than later. Probably after dark tonight. … In the meantime, what say we play some poker?"

"For *real* money?" Robby asked. "We're broke. And we know how you play."

"For chips," Jack said, tossing an unopened box of chips on the table. "Mr. May had a new box of poker chips, and a fresh deck. Must be he never traveled with friends, or he was just antisocial."

Red grabbed a small tablet and a pencil and began writing a note. Typically he would communicate using a text message. But neither he nor Robby had a cell phone.

"No fun," Red wrote. "Must have skin in the game to be fun."

"Yeah," Jack said. "White chips will be a penny, red a nickel and blue a dime. You can pay me later."

"And if we win?" Robby asked.

"Do you actually believe in miracles?" Jack chided.

"Red's beat you before," Robby responded.

"I must be getting old," Jack said. "My memory's got to be failing me."

"You don't *always* win, Uncle Jack. It's just that you're such a good liar."

"It's called *bluffing*," Jack corrected with a smile. "In poker, you're *supposed* to mislead your opponents. It's not lying."

Red penciled a message in very large letters: "JUST DEAL THE CARDS!"

Jack made sure the doors to the van were locked, and the curtains drawn. He then confirmed that the magazine of his Glock was fully loaded.

He opened the deck of cards and removed the two jokers and the information card. He then slid the deck over to Robby and said, "You're the first dealer. And don't be pulling any from the bottom. I've got my eye on you."

While Robby was shuffling, Jack set a burner cell in the middle of the table and pulled a few sandwiches and Cokes from the small refrigerator. "Seven card stud?" he asked.

The boys nodded their approval.

Bill, obviously insecure about losing his best friend, looked up at Red and let out a soft whimper. Red slid his chair back and Bill, all twenty-plus pounds of the *puppy,* found his place of comfort on Red's lap.

Stud poker was Jack's game of choice—five card and seven card. But he knew that the boys preferred seven card stud, and so he deferred to their game of choice.

An hour passed. And then two. Finally Jack made an announcement.

"We're going to do this a little differently from now on. It's getting dark, and I think we're going to have company soon. So I'll tell you how we're going to handle it from here on."

After he had instructed the boys about the changes, all three settled into Jack's plan and waited for Walter Kenny's brother to show up.

Jack had positioned Red in the driver's seat, and Robby in the passenger's, while he stationed himself in a sleeping bag on the roof of the vehicle.

However, before he ascended through the roof hatch, Jack hung one of Mr. May's shirts on a clothes hanger, and suspended it from the ceiling on a piece of string. He then placed his cell on the table and began playing back the recording he had earlier made of their poker game.

He then closed his eyes and fell asleep.

About an hour later he was awakened by a substantial impact against the rear of the van, and by the sound of breaking glass. He had correctly anticipated the *visit*, but he was not certain whether it would be through the rear door, or one of the side windows.

Bill stood to attention and growled, and then barked a warning.

Arthur Kenny had taken the bait. And his point of attack was the rear door.

Jack sat up as quietly as he could, and peered over the rear of the vehicle. There he saw Arthur Kenny leaning through the broken glass. He heard Arthur mumbling, but he could not make out what he was saying.

The dog barking startled Arthur. As he stepped back, Jack spotted a gun extended and pointing into the vehicle. Jack immediately dropped down upon the intruder, using him to break his fall. Both men crumbled to the ground, but with Jack on top.

Removing his finger from the trigger guard on his Glock to prevent an accidental discharge, Jack delivered a crushing backfist blow to the side of Arthur's head, instantly knocking him unconscious.

"Damn," Jack complained as he glanced up to the roof of the Winnebago. "I'm getting much too old for this shit. Or else they're just making those things too tall."

He then rolled Arthur onto his stomach and cinched his hands behind him with zip cuffs.

I'll be damned if I'm going to drag this bastard into the van, Jack determined. *I'll wait until he comes to, and he can crawl in by himself.* After retrieving Arthur's pistol, and thoroughly searching him for any additional weapons, Jack opened the door and tossed it into the van. He then took a seat on the threshold and waited for Arthur to wake up.

After nearly ten minutes, the cool Canadian evening air gave Jack a chill, so he retreated into the motorhome and took a seat at the table where they had been playing poker. He took several deep breaths, and then examined his wounds. He observed that both of his knees were protruding from holes in his pants. While he was confident that he had suffered no severe lacerations, his knees were both heavily bruised and bleeding.

"Why doesn't that bastard wake up," Jack said to himself.

He stood to his feet and walked over to the door to get a better look at the man he had just vanquished. After staring at the killer, and unsuccessfully hoping to detect some movement, Jack reached out and poured half a cup of cold coffee onto the side of Arthur's head.

Still he did not move.

"Damn you, Arthur Kenny!" Jack complained. "I sure as hell hope you didn't die on me."

He closed the door and took a look into cockpit to check on the two boys, both of whom were sound asleep with Bill sleeping between them—a front paw resting against Red, and a hind paw touching Robby.

He then set about securing some clean and hole-less jeans. *How about yours, Christopher May. You were about my size. Have you got any pants I could borrow? You're not going to be needing them. And I didn't bring any extra. Let's see what you've got here.*

How long was this fellow planning to be living out of this motorhome? Jack wondered. *Must be a dozen pairs of pants.* Jack passed up several pair of jeans before he found a brand new pair of khakis. The store labels were still in place.

"36/33," Jack said out loud. "That should be a perfect fit. He *was* just about my size."

Jack quickly slid out of his hole-riddled and bloody pants, ripped off the store labels from the new ones, and pulled them up to his waist.

"Couldn't be a better fit," he said. "How lucky was that?"

After putting his boots back on, he returned to check on Arthur Kenny.

"Still out," Jack muttered as he stepped out of the motorhome and over to where the man was lying.

He dropped to his haunches and felt his neck for a pulse.

"You're alive," Jack said. "But apparently just not *that* eager to wake up."

Jack stood to his feet and glanced up into the motorhome.

"Well, damn you, Arthur. I suppose I'm going to have to drag you up into the van. Sure would have been nice if you could have helped me out with this."

And then, just like clockwork, as soon as Jack began to lift on Kenny, the man began to come around.

"About time, you sonofabitch," Jack said, lightly slapping the man's face. "It's about time you woke up. ... Here, let me help you sit up."

It took a few minutes, but Jack coaxed the man to his feet, and then he unceremoniously shoved him into the van. Jack slid Arthur's legs over to the side so he could squeeze past. He then gripped Arthur's jacket by the collar and pulled him the rest of the way into the van and shut the door.

"What the hell did you do to me? My head is killing me."

"I don't know what happened to you, asshole. I just found you lying by the side of the road. Thought you were sleeping one off. You been drinking or something?"

"Where am I?"

"What do you mean? You know where you are."

"I've got a horrible headache. What did you do to me?"

"You don't remember getting drunk?"

"I've not been drinking. ... My God. It hurts to talk. I think my jaw's broke. Somebody hit me with something. ... And tied up my hands. Where are we?"

"You're on Sugar Island. And the sheriff wants to talk to you. Says you killed two of his deputies, a woman and an old man. What do you say about that?"

"Sugar Island!? I never killed anyone on Sugar Island. ... And what the hell am I doin' on Sugar Island? How'd I ever get here?"

"So," Jack said. "You've never killed anyone on Sugar Island? Is *that* what you're trying to tell me? I've got two boys here who will swear that they saw you shoot and kill two of Sheriff Green's deputies—Deputy Jim Martin and Deputy Donny Cochran. Plus an old man—a buddy of yours, Reynold Wayne Fitzgerald. And an employee of the court system—a female caseworker, Christina Baldwin. The boys saw you shoot all four of them. They *saw* you do it. And then you burned the old man's house down. What do you have to say about that?"

"That was my brother, not me. I don't know any names, but he did tell me that he shot four people at the cottage, and two of them were lawmen. ... But, as for me, I've *never* even set foot on Sugar Island. Not until now. And I don't remember how I got here this time."

"They're positive it was you. They were right there when you did it. They will swear to it."

"It was my brother, Wally. I swear. *He* did it. He told me about it. I do look a lot like him. But I was in Denver when that happened. I can prove it. He was at the cottage to get his money. The old man, he called him Renny, I think. Wally and Renny had robbed a drug dealer a long time ago. And Wally was at Renny's cottage to collect his part. … My brother and I look a lot alike. The boys must be mistaking me for my brother."

"That all sounds like a lie to me," Jack said. "If it was your brother who did those killings on Sugar Island, and not you, where is he now?"

"He's dead. Someone killed him on that freighter. Stabbed him. I was supposed to pick him up after he'd killed the two boys. But, when the boat caught on fire and started to sink, I went on board and found his body."

"That sounds like a bunch of bullshit to me," Jack said. "What did he want with the boys? Why'd he want to kill them?"

"Because they'd seen him. They could identify him as the killer. He had to get rid of them."

"I don't think I believe a word you're saying," Jack argued. "You're telling me that the two boys saw your brother, Walter Kenny, they witnessed Walter Kenny kill the two deputies, the female, and your brother's partner, Reynold Fitzgerald, and that your brother chased the boys onto that freighter, and then tried to kill them there? And that all the while you were in Denver? That sounds like a bullshit story to me."

"I don't know what Renny's real name was. But Wally did kill him, and burn up the cottage. I was in Denver when he did it. And I can prove it. I was working at that time. I can prove it."

"Well, I don't know about it," Jack said, sporting a grin he could no longer conceal. "Let me check this out."

"Check what out?" Arthur Kenny asked.

"Let me check your story out with my good friend."

Jack then picked his SAT phone from off the table and said: "Sheriff Green, are you still there?"

"Jack Handler," Sheriff Green said.

"Sheriff, my buddy here, Arthur Kenny, the brother of Walter Jon Kenny, swears that it was he, Brother Wally, who killed your two deputies, the caseworker, and Mr. Reynold Fitzgerald. And that the two boys were wrong when they identified Arthur Kenny as the killer. Did you hear all that?"

"Yes," the sheriff said. "But, I will need some evidence. Right now I have nothing to prove the brother was ever at the Fitzgerald cottage."

"Okay," Jack said. "Stay on the line and I'll run that by Arthur."

"Arthur," Jack said. "Looks like you're still not off the hook. The sheriff says that there is nothing indicating that your brother was ever at the cottage. … And, the two boys still will pick you out of the lineup."

"There is evidence," Arthur insisted. "Wally told me there was. After he had killed the two boys, he wanted me to go to Sugar Island and pick up some spent cartridges he left there when he was shooting at the boys. He had recalled later that they would have his fingerprints on them, and he drew me out a little map as to where I should look for them."

"Really?" Jack said. "A map. Do you still have that map?"

"It's right here in my wallet."

Jack set the phone back down on the table and slipped the wallet out of Arthur's left hip pocket, and pulled it open.

"Is it this folded piece of paper?" Jack asked. "Tucked in here with these five-dollar bills?"

"Yes. That's it."

Jack removed a Ziploc bag from his pocket and dropped the whole wallet into it. He then picked up the phone and again talked to Sheriff Green.

"What do you think now, Sheriff? Arthur here says that there is proof that his brother was at the Fitzgerald cottage, and that he had admitted to him that he not only had killed your deputies, but that he had tried to shoot the boys. Do you think that might get my buddy here off the hook? After all, he does resemble his brother pretty closely. The boys could easily have mistaken him for his brother."

"As far as I'm concerned, Handler," Sheriff Green said. "This whole thing could be one of your carefully crafted schemes. I don't know who that was talking. Could have been anyone. Could have been *you*, for all I know. I need you to bring those two boys in for questioning. And who ever that was *pretending* to be Arthur Kenny. We'll see where the evidence takes us. But for right now, your boys are my prime suspects. And the longer you harbor them, the more trouble you'll be in when I catch up with you."

"Of course you have to follow the evidence," Jack countered. "And, if this map leads to the cartridges with Walter's fingerprints, then that will pretty much establish that it was Walter who killed all four victims at the Fitzgerald cottage. Isn't that right?

"And, sheriff, let me ask you another question. Haven't you found some latent prints at that stone house that didn't belong to my boys, or the old man? I know it got torched, but using the proper methods, maybe from the office of the State of Michigan Fire Marshal, you'll be able to secure them. I know that they are there. Haven't you pulled them off yet?"

"Just get your ass into my office," Sheriff Green replied. "Then we'll see who's guilty."

"Certainly, Sheriff. I'll give you a call as soon as we get back to the States."

"Back to the States!?" Sheriff Green and Arthur said almost simultaneously.

"Got to go now," Jack said with a grin, "Be sure to go after those latent prints, okay?" And then Jack disconnected the call.

"Did you just tell the sheriff that we were *not* in the United States? Does that mean we're *not* on Sugar Island?"

"Stick a sock in it, Arthur," Jack barked as he called Roger. "I'm busy."

"Hey, Rog, how long before you can get that bird in the air?"

Chapter 41

The Canadian Rescue

When Roger answered Jack's call he was relaxing in his Piper M-350.

"I'm just sitting here at GRR watching the Amway fleet come and go," Roger said. "And reading a good Baldacci book. What's up with you?"

"Need an extraction. ASAP."

"What, exactly, do you have in mind?" Roger asked.

"I need you to get in here as quickly as possible and pull us out."

"By *here,* you're referring to some specific location in Canada?"

"Right."

"And, when you speak of us, how many people would that be? And the total weight?"

"Two adult males—a total of maybe three seventy-five, give or take. ... And, of course, the two boys. Add another two twenty. And then my gear—perhaps another hundred pounds. ... And, we will have another passenger, Bill. He goes maybe twenty-five."

"Bill? Who's Bill?"

"Bill's the boys' new best friend. Bill's an orphaned Labmaraner that the boys are adopting."

"Okay. Am I going to be able to fuel up there?"

"That would be a negative. In and out."

"What are you thinking for a landing strip? I'm guessing that we won't be using any sort of airfield. Right?"

"Good guess. ... What's your range, given the weight?"

"Thirteen hundred nautical miles with stated load, and forty-five minute reserve."

"No problem," Jack said. "Toss a landing and a takeoff in there, and we should still be fine. Provided we don't stretch out the return."

"Want to let me know exactly where I'm heading?"

"Absolutely. But it's going to take me a little time to figure that part out. ... I'd say you should fuel up right now, and take off. It's about eight hundred miles to where we are. And then maybe another hundred to find an appropriate place to land in the U.P."

"I'm all set for fuel. I can be off the ground in minutes. As soon as they'll let me. What's our ultimate destination? ... For the second leg of this flight?"

"Munising looks as good as anything," Jack suggested. "But you can make that call once you pick us up."

"Give me an approximate so I can file an appropriate flight plan."

"Think Katherine's Cove again," Jack said.

Jack's mind was in overdrive.

"Where's your car?" he asked Arthur.

"Close. Probably a hundred yards west of here."

"Gas or diesel?"

"Gas, I think. Didn't stink like diesel."

"Stolen. Right?"

Arthur hesitated before answering.

"What's it to you?" he asked.

"Answer the damn question! Did you steal that car?"

"Yes, of course. I came by boat, just like you."

"What did you do with the owner? ... After you stole his car."

"He's in the trunk."

"Dead?"

"Yeah."

"That's what I thought," Jack said. "And Mr. May—my buddy that you *just* killed. Where's he?"

"I put him in the trunk as well."

"You got the keys on you?"

"I left them in the ignition."

Jack sat silently thinking for a couple minutes. Finally, his expression changed and he said out loud, "This just might work. ... Hell, it damn well has to."

"Boys," he called to Red and Robby. They were both sleeping in the cockpit. He pounded loudly on the divider and called to them again.

"Yes, Uncle Jack," Robby said poking his head back to check out what was going on.

"Who's that?" he asked upon seeing Arthur.

"He's the fellow who's been shooting at us. ... I need you to get busy wiping everything down. Eliminate any evidence of our having been in this vehicle. We're going to be leaving here soon. So be quick. Start right there in the cockpit."

After twenty minutes, the two boys came back to where Jack and Arthur were waiting.

"All set up front?" Jack asked.

"Yeah," Robby said. "I'm pretty sure we got everything."

"Okay, Arthur, it's your turn now."

Jack cut the zip cuffs and attached another set, this time with Arthur's hands in front of him. He then led Arthur into the cockpit and commanded him to grab onto the steering wheel and shifter, and to leave as many fingerprints as possible.

While the two men were busy up front, Jack had the boys wipe down the back.

"Okay, boys," Jack said after studying the maps he had found in the Winnebago. "I think this might work. ... But only if you two come through again. Are you ready for a challenge?"

The boys had no idea what Jack had in mind, but they knew from experience that when he talked like this, life was just about to take on a new and exciting aspect.

The boys looked at one another and nodded. "We're ready for anything, Uncle Jack," Robby said.

"Then let's get on with it."

Jack slipped on a fresh pair of latex gloves and slid in behind the steering wheel. The Mercedes engine started immediately at the turn of the key.

Jack turned the vehicle around and headed back up the two-track toward the car with the two bodies. There was just enough room for him to squeeze by it. Once past, he stopped and said, "Red, Robby, now it's your turn. ... Arthur, you wait here. The boys are coming with me."

Arthur did not say a word.

"This is what you do," Jack said as he opened the car door. "Red, you drive. Robby, you're the communications man. Keep the SAT phone handy. That's the only way we will be able to communicate if we get separated. Don't use it unless it's an emergency. ... Instead, use this short-range two-way radio. It's good for a mile, at least. That should be plenty."

This was not the first time Jack had employed the boys in such a fashion. And when he did, Red was always the driver, and Robby was assigned communications ... all for obvious reasons.

"You guys follow me out. It's quite a ways—looks like about fifteen miles. When we hit the main road, we'll turn right. Stay right behind me. ... About two miles up I'll stop and pull to the side of the road. The map shows a small road there entering from the east. You stop as well. Slide in right behind me. At that point we'll switch vehicles."

As soon as Jack was confident that the boys were going to be able to keep up he called Roger.

"How far out are you right now?" he asked.

"Now that's a good question," Roger replied. "Maybe it'd help if I knew more precisely where I was headed."

"Try these coordinates. They might change once I get a better handle as to the terrain, but plug these in." Jack read the numbers he had plotted from the map: 47.172163 -84.684973.

Roger plugged the coordinates into his GPS, and then said, "That doesn't look much like an airport to me. I think that would be the Trans-Canada Highway. ... I should be able to make a pass in about sixty-five minutes. ... Are you currently at that location?"

"Not yet," Jack said. "But I will be by then. Let me know when you are fifteen minutes out. Exactly."

"Roger that," Roger said.

"How do you intend to pull it off?" Jack asked. "I'm sure the CBSA will not take kindly to your violating their air space."

"I'm cleared to set it down at Chippewa International at Kinross. So that's where I'm headed. When I get there, I'll take one pass, and then drop down over Superior. I figure I can come in at thirty meters or so, I can keep our rendezvous, and then beat it the hell back to the States. ... Provided, of course, you mark where I'm to come down, and keep all vehicles off the road and out of my way."

Roger was intending to fly in under the radar. As long as he remained under thirty meters, he would not be picked up by standard land-based radar systems.

"I've got that covered," Jack said. "You'll spot me without any trouble. The wind is coming out of the north at about seven. So you should approach from the southwest. I'll give you two thousand feet of clear highway."

"That works for me as long as I can find you."

"No problem there," Jack said. But he didn't explain.

Just as Jack reached the main road, Roger announced that he was fifteen minutes out.

"Great," Jack replied.

He had thought that he might have to park and wait, but the timing was perfect. He did not even have to stop. With the boys right on his rear bumper, Jack led his mini convoy out onto the highway, and then toward his destination two miles north.

Traffic is light, he was thinking. *This could be a walk in the park.*

Just as Jack had surmised from the map, from the point he had stipulated to Roger, the highway stretched to the northeast for at least half of a kilometer. *It's straight and relatively level—a near perfect landing strip,* Jack concluded.

He pulled the Winnebago off the road and the boys followed.

Jack then jumped out of the van and moved quickly to the car.

"Let's go, guys," he directed. "Hurry. Take Bill and go get in the motorhome. I'll be right with you."

The three of them scampered out of the passenger door while Jack slid in behind the wheel. He immediately backed the car up until he was confident the boys could not easily monitor what he was about to do, and then he cranked the car to the left and pulled across the highway.

Wasting no time, he hurried back to the motorhome and rummaged through the tool compartment until he found a Dewalt battery-powered drill set. He inserted an eighth-inch bit into the chuck, and looked around until he located a dishtowel.

"This ought to do the trick," Jack said to himself.

He then dragged Arthur out of the rear door of the Winnebago.

"I'm going to help you get out of here," Jack told him. "I'm giving you back the car you stole."

"Really?" Arthur said. "Why's it setting crosswise the road?"

"I'll explain in a minute. First get in and then I'll get you all fixed up."

Jack removed the car keys, shoved Arthur into the driver's

seat, and then fastened his seatbelt. But, instead of removing the zip cuffs, he added a second. This one attached his wrists to the steering wheel.

"I can't drive like this," Arthur complained. "Take these damn things off."

"Later," Jack said. "Everything in its time."

Without Arthur even noticing Jack drawing back his left fist, Jack uncorked a short crushing blow high on his cheekbone. It knocked Arthur out cold.

Jack shoved Arthur's body over the top of the center console so that he was not visible from the outside. He then quickly ducked under the car with the Dewalt and the towel.

Wonderful, Jack thought, after surveying the car's underbelly. *A plastic fuel tank.*

Jack knew that many American automobiles now came equipped with a plastic high-density polyethylene (HDPE) fuel tank, and he was hoping that would be the case with this one as that would simplify the task of drilling a hole in it.

He spread the towel out beneath the tank and commenced drilling.

It took him less than ten seconds to pierce the tank. As soon as the drill bit had penetrated to the fuel, Jack backed it out an inch and released the chuck, leaving the bit in the hole. He did that to slow the flow of gasoline to a rapid drip.

Jack arranged the towel so that it absorbed all of the fuel.

Once satisfied with the leak he'd just created, and with the amount of fuel that had soaked into the towel, he slid out from under the car, removing the towel as he did.

He then unscrewed the gas cap, poked the towel down into the gas tank as far as he could, and lit it.

As he stood to his feet, Jack observed a semi-tractor trailer approaching from the south. He laid the Dewalt on the pavement, placed his right foot against it, and then shoved it like a soccer pass in the direction of the Winnebago. Red watched the drill as it slid to within ten meters of him, but he knew better than to get out.

Jack then turned and trotted toward the oncoming truck to flag it down.

The truck driver had spotted Jack nearly a quarter of a mile away and had already begun braking.

Once Jack was certain the truck was going to be able to stop, he moved to the middle of the highway and engaged his whole body in the effort to flag it down.

"What's goin' on up there?" the driver asked. It was clear to Jack that he was not pleased about being stopped.

"Possible bomb," Jack stated. "We want you to keep this distance. RCMP is aware and is responding.

"In fact," Jack said, looking into the sky, "I expect them to be on scene momentarily. They're coming in by air. So, keep your distance. Or you'll be dealing with their wrath. Got it?"

"Yes, of course. I wouldn't want to interfere."

"Good," Jack said. "Now I'm authorizing you to help with crowd control. Until the RCMP arrive, it is imperative that you do not let anyone get past your vehicle. Is that clear?"

"Yes, sir," the driver agreed. "… Is that smoke I see coming out of the back of that car?"

Just then the flame from the towel in the gas tank ignited the pool of fuel that had accumulated beneath it.

"Got to go," Jack barked. "Remember what I told you. Let no one get past you. Possible bomb. You're safe here. But, get any closer and it could be very dangerous."

Jack circled widely around the flaming automobile as he trotted over to the Winnebago, slowing only briefly to retrieve the Dewalt.

"Slide over," he said to Red.

Jack had left the engine running. He shifted into drive and

sped off to the north.

"We need about two thousand feet," Jack said to the boys. "So, tell me, how many kilometers would that be?"

Red immediately held up six fingers, and Robby said, "Six hundred meters … a little over six hundred."

"Right," Jack said. "Very good. …That means if we head up here between six and seven tenths of a kilometer, we'll be about two thousand feet. Right?"

"Right," Robby said. "Why's it so important that we stay two thousand feet from that car? What's gonna happen to it?"

"It's not so much about what is going to happen to that car. Take a look in the mirror and tell me what you see."

"Holy cow!" Robby shouted. "That's a plane. And it looks like it's about to land right behind us."

"I guess we'd better get out of its way, don't you think?"

"What's happening, Uncle Jack?" Robby asked.

"That's our ride, I think," Jack said. "You did call Uber. Right?" Red chuckled.

"No, really," Robby said. "Uncle Jack, what's the deal with the plane?"

"Okay," Jack said loudly. "That's seven-tenths of a kilometer. That should be perfect."

As soon as he made that declaration he braked sharply and pulled across both lanes of traffic.

"It's time for us to go. Grab Bill and hop out. Stand ready to board the plane when told to."

Roger brought the M-350 in without incident, leaving over three hundred feet of "runway" on the north end. He taxied up to where Jack and the boys were walking, and signaled for them to come aboard.

"Jack," Roger said abruptly. "We've got to hurry. Get your crew in and strapped up. We've got company."

Jack snapped a look at Roger and shouted over the sound of

the engine, "Land, air or sea?"

"Maybe all three. But for right now, we should worry about what's breaking over that hill. Two strobes headed our way at full speed. I spotted them from the air."

Just as Jack was helping the boys and Bill to board, Bill got spooked by the noise of the plane's engine. And then, Bill broke away from Red when the first of the two patrol cars clipped the Winnebago and flipped over in the ditch.

Bill bolted at full speed down the road toward the flaming automobile. At first Red took off after him.

"Red!" Jack barked loudly. "Stop! We've got to get out of here right now. We can't help Bill. Get back here right now!"

Red immediately halted. He stood for a few seconds yelling at Bill as best he could. He then turned around and headed back to the plane. At first he tried to hide his tears, but then it got the best of him. Jack saw Red's despair. He hurried over to him, picked him up and carried him toward the plane.

As he lifted Red into the plane, Jack whispered in his ear, "I know exactly how you feel, Red. Losing Bill rips my heart out too. But this is just one of those tough things a guy has to do."

He then kissed Red on the top of his head, and tossed him in.

Jack, following Red, stepped through and took a seat in the cockpit. He slipped on a headset and said, "You've got just about seven hundred meters. However, that wind is coming from the north-northeast at about twelve. So, you're going to have to stick it to it, as long as you've got to take off with the wind."

"Damn it," Roger complained. "I can't use the whole thing. Got to turn around right here."

The remaining patrol car had managed to get past the Winnebago and was bearing down on them. It would be only seconds before they could force him to abandon his takeoff.

Roger slowed dramatically and spun the plane around. As soon as he had completed the turn he locked on the brakes and kicked it to full throttle.

"Holy shit!" Jack barked. "That can't be much more than a thousand feet. You going to be able to get her up?"

"I think so," Roger said, releasing the brakes at maximum RPMs. "If you and the boys don't put all your weight down. ... And if our engine doesn't overheat."

Just as he reached the flaming car, he lifted off.

The boys looked out of the window trying to get a last glimpse of Bill. And they did. Bill had not slowed down. He was nearing the burning car just as Roger went airborne. At that very moment, just as they lifted, the car below exploded.

Jack cringed.

"Damn, that was close, Rog," he said. "I can't believe the landing gear cleared that car."

"It wouldn't have had we not peeled off to the right," Roger admitted. "Lucky we didn't have any trees to deal with."

Jack then turned around to get a look at the two boys. Both were glued to the windows. The last image of Bill they were left with was his reaching the car just as it exploded. They both witnessed the flames encompassing the dog they had come to love.

"Bill's dead," Red said to himself. "And I did it to him. It's all my fault."

There was nothing they could do. Both were crying. Neither tried to speak. Robby felt badly about losing Bill, and he empathized with Red's grief. He knew that Red blamed himself for losing his grip on Bill's collar. Eventually they would discuss it. But it was no use to attempt it now. Red was in no mood to be consoled, and Robby had no words that could possibly help.

Roger leveled it off at a hundred meters until he reached cruising speed, and then ascended to a hundred and fifty, before turning right and heading out over the lake. As soon as he was over water he dropped it back down to thirty meters.

"Still want to set down in Munising?" he asked.

"What are our options?" Jack asked.

"We're not on reserve, yet," Roger said.

"My Tahoe is still back at Grand Marais Airport. Suppose you could set down there?"

"Don't see why not. Some sheriff is going to have our asses one way or the other no matter where we land. Might as well be your Sheriff Green. We can let him talk to Bob. That might work."

The *Bob* Roger was referring to was their mutual friend, Bob Fulbright, the former president.

"Might work," Jack agreed. "At least we managed to start getting the issue with the boys cleared up. I'm not so sure Green will be alone at Grand Marais, because that's in Alger County."

"Damn it, Jack. Do you see what I see? And I think they mean business."

Approaching at one o'clock was a red and white Sikorsky MH-60T Jayhawk helicopter.

"What the hell are they going to do?" Jack asked rhetorically. "Shoot us down?"

"Oh, they won't do that," Roger replied. "And we could outrun them. But there's no flying under the radar when the radar is above you. ... We'll just press on toward the strip at Grand Marais. No doubt the Canadians have protested our incursion. And it's not going to be easy explaining away the torched vehicle on Trans-Canada. There's going to be some costs involved with that."

"Not to mention the three bodies in the car," Jack added.

"Ouch," Roger cringed. "Who didn't make it?"

"One of them was Arthur Kenny."

"The brother of your killer?"

"Right. He was trying to locate his brother's cash. Don't think he had any luck."

"And whatever he did have—luck that is," Roger said. "It ran out today. ... Who were the other two?"

"The owner of the car. Arthur had commandeered it on the

highway. The third victim was Tremble's man—Christopher May. Nice guy. Arthur shot him as well. He told me he had stuck his two victims in the trunk of the car. I never actually saw them, but he had no reason to lie about it."

"And, Arthur," Roger began to probe. "How was it he decided to stick around after the car caught on fire?"

"You know me," Jack said. "I can be a *very* persuasive fellow. … That chopper is going to intercept us in a minute. That is if I decide to let them. I don't think they know for certain that the boys and I are in this plane. No point providing them with any additional information."

Jack snapped off his harness and slid to the cabin with the two boys.

"Get to the floor, guys," he ordered. "On the double."

Jack recognized the boys' somber mood. *I know what's on their minds,* he reasoned. *Maybe this little emergency will help move them past it. Maybe it'll help move me past it too.*

Just a few moments later Roger flew past the helicopter. He smiled and waved at the pilot as he did. He then continued on with his approach toward the U.S. mainland.

Once safely out of visual contact with the Coast Guard helicopter, Jack and his boys reassumed their seats.

Finally, after several minutes of silence, Roger said with a smile of confidence, "You know what, Jack? I think we might have a way out of this mess. I believe it actually could work. With a little luck, and a lot of subterfuge. … Just wish we had a little more fuel. But, what the hell. What's life all about if it ain't taking a chance once in a while."

"That's right," Jack said as he looked back at his two boys. "And right now, I'm feeling pretty damn lucky."

Chapter 42

Roger's Final Plan

Roger did have a plan. And part of it was to lead Sheriff Green into thinking that he was going to set the M-350 down at Chippewa International Airport just outside of Sault Ste. Marie. So, that's the course he set. But, just before he reached the airport, he turned west toward Grand Marais.

"So," Jack said. "We set down briefly at Grand Marais, and then you take it back up and over to Chippewa."

"Yeah," Roger said. "That's what I had in mind. But only so long as they're not waiting for us at Grand Marais. ... I really can't see them posting guard there. But, if they do, we'll touch down just long enough to drop you and the boys off. A little touch-and-go maneuver."

Roger circled Grand Marais before setting down.

"I don't see any patrol cars at all," he said. "And, it looks like your Tahoe is still there. All is good, I'd say."

"All is sure a hell of a lot better than it was a few hours ago," Jack said. "That's for damn sure. ... Thanks to you."

"Teamwork," Roger quickly added. "It can't be overrated. ... You headed back to Sugar Island?"

"Actually, no. My lawyer is winding up the audit in Chicago. You know, Allison's charade. I figured I should be around in case Randy needs some moral support.

"Besides, I'm not eager to give the sheriff access to the boys until he gets himself convinced that they're not the killers. I think he's almost there, but not quite."

"That makes sense. Stay in touch. I don't think Henry's out of the woods yet. We might have to engage ourselves on his behalf."

"I'm sure he'll need some help," Jack said. "He doesn't think so, but those are some very rough characters he's dealing with. It's going to be difficult to put an end to that matter. … Anyway, I will stay in touch."

Chapter 43

The Audit

Tuesday rolled around quickly. Calibret had moved all the file cabinets out of Jack's first-floor office, along with his desk, potted plants, and wall hangings. The four file cabinets he had loaded into an enclosed trailer for Jack to relocate, while the rest of Jack's office he arranged neatly in what had formerly been the third-floor apartment's living room. The specific files that Abraham Stern, Allison's lawyer, had requested—these Calibret had packed up in six drawer-sized storage boxes and set out neatly on an eight-foot table in the third-floor "office."

Initially all was friendly. Calibret met and greeted the two well-dressed accountants, and the attorney who accompanied them. He was surprised when the attorney introduced himself: "My name is Abe Stern. I am representing the interests of Mr. O'Donnell in the proper transfer of his share of the bar to Mr. Handler. And these are my two associates, Mr. Jeffry Stokes, and Mr. Kenneth Wilson. Mr. Stokes is the founder of the accounting firm of Stokes, Craig and Smith. And Mr. Wilson is a junior partner in that same firm. They are both members in good standing of the bar in the State of New York, as well as certified public accountants. They're here to help me get a handle on just what the price of this establishment ought to be.

"And the fourth gentleman, the young man who stopped off at

the bar, if you haven't yet met him, he is Mr. Conrad O'Donnell, Jr. He said he would be around to answer questions, if we had any. But he really didn't think that he could be of much help in what we're going to do today."

Calibret had not expected Abraham Stern himself to show up. And neither had Jack.

Of course, Jack was not physically onsite. Initially he had thought that he would still be busy winding up the details regarding the two boys and law enforcement. However, he decided at the last minute to drive to Chicago to be available should Randy need him. He and the two boys had just arrived.

However, even if Jack had been able to be present during the audit, he would have absented himself from the event. His lawyer had, in fact, insisted that he not be present.

"We don't need for you to be hurting some rich accountant," Calibret told him. "If you stick around while these guys are here, you're going to be asked questions that you do not want to answer, and you'll probably end up shooting somebody. So make yourself disappear until it's over. As long as this audit is still taking place, find something else to do. And don't answer your phone unless you can identify who's calling."

"I understand," Calibret continued. "You want to know what's going on. That's why I'm wearing this fancy pocket liner."

He then pointed his cell phone at what looked like an ordinary pen.

"Check this out," he said. "This is a real, functioning ballpoint pen. Except, it has a camera built into it. It also has a miniature microphone. So, wherever I go, you can watch what I'm watching, and hear what I'm hearing. Pretty cool, huh? There is a battery pack and cellphone transmitter in the bottom of the pocket protector. So, you can go anyplace in the world, as long as it has cell service, and it will be just as though you're there with me.

"That means you will be able to hear everything the lawyers

and accountants throw at me."

"And if they shoot you," Jack chuckled. "I suppose I'll be forced to testify against them. … Or, maybe against you."

Shortly after Calibret's call ended, Jack received a phone call from Harry Weinstein.

"Well, Jack, how's it going so far?"

"Damn, Harry, you don't waste any time. I'm not in my office today. But, Randy set me up with a little camera and mic, so I can hear and see how the meeting goes. I can even check out the expressions on their faces. They just arrived. Randy has not taken them up to the office yet. So I really don't have much to say about it."

"*Up* to your office? I thought your office was just off the bar."

"It used to be on the main level. But we moved it to the third floor."

"I knew you had a second level. That's where the banquet halls are. But a third floor. What's up there?"

"Right now, just my new offices," Jack said. "It's quite a long story. Someday I'll tell you all about it over a beer. But, for right now, Randy and the lawyer, Stern, are still exchanging pleasantries. The kid is there too. He's drinking at the bar. He'll probably end up on all fours before this day is done."

"The bar's open?"

"No. Not officially. It opens at noon. But the kid serves himself during off hours. The piece of shit is a serious boozer."

"Does he do drugs, too?"

"Connie said his boy drank a lot, and smoked a little weed. But as far as hard drugs—I don't think he's got a habit. At least, his dad never mentioned one to me. His biggest problem is that he's lazy. Never had any sort of paying job. … I know Connie didn't want him hanging around the bar. All he wanted to do is get drunk, play pool, and fight with the regulars. Everyone knew he was Connie's son. So, when he'd get in debt to them, they'd want to collect at the bar. Connie totally banned him for almost a year … right up until he died. Now, since I've offered to buy him out, he's starting to show up again. But we don't let him play pool. Or poker. It's okay if he drinks some beers. I'll spot him that much. But, if he ever starts expecting me to cover his losses, I'll kill him myself."

"I'm surprised you even let him through the doors."

"Yeah. It'll end. Right now, it just doesn't seem the thing to do. To kick him out. … His dad was one of my best friends. It wasn't his fault that the kid turned out like this. Like I said, he's nothing like his father."

"Well, I'll probably check in later. Let me know if anything interesting happens."

"Probably won't be doing that," Jack said. "But I will let you know when it's all over. I think I'll be letting a bunch of people know when this farce is over with."

"Okay, Jack. You do that. And if you need a hand with anything. I still have friends in the city. You know, the kind of friends that can make things happen. If you need anything, just let me know."

"Right," Jack said as he disconnected.

"Damn it all," Jack then mumbled to himself. "I just don't like that guy."

"Where are you taking us?" Abraham Stern asked as they got on the elevator and hit the third floor button. "I thought the office was on the ground floor. Just off the bar."

"That's right. It did *used to be* down by the bar. But, Jack was getting a little cramped down there, and, since he wasn't using the third floor for anything, he decided to move his offices up there. Connie used to rent it out. Years ago he had an apartment on the third floor. But when the old guy who lived there passed away, Connie just locked it up and forgot about it."

"That's interesting," Stern said. "I don't recall seeing anything about a rental unit on the description. That would definitely increase the property's value, I should think."

"It's not been rented out for years. Quite recently Jack had it all cleaned out, and he moved his office up there. Besides, he needed the old office space by the bar for storage. So, it all worked out perfectly. He made use of the empty apartment, and it freed up some additional pantry and storage for the bartender. It made everybody happy."

"I suppose it's okay. We did bring our own printer, so we should be fine, as long as we have power."

"There's power, bathroom, kitchen, and the files you requested. Should be perfect. Jack does want me to lock it up at five. I trust that will be okay with you."

"We'll be out by five. No problem there. Tomorrow, we'd like to get started a little earlier—maybe nine. If that's okay. We'd like to wind it up a little early."

"Nine's fine."

"So, will Mr. Handler be available if we need additional documents?" Mr. Stern asked as they exited the elevator.

"Jack's on some sort of assignment for the week. I really have no knowledge of his whereabouts. But *I'll* be around if you need something. I think you'll find that we've provided all the information you requested. If you can justify additional documents, I'll be happy to accommodate. … When do you anticipate winding this audit up?"

"I think tomorrow. But, technically, this is not an audit. Our only purpose here is to accurately establish the value of the property in question in order to determine a fair and equitable buyout price for our client. That's all this is about."

"Bullshit!" Jack grumbled as he jumped up from the table. "You lying asshole. Your whole mission is to get me killed. You don't give a shit about the kid."

Jack angrily flung the cooling coffee from his cup into the kitchen sink and poured a fresh cup from his coffee maker.

"Can't believe I'm talking to myself," he said, again audibly. He then assumed a sardonic grin and shook his head. "Don't know if I should even be monitoring this charade," he said, this time in silence.

"I'll give you a quick tour of the offices," Calibret said. "And then I'll leave you to your work."

The three men followed Calibret through the door, turned on the light switch, and walked a few steps into the dingy work area, and then stopped.

"The boxes on the tables contain all the files you requested," Calibret announced, struggling to keep a straight face. There is a printer with a couple reams of paper, but if you have your own—"

"Are you kidding me!?" Stern grumbled. "You can't expect us to work out of this shithole! This place is filthy."

"Actually, it's quite clean. Jack brought in a professional cleaning crew to spruce it up for you. Granted, it's a bit Spartan. But it's very clean. If you follow me I'll show you where the bathroom and kitchen are."

"We're not following you anywhere," Stern barked, "because we're not working here. You need to provide us with a reasonable working environment. Not some crappy attic."

"I'm sorry you're not pleased with Jack's office. If you'd prefer, you're welcome to take these file boxes downstairs and work in the bar. It will be a bit noisy, but it's fine if you wish to do your work down there."

"How about a banquet room?" Stern declared. "We'll use it."

"Can't let you do that," Calibret said. "Sorry."

"You sure as hell can. We're *not* going to work up here. It's a filthy hellhole. I don't care who you say cleaned it up. It stinks like an outhouse."

"I'd be happy to let you use one of the banquet halls, but city ordinance permits single use only. If we start using one of the halls as an office we'll have the city come down on us and jerk our permits. … It'll have to be here, or the bar."

"This is just bullshit," Stern complained. "Then, we'll pack up the files and work out of our hotel. That's certainly not convenient for us. But, we're not going to subject ourselves to this shit."

"I'm so sorry you feel that way, Mr. Stern. But these files must not leave the building. That's stipulated in our agreement. You may make copies, but you must not remove the originals. … As I said, if you're unhappy about working out of Jack's office, then you can use the bar. But those are your only two choices."

Stern was furious. He slammed his briefcase down on the nearest table so hard that it slid entirely across the surface and crashed into the back of a folding chair knocking it over backward. Both the chair and Stern's briefcase slammed to the floor.

"I know exactly what you're up to, you sonofabitch," Stern shouted. "You think you can discourage us from doing our investigation. I'm from New York. I've worked in worse places than this, so your punk ass tactic won't work on me. We'll do what we have to do right here. But, you can take this to the bank, not only is Handler's stupid trick not going to discourage us, we will see to it that he receives no breaks. None. He's going to pay for this shit!"

"I hope you are not threatening us, Mr. Stern," Calibret said in a very calm voice. "Is that what you're doing? Because, if it is, then we should terminate our agreement right here and now. I think that a threat would be considered adequate grounds for terminating it. Tell me, are you threatening us?"

Mr. Stern walked over and picked up his briefcase and returned the chair. But he didn't respond to Calibret's question.

"If you'll excuse me for a moment," Calibret said, "I'll use the restroom. And then I'll leave you to your work."

He went into the bathroom and fastened the hook-and-eye latch. He then removed a plastic jar from his jacket pocket and released three dozen cockroaches. Four of them were already dead. At first he considered scraping up the corpses, but decided against it. *What the hell, might as well leave the dead ones for these bas-tards to deal with,* he determined. *A few dead roaches might even be more disgusting than live ones.*

He then flushed the toilet and washed his hands.

Looking into the mirror he began to chuckle. And when he realized that he was not able to put on a serious face he had to look away.

Turning to face the door, he began carrying on a conversation loud enough for only him to hear:

"Stink? I don't smell anything. Maybe it's the disinfectant. Some of those newer ones do have a powerful scent. A dead rat? No. I don't think so. Probably something the cleaning people used. But I don't really smell anything."

Forcing himself to put on a straight face, he opened the door and walked out.

"Here's my card," he said, holding it out for Mr. Stern to take.

Stern just sneered and did not even look at him.

Calibret set the card on the table and said, "If there's nothing else, then I'll be going down to the bar."

No one responded to him.

Downstairs at the bar, Conrad O'Donnell Jr. was racking up the balls on a pool table. He had just granted access to a man who had been pounding on the locked front door.

"I'll break," Conrad said. "That is, if you don't mind. I always like to break first. And it is my table. So we play by my rules. Okay?"

"Sure," the short muscular man said. "I don't mind at all. I'm more of a counterpuncher, anyway. ... So, what are your rules? BCA or APA?"

"I call them Conrad's bar rules. Call your shots. Drop the eight on the break and it's a winner. That's about it."

"Good enough," the man said. "Let's see what you got."

Chapter 44

The Pool Shark

W e should make it interesting, don't you think?" Conrad said. "How about twenty. You can do twenty. Right?"

"Sure," the man agreed. "Twenty is fine."

"Well, then, put your twenty on the table," Conrad said. "By the way, I always like to know whose money I'm taking. You do have a name?"

"Sure," the man said. "My name is Harley."

"No shit," Conrad said. "Just like the motorcycle?"

"Just like."

"Don't tell me your last name is Davidson."

"No such luck. My last name is Johnson. Harley Johnson."

"Okay, Harley. Game on."

Conrad had an unusually good break, for him. Both the eleven and the thirteen dropped. The eight ball rolled near the far right corner pocket, but did not go in.

"I guess that makes me high," he said.

"Guess it does," Harley said. "Nice break."

"Would have been nicer if the eight would've dropped. But I'll take what I can get, when I can get it."

"Ten in the side," Conrad said.

The cue ball grazed the ten ball, but it did not fall into the pocket.

"Shit!" Conrad groaned. "Damn table must be off. That should've dropped. No doubt, the table's off. I'll have to get it fixed. … Just not right now. I gotta take your money first."

"Right," Harley said. "Looks like you might just do that. If I don't start sinking some shots, you'll be taking my money."

Harley walked to the other end of the table and said, "Doesn't look like you left me with much."

Harley was an enigma. He blew into the bar with his Chicago Bears cap, a denim jacket, blue jeans and a blue and orange Soldier Field tee shirt. He was six three with a three-day scruff beard. He was more confident appearing than Conrad would have wanted.

"Just like I planned it," Conrad boasted. "That's how I play the game. If I don't make my shot, at least I set it up so my opponent doesn't have a good one. That's how good players do it."

"Well, that's sure as hell what you did to me. I don't have a decent shot. Not even a half-decent one. … Maybe I'll do this. How about the three in the corner. That might be my best bet."

"You can't hit that," Conrad said. "The eight ball's in the way. That's a sucker shot. I'd recommend against it. But, do what you want. It's just a game. Might as well take the shot. I can use your twenty."

"Three in the corner off the eight."

"Oh, shit! You gotta be kiddin' me. Off the eight? You're playing with fire, my friend."

Harley's shot cracked loudly. The cue ball struck the three firmly and knocked it into the eight ball, just as Harley had called. And then the three ball dropped in the corner pocket, also just as he had called. But his shot had been too firm, and the eight ball continued to slowly roll until it dropped into the side pocket.

"Oh!" Conrad cried as he scooped up the money. "Tough luck, Harley. Looked for a while like you'd made a good shot. But, like I said, it was a sucker shot. Would've been good if you hadn't hit it so hard. Right angle, just too hard.

"You look like you might be a pretty good pool player. How about another game? But this time let's double it. How's forty sound? You can get your money back and then some."

"Sure, why not? But before you break, let me run out to my car and get my own stick. I think I might do better with it."

"Oh. Really? Got your *own* stick? You some kind of hustler?"

"No. Not at all. You saw me play. I'm no hustler. But, like you said, the table might be a little off. I don't know. I just think that I might do better with a stick I'm familiar with. Is that okay? I can use one of the bar's sticks. But I'd prefer my own. If that's okay."

"No problem, Fast Eddie, you go get your special custom stick. I'll just play with one off the rack. And I'll still kick your ass."

"Then you don't mind?"

"No. Go get your own stick. That's fine."

Harley excused himself and left. While he was gone, Conrad walked behind the bar and poured himself a shot of whiskey. He scrunched up his face when he tasted it.

"Damn, I hate that stuff," he said.

He poured the shot back in the bottle and drew himself a draft beer.

Five minutes later Harley returned. Because the bar was not yet officially open, Conrad had to let him back in.

"Wow!" Conrad said. "That sure is one fine looking case. You sure you don't have a machine gun in there? Looks more like a violin case than a pool cue. … Open it up. Let me take a look."

Harley walked over to the table and set it down.

"That's amazing!" Conrad said. "I've never seen a cue stick that fancy. And you've got two of them. How much did they set you back? A lot, I bet."

"I didn't buy the sticks. My father gave them to me when he … when he retired."

"Why two of them? In case one gets broken?"

"One of them is for muscle—like when you break. And the other for finesse."

"You said your dad gave you his sticks when he retired. Retired from what? I can't imagine anyone having a set up like that who wasn't a hustler. Was he a hustler?"

"No. Far from it. My father was a professional billiards player. He was actually ranked in the top ten back in 2002. These were his sticks. ... He didn't think much of straight pool. But he was great with his billiards."

"Ready to play?" Conrad said. "I'm anxious to see if those sticks improve your game. Should I be scared?"

"No. Not scared. But I think using a quality stick does improve my game a little. Probably just because it belonged to my dad. ... Break whenever you're ready. We've each got forty on the table, so do give it your best."

Conrad kept talking as he racked the balls.

"I suppose I'd better play my best from now on, if that stick is as good as you claim. But, you know, I can afford to lose. I'm very rich. I own this bar right now, and I'm selling it ... for millions. I've got an offer. Millions."

Crack.

Conrad did not have as good a break as he did in the first game. Nothing went in.

Harley stepped up and called for the nine ball in the corner pocket, and so it was. The sound of the stick hitting the cue ball was crisp. And the nine dropped right into the corner. The same happened after he called the ten in the corner, and the fifteen in the same corner. In fact, he correctly called and sunk all the high balls—all before Conrad was able to take his second shot.

"You gonna run the table with that fancy stick, aren't you?"

"Pure luck," Harley said. "Sometimes I just get lucky. ... Okay. Eight ball corner."

Taking careful aim, Harley finally pulled the trigger. Unfortunately, he pulled it too hard. The eight ball was in and out before it had a chance to drop. Quickly Harley lifted his hands off the table so as not to obstruct the path of the eight ball. It rolled and rolled, until it slowly tumbled into the opposite corner pocket.

"Can't believe I did that *again*," Harley quipped. "Guess this just isn't my day. I'm done. Thanks for the games."

"You can't quit now. You played a great game. Right up until you didn't. That was just bad karma. I'm sure you'll win the next one. Give it a try."

"I don't have any more money to lose. I've got to be done."

"Let's play for your stick. Both of them, along with that fancy case."

"They're worth a lot of money. I don't think you want to gamble that much."

"How much do I need to put down? You tell me."

Conrad pulled out a hundred dollar bill and laid it down on top of the eighty that was still on the table.

"That's one hundred and eighty dollars. Is that enough?"

"Double it, and it would be close enough."

Conrad said, "Fine. Here's another two Franklins. Does that do it? That would be three hundred and eighty dollars. Against your pool sticks. Does that work for you?"

"Sure. Why not? I'll never be a professional billiards player. And I seldom shoot pool anymore. I'll give it a go for that. I almost won that last game. ... So, kid, do what you do best. Break 'em up."

"Look, you asshole. Don't call me kid. I just beat you two games. Fair and square. And you are playing pool in my bar. So show me some respect. My name is Conrad O'Donnell. I own this piece-of-shit bar. So call me Conrad, or Mr. O'Donnell. But don't call me kid. I ain't your shit-ass goat. That's what they call a goat. Kid. Got it?"

"Sorry about that, Mr. O'Donnell. I meant no offence. Okay?"

"Sure. No problem. But I'd be more comfortable if you just

called me by my first name. Conrad. Nobody ever called my dad Mr. O'Donnell. It was always just Connie. Or Sticky. His friends called him Sticky. So just call me Conrad. Okay?"

"You got it, my friend. Conrad will be it from now on. Now, go ahead—rack 'em and break 'em."

Conrad set the cue ball down just right of center, and pulled the trigger. The break was extensive, but nothing found a pocket.

Obviously disappointed in his shot, Conrad backed away from the table and grumbled, "Your turn, hotshot. See if you can put something in."

Harley took aim on the three ball. "Three in the corner."

Softly he delivered it right where he'd predicted. The same happened to the five, the six, the two and the one. All that remained were the four and the seven.

"I really don't see anything," he said. "I suppose I'll go for the four in the side. Maybe I can at least park the cue ball."

And that's what happened—at least the parking part. He touched the four, but it did not drop. The cue ball ended up against the eight ball on the opposite end of the table.

Conrad did not have a good shot. His best chance was to wrestle the nine ball into the corner. He tried it, but it didn't fall.

Harley was left with a clear angle for the four in the side. It dropped. The seven was straight in for the corner. He made that as well.

"Damn," Harley said. "I can't believe this. All I need to do is sink that stupid eight ball, and I win. Finally!"

"Eight in the corner," he said confidently.

His stick exploded into the cue ball, and it struck the eight, and the eight dropped perfectly in the corner. But he did not cheer his apparent victory. He couldn't. Because, again, the cue ball rolled slowly toward the same corner pocket. It reached the edge. It seemed to hesitate without falling.

When the cue ball seemed to stop, Harley slammed his fist

down on the table.

"At last! I win the game," he boasted.

But the shock of his fist on the table was all it took to loosen the cue ball, and it toppled into the pocket.

"Hah!" Conrad yelled. "Well I'll be damned. Scratching on the eight ball. You, *kid*, lose again. Looks like I got me a couple fancy assed pool cues. … No hard feelings. Right? I won this fair and square. Right?"

"Damn straight," Harley said. "Fair and square. You're the winner."

"You don't mind if we call it quits," Conrad said. "I've got to check up on my lawyer. He's upstairs somewhere, doing some work for me. Stop in again if you ever want to lose some more money. I'll help you out."

"Sure thing," Harley said, reaching out to shake hands with the kid. "You take good care of my dad's billiards sticks. Okay?"

"You can be sure I will. You can let yourself out. The door will lock behind you."

Harley walked toward the door. When he got there, he turned and watched Conrad separate the stick and slide it into the case. He then snapped closed the two latches, and picked the case up by the handle. He held it out in front of him to admire it. However, he abruptly set it back down on the pool table, looked at his hand and quickly walked behind the bar to the sink.

Harley stopped at the door for just a moment to observe young Conrad, and then he smiled and walked away.

Chapter 45

We're Outta Here!

Mr. Stern and the two accountants worked until lunchtime, and then abruptly headed down to the bar. Calibret spotted them as they inquired of the bartender about Conrad Jr. He asked them if they planned to return after lunch, but they did not acknowledge his question.

The bartender explained to the men that the young man had told him that he was not feeling well, and so was going back to his apartment.

"But he says he plans on returning before five."

Mr. Stern expressed his dismay with a shrug of his shoulders and a two palms up hand gesture.

Calibret immediately stood and began walking toward them. "Can I assume you'll be back in the morning?" he then said.

Again, Stern and the two accountants ignored him. They slid past him and headed toward the door.

Calibret turned and followed them for a few steps. He laughed as the door closed behind them.

"Jack," he said. "If you're listening, what do you suppose might have irritated them? The cockroaches, or the dead rat? My money's on the cockroaches."

But Calibret's question was not heard by anyone. Twenty minutes earlier Jack had been summoned to the hospital by Mercier O'Donnell, his late partner's younger brother. Apparently Conrad O'Donnell Jr. had just been admitted into emergency. The cause of his distress had not yet been diagnosed, but the young man's heart seemed to be failing, and he could not breathe properly.

"Jack," Mercier said. "Please meet me down here. The doctors don't know what's going on. It's like he's developed a bad case of the flu. They're even talking like my nephew might be dying. It's crazy! He's barely thirty. Can you please meet me at the hospital?"

Jack dropped everything and caught a taxi.

By the time he reached the hospital, the young man had already slipped into unconsciousness.

"Jack," Mercier said, looking down at his watch. "This is absolutely the most weird thing I have ever seen. The hospital called me a little over an hour ago. Right before I called you. They told me to get down here as quickly as possible—that Conrad had asked for me. I'm his only relative, now that Connie has passed. They said that he had admitted himself an hour earlier, with what looked like flu symptoms. No matter what they did he has progressively grown worse. They don't know what's wrong with him. They asked me if he'd been out of the country recently, or if any of his friends had.

"I told them that the kid and I weren't very close. But that as far as I knew he had been hanging around in Chicago. I don't think he's ever traveled. And, as far as his friends, I don't have any knowledge about that stuff. I know he hangs around the bar drinking beers and shooting pool. But he doesn't have a job. I don't think he has many friends. And he doesn't have a girl as far as I know. I told them all that."

"Did you get a chance to talk to him when you first got here?" Jack asked.

"No. They had him in a room by himself. And they were all wearing what looked like hazmat suits. It's like they had him quarantined … until they figured out what it was exactly that was making him sick. … What do you suppose they think he's got? The plague or something? It's just very weird."

"I would really like to talk to one of his doctors," Jack said as he looked around.

When he spotted two nurses talking he bolted toward them.

"Excuse me, ladies," he said to them. "Could you tell me anything about my good friend, Conrad O'Donnell? He was admitted earlier with something like flu symptoms. Do you have any information about his condition?"

"Are you a relative?" one of the nurses asked.

"Almost," Jack replied. "He's the son of my good friend and business partner. Conrad is like my own son."

"Wait right here," she said. "I think Dr. French will want to talk to you. … Stay right here. Okay?"

"That's why I asked you to come down here," Mercier said. "People always pay attention to you."

A minute later a doctor approached. Every inch of his body was covered. "My name is Dr. William French. I'm treating Conrad O'Donnell. I understand you are a close relative of Mr. O'Donnell. Is that right?"

"Almost," Jack said. "He's a close friend and business partner. We own a bar on the Southside. How is he?"

"When's the last time you saw him?"

"He was in the bar earlier today. But I didn't see him there. I haven't been in yet. How sick is he?"

"He's pretty ill. We're doing some tests right now to determine what exactly it is that is making him so ill. Frankly, whatever it is, it's not good. Nothing we've done so far has helped. If we can't get a handle on it within the next hour, he might not make it."

"Mercier, my friend, and the boy's uncle, said that he looked like he had the flu. Is that right? Has he got the flu?"

"We really don't know what's making him ill. The symptoms

are flu-*like*. But we just don't know yet. ... There is one thing that is particularly puzzling. There is a pimple like sore on the inside of his right hand. Specifically on the upper portion of his middle finger. There appears to be a small puncture wound. ... Do you have any idea what that could be? Did he suffer an injury to that hand recently?"

Jack looked over at Mercier and said, "Do you know about any injury? I don't."

Mercier just shook his head. "No. I don't know anything about that."

Just then one of the other doctors who was treating the boy walked out of the room and called over, "Dr. French. Would you step back in here? We need to consult."

"Excuse me," the doctor said as he walked back toward the room where Conrad was being treated.

Two minutes later Dr. French stepped back out of the room. He looked around until he saw Jack and Mercier, and then he walked over to them.

"I'm very sorry," he said softly. "I'm afraid we lost him."

Mercier's shoulders dropped. Tears began forming in his eyes. Jack put his arm around the man to steady him.

"I am so very sorry that we could not help him."

"Still not certain what it was that made him so sick?"

"Not yet. It happened so fast. We should know more as soon as we get the results back on our tests. And, of course, there will be an autopsy. That will undoubtedly tell us what was going on. But, right now, we're not sure about what we're dealing with. ... I am very sorry for your loss. But I do need to get back. We've got to get to the bottom of this. Right now we see no reason to think that we're dealing with a communicable disease. But we don't know. If you learn anything about that irritation on his right hand please contact us immediately. It had become progressively worse right up until the man passed away. We think that it might be significant. Let us know if you find out anything about it. Okay?"

After the doctor walked away, Jack suggested to Mercier that they head down to the coffee shop. "Are you up to it?" he asked. "There's nothing more we can do up here."

"Yeah, sure. I think I need to talk to someone. I never expected anything like this to happen. ... Jack, in less than two months I've lost my entire family. I was not particularly close to the boy, but Connie and his son are ... they were my only family. As far as I know, I'm the last surviving member of the O'Donnell clan. I'm it."

Jack pondered his words as they walked to the coffee shop. He recalled the wording used in his partner's will. It seemed a little awkward to Jack at the time—probably because Connie had penned it himself. To the best of Jack's memory, it read something like this: "In the event of my death, if my son, Conrad O'Donnell Jr., is living, he will inherit all of my possessions. This would include, but not be limited to, my share of the bar (Sticky's). If, however, at the time of my death, my son Conrad Jr. is not living, my brother Mercier O'Donnell should inherit everything.

"Should Conrad Jr. inherit my possessions, and then pass away, my share of the bar shall pass to my brother Mercier. If both Mercier and Conrad pass away, my share of the bar shall in all cases revert to my partner, Jack Handler, or his heirs.

"If Mercier or Conrad choose to sell their interest in the bar to Jack Handler, they may do so. But, under no circumstance might my share be transferred to any party other than Jack."

"That, in a nutshell, is it," Jack said to himself. "Connie did not want his share of the bar to be sold to a stranger. That's why he made provisions for it ultimately to revert to me. That means Mercier, here, is my new partner. ... What a truly weird chain of events."

The two men chose a small booth toward the rear of the shop.

"Well," Jack said to Mercier once they were seated, "what would my new partner like to eat with his coffee?"

Mercier smiled and said, "Yeah, right. I think I'll have a bagel. I'd really like a donut, but the donuts here are pretty bad."

"Then bagels it is. I'll have the same. I think we should order donuts too. Maybe they got some decent ones in today. ... By the way, partner, have you ever read Connie's will?"

"Hell no. I never expected him to kick the bucket. It was all a huge surprise to me. And now the kid. ... What's this shit about your calling me your partner? What's that all about?"

"You *are* my new partner at Sticky's. Hope you like to tend bar. How about it? Can you make a martini?"

"You're not shittin' me, are you? Did I inherit the bar? Or, Connie's share of it? Is that what has happened?"

"The lawyer will have to make the call, but I'm positive that's what Connie's convoluted wording calls for."

"Well, I'll be damned. Are you sure?"

"Yeah. I'm sure. Like I said, the lawyer will make the call. Or, rather a judge will, if it gets challenged. But it was pretty cut and dry. And there's no one around who's going to challenge it. ... The kid was first in the line of succession, and then you.

"The way he wrote it up, neither you nor his son can transfer the ownership of his share to anyone but me. But, as long as you want to own it with me, it's yours. ... Like I said, can my new partner mix a martini? If not, then I'll have to teach you."

"What was this business about you buying the kid out? I never did quite understand that."

"I think his son wanted to cash out quickly. He doesn't really like working. And so he thought he could collect a little cash, and not be stuck working in the bar."

"Sounds like the kid," Mercier said. "He was one lazy boy. Always was. And Connie knew it. He knew the kid hated working. What a disappointment. And now he's dead. ... I never had kids. Don't know what I'd of done if I would have had a son like that one. All very sad.

"But, yes, I can bartend. Back in the early days, when Connie first opened the bar, I used to work with him. I had a lot of fun working bar. And then, when I started driving taxi, I didn't have the time, or the energy."

"I was just kidding you," Jack said. "You wouldn't have to tend bar. Connie didn't do much bartending the last few years. More than anything he just mingled with the clientele. The customers loved him. He was quite a guy."

Mercier just sat silently for a few long moments. And then he said, "You know, I really wouldn't mind doing what he did. We were a lot alike, you know—Connie and me. He was a little more outgoing. But the customers used to tell me that they liked to come to Sticky's just so they could talk to me."

"Man," Jack said. "If you could start stopping in, it would help take the edge off the loss they are sensing with Connie's death. I'd really like to see you do that, if it's something you'd want to do."

"Yeah, sure, I'll give it a try."

Both men sat silently for several minutes. Jack was thinking about what the doctor had said regarding the pimple on the kid's hand. And, Mercier was wondering if anyone got the license plate number of the Mack truck that had just hit him.

Finally, Jack broke the silence.

"You're going to have to make the arrangements for the kid's funeral. Are you up to it?"

"Yeah, I can handle it. I just buried his father. So I know exactly what I'm doing. You could say that I'm well practiced at the art of death and burial. There's a plot right beside Connie. It already has a headstone with my name on it. And there's another one on the other side of Connie's wife. It's for Conrad O'Donnell Jr. All I have to do is put a date on it. … That's all there'll ever be of the O'Donnells. It'll be the end of our line."

Jack reached over and gripped Mercier's bicep.

"Partner," Jack said. "Your brother was one of the best friends a man ever had. And he always spoke highly of you. He truly loved you. I am really looking forward to working with you. It'll be almost like working with your brother. We had some great times. You and I will have some great times too."

Jack then stood up and prepared to leave.

"We've got some great help in place at Sticky's. So don't think you have to dig in and start working. Just do what you have to do, and when you feel the time is right, we'll work out the details.

"I'll make sure you get on the payroll as of today. But, you take your time. You've been through a lot."

Mercier looked up at Jack. His eyes were red and glazed, and his mustache had grown moist.

"Thanks, Jack," he said snatching a napkin and wiping his nose. "But I'd really like to jump right in. I need a diversion."

Jack knew that not another word was necessary. Mercier was very much like his older brother. And with Conrad out of the picture, that would mark the end of the audit. Mercier would not be open to any outside interference. Allison had lost her leverage. And all of Jack's clients, including Harry Weinstein, could now sleep more comfortably.

Chapter 46

Lawrence Reports

Where are you right now?" Carl asked.

"Picking glass out of my face. That sonofabitch somehow came back to life. I've never hit a man that hard and had him live."

"Well, now you know what you're dealin' with. He's some kinda superman. He took out three of our best last year ... all by himself."

"I know I screwed this up," Lawrence apologized. "But, I'll make it right. I'll get him, and then I'll take care of his boss."

"I know you will. ... What happened, anyway?"

"I wasn't counting on his daughter. He had his daughter with him. She interrupted me right after I nailed the guy. ... But, that's not a good excuse. I thought I'd killed him, so I didn't slice his throat like I should have. He was just tougher than I expected. My bad. I'll fix it."

"At this point it's okay to finish him off in any way you see fit. If you decide to blow up his car—go for it. Use whatever means you choose. Just get him gone. ... And if the kid gets in the way, take her out too. ... I realize that I messed this up by not knowing about the kid. So, I'll take some of the blame here. But, now you know. So get the contract done. And do a better job this time. Got it?"

"Yes, boss."

"I would have preferred that it looked like a random killing—like a robbery gone bad. But that option is now off the table. So, just kill the bastards ... both of them."

"Yes, boss. I will take care of it. ... Right away."

"I'm sure you will. But, it might be wise to lay low for a little while. He's gonna be looking for you to come after him right now. So, maybe you'd do better to bide your time, let him start to relax, maybe convince himself that he wasn't the target after all, and then strike. ... That's how I'd do it."

Lawrence was a little surprised that Carl hadn't ripped him a new one. That was the reaction he'd expected. *I think that Carl might be right,* he thought. *This Henry guy might not be sure what this is all about. Given a little time, he might start thinking that it actually was just a robbery. Makes sense. I did take his money. So he really doesn't know. ... I gotta torch this car and get me a new set of wheels.*

And that's what he did.

The first thing he did was to pull into a motel along US-131 North and he there exchanged the plates from his car with one in the parking lot. And then he drove north to another motel. There he managed to jump start an older but well-kept Chevrolet Malibu. But, before he drove it off, he replaced the plates that were on it with the ones he had stolen earlier. He then drove the Toyota with the shattered driver's side window to the far end of the parking lot, cut the fuel line, and ignited the fuel beneath it.

He reasoned that the best way, at this point, to ensure that Henry and Jack Handler would be at the same place at the same time would be to relocate himself closer to where his targets resided—Sugar Island.

Need to do something about this face, he decided. *Got to get the blood off. And pick some of this glass out. Damn lucky I didn't get any of it stuck in my eyes. Damn lucky. But the blood on my neck, and on my shirt. If I get stopped, it'll be hard to explain. Gotta hit a rest stop and see what I'm dealing with.*

"I wonder if there might be some clothes I could wear in the back seat?" he asked himself out loud. He did recall that there was a large suitcase.

He was just south of Grand Rapids on US-131 when he spotted a safe place to stop—a McDonalds restaurant. *This'll do just fine,* he reasoned.

After he'd parked he reached back and unzipped the gray fabric suitcase. It was a cheap looking oversize bag—the type the air carriers always overcharge for stowing.

"Would you look at that," he said, obviously quite pleased with his find. "They all look like they're extra-large. A little big for me, but they'll work just fine."

He immediately stripped his shirt off and put on one of the less offensive looking shirts that he had pulled from the bag.

Looking around the car a little more closely, he found an adjustable Detroit Tigers baseball cap lying on the floor in the back. He put it on and looked at himself in the visor mirror.

That works, he figured. *Could stand to get my faced cleaned up a bit, but this will at least get me into the toilet without drawing attention.*

His next order of business was to make a stop at a twenty-four-hour Walmart Superstore. There he bought a box of bandages, some sterile gauze, and a bottle of hydrogen peroxide.

He then picked up a small can of spray of gray primer paint.

After he'd paid for his shopping, he returned to the car he'd stolen. Popping the cap off the paint, he sprayed the area where the trunk closed, and then followed the line between the trunk and the two rear quarter panels.

This car is sure to be reported as stolen, he figured, *but the car the owner will be describing won't look much like the one I'm driving.*

He then sprayed primer paint at various locations on the side of the car, such as along the edge of the fenders—places commonly found to rust out.

He tossed the near empty paint can on the floor in the back of the car, and then quickly blotted the spots on his face that had been cut by the glass when Henry delivered his flying kangaroo kick.

Lawrence found that all of his injuries were superficial except for a rather deep laceration just above his left ear. So he paid special attention to cleaning it up.

"At least the cap will cover that cut," he told himself. "Once it totally stops bleeding, it will not be noticeable at all. … And, as for you assholes—Henry and Handler, you're dead men already. You just don't know it yet."

Chapter 47

Henry on Jack's Mind

As soon as he had the opportunity, Jack called Henry.

"What are you up to?" Jack asked. He did not want to pry into Henry's private life, but he wanted to get a handle on how his friend was dealing with the robbery, and the attack on his daughter.

He knew that Henry would not be satisfied until he caught and punished his attacker, but he was also aware that his friend did not want Jack to interfere—the man who Tasered Lily, and nearly killed him, would be made to pay for what he had done. But Henry was insistent that it all be carried out by his own hand.

Jack, however, was equally convinced that he was in a better position to pull it off than was Henry. Therefore, Jack had to pursue the matter in a substantially more subtle manner than was his custom.

"Grace, Lily's aunt, drove up from Missouri and picked up Lily earlier today. They're already halfway back by now. And my doctor said that I would be released as early as tomorrow morning. So, it's all good news."

"And then what?" Jack asked.

"What do you mean?" Henry asked. "Where am I headed

when I get out?"

"Right. Are you headed back home? Or what?"

"Yeah. I suppose. ... Have you got a project for me?"

"Maybe. I'm heading back to the resort later today. I've got the two boys with me."

"That's terrific," Henry said. "Are they going to be able to stay with you at the resort? Or is that just a temporary arrangement?"

"It's still up in the air. The sheriff no longer suspects them in the killings. So that's not a problem. But, as far as CPS is concerned, I'm not sure what to expect. That's why I was wondering about your plans. I might need some help when I get them up there. ... For sure I'm not going to voluntarily surrender them without an argument, but I'm not about to buck the system, either. I could lose them for good."

"And you think I might be able to help out?"

"Power in numbers, you know. I'd just feel more comfortable having you around when I'm dealing with it. There's still the matter of finding out how that sonofabitch found out that the boys were on the freighter. Someone volunteered that information. I'd like to know who it was, because it could present us with a security problem down the road ... if there's someone out there who has sinister motives as far as my boys are concerned.

"And then, there's the matter of all that money."

"Money? What money?" Henry asked.

"The loot that Walter Jon Kenny came after. I think it's still somewhere on Sugar Island. And it's a bunch—maybe as much as several million."

"And you suspect that it's hidden on Sugar Island?"

"That would make the most sense," Jack replied. "The brother had killing me and the boys in mind when he pursued us into Canada. And then he intended to go back to Sugar Island for the cash, after the three of us were dead. As I understand it from what the brother told me, that's what Walter Jon Kenny had in mind as well.

"I think that once we figure out who ratted the boys out, we'll know where the money is located as well."

"Tell me," Henry said. "Is there any chance that the guy who attacked me, that he might somehow be connected with this Kenny character?"

"None," Jack replied without hesitation. "Your guy, whoever he is, I'm sure never met Kenny, or even heard of him. ... But, that is not to say that your guy targeted you merely by chance."

"Okay," Henry said in a slow and deliberate fashion. "Then, robbery was not the motive. Is that what you're suggesting?"

"I don't think it was the *principal* motive. I think your unsub wanted it to look like a robbery. ... And, I think that he has done this before—attacked and robbed men who were taking a leak in a public restroom. Think about it. It's a good plan. When a man walks up to a urinal while he is driving cross country, he has one thing on his mind—relieving himself as quickly as possible. His back is turned, so he has no idea as to who might be approaching from the rear. And, his face is only inches away from some very hard objects. I can't think of a more vulnerable position that a man could be in."

"You're right," Henry agreed. "I always use a stall for that very reason. This one time I didn't. Lily was right outside the door, and I wanted to be close enough to hear her if there were to be a problem. ... And, that's all it took. I totally get it.

"But, what makes you think that there was more to it than just a robbery? He got five hundred dollars from me. That's a pretty good haul."

"I don't doubt that this guy has done this before," Jack said. "And those times robbery might have been the driving force. That will be one of things we will be checking on. But, in this instance, it looks to me like he had something else in mind for you. Other than simply robbing you.

"For instance, if robbery was his only motive, he would have most likely just knocked you out, lifted your cash, and then split as quickly as he could. But he didn't do that. He dragged you into a stall, secured your hands to the plumbing, gagged you, and then almost surgically stuck you with his knife. One single stab wound to the gut.

"It looks almost exactly like a prison hit. Except in lockup, he would have used a shiv with a notched handle, so that it would break off inside the body where you would be unable to pull it out and stop the bleeding. ... The only thing that saved you, Henry, is that when he removed the blade, your wound closed up enough so that you didn't bleed out internally. I think that was a prison-style hit that just didn't work so well using outside technology. You're just lucky. If he'd used a sharpened toothbrush you'd be dead."

"Damn it, Jack. The way you explain it. I think you just might be right. ... And, if you are, if this guy was trying to kill me, then, who would he be working for? For himself, do you think?"

"We'll know more about the *whys*, once we figure out *who* he is. Roger's going to have to help us with that. Once we get a fix on exactly who this guy is, and where he did his time, then we'll be in a better position to trace him back to his associates.

"His prison tats, especially the spider web on his elbow, and the Neo-Nazi tat, that already tells us a lot. ... I think it was a contracted hit. And, I would even go so far as to suspect it relates to your having beat up those three guys who were trying to kill me. They were all members of the Aryan Alliance. And one of them ended up dying. I think the attempt on you was payback. They've got a reputation to protect."

"Then they aren't finished with me, are they?"

Jack did not immediately respond to Henry's question. But, finally, he said, "That, my friend, I would characterize as an unpleasant, but astute observation. ... I'd say that what you did embarrassed the organization. They can't be very happy that I'm still walking around, either. … No other realistic way to look at it, in my opinion. Someone with connections contracted the original hit on me. You can be sure they haven't gone away. They still want me dead. And the guy who took the contract on you, he has to honor it. Even though he failed on his first attempt. … We're going to have to go after the head of this snake. Otherwise, they will eventually get both of us."

Chapter 48

Henry to be released

Find out anything about my *buddy*?" Henry asked. "Oh. And by the way. It looks like I will be released tomorrow morning. They've been waiting to see if I was going to develop any kind of infection from the stab wound. And, so far, it looks clean. Strange how it missed everything. ... And there's no temperature. So no infection. Might not happen in the morning, but I'm pushing for it. ... So. I'm just wondering if you and Roger came up with anything?"

"According to what Roger found out," Jack said, "No one seems to recall anyone exactly fitting your description. At least, not closely enough to warrant any exhaustive search. The Louisiana system has engaged in a boxing program, but your guy, the way he threw that elbow, sounds more like a street fighter, or maybe someone with MMA experience. ... But, Roger was able to put together a list of candidates. And, when we couple the names on that list with recent releases, we're left with only a few who stand out.

"Now, that is *not* to say that the guy we're looking for *has* to have got out only a short time ago, but it seemed logical to both Roger and me that our unsub has not been on the outside for very long. Fresh releases are often easily recruited for jobs like this.

"So, Roger and I both like one guy in particular. He's damn near crazy. Had the reputation of an enforcer in the system. The Missouri system. No professional boxing experience, but he was preoccupied with fighting. Sparred every day. Was known to have calcified both of his elbows by slamming them into the concrete walls of his cell. For hours at a time. He was suspected of killing half a dozen inmates while serving out his sentence. He did a total of twenty-three years. No early release. ... And, most telling of all, he seems to have dropped off the edge of the earth almost immediately after release."

"Really?" Henry said. "He must be living under a different name. That kind of stuff requires help. He's got to have some major connections on the outside."

"Exactly," Jack agreed. "And with his Aryan Alliance affiliation, we can assume that they were the ones who arranged everything for him."

"What's his name?"

"Raymond Lee Munson. That was the name he used right up to the day he was released. After that—there's absolutely nothing. We have to assume he has acquired a new identity."

"What did he go in for—originally?"

"He was convicted for beating up the star quarterback at his high school."

"So, what was he? Seventeen? Eighteen?"

"He was eighteen when the judge sentenced him. Could have been out in three, but beat a man to death inside. He got a twenty-year sentence for that."

"So, that would make him how old?" Henry asked. "Pushing forty?"

"He was forty-one when he walked out the doors of Potosi Correctional Center."

"Potosi!" Henry said. "Holy shit! I thought only lifers got sent there."

"That's about it. But our guy made the cut. He created such a reputation for himself, he was deemed a menace, and finished out his sentence at Potosi."

"That sounds about right. Aryan Alliance, you say. Then he was a skinhead?"

"Right."

"Well, the only good look I got of him was when I was kicking the window out of his car. But he sounds just about right. Any idea how we can go about finding him?"

"Roger seems to think, and I would agree with him, that anyone doing his time in the Missouri system, would most likely settle down somewhere in the general vicinity. If not in Missouri, then in one of the surrounding states.

"How active is the Aryan Alliance down there?"

"It's all over. But my guess is that if he got a new identity, chances are that he would not be living in Missouri. Might be too easily identified."

"Whoever he might have hooked up with on the outside … that's what we'd like to figure out. Someone helped him out with a job, place to live, and, of course, almost certainly obtained a new identity for him. He probably knew someone of importance on the inside. Most prisoners at Potosi are lifers with no possibility of parole, or are on death row—they have a very large contingent of inmates awaiting execution. Some, like Munson, are just really bad actors who get themselves sent to Potosi because they can be dealt with best in a maximum security prison.

"It's possible that he never actually met his handler—that someone of significance on the outside simply heard about him through the Alliance, and sought him out for his special talents.

"However, we are running down some names that we've been able to tie to former inmates through fingerprints. These would be people that Munson knew personally—other former inmates of the Missouri Department of Corrections."

"Any that stand out?" Henry asked.

"Like I said, there are a few we're following up on. But, there is one in particular. A fellow by the name of Carl Milton. Currently we've learned, that he goes by the name of KJ Kuiper. Lives in Little Rock."

"And so, how does Munson know him?"

"Milton slash Kuiper was serving a life sentence at Potosi—rape and murder. A bit of a sad story. He was suspected in the killing of another inmate at Potosi, but since he was already serving a life sentence without the possibility of parole, the case he was suspected of on the inside was not pursued as thoroughly as it might have been. At least, that's the story Roger tells. At any rate, his lawyer managed to get his original conviction overturned on a technicality, and four years ago he walked out. Doesn't often happen, but in this instance, it did.

"And, much like in Munson's case, Milton dropped out of sight. Completely. Until he was picked up driving a car with a questionable registration. When he was fingerprinted, his identity came back as Carl Milton. Since that time the FBI has had him on their radar. ... He's the fellow Roger and I like in this. He has close connections with the Aryan Alliance."

"With his conviction being totally overturned," Henry added, "he's not on parole, so he has no problem associating with known felons."

"Exactly."

"Can we connect him with Munson?"

"Not so far. At least not on the outside. If we can come up with the name that Munson is currently using, we might then be able to tie him to Kuiper. But nothing so far."

"How do I find this Kuiper guy—Carl Milton?"

"You don't want to do that," Jack advised. "If Kuiper ever learned that we were on to him, he'd have Munson killed, and he'd award the contract on you to someone we don't know anything about. Better the devil we know than the one we don't."

"So," Henry asked, "How do you propose we proceed?"

"As soon as they release you," Jack said, "I'd like to have you head back to Sugar Island. ... If Roger is right, this Munson guy won't put it off. He's not been out of prison very long, so he's going to want to impress his boss. Kuiper can't be very happy about the failed attempt on you, so Munson will most likely follow you to the resort, and there seek to finish the job.

"Kuiper might like that scenario, because I'll be there as well, and I'm sure I'm part of the deal—*two for the price of one.*"

"And you're gonna have the boys at the resort?" Henry asked. "How's that gonna go over with CPS?"

"Like they say, we're just going to have to play the cards we're dealt. ... The boys will be a lot better off if we can put an end to this shit. Not sure we can do it, or how to best approach it. Not yet, at least. But we're going to have to give it our best shot."

"Well, if they let me, I'll leave for the U.P. in the morning."

Chapter 49

Battle Lines Drawn

Sitting in his office in Little Rock, and talking to Lawrence Christian, was Carl Milton.

"Lawrence. I want you to be ready. Our guy is checking out in the morning. After his doctor makes his rounds. Not a for sure thing, but my sources indicate that most likely he will be released. When he does, I'll let you know."

"Should I hit him as he leaves?" Lawrence asked

"No. You should follow at a distance. I'll tell you where he's at. And which way he's headed. I have a tracker on his vehicle, so there'll be no need to be glued to him. ... Chances are he will be going back to the U.P. If so, that will give us a shot at both him and his boss."

* * *

"Jack," Roger said. "You'll find this interesting. Someone, quite probably KJ Kuiper, AKA Carl Milton, has placed a tracking device on Henry's car. We're able to monitor it as well. When does he get out of the hospital?"

"He might be released in the morning," Jack replied. "Anything specific as to why you suspect Milton?"

"The tracking device that was used is a simple cell-based product. You can buy them over the internet. I have no good reason to suspect Milton, though. I'm just suggesting that the tracking device is nothing sophisticated."

"That's good information," Jack said. "But it will make locating the unsub more difficult, because he could just sit back and wait until Henry gets to wherever he's going. And then attack. Is there any chance that we could trace the cell at the receiving end?"

"Not that easy. The way that system works is that it dumps its info into a monitor at a neutral location. One monitor can service hundreds of devices. And then when a person wants to access the data, he calls in to the monitoring station. We would have no way of detecting which set of data any individual party was wishing to download. ... When Henry leaves, where is he headed?"

"Sugar Island. To the resort."

"That's what I suspected. We won't know where to expect the next attempt. Because that tracking device can be monitored from anywhere. I'm here in New York, and I'm logged on. Milton is in Little Rock, and we don't know where Munson is right now. Or, even if it is actually Munson that we're looking for. We could be wrong about all of it. You'll just need to be ready all the time. You *and* Henry."

* * *

"Here you go, Henry," Jack said as he slid a copy of the local Sault Ste. Marie newspaper in front of his friend. "What do you make of this?"

It was Monday night, and the two men were having a beer at their favorite bar in Sault Ste. Marie, MI.

Henry stared blankly at the obituary page, not quite understanding what Jack had intended.

"Right there," Jack said as he pointed to a specific article. "Capt. George Geraldson's obit. Read it. Let me know what you think."

Henry then focused in on that obituary:

Capt. Geraldson, George R. "Cap" of Sugar Island (in Michigan's Upper Peninsula) passed away unexpectedly at his home on Tuesday night. Capt. Geraldson was born December 24, 1948 in Chicago IL. The only child of George and Carol (Owen) Geraldson, Cap served his country as an Army Ranger during the Viet Nam War. After he left the service in 1983, he studied at Loyola

University receiving a BA degree in 1987. From 1987 until he retired in 2007, Cap Geraldson worked in law enforcement for the City of Chicago, retiring as a captain of detectives, homicide division. Immediately after leaving the Chicago Police Department, he busied himself working as a private investigator in Chicago. In 2014 Cap bought a house on Sugar Island, and from time to time assisted his life-long friend, Jack Handler, who is also a private investigator. Cap enjoyed fishing and hunting, but working on difficult investigations was where he always found the most enjoyment. He married Shirley Holt (Caramel) in 1972. The couple had one child, a son (George III.), who was killed in 2012 serving his country in Afghanistan as an Army Ranger. His wife Shirley passed away in 2013 after a long bout with cancer. Funeral arrangements are being overseen by his life-long friend, Jack Handler. Handler will receive Cap's friends on Thursday, 4:00 - 7:00 P.M. at the Sugar Island Resort. Internment will take place immediately afterwards at Mission Hill Cemetery in Brimley, MI. Memorial contributions to St Jude Children's Research Hospital will be appreciated.

"Okay, Jack," Henry said, "I'm not quite sure what you want from me. Of course, I'm very sorry for your loss. That goes without saying. Obviously, he was a good friend of yours. But, I'm really surprised that you never introduced us. Sounds like a guy I'd like to have met."

"Sounds like I guy I'd liked to have met too," Jack chuckled, and then ordered another beer.

Henry slid back on his chair a little, crossed his arms and stared at Jack.

"What exactly does *that* mean?" Henry asked. "This article makes it look like you two were great buddies. Those years in Chicago, those were the same years you worked homicide there. Isn't that right?"

"Those were the years I worked homicide, all right. Except, Cap here, he just wasn't there. In fact, he wasn't anywhere. ... Cap never existed."

"Who the hell is he, then?" Henry asked.

Jack did not immediately respond. Instead, he buried his grin and stared into his beer.

"Oh, shit!" Henry said. "I totally get what you're doing. You're baiting those guys who are targeting us. Right? Isn't that what you're doing?"

"Think it will work?" Jack asked. "*I* think it just might."

"Are you telling me that this Cap, this supposed *best friend* of yours, never existed? How'd you get the paper to print that? Doesn't that violate some law?"

"I've got friends in the press. And mistakes are published every day. ... I suppose we'll have to issue a retraction in a couple of days, or an apology. But, by then, maybe we'll have got this whole thing sorted out."

"How are you planning to pull this off?" Henry asked. "If we have a crowd, either at the resort, or at the cemetery, how will we deal with that?"

"The only people who know this guy are you and me. He has no living family. So, no one in the area could possibly have known him. Hell, this guy never existed. ... Now, as far as the attack taking place *at* the resort, I don't think that's likely. At least, I wouldn't plan a hit where the only means of escape would be on a slow-moving ferryboat. Wouldn't make sense.

"No, the only way to pull off a kill like this, under these circumstances, would be to set the stage at the burial. That's where I'd do it. Mission Hill is isolated late afternoon and evening. We shouldn't have any company. Since I'm in charge of the proceedings, I will have to be there. And, it would be only natural to expect you—my *other* best friend—to be there as well. If these guys take the bait, they will make their move at the cemetery."

"How do we go about controlling the battlefield?" Henry asked. "If we are exposed, and we will be, what's to stop them from simply picking us off with a sniper rifle?"

"I know what you mean," Jack said. "We'll have to cover all contingencies. I've actually opened the ground already. A friend of mine owns several plots at the cemetery. And Mission Hill allows you to open and close a grave yourself. ... Tomorrow. Tomorrow, we'll have to get started early. I do have a plan, and in the end, I think you'll like it. But it'll be easier to show you than it would be to describe it. ... One more beer, and then we'll head back and get a good night's sleep."

Mission Hill Cemetery is exceptional, as far as Native American cemeteries go. Located atop a large Bay Mills hill, it serves as the final resting place for over four hundred and fifty souls, including the seventeen sailors who lost their lives on board the SS Myron, a wooden freighter that went down in a storm near Whitefish Point in 1919.

Due to its substantial elevation, the view from the cemetery to the north is flat out breathtaking as it provides a spectacular view overlooking Spectacle Lake in the foreground, framed from behind by Lake Superior and Canada.

There were several reasons why Jack chose Mission Hill Cemetery for his trap, the main one being that it was substantially isolated, particularly from the boys and their Sugar Island residence. *No matter what route they choose to get to Mission Hill,* Jack determined, *it will take those skinheads over an hour to drive from Sugar Island to the cemetery. Odds are overwhelming that they will want to scout out the area in advance in order to obtain an optimal position, and then stage an ambush.*

There are only two practical ways to get to Mission Hill Cemetery—that is, of course, if you are willing to discount the use of a helicopter. And Jack was. That left West Lakeshore Drive, either from the east by turning onto West Tower Road at Bay Mills, or from the west from Dollar Settlement. The west approach would be less direct and would involve a long drive on dirt roads.

The most logical route for a person arriving from Sugar Island would be from the east. The problem with that approach would be a substantial stretch of single-lane pavement, rising in elevation at a precipitous rate for over a quarter of a mile. That stretch of the road is so narrow that it is virtually impossible to squeeze past an oncoming vehicle. In other words, it would make a perfect place to stage an ambush.

If they were to opt for that strategy, Jack was thinking, *they would position observers to lay in wait, and then when we approached the incline they would pull in ahead of us. They would have two gunmen stationed in the woods on the elevated side. As they reached the point of attack, the lead car would suddenly stop, and the attack would commence from the shooters in the woods.*

This would provide a near perfect point for an ambush—it would be virtually impossible to defend against.

However, that approach would not account for the possibility that Jack and Henry just might approach from the west—on West Tower Road from Dollar Settlement.

"They're going to have to assure themselves that we are opting for an entry from Bay Mills," Jack said. "That means they will tail the vehicle bringing Cap's "body" from Sugar Island. They would need to be convinced that the approach would be from Bay Mills. They would be able to conclude that once the vehicle transporting the body turned off M-28 onto M-221 toward Brimley Road. That's where they would position the spotter. And then, once we turn toward Brimley, the spotter will fall in behind us and provide updates to the skinheads.

"However, were I to continue west on 28 past 221, they would know that I was trying to avoid the one-lane incline by taking the long route and coming in from Dollar Settlement. In that case, they would adapt an alternative approach—such as hitting us at the gravesite itself. That could get messy."

Chapter 50

Mission Hill Funeral

When the time for the funeral arrived, Jack and Henry walked out of the Sugar Island Resort at exactly seven P.M.

"What is this?" Henry chuckled. "Where in the hell did you find this ... thing?"

Henry was stating his astonishment with what Jack had waiting for them. It was a custom built Rolls-Royce Phantom Hearse B12. The vehicle, which was recently constructed in Europe, measured a whopping two hundred and seventy-six inches.

"What's the big deal?" Jack said through his smile. "Don't you think my old buddy Cap deserves nothing but the best?"

"Will this thing even make it up that hill at Mission Point?" Henry asked. "This is the biggest car I have ever seen."

"Power's no issue," Jack replied. "It's got a Rolls-Royce 6.75-liter V12 engine. But let's hope we don't have to go that far."

"I thought we'd be driving up there in your Tahoe. Why the big fancy car?"

"Safety glass," Jack said. "The windows can withstand a high-velocity .223. And so can the entire body. It was put together for a friend of mine—a Saudi prince. He asked me to test it out ... to make sure it'll do the job for him."

"Does the prince have any idea what might happen to it today?"

"He asked me to test it. What better way than with live ammo? But I don't intend to keep it very long. We should be done with it by the end of this day. Hopefully without any scratches, dents or dings. Old Cap's budget wouldn't cover much in the way of repairs. ... So, check your shoes before you get in."

The ferry ride back to the mainland was uneventful. In fact, the entire trip went as planned, right up until they reached the intersection of M-28 and Brimley Road—M-221.

"Did you spot that car?" Henry asked.

"Sure did. Two men. I'm pretty sure there were only two of them. I didn't want to stare, but that's how it appeared to me. What did you see?"

"There were two—just as we anticipated. ... Did they fall in behind us?"

"Sure did. Again, no surprise."

Five minutes later they reached West Lakeshore Drive at Brimley.

"Still behind us?" Henry asked.

"Absolutely," Jack said. "They are definitely our guys. I'd doubt that either one of them is Milton or Munson. But I'm pretty sure they're skinheads. ... We'll see if they fall in behind us at West Lakeshore. If they do, then that will tell us that they probably do not have an alternate tail vehicle. That being the case, we'll likely be dealing with a minimum of five individuals. Two in the car tailing us. Two lying in wait on the hill. And one in the lead vehicle. Could be more, but I think we can count on at least five—"

At that point Jack was interrupted by his cell phone.

"Kate. You in position?"

"I am. And so are they."

"What are we looking at?"

"Three that I know of. At least that's all I've seen. You've probably picked up a tail by now. What's your 10-20?"

"We're just turning onto West Lakeshore, at Brimley. That

would make us about six miles out. Eight minutes, twelve minutes at most. … And, yes, we do have a tail with at least two occupants. Describe the lay of the land."

"We've got a single vehicle—late model Silverado Crew Cab— at the bottom of the incline, but they've pulled it off to the side. I've seen three subjects with that vehicle. One of them looks like your main suspect, Carl Milton. All three have shaved heads … and ample tats. I expect that they will wait until they hear from your tail car, and then they will take up positions … probably a little further up the incline. It would be impossible to get around them if they stop even close to the center of the road. You'll have the woods to the left, and the sharp drop off to the right. Be no place to go. The tail pulling in behind you would block your escape. You'd be sitting ducks."

"It's a good plan," Jack said. "But ours is better. Let me know as soon as—"

"There they go," Kate interrupted. "All three of them got in the truck and they are preparing to head up the incline. They're just holding that position right now. Probably waiting until you get a little closer. … Okay—they're on the move. They're just pulling up the hill. How far out are you?"

"We're just turning onto West Tower. You can probably see us."

"Yup. There you are. … Time to rock and roll."

"Kate. Is that how they put it in New York?"

"No. I just thought you'd like it. … And, for the record, who's buying tonight? You or Henry? This is *his* gig, you know."

"You're on speaker. I think you just told him. … He's nodding. I think that means he's buying."

Kate could not monitor the location of the Silverado once it entered the incline, but she assumed that the driver would drop off the two shooters, and then proceed on up the hill a short distance, and then stop.

Their plan was for Jack and Henry to start up the hill and pull in behind the truck. And when they got out of the hearse to scrutinize the situation, the men in the woods would open fire, as would the driver of the pickup.

Should Jack and Henry try to escape by backing down the hill, the tailing vehicle would have the road blocked. There'd be no escape.

But that was just *their* plan. Jack had one of his own.

"This ought to do it," Jack said pulling up to where West Tower turned right onto the approach to the incline. There he stopped.

"You got my back?" he said to Kate using radio communication.

"Got you covered."

After a minute he popped the hood and got out of the hearse. He opened the hood fully and began tugging on cables and hoses. And then, feigning frustration, he stood straight up and looked into the front windshield. As he did, he sneaked a quick glance down the road behind them. He then looked back at Henry and winked.

Jack had spotted the tail vehicle pulling to a stop less than fifty yards behind them.

The wink was Henry's signal. He quickly slid open the door that separated the cockpit from the casket compartment. Assuming a kneeling position in the rear of the hearse, he prepared his AK-47 for firing. The rear window on the hearse, which was constructed of a bullet-proof glass-clad polycarbonate, was still closed. All the windows in the hearse except for the windshield were the same—one-way, allowing occupants to see outside, but tinted and mirrored to anyone trying to look in.

Five minutes passed.

Finally Kate spoke into Jack's earbud.

"We've got some movement on the hill. The Silverado is slowly backing down toward you."

"Don't give your position away," Jack said. "Wait until I give the signal. … How far along are they right now?"

"Thirty yards from the bottom. Moving very slowly. I think they are coasting down. All three of them are in the truck. Two in the back."

Jack remained under the hood.

"And now?" he asked. "How close are they?"

"They are nearing the bottom. Time for you to take cover."

Jack did not look in their direction. Instead, he casually walked back to the driver's side door, which he had left open, looked over to where Henry had been sitting, shrugged his shoulders and pretended to be talking to him.

"Anything from the rear?" Jack asked.

"Nothing yet," Henry replied.

"How about you, Kate. What do you see?"

"Strange," Kate said. "They're just sitting there, almost at the bottom of the hill. Still two in the back, and one, the driver, in the cab. Just sitting there."

"Dad!" Kate said interrupting herself. "Above you! You've got a drone directly overhead. It's descending right over you. … It looks like it's dropping right on the hearse."

"Damn it!" Jack moaned as he slid behind the wheel and shut the door. "What the hell are they doing? I'll bet they have some sort of explosive device in it. Shee-it!"

Jack remained silent as he contemplated his situation.

"Hadn't planned on that," he complained to Henry. "They're setting a drone down on the hearse. Probably has some explosive in it. Maybe shrapnel."

Henry absorbed everything Jack was saying, but he did not alter his firing position.

"Kate," Jack finally said. "Where is that drone right now?"

"It's hovering about ten feet off the roof."

"Can you tell if it's carrying a payload? Or just a surveillance camera."

"It's a pretty large drone. ... And it does appear to have a package underneath. Pretty good sized, too. Maybe three inches thick, and six inches square."

"C-4, I'd guess."

"If it is, it could do a lot of damage. Even though that hearse is built like an Abrams tank. ... It landed on the roof of the hearse, and then went up again. ... There! It did it again—it landed briefly, and then took off."

"That's weird. Do you have a clear shot? If so, the next time it lifts, take it out."

Kate did not hesitate.

"Crack!"

The same millisecond that her shot rang out, the package on the drone exploded. And Jack was right. The package did contain nearly three pounds of C-4 explosive—one of the most deadly explosives known to man.

The force of the blast knocked Henry off his knee momentarily.

As soon as the dust began to clear, Jack spotted the three men from the truck running full speed toward the hearse. He immediately recognized one of them from the pictures Roger had sent to him—it was Carl Milton.

Beside Milton was a particularly tough-looking man with a large number of tattoos. *That might be Raymond,* Jack reckoned. *I'll bet it is.*

No sooner had that thought crossed Jack's mind, than Henry opened fire on the two men approaching from the rear. Two bursts of 7.62 took them both out.

Jack waited inside the hearse while the three men sped toward him from the truck. But, just as they reached the Rolls-Royce, Kate's voice rang out: "Hey, boys, drop your weapons or die right here."

Carl Milton swung around to fire, and she hit him with three rounds from her AR-15. Lawrence and Slim stopped in their tracks.

"Drop 'em right now!" Kate shouted. "Do it now! Or I'll drop you!"

Both tossed their weapons on the ground.

Jack then opened the door of the hearse and stepped out.

"Wise men," he said. "She's a very deadly kid."

"Kid? Dad, really? *Kid*?"

Jack just smiled at his daughter.

"Okay, boys, toss your buddy in the back of the pickup. ... After you do that, go back there and pick up your other friends. Put them with your boss. ... And get a move on!"

After they had tossed Milton in the bed of the pickup, the two men walked slowly back to retrieve the other dead comrades. As they passed, Jack kicked Raymond in the butt and said, "Get your ass moving or I'll turn my daughter loose on you. And it won't be pretty."

Both men ran back and retrieved one of the dead bodies. After they had dumped it into the truck, they then returned to retrieve the last one.

After they had deposited the third body into the pickup, Jack barked at them, "Okay, you, the skinny one, you, jump in the back of the truck with your buddies. Do it! Now!"

As quickly as he could, Slim jumped in the truck and lay down.

"Now, you, Raymond ole buddy, you come over here by me. I want to introduce you to my friend."

Just as Raymond was nearing the hearse, Henry opened the rear door and stepped out.

"Hey," Raymond said. "Man, I hope you don't harbor hard feelings. It was just a job. I was supposed to rough you up a little. And that's what I did. I could have killed you, but I chose not to. It was just a job. Nothing personal."

"I get it," Henry replied. "You sucker punched me from behind. But you did it pretty well. No hard feelings about that punch. It was a good one. I don't always fight clean either. ... No doubt about it, dude, you pack some serious power. That was the best elbow that's ever been landed on me. You knocked me out clean. Not very many people can boast of that—knocking me out like that. That was one hell of a strike. ... Come here. I want to shake your hand and congratulate you. That was a world-class elbow you laid on me."

Raymond hesitated, but with Kate's barrel aimed directly at his midsection, he walked slowly over to Henry to shake hands.

Smiling broadly, Henry yanked Raymond's arm over his shoulder and jerked it down with so much force it shattered not only his elbow, but both bones in his lower arm.

Raymond screamed like a little girl.

Henry then crushed his face with a powerful back kick.

"That one's for Lily," Henry said as Raymond slumped to the ground.

Not only did the blow silence the screams, it instantaneously killed the man with the web tattoo.

"Like I said, buddy, I don't always fight fair either. Hope there's no hard feelings."

Henry then spread his feet, and power-lifted the dead man over his head. He walked over to the truck and flung the dead body on top of Slim. The force of the flying body snapped Slim's skinny neck, killing him.

"Kate," Jack said. "Dump your weapons in the truck and get the hell out of here now—before we have company. No point getting you any more deeply involved. We'll reconvene tonight at the bar. ... And, Henry, you drive the hearse. I'll take the pickup. Meet you at the top of the mountain. We have to give these boys a proper Aryan Alliance funeral."

Chapter 51

Yes, Henry Buys Tonight

So," Kate said, "did we decide who's going to be buying tonight? If I remember correctly, I think we decided that Henry was doing the honors."

"Yeah," Henry said. "Drinks will be on me tonight. No problem."

The three of them, Jack, Kate and Henry, were sitting at a table in Moloney's Alley in Sault Ste. Marie—one of their favorite spots to unwind when they got the chance.

Henry flagged down the waiter and ordered a round of Two-Hearted Ale for the three of them.

"Their vehicles are gone?" Henry asked. "Probably on a truck headed out of town. Right?"

"I'd say that by now they'd be compressed into cubes," Jack said. "And by tomorrow—who knows. They might be on their way to China."

"And the five skinheads—where are they?" Kate asked.

"They lie at rest under a single headstone near the east end of Mission Hill Cemetery," Jack said as he removed a small piece of paper from his wallet. "... I'll read to you what's inscribed on the headstone: 'The final resting place for Capt. George R. Geraldson (1948-2018), known to his friends as "Cap Geraldson. Cap was loved and respected by all that knew him. May he rest in peace."

Michael Carrier

"Perfect ending for those boys," Henry chuckled. "... But, do you think that this is really over now? Or will the guys who hired them still come after us?"

"Possibly, but I really doubt it," Jack said. "For sure, there are those who still want us dead. But I can't see them avenging that failed hit. This Kuiper fellow—aka *Milton*—was the leader. And he's gone. He and his buddies failed to avenge the beating Henry had meted out to their members at the prison camp. ... Those things happen. Besides, as far as anyone knows, those assholes we buried are just vacationing down in Barbados."

"Dad, do you know definitively just who it was that hired them—the ones that Henry beat up at the camp?"

"No. Not for absolute certainty. I have my theories, but I can't prove anything, yet. It all started when certain people found out that I was being released from prison camp.

"There's one other thing I still haven't figured out," Kate said.

"Only *one* thing?" Henry chuckled. "There are a few items that have me stumped."

"Yeah. I'm with you, Henry. I have questions about much of what went down on Mission Hill. Actually, for the rest of you, this whole week was hectic. ... But, my biggest confusion has to do with that drone. Why did it keep taking off and landing on the top of the hearse? I don't get that."

"I didn't either," Jack confessed. "At least, not at first. But then I got to thinking about it. A bomb like that works best if the blast can be directed. That's what the drone pilot was trying to do ... I think. The explosives were most likely encased in a metal enclosure—perhaps weakest at the bottom. If he removed the landing gear, and installed magnets below the bomb, it would attach itself to the roof of a vehicle, and the major force of the explosion would then be directed downward. It would have destroyed a normal steel-clad vehicle and killed all the occupants."

"So," Henry asked, "why didn't it land on the hearse, and stay there?"

"Aluminum. That Rolls-Royce is built out of aluminum. Milton, or whoever was piloting the drone, probably could not understand why it didn't stick to the roof. And then, when he finally *did* figure it out, he started looking for a steel cross-member. That's why he kept moving it around."

"And then I shot him out of the sky," Kate added. "I just hope my boss never hears about this whole episode. I could lose my job."

"I'm sure you'd lose a lot more than your job," Jack added.

"Even though it didn't land on the hearse," Henry said, "It still delivered a hell of a punch. When Kate shot it, the blast knocked me down. I looked over at you when I got up. I expected to see you splattered all over the inside of that hearse. But you were fine. What the hell is that thing made of? Can't just be aluminum. The roof was pretty messed up, on the surface, but nothing got through it. What is it? Kevlar?"

"Actually, this one's lined with rock—basalt."

"Really?" Kate said. "Basalt. Isn't that the gray stone we see all over the Lake Superior shoreline?"

"It is. But, the basalt used here has been converted to a fabric, and then mixed with a special resin. The process was perfected in Eastern Europe. They melt the basalt and form it into a fiber. They then weave it into a fabric, and add resin. There are several layers of this basalt fiber positioned beneath the aluminum shell. It's incredibly strong. The U.S. military has tested it out and it compares nicely with anything else available—such as Kevlar. ... We're just fortunate that this vehicle was well-protected against an attack from above."

"How about a Hellfire?" Henry asked. "Would a Hellfire missile have taken it out?"

"Oh yeah. A Hellfire would take out a tank. But they weigh over a hundred pounds. A standard small drone is very limited as to ordinance. The one these skinheads used was really quite sophisticated, for a non-military attack. It would have worked against any ordinary domestic vehicle."

"Except, not against my father's Rolls-Royce hearse," Kate chuckled.

"It wasn't *my* hearse," Jack said laughing out loud. … "Anyway, I'm shipping it back to the prince just the way it is. … With this message attached: 'Great vehicle. Armor worked perfectly. Field test was one-hundred percent successful.'"

"What's it going to cost to get it repaired?" Henry asked.

"The original out-the-door price was about three-quarters of a million. I would imagine it'll cost a hundred grand or so to repair it."

"You going to send him a bill for your services?" Henry asked.

Jack just smiled. He was obviously deep in thought.

No one talked for a long moment, and then Kate said, "What's up with your audit? I heard Connie's kid had been giving you a hard time."

"That's all a very sad story," Jack said. "Looks like poor Connie was just a pawn in someone else's power play. I hated losing him. We'd been friends for a lot of years. … But that kid of his—he was a waste."

"I gather that your partner's death wasn't really just a random robbery," Henry said.

"Looks like you might be right," Jack agreed. "But it'd be impossible to prove."

"Do you suppose that his kid, Conrad, might have been in on his father's death?" Henry asked.

"We'll never know about that. I think I'll give his memory the benefit of any doubts. The kid was a loser. Connie certainly deserved better. But I wouldn't tarnish the kid any further than he's tarnished himself. He's gone. And his father's gone. The only O'Donnell left is Connie's younger brother, Mercier. And I know him to be a straight shooter. ... So, I suppose you could say that all is well in Chicago tonight."

"Have the cops figured out what killed the kid?" Henry asked. "He was so young. Too young for a heart attack. They got any ideas about what he died from?"

"You two are just full of questions tonight, aren't you?"

"I don't mean to pry," Henry said. "But, the death is a little suspicious. Is it being investigated?"

It was clear to Kate and Henry that Jack did not want to discuss it. But the question was asked, and Jack always tried to accommodate his friends.

"Look at it like this," he said. "Have you ever heard of the *Bulgarian Umbrella*? ... Well, I suppose you could call this the *Deadly Cue Stick Case*. I suspect it was somehow provided to the kid compliments of one of my old clients—probably my old buddy, Harry. I don't know that for a fact, but it sounds a lot like his handiwork. ... I found this fancy case in the bar after the kid had died. It had a spring-loaded hypodermic in the handle. Apparently it could be triggered remotely. The needle apparently injected a poison into the kid. Probably ricin."

"Is that what was burning down by the river last night?" Henry asked. "That mysterious case?"

"Could have been," Jack said. "You never know."

Kate, wanting to change the subject, said: "Well, I think it's just wonderful news that the court has seen fit to give the boys back to us. With no strings attached."

"It was the right decision," Jack said. "Once the sheriff realized that he had been totally wrong about them from the start, he really had no choice. Had he forced us to petition the court to get them back it would have compounded his embarrassment. ... I have to give him credit—in the end, he did the right thing."

Jack did not wish to respond further, so he didn't.

It was clear that his eyes had glazed over. Finally, after an uncomfortable minute, he snatched a napkin from off the table and blew his nose.

"I'll be damned," he muttered. "I must be catching a cold."

He then flagged down the waitress and said, "One more round for my friends and me. … And, Kate, I hope you don't mind my calling you my friend. Because you are more than just my daughter, you know. You are my friend."

Kate smiled. "That's cool with me. I'll be your friend every day of the week. … But, I do have one last question. And I promise this'll be the last one. … Henry and I were talking. We heard something about that Kenny guy—Walter—having a lot of money. And he apparently stashed it somewhere on the Island. Is that true?"

Jack looked up at her but did not respond to her question.

Kate looked over at Henry, and then said to her father, "Do you think that might be something you'd like to share with a couple of good friends?"

Jack looked down into his beer and remained silent. But his *friends* could not help but notice his smile.

Henry and Kate knew exactly what Jack's demeanor meant—if Jack knew where Kenny's cash was, he wouldn't be announcing it on this night.

"Look, kids," Jack said as he leaned back in his chair, "the morning's going to get here sooner than we think. And, Kate, you've got a plane to catch. I say we call it a night and head back to the island."

"Dad!" Kate blurted out. "Check out the TV behind the bar. I think they're talking about you and the boys. That looks like the Winnebago you told us about. And the flaming car. Isn't that it? It says it's in Canada."

Jack stood and walked toward the bar. By then the reporter was interviewing a man at his house in Winnipeg. It was the truck driver Jack had used to stop traffic while Roger was picking them up. The sound was off but it was captioned: "…This guy flagged me down and had me get outta my truck and stop traffic. He said that I should keep everyone back because this car that was on fire, that it might explode. So, I did what he said. And then this airplane landed to pick him up. When it took off, the car did explode, just like he had warned me. And when it did, this dog came running out of it. His hair all singed and sooty. He just jumped in my truck. He was scared, but not hurt. He won't leave my side now. Goes with me everywhere."

"Holy shit!" Jack mumbled. "That's *Bill*! ... Talk about Dog Rescue ... Can't wait to tell the boys about this."

Cast of Main Characters in the "Getting to Know Jack" Series

(Characters are listed in a quasi-chronological order.)

This book, *Superior Shoal*, is the fifth book in the second Jack Handler series—*Jack's Justice*. *Ghosts of Cherry Street—and the Cumberbatch Oubliette* was the first book in the series. All told, at this time there are a total of twelve Jack Handler thrillers.

While many of the characters encountered in this book have already made appearances in one or more of the previous Jack Handler books, if you want a deeper understanding about what makes a player tick, you can refer to *The Cast* to answer additional backstory questions.

Main characters are listed in quasi-chronological order.

Jack Handler:

Jack is a good man, in his way. While it is true that he occasionally kills people, it can be argued that most (if not all) of his targets needed killing. Occasionally a somewhat sympathetic figure comes between Jack and his goal. When that happens, Jack's goal comes first. I think the word that best sums up Jack's persona might be "expeditor." He is outcome driven—he makes things turn out the way he wants them to turn out.

For instance, if you were a single mom and a bully were stealing your kid's lunch money, you could send "Uncle Jack" to school with little Billy. Uncle Jack would have a "talk" with the teachers and the principal. With Jack's help, the problem would be solved. But I would not recommend that you ask him how he accomplished it. You might not like what he tells you—if he even responds.

Jack is faithful to his friends and a great father to his daughter. He is also a dangerous and tenacious adversary when situations require it.

Jack Handler began his career as a law enforcement officer. He married a beautiful woman (Beth) of Greek descent while working as a police officer in Chicago. She was a concert violinist and the love of his life. If you were to ask Jack about it, he would quickly tell you he married above himself. So, when bullets intended for him killed her, he admittedly grew bitter. Kate, their daughter, was just learning to walk when her mother was gunned down.

As a single father, Jack soon found that he needed to make more money than his job as a police officer paid. So he went back to college and obtained a degree in criminal justice. Soon he was promoted to the level of sergeant in the Chicago Police Homicide Division.

With the help of a friend, he then discovered that there was much more money to be earned in the private sector. At first he began moonlighting on private security jobs. Immediate success led him to take an early retirement and obtain his private investigator license.

Because of his special talents (obtained as a former army ranger) and his intense dedication to problem solving, Jack's services became highly sought after. While he did take on some of the more sketchy clients, he never accepted a project simply on the basis of financial gain—he always sought out the moral high ground. Unfortunately, sometimes that moral high ground morphed into quicksand.

Jack is now pushing sixty (from the downward side) and he has all the physical ailments common to a man of that age. While it is true that he remains in amazing physical condition, of late he has begun to sense his limitations.

His biggest concern recently has been an impending IRS audit. While he isn't totally confident that it will turn out okay, he remains optimistic.

His problems stem from the purchase of half-interest in a bar in Chicago two decades earlier. His partner was one of his oldest and most trusted friends—Conrad (Connie) O'Donnell.

The principal reason he considered the investment in the first place was to create a cover for his private security business.

Many, if not most, of his clients insisted on paying him in cash or with some other untraceable commodity. At first he tried getting rid of the cash by paying all of his bills with it. But even though he meticulously avoided credit cards and checks, the cash continued to accumulate.

It wasn't that he was in any sense averse to paying his fair share of taxes. The problem was that if he did deposit the cash into a checking account, and subsequently included it in his filings, he would then at some point be required to explain where it had come from.

He needed an acceptable method of laundering, and his buddy's bar seemed perfect.

But it did not work out exactly as planned. Four years ago the IRS decided to audit the bar, which consequently exposed his records to scrutiny.

Jack consulted with one of his old customers, a disbarred attorney/CPA, to see if this shady character could get the books straightened out enough for Jack to survive the audit and avoid federal prison.

The accountant knew exactly how Jack earned his money and that the sale of a few bottles of Jack Daniels had little to do with it.

Even though his business partner and the CPA talked a good game about legitimacy, Jack still agonized when thoughts of the audit stormed through his mind. This problem was further complicated when Conrad was murdered in what was thought a botched robbery. Connie's lazy son, Conrad Jr., inherited his father's share of the bar.

A year earlier Jack had been convicted and sentenced for attacking a veteran detective, Calvin Brandt. The day that his conviction was overturned, an attempt was made on his life inside a federal prison camp. He believed at the time, and still does, that Calvin Brandt had been responsible for contracting the Aryan Alliance to carry out the hit.

Fortunately for Jack, Chuchip (Henry) Kalyesveh a Native American of the Hopi tribe, who was also an inmate at the prison camp, came to his rescue.

Kate Handler:

Kate, Jack's daughter and a New York homicide detective, is introduced early and appears often in this series. Kate is beautiful. She has her mother's olive complexion and green eyes. Her trim five-foot-eight frame, with her long auburn hair falling nicely on her broad shoulders, would seem more at home on the runway than in an interrogation room. But Kate is a seasoned New York homicide detective. In fact, she is thought by many to be on the fast track to the top—thanks, in part, to the unwavering support of her soon-to-retire boss, Captain Spencer.

Of course, her career was not hindered by her background in law. Graduating Summa Cum Laude from Notre Dame at the age of twenty-one, she went on to Notre Dame Law School. She passed the Illinois Bar Exam immediately upon receiving her JD, and accepted a position at one of Chicago's most prestigious criminal law firms. While her future looked bright as a courtroom attorney, she hated defending "sleazebags."

One Saturday morning she called her father and invited him to meet her at what she knew to be the coffee house he most fancied. It was there, over a couple espressos, that she asked him what he thought about her taking a position with the New York Police Department. She was shocked when he immediately gave his blessing. "Kitty," he said, "you're a smart girl. I totally trust your judgment. You have to go where your heart leads. Just promise me one thing. Guarantee me that you will put me up whenever I want to visit. After all, you are my favorite daughter."

To this Kate replied with a chuckle, "Dad, I'm your only daughter. And you will always be welcome."

In *Murder on Sugar Island (Sugar)*, Jack and Kate team up to solve the murder of Alex Garos, Jack's brother-in-law. This book takes place on Sugar Island, which is located in the northern part of Michigan's Upper Peninsula (just east of Sault Ste. Marie, MI).

Because Kate was Garos's only blood relative living in the United States, he named her in his will to inherit all of his estate. This included one of the most prestigious pieces of real estate on the island—the Sugar Island Resort.

Reg:

In *Jack and the New York Death Mask (Death Mask)*, Jack is recruited by his best friend, Reg (Reginald Black), to do a job without either man having any knowledge as to what that job might entail. Jack, out of loyalty to his friend, accepted the offer. The contract was ostensibly to assassinate a sitting president. However, instead of assisting the plot, Jack and Reg worked to thwart it. Most of this story takes place in New York City, but there are scenes in DC, Chicago, and Upstate New York. Reg is frequently mentioned throughout the series, as are Pam Black and Allison Fulbright. Pam Black is Reg's wife (he was shot at the end of *Death Mask*), and Allison is a former first lady. It was Allison who contracted Reg and Jack to assassinate the sitting president.

Allison:

Allison is a former first lady (with presidential aspirations of her own), and Jack's primary antagonist throughout the series. Usually she fears him enough not to do him or his family physical harm, but she and Jack are not friends. She seems to poke her nose into Jack's business just enough to be a major annoyance.

On a few occasions, however, Allison's anger at Jack reaches boiling point, and she strikes out against him. To this date, she has been unsuccessful.

Over a year ago Allison suffered a severely debilitating stroke, so her current activities have been dramatically limited, a situation which has provided Jack a bit of a reprieve in his having to worry about what she might be up to vis-à-vis his well-being.

Roger Minsk:

Roger is a member of the Secret Service, and a very good friend to Jack. Roger is also friendly with Bob Fulbright, Allison's husband, and a former president.

Red:

This main character is introduced in *Sugar*. Red is a redheaded fourteen-year-old boy who, besides being orphaned, cannot speak. It turned out that Red was actually the love child of Alex (Jack's brother-in-law) and his office manager. So, Alex not only leaves his Sugar Island resort to Kate, he also leaves his Sugar Island son for her to care for.

Red has a number of outstanding characteristics, first and foremost among them, his innate ability to take care of himself in all situations. When his mother and her husband were killed in a fire, Red chose to live on his own instead of submitting to placement in foster care.

During the warmer months, he lived in a hut he had pieced together from parts of abandoned homes, barns, and cottages, and he worked at Garos's resort on Sugar Island. In the winter, he would take up residence in empty fishing cottages along the river.

Red's second outstanding characteristic is his loyalty. When put to the test, Red would rather sacrifice his life than see his friends hurt. In *Sugar*, Red works together with Jack and Kate to solve the mystery behind the killing of Jack's brother-in-law (and Red's biological father), Alex Garos.

The third thing about Red that makes him stand out is his inability to speak. As the result of a traumatic event in his life, his voice box was damaged, resulting in his disability. Before Jack and

Kate entered his life, Red communicated only through an impro-
vised sign system and various grunts.

When Kate introduced him to a cell phone and texting, Red's
life changed dramatically.

Robby:

Robby is Red's best friend. When his parents are murdered,
Robby moves into the Handler home and becomes a "brother" to
Red. Robby and Red are now virtually inseparable.

Buddy:

Buddy is Red's golden retriever.

Bill Green:

One other character of significance introduced in *Sugar* is Bill
Green, the knowledgeable police officer who first appears in Joey's
coffee shop. He also assumes a major role in subsequent books of
the series, after he becomes sheriff of Chippewa County.

Captain Spencer:

Captain Spencer is Kate's boss in New York. The captain has
been planning his retirement for a long time, but has not yet been
able to pull the trigger. Kate is his protégée, and he almost seems
to fear leaving the department until her career is fully developed.

Paul Martin and Jill Talbot:

Two new characters do emerge in *Sugar Island Girl, Missing in
Paris (Missing)*. They are Paul Martin and Jill Talbot. They do not
appear in subsequent stories.

Legend:

Legend is one of the main characters in the sixth book of the
series, *Wealthy Street Murders (Wealthy)*. In this story, Jack and
Kate work with Red, Robby, and Legend to solve a series of murders. Wrapped up in a rug and left for dead at the end of *Wealthy*,
with Buddy's help he lives to play an important role in *Ghosts*.

Mrs. Fletcher:

Mrs. Fletcher, one of the caretakers at Kate's resort on Sugar
Island, progressively plays a more prominent role as an occasional

care-provider for the two boys. And, of course, she becomes embroiled in the intrigue.

Unfortunately, Fletcher and her husband are murdered in an earlier segment of this series: *Dogfight*.

Sheriff Griffen:

The sheriff first appears in *Murders in Strangmoor Bog (Strangmoor)*. He is sheriff of Schoolcraft County, which includes Strangmoor Bog, and Seney Wildlife Preserve.

Angel and her mother Millie:

In *Strangmoor*, the seventh and last book in the "Getting to know Jack" series, two new main characters are introduced: Angel and Millie Star.

Angel, a precocious fun-loving redhead (with a penchant for quick thinking and the use of big words), immediately melts the hearts of Red and Robby and becomes an integral part of the Handler saga. You will probably see Angel and Millie in other subsequent books in the "Jack's Justice" series as well.

Lindsay Hildebrandt and Calvin Brandt:

These two significant new characters are introduced in *Ghosts of Cherry Street (and the Cumberbatch Oubliette)*. Lindsay, a rookie detective in the Grand Rapids Police Department, quickly becomes a special person in Jack's life. If you were to ask her if she is dating Jack, Lindsay (who is about two decades younger than Jack) would immediately inform you that people their age don't *date*. But she does admit that they are good friends and occasionally see each other socially.

They have in common the fact that they both lost their spouses in a violent fashion. Lindsay's husband, also a Grand Rapids detective, was shot and killed several years earlier. This crime has not yet been solved.

Calvin Brandt, a veteran Grand Rapids detective, does not get along with anyone. And that is especially true of Jack Handler. Jack would be the first to admit that he was not an innocent party with regard to this ongoing conflict.

Chuchip Kalyesveh:

Chuchip generally goes by the name of Henry because he has found most people butcher his Native American first name.

Jack first met Henry in a federal prison camp where both were serving time. They became good friends when Henry saved Jack's life by beating up four other inmates who had been contracted to kill him. Jack says he has never met another man as physically imposing as his friend Henry.

Now that both are free men, Henry works for Jack at the Sugar Island Resort. And, sometimes, he partners with Jack (unofficially, of course) to help out with some of his tougher private security cases.

Expect to learn more about Henry as subsequent Jack Handler books roll off the press.

Emma:

Emma (Legs) is a very attractive thirty-something-ish contract killer. She makes her first appearance in *Dogfight*. Expect to see her again.

* * *

Here are the Amazon links to my previous Jack Handler books:

Getting to Know Jack Series

Jack and the New York Death Mask:	http://amzn.to/MVpAEd
Murder on Sugar Island:	http://amzn.to/1u66DBG
Superior Peril:	http://amzn.to/LAQnEU
Superior Intrigue:	http://amzn.to/1jvjNSi
Sugar Island Girl Missing in Paris:	http://amzn.to/1g5c66e
Wealthy Street Murders:	http://amzn.to/1mb6NQy
Murders in Strangmoor Bog:	http://amzn.to/1IEUPxX

Jack's Justice Series

Ghosts of Cherry Street:	http://amzn.to/2n3lrRf
Assault on Sugar Island:	http://amzn.to/2n3vcyL
Dogfight:	http://amzn.to/2F7OkoM
Murder at Whitefish Point:	http://amzn.to/2CxlAmC

Made in the USA
Las Vegas, NV
03 February 2024